The Wretched

Russell J. Carpenter

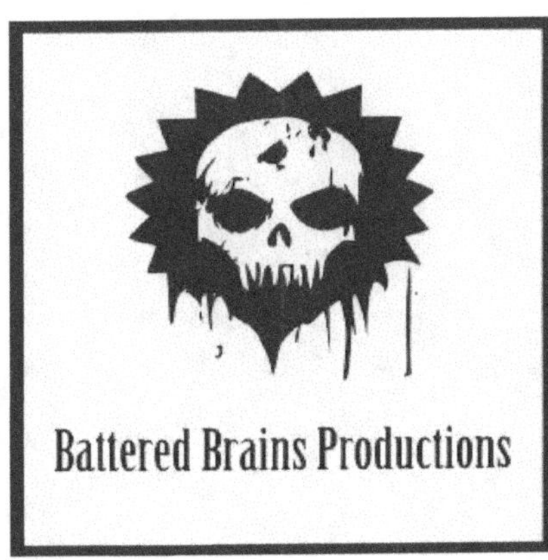

Battered Brains Productions

THE WRETCHED

The Wretched

By **Russell J. Carpenter**

Cover designed by John Schwegel.

https://www.johnschwegel.com

FREE AT LAST EDITION

ISBN Paperback: 979-8-9909971-1-0

THE WRETCHED

This book is dedicated to Jesus Christ who gave me the itch, to my wife who helped scratch it. And of course, my two lovely children – both nerds.

THE WRETCHED

PART ONE:

Rise of the Fall

CHAPTER 1

"Wake him up."

Lucious was awake, but his abductors didn't know it. How could they? His head was stuffed inside an old bag reeking of mothballs. The stench was so pungent it made his eyes water, and his nostrils burn. He heard someone approach, their footfalls unrushed. There was a wheeze of an air conditioning unit, which reminded him of the last breath of a dying man.

I'm inside. But inside where Lucious wondered.

"I'm awa…" he began, but a hard slap cut off the sentence. Fire rushed up the left side of his face as blood flooded his mouth. Licking around some, he found the source of the gush. One of his canines was knocked loose.

"It is a great honor to stand before someone of your special magnificence, Lucious. To bask in your glory, the majesty of your grandeur…"

"Yadda-Yadda-Yadda," Lucious grumbled. "Get to the point. Your voice is like an iron hammer driving nails into my brain."

The room filled with the taunting laughter of bullies. Lucious wanted to spring from his seat so he could unleash disgusting levels of violence on his abductors, but the hell-forged chains wrapped around his chest weighed him down in his seat. He couldn't even lift his arms.

"Squirm all you like, Lucious, but escape is not in your immediate future. Death is."

Thunderous applause erupted from those in attendance as Lucious tried to figure out their numbers. If he had to make an educated guess, there were many. He eased back into his seat as sweat poured down his face. He said, "You have not earned the right to call me that and never will. Call me Lucifer."

More laughter this time, hollow and menacing. He clenched his fists, causing the nails to leave indentations in his palms. They were slick with a cold sweat – a rage sweat. "Which of you idiots actually believes they can kill me, the Fallen Star?"

"That would be me…Mastema."

Lucious recognized the name. It belonged to a former angel handpicked by the Eld to challenge mankind with an army of prankster spirits known as Nonentities. Most of the crap he got blamed for had nothing to do with him; it was these assholes.

"Surprised?" Mastema asked.

"More like relieved. It's going to take someone with bigger balls than you got to kill me. I'll tell you what: I'm feeling generous, so I'm going to give you a chance to end this before it passes the point of no return. Let me go now, and I'll just chalk this tiny transgression up as a prank, nothing more."

"And if we don't?"

"I'll kill you all."

They laughed.

The grooves in his palms grew deeper as the nails punctured flesh. And then, above the roar of mocking laughter, he heard a voice cut through the snickers like a chainsaw through bone. It ended the merriment instantly and moved the hand of Lucious's Doomsday Clock closer to midnight.

"Can we get on with it, Jesus Christ?"

It was his wife. Hearing her voice sent an atomic shockwave up his spine. He shifted uneasily in his seat, head cocked, trying to pinpoint her location. They could do what they wanted to him, but he vowed a bloodbath if they harmed his beloved Agrat.

"Why is she here?"

"You still don't understand the gravity of your situation, do you?"

"Kind of hard to do that with a bag on my head," he said as he ran his tongue across his damaged tooth. That's when he noticed the smell. Faint but still noticeable enough inside the sack. It was the repugnant aroma of mankind – the air was thick with it.

"I think he gets it," Mastema taunted.

"I'm on Earth."

"Bingo."

Death in Hell worked as a temporary inconvenience, nothing more. Depending on how you died, resurrection took less than twenty-four hours. Here on Earth, however, death was an absolute.

"I had you brought to the one place I could kill you," Mastema said, his voice ripe with maliciousness.

"Well, la-di-da."

"I'm going to swallow your soul."

He didn't like the sound of that.

"You can do what you want with me, but let my wife go."

"How romantic. I never took you for the sort, Lucifer. I'll tell you what I'll do; I'll let her watch you die before I slit her slutty throat. How's that sound?"

Lucious started to rise when someone grabbed him by the shoulders and shoved him hard back into the seat. This was followed by another slap, but this time, it was the assailant who got hurt. He heard the snap, crackle, and pop of the attacker's hand as the bones were pulverized against his thick skull.

"My hand," they squealed.

He recognized this voice, too; it belonged to one of his wife's lieutenants, a brown-nosing little creep named Orthon. The bastard must have sold them out to the Nonentities. Lucious made a mental note to kill him first once he got the chance.

"It's broken," Orthon cried.

"It's your own damn fault," Agrat interjected. "Who told you to strike him in the first place? Nobody. So, sit down and keep that sewer grate you call a mouth shut."

The dejected footfalls of Orthon's retreat made Lucious laugh. It came bubbling out of him like molten rock.

"Enjoying yourself?" Mastema asked.

"A bit. But if you want to get this party started just unchain me."

"Not in a million years."

He would have shrugged if the chains had not weighed his shoulders down. The only bright spot was his tooth had stopped bleeding. His mouth still had the taint of rusty copper, the sort of flavor cannibals loved. Lucious wanted to rinse his mouth out and then grab a nice glass of Domaine de la Romanee Grand Cru to take the edge off. And should this day be his last, he wanted to toast his farewell.

"I'll tell you what…I'll remove the bag."

"Knowing it's you, I'd rather keep it on," Lucious said.

"I want you to see what death looks like."

Mastema charged over and ripped the bag off. It took a moment for Lucious's eyes to adjust, but once they did, he came face to face with Mastema. Jesus, he thought, what the hell happened to you? The man looming over him, his nose just a few inches away from his own, bared no resemblance to the angel he once knew.

All the beauty and majesty had been replaced with a lot of ugly. Mastema's face was heavily pot-marked and covered with giant, black tumors. His beard was alive with the squirming, wiggling bodies of plump lice, and his breath reeked of hot beer shits.

"See me. See me well, for this face will be the last you ever see."

Mastema straightened and stepped back, his arms outstretched like the crucified Christ. His clothes were in tatters, kept together by patches and drunken stitchwork. His jeans were ripped at the knees, allowing Lucious to glimpse maggots feasting on the rotten flesh beneath. Behind him was a brutal crime scene.

They were in a diner turned slaughterhouse. There were body parts strewn everywhere. A man dangled from the bar lights by his intestines, his dead face still twisted in terror. On one table was the head of a little girl. Her eyes were rolled back in their sockets until the whites gleamed like hard-boiled eggs. Lucious had no issues with mass murder, but the butchering of children never set well with him. He turned away, gagging on the overpowering blood stink.

"We had a bit of a pre-party before you arrived," Mastema gloated.

Sitting in a booth with his shattered hand pressed against his chest was Orthon. Next to him, smoking a cigarette, was Chemat – one of Beelzebub's most decorated soldiers. The demon's oddly shaped head had the texture and contour of a poorly made meatball. Straining his neck, he spotted two additional guards positioned outside, looking like club bouncers. He was just about to ask about Agrat when she came strolling in from the back of the diner holding a slice of what looked like apple crumble.

She was unchained.

Alone.

Free.

"Agrat?"

"How else do you think we got to you? Do you think we lowly Nonentities can simply cross over and kidnap the King of Hell undetected? We're good, but we're not that good," he said with a monstrous grin, which revealed a mouth riddled with broken, yellow teeth. "She was our insider, the keeper of all the keys. Without her…none of this would have been possible."

"Shut up, Mastema," Agrat snarled as she came around the counter, setting the pie down as she came. She wore black pants and a Ramones t-shirt, faded and crimson splattered.

CHAPTER 2

An explosion rocked the building and sent Lucious to the floor. He hit hard, cracking his skull off the linoleum. With his ears ringing, he turned towards the front of the diner. It was completely blown out. Lying among the debris, their bodies still smoking were a pair of dead demons.

Hoping the fall loosened the chains, Lucious tried to slip free. He twisted and squirmed, but instead of slacking, the chains restricted.

He heard Mastema screaming for someone to secure him.

Lucious rolled onto his side just as Chemat slid out of the booth, armed with a gold-plated Glock. He started running towards him, but the dumb bastard got mowed down by a barrage of gunfire. The demon's corpse landed near him with a wet plop.

Wanting his gun, he rolled towards the body like a man in a barrel as the diner descended into chaos. On his fourth dizzying rotation, he slammed into the demon's body. With his back turned to the corpse, he searched for the Glock blindly as bullets tore into the building. He found the gun. When he tried to pull it free, it misfired with a monstrous thunder crack – the bullet just missing his ass.

Back at the booth, Orthon was struggling to get out with his crippled hand still pressed against his chest. In his one good hand, Lucious spotted a knife. The blade engulfed in hellfire. The look in the turd's eyes boiled with madness, the type of crazy reserved for those locked inside a mental asylum's solitary confinement.

Battling against the strangulation hold of the chains, his fingers snaked down to Chemat's hand, which still clutched the gun in a death grip. Instead of prying the fingers loose, he snapped them off.

Orthon scrambled towards him, his lips drawn back to reveal a mouthful of daggers swimming in white foam. The demon cried out madly as he ran the last few feet, knife raised for the master's death stroke. Lucious fired.

The bullet slammed into Orthon's chest, causing him to moonwalk backward with his face twisted in stunned horror. Grinning, Lucious unloaded the mag into the demon, making him dance.

"Lucifer!"

He turned just as Mastema leveled a Magnum .357 at him, its entire length immersed in oily black smoke. Lucious half-expected a glorious montage to flash before his eyes, highlighting his existence in one final great blowout before the hammer fell.

He got nothing.

And then, just when he thought he was beyond hope, something zipped past his head toward Mastema. A strange glowing disc, burning a glorious amber. Before the Nonentity pulled the trigger, it came down at a kamikaze arch and cut the bastard's hands off at the wrist. Mastema howled in agony as he lurched back, painting the floors and nearby tables in dark crimson.

Lucious saw his savior standing in the skeletal remains of the doorway as they plucked the disc out of the air. Thanks to the lingering smoke, he couldn't make out much about them outside of their gender. They were female – the curves of her body told him that. She secured the disc to her belt and then unslung her rifle. Storming into the diner, she discharged her exhausted magazine and jammed in a new one. It was clear that whoever she was, she was here to kick some serious ass.

"I won't let it end like this," Mastema screamed. He was leaning against the remains of the counter with his amputated stubs held up in front of his face.

"Shouldn't have monologued so long."

Mastema snarled as his eyes burst in their sockets. Flames flickered from the holes as he stampeded towards Lucious, his footfalls shaking the building.

"This would be a good time to shoot," Lucious shouted to his hero.

Mastema drew closer, the stumps of his hands spewing fire like a flamethrower low on gas. Lucious watched in horror as those flames turned into a pair of phantom hands.

"Shoot," he yelled, "SHOOT!"

A single shot cut through the silence like the roar of many waters, culminating in a central, violent surge. For a moment, Mastema rushed towards him with his phantom fingers outstretched, hungry for murder; the next, he was airborne. He slammed into the counter and collapsed between some stools with his entrails resting in his lap.

In the momentary hush, Lucious searched for Agrat. He expected to find her dead, lying on the floor with her brains painting the linoleum like a spilled bowl of jelly.

But he didn't see her.

He didn't sense her either. She was gone.

"Oh. My. God."

Bathed in the ugly diner's fluorescent lighting was his heroine. It had to be a trick, some sort of master illusion because there was no reason why she should be risking her neck to save his. It made zero sense.

"Lilith?"

"This has got to be a mistake," she said. Lilith stared down at him with her lips curled in disgust. She flung her rifle over her shoulder and reached into her pocket. She fished out a mobile phone and punched in a few numbers, her eyes never leaving his.

"Hey, it's me. Yeah, it's done. Can I ask you something real quick? Did you actually send me here to liberate that piece of shit, Lucifer?"

"Be nice," Lucious said.

She flipped him off.

Lilith had changed a lot since their last meeting, which happened shortly after her fall from grace. Back then, she was a terrified young woman wandering the wastes of the new Earth alone. His appearance to her served no sinister purpose, no secret agenda or meaning; it was out of genuine concern. He offered her a place to call home and a rebellion to join, but she refused.

"Still as tenacious as ever, Lilith."

"Yeah, that's him. Can you hold a second? Great," she said as she cupped the phone. "Do you mind, dude? I'm on the phone. Shut the fuck up."

He was happy to see her attitude hadn't faded with the steady pendulum swing of time. He wished he could say the same for her looks because those suffered greatly. Her once fair skin was leathery and scar-laden, and her once long raven black hair was cut short and dyed an ugly green.

"This world hasn't been kind to you, has it?"

"I told you to shut your mouth," she hissed, kicking him full-on in the dick. As he writhed around in agony, she got back on the phone. "I'm back. So, this whole Lucifer thing…you knew? Why didn't you tell me? No, I get that. Damn straight, I would have refused; he's a piece of garbage. Yeah, yeah, whatever…I got to go. Laters."

She hung up and put the phone back into her pocket.

"Who were you talking to?"

"None of your business. Can you walk?"

"Walk? I can't even pee."

"Get up."

"You kicked me in the junk."

"I'll grind your junk into pudding if you don't get up in the next three seconds."

This wasn't an empty threat; she meant business. She was a no-nonsense, take no shit, stand on Superman's cape sort of girl, and grinding his junk was nothing to her. Neither was putting a bullet in his brain.

"How do you expect me to rise when wrapped like a burrito?"

"Not my problem," she said.

"Do you not see these chains?"

"Yeah. Kinky."

"You could cut me loose?"

"I'd rather get cervical cancer."

Sirens wailed in the distance, the calling card of approaching law enforcement. Lilith rushed over, grabbed the chains where it wrapped around his shoulders, and tried to lift. She didn't get him up very high before dropping him flat on his rump.

"Too heavy?"

"Your chains burned my hands asshole," she snapped, shaking her hands wildly as wisps of smoke rose from her palms.

Outside, the sirens drew closer.

She took a deep breath and tried again. She yanked hard, fighting against both gravity and her own burning flesh. Smoke bellowed up from her hands as she struggled to get him up. If she dropped him again, Lilith knew escape would be impossible.

"Just a little more, and I can get my feet under me."

"I hate you," she grunted. She gave one last mighty heave-ho, praying it would be enough because Lucifer wouldn't get another one.

"I'm up."

"Thank God," she said. She released the chains.

"Let me check your hands."

"You a doctor?"

"No."

"Then eat a bag of dicks. Let's leave before the cops show up and ask questions we can't answer."

"You got a car?"

"Follow me, and you'll find out," she said as she pushed past him.

He raced after her into the diner parking lot, which was littered with a few cars scattered here and there. Lilith ran past most of them on her way toward a beautiful 1953 Plymouth Fury parked on the far side of the lot. And then passed that one, too.

"Where did you park – the dark side of the moon?"

She ignored him as she hurried across the road like a chicken from a poorly constructed children's joke and up a slight embankment. And she was then gone, vanishing from view behind a row of dead bushes.

He stopped in the middle of the road, licking his lips as the weight of the world hung on his shoulders, ironically like a heavy, cold chain. Truth was, he didn't want to go with Lilith. Something about all this didn't feel right.

Lucious looked back at the diner. Scrawled across the front in blazing neon greens, yellows, and reds was the name – Rays. On a normal day, he suspected from where he stood, he'd be overwhelmed by the alluring aromas of burgers frying on a hot grill, but tonight, it reeked of death.

"You coming or what, Lucifer," Lilith shouted from the dark. "I don't have all damn night. Places to go, places to be!"

"I'm coming."

CHAPTER 3

Everything ached with stubborn persistence as Lucious trudged up the embankment. Behind him, he heard the angry screech of tires as a handful of police cruisers arrived. He felt kind of bad for the officers, seeing as they had no idea what horrors awaited them inside Rays.

Following a narrow path cutting through the weeds and overgrowth, Lucious entered a dark field. In the blue of the police lights, a couple of tires materialized out of the murk, their treads ripped and torn like a rabbit chewed up by a lawnmower. He spotted discarded beer cans, a pair of panties, and a used condom stuck on the end of a tree branch. And up ahead, sitting on a large rock with her rifle lying across her lap, was Lilith. The first wife of Adam, he thought, the original she-bitch.

"About time."

"You got somewhere to be?"

"I do, actually. And guess what, you're coming with me."

"Are we going to Disneyland?"

"Don't be a retard," she said. She hopped off the rock.

Lucious got a good glimpse of her weapon, this strange hodgepodge of different parts molded together to create something new and deadly for those of the demonic persuasion.

"That's an interesting weapon."

"Designed with the sole purpose of killing demonic pricks."

"Did you make it?"

"No."

"Who did?"

"Your mother," she said, annoyed. "Stop asking so many damn questions."

"What now?"

"We get the hell out of dodge genius. My car is over there," she said. She pointed towards a distant highway.

"That far?"

"It was a tactical decision, dude. The local donut patrol would be all over us by now had I parked any closer. Instead of complaining, you should be thanking me for saving your ass."

"Why did you?"

Groaning, she started walking towards the highway. Lucious followed, feeling like a scolded child trailing behind an angry mother.

"When did you get there?"

"I don't know."

"Long enough to watch Mastema and his goons slaughter a bunch of innocent people?"

"They weren't my business."

"That's cold."

"No, that's life."

"How could you let them butcher a child?"

She didn't answer.

It felt good taking the knives to Lilith. Her discomfort made him feel better because it allowed him to put some much-needed mental distance between himself and his own miserable existence. All he wanted to do was see her confident exterior shatter like a mirror introduced to a brick.

"I wouldn't have allowed it," he continued. "You can think as lowly of me as you will, but I would never harm or allow harm to befall a child. I don't have many principles, but that is one I hold dear."

"Good for you," she replied flatly. "You want a cookie?"

"Yes. Yes, I would. You have any in yonder transport?"

"Nope."

"Where are we? I'm guessing somewhere in the West, like California?"

"We're in a field, right on the border of Eat a Dick and Shut Your Mouth. From what I've heard, it's a great place to raise your kids. Good schools."

"You're a bit touchy."

He thought bitchy was a better word to describe her but decided it best not to say it. He wanted her broken, not homicidal. For a while, nobody spoke as they marched across the field. Lilith found the temporary silence blissful, while Lucious found it intolerable.

"If you won't tell me where we are — will you at least tell me where we're going?"

"Wouldn't want to spoil the surprise."

"Yeah, the tragedy of it all," Lucious mocked.

"You done with this round of twenty questions?"

"Nope, not even close. Who are you working for?"

"I'm not at liberty to say," she said, even though she totally was. Instead of telling the answer, Lilith decided to bust his balls. "My employer is like extremely mysterious."

"You do realize you're speaking with the Father of Lies, right? You don't think I can see past your fabrications? You can tell me. You're just choosing not to."

"Bingo!"

"What's your problem?" Lucious asked.

"You seriously want me to answer that question?"

"Inquiring minds want to know."

"Inquiring minds end up splattered on walls."

She left the threat hanging between them like a suicide victim, their feet dangling above an overturned stool. Most people would let things slide, zip their mouths, and walk quietly. But Lucious was annoyed, and when he got annoyed, his senses vanished in a puff of sulfuric smoke.

"I'll take a stab at it. You're jealous."

"Of you? Don't make me laugh."

"I won't because the reality of the situation is as grim as it is ugly. We both revolted against the Eld with totally different outcomes. I became the King of Hell, a god in my own right, while you got smacked with immortality and an eternity on this rock. Thanks, but no thanks. I'd rather get dipped headfirst in a vat of boiling piss with my mouth opened than spend 24 hours exiled here."

"Oh. My. God. Do you ever shut up?"

"I bet you were alone most of that time, too, huh? With nothing but the ghosts of your past to accompany you. And how much of a sting was it when the children of Adam started populating the earth? I bet you saw your ex in a million faces. Is that why you refused to save that girl, Lilith, because she reminded you of someone you wanted dead? Eve, perhaps?"

She spun around and pointed the rifle in his face. Her lips were curled back in a vicious, mad dog snarl. In the darkness, her eyes glowed a creamy violet. Lucious recognized it for what it was: a residue from her divine creation.

"I really should kill you. Nobody would care."

"Your mysterious employer might."

"I can lie. Tell him you got shot while trying to escape," she said.

"You could. I doubt he'd believe you, though."

"Why?"

"You're a horrible liar," Lucious said with a grin. "You mind lowering that boom stick?"

"I hate you."

"Feeling's becoming mutual."

She lowered her weapon and stormed away, marching through the tall grass with a little less gas in her tank. Lucious smiled as he followed, his goal accomplished.

They reached the highway. The lights, which generally bathed the snaking road in the color of dying sunlight, were dead. He wasn't sure if it was done by paranormal forces or the result of municipal economic death throngs, but he didn't like it.

And then came the thunder-like rapport of gunfire.

Lilith turned, crouched low, her weapon raised. She flicked something on its side, which made it sing in a low, electronic hum. Not wanting to take any chances, Lucious slipped behind her and scanned the horizon for movement. He half expected to see Agrat or some other demon charging at them from the direction of the diner, but nothing came. The gunfire died out suddenly, leaving them in the darkness as the night grew eerily silent.

"We should go," Lilith said.

"I agree. Cover me," Lucious said as they bolted towards the highway in a mad dash. He wanted to go faster, but the weight of the chains and his own exhaustion made his sprint more of a clumsy, weak jog. Two seconds later, Lilith passed him.

Up ahead was a barbed wire fence running the entire length of the road, and beyond that, a car. He followed Lilith through a gap in the fencing, huffing and puffing.

In front of him was the most wretched hunk of junk ever to be mislabeled as a car. The thing was covered with huge spots of rust and contained massive dents and dings running the entire length of its body like a murder victim. The thing that really made his jaw drop was the sticker plastered to the back window. It read, God Saves.

"You came in this?"

"Dude, if it doesn't fit your fancy – you can walk," she said as she took the keys. "It's your choice."

She disappeared inside, slamming the door behind her. He was about to head towards the passenger side when the car rattled to life and blew a thick cloud of exhaust right in his face.

Nice.

Lilith opened the passenger-side door for him as he came around. He knelt to climb in but froze when he saw the dreadful state of the interior. The bucket seats were ripped and horribly stained, and the floor was littered with old newspapers and empty soda cans (mostly Dr. Pepper). With a bit of trepidation, he climbed in.

Lilith reached over and tried to close his door. It resisted at first, but with some effort, she eventually managed to swing it shut. She grabbed the limp seatbelt dangling from overhead and pulled it down across the chains, locking Lucious in place.

"Seriously?"

"What can I say," Lilith said, "safety first."

"If safety were your concern, you wouldn't have picked this car."

She laughed as she got back behind the wheel. She checked her mirrors and then turned onto the road, which was mostly dead due to the lateness of the hour.

From where he sat, Lucious noticed all the dashboard's emergency lights were on, warning them of their impending doom. "This car is a death trap," Lucious said.

"Yeah, what do you expect? It's a Ford."

"And you're driving it because?"

"It's clean."

"Your definition of clean must be different than mine because…"

"Not clean-clean, you moron. Clean, as in off the books. And besides, it'll…"

"Get us to point B," he finished, "yeah-yeah, I remember. Right now, I'm a little more concerned with your driving than the actual state of the car."

"There's nothing wrong with my driving," she said as she swerved around a van lagging in the center lane. The engine coughed and wheezed like a man dying of lung cancer as they zipped past it in a fury of pissed-off sparks. "I've been driving since the first automobile," she continued, "and haven't received a single citation. My record is immaculate."

She reached between them, flipping on the radio. She cranked it up until the car pulsated with the electronic beats of Send Me an Angel by Real Life. Almost immediately, Lilith started tapping on the wheel to the fabulous 80's synth classic.

"I love this song. It's my jam."

"You would."

"Oh, does the big, bad evil Satan not like 80's pop?"

"I like Oingo Boingo."

"What? I figured you to be like the rest of your braindead followers, being all about the dark side, you know. Stuff like heavy metal, something you can bang your head to."

"I like a lot of stuff."

With a sputter of sparks, the radio died.

When Lucious started laughing, that's when Lilith finally snapped. Without a word, she reached over and grabbed a fistful of his sweaty, oily hair and smashed his face into the dashboard with a sickening slam. The first blow broke his nose; the second knocked him out. The next five were simply therapeutic.

CHAPTER 4

Lucious woke up in a small room.

Somewhere.

He was lying on the floor, still bound in his chains, his personal metallic straitjacket. He tried to sit up, but a flash of searing pain sent him back to the floor, battling against a mounting scream. He didn't want to give that she-bitch the pleasure of his discomfort, so he bit his bottom lip hard enough to draw blood.

Lucious closed his eyes, took a deep breath, and let his mind drift to its gooey, dark center. Almost instantly, he felt an intense power building at the base of his spine. When he exhaled, the energy traveled through his entire body, curing him of all his aches and pains. It even fixed his nose, but his tooth was still screwed up.

Feeling better, Lucious took in his surroundings. His cell's walls were cracked and covered in the hieroglyphs of the insane. Drawn in charcoal black were thousands of crosses of various sizes. Some were nothing more than frantic slash marks, while others were complicated compositions bordering on brilliance in both design and execution. The room was bare except for a badly soiled mattress in one shadowy corner and a broken toilet in the other, its seat speckled with dry shit.

He sat up.

"I'm awake," he shouted, his voice booming off the walls. "If you're not going to talk to me, then go ahead and kill me; I'm bored. Lilith? Lilith's mysterious employer? Anyone?"

No answer.

"Perfect," he muttered, leaning against the wall. He closed his eyes.

With nothing to keep his mind occupied, it began to wonder, drifting down synapses less traveled where dark reflections hung by their necks. One memory bubbled to the surface like a bloated whale carcass, demanding his full attention.

It was the day of his expulsion.

Not his best day.

He remembered standing on the narrow plank of the Eld's behemoth airship as it circled over the Vraga, a vaginal gateway leading to a netherworld full of living nightmares – a place he would eventually conquer and call home.

The air space above this corner of Heaven was typically a no-fly zone, but today, it was cluttered with hundreds of similar ships of various makes and sizes. And flying amongst them like flies around a pile of dog crap were thousands of angels.

Before his turn came, he watched his supporters make the fateful leap. Most went willingly, while others were cast down kicking and screaming. A few gutless cowards begged the Eld for forgiveness before being cast down, down, down.

When it was his turn, he went freely.

He walked out onto the plank, which extended out over the Vraga as the sky filled with boos. He didn't care. To him, those loyal to the Eld were nothing more than brainwashed slaves — too afraid, too stupid to free themselves from the Eld's unjust shackles.

He hated them all.

He strode to the end with his arms outstretched like a future crucified Christ and then stopped to take in the moment's grandeur. Feeding on their hostility like a hot plate of spaghetti. And then, right before he stepped off, someone called his name.

Sort of.

"Hey, Lucy!"

He stood back on the ship dressed in golden armor with his majestic wings unfurled to taunt him, for his were cut off the night before. At his feet was a leathery black sack, which leaked a dark liquid all around it.

"Just when I thought this day couldn't get any worse."

"Not happy to see me?"

"I'd rather have my eyes gouged out than look at you. Why are you here? Come for the show, or did you come to beg me for a job? I could use an obedient dog like you to fetch my slippers and clean my privy."

"I'm just here for the show. Your lucky Lucy, the Eld is letting you off pretty light for your treachery. If it were up to me…"

"Too bad it isn't up to you," Lucious said as he cut him off. "Slaves aren't allowed to think for themselves. You're designed to obey. To serve. To follow. Me, I'm a free thinker, baby. I do what I want when I want. It's funny; all I tried to do was liberate you all from the irons of oppression, and yet I'm branded the villain. If anyone should be flushed down the Vraga, it should be the Eld. Not me."

"You can't liberate those already free Lucy. None of us asked for your rebellion, and none of us wanted it. Your little insurrection failed because your dogma is flawed. We don't serve the Eld because we have to but because we want to. We love him. And I know for a fact, though you don't deserve it, He still loves you, too."

"I wipe my ass with His love. We done here, Michael?"

"Almost. I just wanted to make sure you didn't leave without these," he said. He dumped the sack's contents on the plank with a heavy thunk.

It was his wings lying in a pool of congealed blood.

Three days ago, Kushiel removed them before the Eld and His family, His good-for-nothing son and His fat cow of a wife. While they ate, drank, and laughed like jackals. They watched him as he was strapped to a pillar and flogged damn near dead. And then Kushiel severed his wings with a big, fiery axe.

"Give Him a message for me."

"Why should I?" Michael asked, crossing his arms.

"Don't I deserve as much?"

"Not really. But go ahead."

"Tell him I won't rest until I have destroyed everything He loves. I'll start with the children of Adam, who will stink with the rot of their sins when I'm finished. And then, I'm coming back for Him."

"Is that right?"

"Damn right."

"Well, I'll try and remember," Michael said with a sneer. "In the meantime, don't you have a hole to throw yourself into?"

"I'd rather rule in darkness than be a slave in the light of the Great Prevaricator," Lucious said as he threw himself off.

One moment, he was plummeting toward the Vraga and the next, he was being carried up and away from its awaiting maw. Someone had caught him.

It was Agrat.

She was trying to fly him to safety.

"What are you doing?"

"Saving your life."

"They'll kill you! Let me go."

"Let them," she said. "Life without you is no life I wish to live."

Beneath them, Lucious's feet hung dangerously close to the lips of the Vraga. Not wanting to be denied its offering, a pair of wispy tendrils crept up towards his legs. He kicked at them, which temporarily disrupted their smoky physicality.

"You got to get higher," Lucious pleaded.

"I'm trying."

"Try harder."

Suddenly, they began to slowly rise upward. Each inch was a fight, an epic war between two stubborn wills, the will of love against the will of physics. And physics was winning.

"It's no use," Lucious said. "Drop me."

"No."

"There is no place we can go. If you love me, you'll let go."

Agrat's fate was determined by a massive arrow, which slammed into her wing. She screamed as they started a madman's spiral towards the Vraga's opening.

And then the memory was gone.

In its place came others, all focused on a solitary entity at its collective center – Agrat. He was bombarded with snippets of conversation and shared moments so sweet and blissful that it broke his heart and crippled him with melancholy.

"Oh. My. God. Are you crying?"

Lilith was peering in at him through the glassless window of his cell door. She unlocked it and stepped inside wearing fresh garbs – a pair of blue jeans, cowboy boots, and a faded Batman t-shirt.

"Do my tears surprise you?" he asked.

"Not really. I always suspected your mythos to be based more on fluff than fact."

"Your employer clearly thinks differently."

"It's a free country," she said. She pulled out her mobile phone. "Let him think what he wants; I don't care. In my book, you'll always be overrated."

"What are you doing?"

"Capturing the moment," she said, snapping off a picture. "This is absolutely golden. It's definitely going on my Facebook page, she said, eyes locked on the photograph.

"I hate you."

"Feelings mutual, Lucifer."

"Call me Lucious."

"Call you…what?"

"Lucious."

"What the hell is Lucious?"

"My free name."

"Well, it's stupid," she said with a laugh. "Now that we've got that crap cleared up, how about you get up and follow me. We have places to go and people to meet."

"You mind giving me a hand?"

She clapped.

"That's not what I meant."

"I know."

"Why do I feel this will be a long day."

"If things don't work out how my employer hopes it does, it might prove a lot shorter than you think," Lilith said.

"What did they offer you?"

"None of your beeswax babe. Now, get up."

"I'm too exhausted."

Lilith stormed over, grabbed a fistful of his oily hair, and tugged. It took everything remaining he had left in the gas tank to stand, but somehow, he managed.

"Look," she said, grinning. "I helped."

"Thanks."

"My pleasure. At least your demonic friends didn't bind your legs because I sure as hell wouldn't be carrying you."

"I bet you'd change your tune if your employer demanded it. Am I right? Good dogs always follow their master's commands."

"And the disobedient ones always end up abandoned or dead."

"Speaking from a place of experience?"

She flipped him off and then stormed out.

Lucious stepped out into the hall. Here, the sunlight was intense and came spilling in from grime-covered windows running every five feet down a dilapidated hallway. Like his cell, the walls were completely covered in graffiti. Most were obscene illustrations of big pink dicks or cartoon-sized tits, but scattered amongst them were more religious paraphernalia in that same charcoal black.

"Someone clearly had too much time on their hands," he said. He walked in silence as he surveyed a madman's artwork. He passed more rooms like the one he was held in, but they stood empty. The one constant, besides the decaying similarity they obviously shared, was the crosses.

They were everywhere.

He passed through a pair of swinging doors and into another corridor. Unlike the previous one, this hall was in a lot better shape. Though it still looked like absolute ass, at least the walls still contained most of its tacky green and white tiles.

The next set of doors opened into an apocalyptic waiting room, which included rustic plastic chairs lined up like forgotten church pews. Most were broken and covered in white specks of fallen plaster and cobwebs long neglected. There was an old nurse's station, and painted on its counter was a monstrous, lidless red eye made with enormous insane spirals. Beneath it in fading pink spray paint were the words I am the Eater of Worlds. Behind it was another room, where light flickered on and off overhead, throwing up light on rusty filing cabinets. Lilith stood on the far side of the room, leaning against the wall, drinking a Pepsi.

"Nice place."

"Best get used to it," Lilith said, "for it might become your tomb. I already found a nice spot in the basement to store your body."

"Is your employer here?"

"Lucifer," a voice called.

He recognized the voice instantly – it belonged to the Archangel Gabriel. Turning around, he saw the prick as he materialized behind the nurse's station, wearing long, white robes embroidered in gold and silver. He was tall and toothpick thin and had a face soccer moms drooled over and husbands dreamed of beating to a pulp.

"I can't believe this," Gabriel said jubilantly as he approached. "Is this really happening? You and me standing beneath the same roof? How glorious. How beautiful."

"How annoying," Lucious snarled.

"Stop being a glum-drum, Lucifer, and embrace this for what it is."

"You mean a nightmare?"

"The first infantile steps towards peace."

"Peace," Lucious repeats with a dry chuckle. "Are you serious or drunk? I'm guessing drunk."

"Lucifer…"

"If you want to keep addressing Gabe, call me Lucious."

"Lucious?" Gabriel repeated, confused. "What is that?"

"My name."

"He gave himself a dumb stripper's name," Lilith said.

"It's not a stripper's name."

"I hate to say it," Gabriel said, "but it does sound like one."

"You ever step inside a strip club before?" Lucious asked.

"No."

"Then how do you know what a stripper's name sounds like?"

"I've seen Showgirls," Gabriel said. "Did you choose that name yourself, or was it a kind of penance for your sins?"

"I chose it dickhead. It's a symbol of my freedom, my rebirth."

"It's a symbol, alright," Lilith said, "a symbol you got bad taste."

"And what is all this talk of freedom, Lucifer, when you had more than enough in Heaven? You were loved and honored more by the Eld than the rest of us."

"Bullshit."

"You sat at His side," Gabriel continued, "you shared His wine, His ear, His respect, and most importantly, you ingrate, His adoration. He worshipped you. And for all His love, what did you offer Him in return? Nothing but a knife in the back and centuries of absolute misery and grief."

"He should have killed me when He had the chance. If He had done that, Adam and Eve would still be in that stupid garden of His talking to animals and screwing like monkeys. His error brought death to the world. Screw the Eld and screw you too, Gabe."

Gabriel surprised him when a curved dagger appeared in his hand in a bright flash of fire. The Archangel rushed forward, putting the blade close enough to Lucious's face that he could feel its heat.

"I should cut your throat."

"Then do it already and stop wasting my time."

Lilith, shocked at what she was witnessing, ran over to them. "What are you doing? Put the knife away!"

Lucious noticed the sour scent of wine permeating off the Archangel's breath. It was ripe with it. "You really have been drinking, haven't you, Gabe? Does the Eld know? I bet He doesn't. Maybe we should call Him, see what He thinks?"

"Can you stop egging him on," Lilith pleaded.

Lucious ignored her and continued to dig into Gabriel as if he were a juicy steak. "You pull a weapon on me you better use it, because I won't return the mercy."

Gabriel licked his lips as sweat poured down his face. In his hand, the knife trembled.

"Get to carving whelp or get that pig sticker out of my face."

"I'll…"

"Do nothing and like it," Lucious said. "You got no balls, which is probably why you drank before this encounter. You needed some liquid courage because you're weak. You're nothing."

"Don't let him get inside your head," Lilith pleaded as she put her hand gently on Gabriel's shoulder. "You do it, and he wins."

Her words seemed to knock him out of his murderous psychosis. He staggered back, blinking wildly. A second later, the knife vanished. To Lucious, he looked like a man waking from a deep nightmare.

"You okay?" Lilith asked the angel. "You had me worried there for a second. Your face looked different, almost demonic."

"Really?" he asked confused.

"Demonic? I thought he looked more like an asshole."

Leaning close to Gabriel, Lilith whispered something. Most mortals wouldn't have heard a peep, but Lucious heard everything.

"We should kill him."

"No."

"We can't trust him. He's too dangerous, Gabriel, I mean, look what he did to you."

"We can't."

"Why the hell not?" she asked, stepping back. "Even He's got to understand the risk of having Lucifer involved in this endeavor."

"Hey guys," Lucious said, "I'm still here. And who is this 'he' you keep referring to? Shouldn't he be here overseeing this thing before one of you gives into your blood lust and kills me prematurely?"

"Who do you think wanted you saved?" Lilith asked.

"Elvis?"

"Oh. My. God. You're retarded."

"Enough with the damn pronoun game – one of you, I don't care who, tell me who wanted me saved?"

"The Eld," Gabriel said.

"The Eld? Stop joking around Gabe, I'm in no mood for it."

"You might not like it, but He did."

"Why?"

"What do you know about His status?" Gabriel asked.

"Aw man, I totally forgot to check his Facebook status this morning. How is the old bastard?"

"He's dying," Gabriel answered coldly.

"Is this a joke?" Lucious asked with a chuckle. "Am I being punk'd? Where's the camera?"

"Search yourself," Lilith said, "you're the Father of Lies; tell me if Gabriel's lying."

"Holy crap – you're serious. He's really dying."

Gabriel nodded.

"Good. You think I can go to the funeral?"

"Can I gag him?" Lilith asked Gabriel.

"No."

"So, he's dying, big deal. What does that have to do with me?"

"You're going to help save Him," Gabriel said.

Lucious laughed until his sides hurt, and his cheeks were slick with tears. The entire time he did, he felt death glares coming from both of them, making him laugh even more.

"You done?" Lilith asked.

"Seeing as I'm retarded, let me see if I got this right. The Eld wants to make a deal with the Devil, so He can, what, save His own skin?"

"He has an offer," Gabriel said.

"I bet He does. So…what's killing the turd?"

"We don't know what you call it," Gabriel explained, "but you and your devilish consorts have shielded His children from the light and love of their Heavenly Father. And it has weakened Him to the point of death. We need it removed."

"The Shroud?"

"Is that what you call it?" Lilith asked.

Lucious didn't know how to react to this revelation. Victory over the Eld was just a stone's throw away, and it didn't even come with a military conquest of Heaven, but the stupid Shroud. Created not long after his banishment, it was designed to cut off God's children from His love and grace and ultimately make them easier to corrupt. He implemented it to annoy the Eld, not kill Him.

"Something like that," he said eventually, still shocked at the news. He shifted uneasily on his feet as the weight of the chains bogged him down, hurting his feet and legs.

"That's it?" Lilith asked. "You just found out you killed God, and that's all you've got to say?"

"You were expecting a bigger reaction? I could do the jig if it makes you feel better," he goaded as he kicked his legs around frantically like a drunk at an Irish wedding. "Is that better? If not, I can always do the moonwalk."

"We're not going to let Him die," Gabriel said.

"Happy to see you're setting goals. I'd give you a round of applause, but as you can see, I'm a bit tied up at the moment," Lucious said as he glanced down at the chains wrapped around his body like a giant, metal python. "If you want to put His death on me, I got no qualms with that, but to place it entirely on me is a bit of a stretch, Gabe, and you know it."

"What are you blathering about?" Lilith asked, annoyed.

"He killed Himself," Lucious said. "I might have had the gun, but it was He who stuck it in His mouth and pulled the trigger. He went quiet. His miracles appeared less and less, and after His precious lamb got crucified to some hunks of wood, He vanished. People lost faith in Him and put it in things they could see, things they could experience. All I did was make it available."

"You turned his children against Him!" Gabriel shouted.

"Why didn't He stop me then?"

Gabriel stared.

"There is no masterful plan, just a driver asleep at the wheel. We both know that. He became a hermit, an odd recluse living off His former glories in a world that grew up in the grandeur of science. What can be said, He's become obsolete, a relic, and soon He'll be nothing more than a corpse in need of burial. You won't blame Him for his failings, so you put it on my shoulders. My suggestion, Gabe, is to let Him die. Start over."

"You can twist the truth to fit whatever morbid narrative you like, but in the end, it doesn't really matter. The only thing that matters," Gabriel said, "is saving the Eld. And to do that, we have to liberate His children and destroy this Shroud of yours."

"Do what you want, Gabe," Lucious said as he sat on one of the dust-covered chairs, his back on fire. "But I'll tell you this: you'll do it without me. I'm glad He's dying. Couldn't have happened to a bigger piece of shit."

"I told you this would be a waste of time," Lilith said. "He isn't going to help us. We might as well kill him and get it over with. Move on to plan B."

"Will you listen to His offer?" Gabriel asked. "Or should I let Lilith satisfy her blood lust and kill you right here, right now?"

"I guess I'll hear it. I mean, the dumb bastard did save my life. What is His offer, a brand-new pair of Nikes?"

"A full pardon for services rendered. Complete absolution."

"Redemption?"

"Oh. My. God. Are you kidding me? After all the crap he's done, you guys are just going to what, let him waltz back into Heaven like nothing ever happened?" Lilith asked.

"Yes. The Eld has spoken," Gabriel replied.

"It's the Eld's way or the highway," Lucious said. "You should know that considering your own personal history with the prick. Look how he treated you when you refused to be Adam's silent slut. He may be our creator, but the dude has some serious anger management issues. As for the offer, is that it? Is that all He's offering me to save His life?"

"Redemption isn't enough?" Lilith asked, shocked.

"You're blinded by the word, but I see through the glam. It's just another way for them to slap the shackles back on and return me to bondage."

"That's unfair. We…"

"I'm not interested! Redemption, are you kidding me, Gabe? I did nothing wrong except stand up against a tyrannical dictator. People like me are usually considered heroes."

"Lucifer…"

"No. You tell Him if He wants to save His worthless ass from the Grim Reaper, He's going to pay big-big."

"I'm listening," Gabriel replied coldly. "What is your counter-offer?"

"I want what was stolen from me. I want my daughter Eisheth released from prison, and the keys of Hell returned. And if the Shroud is going to be destroyed, I will be leading the charge, no one else. Your deal may moisten some lips," he said as he looked back at Lilith, "but I'd rather reign in Hell than serve in Heaven."

"You are asking much."

"So is He," Lucious fired back.

"I will present it to the Eld," Gabriel said, "but what happens next is out of my hands."

"No surprise there."

Gabriel nodded and then walked away with his entire body engulfed in golden light. With each step, his physical essence faded until he eventually appeared phantasmal. Lucious noticed the room had a chill to it, and the faint smell of flora hung in the air. Just before disappearing into the light completely, the angel turned around.

"Escort our guest back to his cell. Unchain him. And get him something to eat."

"Unchain him?" Lilith asked. "Are you serious? He might…"

"Do as you're told," Gabriel ordered and then vanished.

The temperature in the room returned to normal as the unpleasant scent was quickly oppressed by the delicacy of decay and ruin. To Lilith, Lucious said, "Unchain me."

"Eat a dick Lucifer," she fired back.

"Now you see why I rebelled."

"Keep talking, and that dick you eat will be your own," she said. She stormed off back towards the cell area.

Lucious followed.

Again.

They didn't speak as they ventured down the halls of ruin. The sunlight in his wing, which had been blazing before the encounter with Gabriel, was now dying. He wasn't sure of the time, but he figured it had to be late afternoon.

Lilith was standing outside his cell. "Home sweet home, at least until Gabriel returns. After that, who knows, this might just become your tomb."

"I doubt it."

"You seem pretty confident."

"The Eld has no choice but to agree with my terms because dying men are the most desperate."

"The Eld is no man."

"Funny, He's still dying like one."

"Whatever, Lucifer," she said, throwing up her arms in frustration. "You going to get in there on your own or what? I'm tired, hungry, and sick of listening to your endless jabber-jawing."

"I'll go in after you remove these chains."

"And how do you expect me to do that, genius? I don't have the damn keys."

"No, but you've got some pretty impressive contraptions in your arsenal that should make short work of them. Cut me loose."

"I will, but before I do, I want you to understand something first."

"I'm listening. Kind of."

"First of all, dude, I know every type of hand-to-hand combat known to man – I'm talking Kung Fu, Savate, Kalarippayattu, Taekwondo, Jujitsu, and a bunch of other stuff long lost to antiquity."

"Good for you. And you're telling me this because…"

"You try something stupid, and I'll beat your ass. Secondly, you try and pull a Shawshank…you see those crosses?"

"Kind of hard to miss."

"They'll roast you like a witch on a stake with divine energy."

"Wonderful," he said. He stared at the wall with new, dark interest. What once he took for a madman's sketches were actually angelic in nature and were actually dangerous.

Lilith walked towards him with a small device in her hand. It looked to Lucious like a garage door opener. Or a pocket vibrator. She pressed a button on it, and a small, pencil-thin blade appeared comprised of solid indigo light.

"If you want to get out of these chains in one piece, don't move," she said. "You've seen Star Wars, right?"

"Who hasn't."

"Think of this thing here as a mini lightsaber."

She placed the glowing blade against the chain, crisscrossing his shoulders and neck. There was an angry hiss when it touched the metal. Afraid he might lose an eye; Lucious quickly turned his head.

"What did I say about moving?"

"Something about not doing it."

"You're such a child."

The metal snapped with a loud pop. Almost immediately, he felt the grip around his midsection slack. After cutting a few more places, Lucious could slither out of them like a snake shedding skin. Done, the chains collapsed around his feet in a heap of butchered metal.

"Okay, the chains are off – now get in there like a good doggy, and we'll see about getting you some chow. I suggest keeping your expectations low because this isn't the Ritz."

"Yeah, no shit," he said as he stared inside his decrypted cell. "I know you're just following orders, but can I stay out here? I promise I won't run."

"Get your ass in there, Lucifer, or I'll break your arm."

He raised his hands as he moonwalked back into the cell.

THE WRETCHED

PART TWO:
South of Heaven

CHAPTER 1

Agrat carved out a generous portion of apple crumble as the fry cook bled out at her feet from multiple stab wounds, 19 in total. When one of his weak hands reached out towards her foot, she crushed it beneath her heel, grinding his knuckles into pulp. The entire time she did this, she hummed the tune to 'Walking on Sunshine' by Katrina and the Waves.

She felt amazing.

Better than amazing, floating somewhere between that and pure euphoria. And why not? She was moments away from dropping the dead weight of her ex-husband. She felt no guilt betraying Lucious after selling his ass out to his enemies for a shot at freedom. The love for him was gone, and in its concavity was a deep abhorrence. One day, she woke to see him standing by the window, his body bathed in the predawn light – the color of menstrual blood – and felt nothing.

After a long year of plotting passed, she stood upon the precipice of a new life, and like a child on Christmas Eve, the anticipation of the next glorious dawn was torturous. Hence, the slaughter. The maliciousness in her attack, the savagery behind each brutal stab, was a direct result of that growing, gnawing madness of the delayed start.

She picked up the plate of crumble and ate while Mastema taunted her ex like some knock-off Bond villain. She wished he'd shut up and get to the murdering already, for there were better places to be than stuck at Ray's Diner in Elephant Head, Arizona.

"Squirm all you like, Lucious, but escape is not in your immediate future. Death is."

"Jesus," she grumbled as she crossed the kitchen. Shoveling more food into her mouth, she heard the idiots hooting and clapping like monkeys. It was clear they were enjoying themselves with the little game they were playing; she just hoped they did so with caution. Lucious was a master manipulator, so she put the sack on his head.

When she reached the door separating the kitchen from the front of the house, she heard Lucious rant to Mastema about his stupid name. Ever since his expulsion and subsequent name change, he had steadily grown increasingly preoccupied with it.

And it drove her nuts.

At first, she thought it was sort of cute. But she was done after a millennium of listening to him babble about it. Talk about something she wouldn't miss about the asshole.

"Which one of you believes they can actually kill me?"

She hoped this was where Mastema would do it. Cut his throat, lop off his head, shoot him – whatever. Just finish it. She listened, her mouth full of sweet apple and cinnamon.

Do it.

Do it.

She felt her heart pounding against her rib cage. No more games, she thought, no more childish taunts – just kill the prick.

"That would be me, Mastema."

"Why are males such useless creatures," she grumbled. Agrat figured she better get back out there because if Mastema didn't kill him in the next five minutes, she figured she'd have to do it herself.

Annoyed with the progression of the night's events – or lack thereof – she stormed out of the kitchen. With the door swinging loudly behind her, she asked, "Can we get on with it, Jesus Christ?"

She saw Lucious straighten in his seat.

"Why is she here?"

"You still don't understand the gravitas of your situation, do you, Lucifer," Mastema taunted.

The threat was true enough, but she was beginning to doubt the Nonentities' follow-through. Mastema talked too much, and the more he did, the more anxious she felt. This had to end sooner rather than later. She took another spoonful of crumble, but the sweetness was gone. The texture was like sticky sawdust.

"Kind of hard to do that with a bag on my head."

"I think he gets it."

"I'm on Earth," Lucious gasped, surprised.

"Bingo."

She set aside her food and hopped up on the counter, bored. The guys were having fun, but all she wanted was to slip back to the safety of Hell. And to him.

"I had you brought to the one place I could kill you," Mastema was saying. It was clear to her he was just showing off in front of the others, trying to flaunt his stuff.

It was pathetic.

"Well, la-di-da."

"I'm going to swallow your soul."

"You can do what you want with me, but let my wife go."

That surprised her.

For about half a second, Agrat felt a pang of guilt for betraying her husband. Just a single, lonely pang – more of a blip, really. And then it was gone, swallowed by her desire to see him dead.

"How romantic," Mastema said, "I never took you for the sort Lucifer. I'll tell you what I'll do. I'll let her watch you die before I slit her slutty throat. How's that sound?"

After that, she wanted Mastema dead too.

On the far side of the diner, she watched Orthon walk over to Lucious and then strike him across the head. Almost instantly, he scampered off with his hand cradled against his chest, his face twisted in agony.

"My hand. It's broken."

"It's your own damn fault," Agrat interjected. "Who told you to strike him in the first place? Nobody. So, sit down and keep that sewer grate you call a mouth shut."

She watched Orthon retreat to his booth as Mastema continued tearing into Lucious like a high school bully. It was clear to her this dick-measuring contest was far from over, so she decided to take her crumble back to the kitchen to see if she could find some ice cream for it. Entering the ransacked kitchen, she saw several bodies lying on the floor, their bodies still warm.

Agrat was about to head to the large walk-in freezer when she heard Mastema say something mind-bogglingly stupid.

"I'll tell you what...I'll remove the bag."

She froze, thinking she might have misheard what the King of Nonentities said because there was no way he was that dimwitted, was there?

"Knowing it's you, I'd rather keep it on," Lucious said.

"I want you to see what death looks like."

"Keep it on, you idiot," she muttered through clenched teeth.

Judging by the reaction that came next, she realized the error in trusting the Nonentities, for they just screwed up.

Royally.

"See me. See me well, for this face will be the last you ever see."

Shit.

She spun around and darted for the door, knowing she'd be the only one capable of reining in the madness. Agrat burst through, her eyes meeting his, and stopped.

"Agrat?"

She was about to say something when Mastema beat her to the punch. And like a total jackass, he confessed everything to Lucious like a little bitch. Agrat listened as he boasted about how she assisted in his abduction and planned to have him killed on Earth.

What a douchebag.

"Shut up, Mastema," she snapped as she came around the corner in a hot fury.

"I thought…"

"Wrong," she finished coldly. She looked at Mastema, "How long are you planning to drag this out? Kill him and be done with it."

That's when death came calling.

It just happened to come on the wrong side as the front of the diner exploded in a flash of blinding white. The impact sent Agrat over the counter and deposited her on the floor, hard enough for her to see the entire cosmos dance before her eyes.

What the hell was that?

With her ears ringing, she slithered across broken plates and shattered glass on the way toward the kitchen area. Mastema screamed something just before the night filled with the ratta-tat-tat of gunfire. Reaching the end of the counter, her hands sliced and diced, she waited for a break in the shooting.

When it came, she bolted.

And didn't stop.

She raced through the kitchen, passing prep tables and leaping over dead bodies as she headed towards the back door. She was nearly there when she heard Mastema's primal roar rise above a short burst of gunfire. There was a heavy crash as something massive fell in defeat.

She knew it was Mastema.

Agrat opened the backdoor and took off across the pitch-black parking lot, passed a pair of dumpsters reeking of rotten vegetables and maggoty meat, and into a field beyond.

CHAPTER 2

Agrat might be a demon, but an Olympic sprinter, she was not. It didn't take long for exhaustion to set in and reduce her run to a trot and then a walk. That ended, too, as her lungs became leaden and her breath acidic. Even though she had no desire to stop, she did. She doubled over, resting her hands on her knees as she struggled to catch her breath.

The diner was behind her but still too close for comfort. The ugly building was now covered in the revolving reds and blues of arriving police cars. Crouching low in the tall grass of the vacant lot, she watched them like a predatory cat observing prey. Officers spilled out of their vehicles; weapons drawn. Most of them bravely ran into the diner, but one lingered back, half-hidden behind one of the cruisers.

She hoped Lucious was still inside so the cops could nab him. Then it would be easy pickings. She'd simply stroll inside the police station with an army of demons and slaughter everyone. Agrat closed her eyes and tried to pinpoint his location inside the building, but she couldn't find him. The bastard was gone.

"Damn it," she snarled bitterly.

They had come so far and done so much to sneak him out of Hell to this Podunk town in the middle of nowhere, and for what? For him to escape because Mastema had gone off at the gums rather than the knife. Leave it to a male to fuck up what should have been unfuckable.

As much as she didn't want to return to Hell a failure, she knew she had to bite the bullet and get back there lickety-split. But she needed transport. Her ride, a 1983 black GMC Vandura van, was back at the diner. As she cleaned the sweat from her brow and contemplated what to do next, fresh gunfire filled the night.

And that was followed by death howls as a fresh wave of butchery began at Ray's. Not wanting to take any chances, Agrat decided she better arm herself. She held out her hand and flicked her wrist. A second later, a big bastard of a sword appeared in her hand from a cloud of oily smoke.

She called it Misandry.

Staying low, she crept back towards the diner, her eyes locked on the cop by the cruiser and his drawn weapon. Suddenly, from out of nowhere, he took a knife in the eye. He screamed as he staggered back, his hands fumbling with the projectile. Figuring this was as good a time as any; she sprinted for the diner as the cop struggled to remove the knife.

When she reached the building, she pressed herself hard against the wall to melt into the shadows. After all the noise and screams of the dying, the night took on a vacant, almost haunting ambiance that made her feel uneasy. Taking a deep breath, she pushed open the back door and entered the crime scene, unsure what to expect.

Slowly, she made her way down a narrow hall with grease-covered floors, passed a couple of large freezers, and back into the prep area. She stopped beside a massive rack containing spices, condiments, and other dried goods. Off to her right was an industrial-sized dishwasher with steam oozing from its open metal maw.

She saw the fry cook lying face down on the floor and a few other dead kitchen staff, sprawled out and gutted. Agrat was about to make her next move when the door leading to the kitchen opened.

A waitress shuffled in, looking like an animated corpse. Her skin was pale, and her uniform blood splattered. Though her outward appearance was human, Agrat sensed something demonic lurking beneath her exterior.

"Mastema…is that you?"

"The one and only," the girl said in Mastema's dark, brooding voice. "I thought you darted back to Hell with your tail tucked between your legs."

"And I thought you got your dumb ass killed."

Mastema snickered.

"Any other survivors?"

"The rest are dead. And as far as your husband goes, he's gone with the wind. Escaped with the assassin."

"You mean to tell me that one person did all that damage?"

"That I saw."

"You saw him?"

"Her," Mastema corrected. "It was the first wife of Adam, Lilith."

Though far from an expert on Lilith's life, the one thing she knew about her without question was her disdain for Lucious. He often bored her with the story about how he once offered her a chance to join the Fallen after her exile from Eden. She refused and emphasized the rejection by kicking him right in the old grapefruits.

"That's impossible."

"You calling me a liar?" Mastema asked.

"Maybe you saw wrong."

"Murdered men have photographic memories when it comes to those who kill them. I know it was her. I've encountered her before, many times."

"I don't want to hear your life story, Mastema; sorry, I really don't care. I want to figure this out – how did they know we were here? Do you think any of your Nonentities might have sold us out?"

"I'm their King…they would never betray me."

"Your trust blinds you. Lucious was confident too, but look what that got him?"

"That's why I stay away from my Shedim," Mastema said.

Agrat knew Shedim was a powerful Tempestarri and Mother of the Nonentities. She was a vicious, uncaring conjurer of storms and, no doubt, a female you did not want to piss off.

"Rumor has it you have access to a spy network…is that true?" Agrat asked.

"What about it?"

"How does it work? Can you use it to find Lucious?"

"You ask a lot of questions. Look, I'm too tired to go into detail about it; just know I can access the minds of lesser animals."

"Have they seen anything?"

"Enough! I'm tired. Remember, one of us almost died tonight. Getting my soul transferred into this vessel was incredibly exhausting," he said as he gestured to the waitress's body. "I need to feed and rest. Where I'm at right now, I couldn't track Lucifer to the bathroom."

Mastema staggered out of the kitchen.

And Agrat followed.

The dining area of Ray's was a bloodbath, with the floor covered with the remains of Arizona's finest. As for the demons, their bodies were melting into puddles of sticky, icky black pools.

"Hard to believe Lilith could do so much damage alone."

"You don't know Lilith."

"I guess not," she replied, maneuvering around an overturned table. Doing her best not to step in anything foul, Agrat followed Mastema out into the parking lot. It was funny watching the dumb bastard trying to walk in the possessed girl's high heels.

"You coming with me?" he asked.

"I need to go back."

"Back to Hell?"

"Where else would I go numb nuts? Of course, Hell," she said as she fished out her keys. "Beelzebub needs to know what happened. Besides, there isn't much for me to do here unless you want me around to hold your hand."

"Oh God no. By all means – piss off back to Hell."

"Good. Glad to see we're on the same page."

"When will you return?"

"When you find them. Remember," she said, jamming her finger in his face, "track them down, but under no circumstances will you engage them until I return. Is that clear?"

He raised his head, the lights catching the darkness in those beautiful young eyes of his stolen body. He might have had the tender appearance of an attractive twenty-something, but the beast lurking beneath the soft exterior was pure malevolence. Agrat expected him to protest, but he stunned her by nodding in agreement.

"Swear to me," she insisted.

"I'll swear to nothing. Remember, this is my kingdom, and you're a guest here. Show me the damn respect I deserve, or you can take this alliance and shove it up your ass."

She swallowed her venom with bitter reluctance and gave the King of the Nonentities a respectful half-curtsey. Tonight, she would take his verbal lashing and like it, but she would not forget and never forgive. In a more sympathetic tone, she said, "I beg pardon, Mastema. I just want to be there when you kill Lucious. I think I deserve that much."

"You do, but I still make no promises. My suggestion is you go do what you've got to do and then get your ass back up here lickety-split, especially if you want to partake in the slaughter."

In the distance came the electric moan of an army of sirens. Time was short and growing shorter by the second; soon, the place would be crawling with additional law enforcement. She bolted towards her van, shouting, "I will contact you soon!"

"And I'll try to remember to answer," he said. "Just remember things changed when that bitch killed me."

CHAPTER 3

"Where we headed?"

"We're almost there, doll face," Agrat assured sweetly as she squeezed Brad's inner thigh. She watched his youthful face relax as the tension drained. She knew where the blood was going. She could see the bulge grow in his tight jeans.

Men, she thought with bitter disdain.

The sky up ahead turned a rotten orange as the sun began peering on the horizon. Time to access the gate was rapidly shrinking, and if she wanted to get back to Hell, she needed to get there now or be stuck topside until dusk. She hit the gas, and the engine groaned angrily like a kicked dog. Brad sat up with a start, his eyes wide and alert. Agrat was certain if he was sober, the alarm bells would be ringing inside his head, but thankfully, they remained dead and silent.

"Relax, babe," she cooed seductively, "we're almost there. How about you close your eyes and think about all the naughty little things I'm going to do to you."

He closed his eyes with a half-drunken smirk plastered across his big, dumb face. Back at the San Cayetano Saloon in Rio Rico, she managed to hypnotize him with her immense sexuality. The poor, small-town hick was clearly not accustomed to seeing someone of her caliber outside of porn movies. One glance at her, and he was lost to lust. He approached her as soon as she sat at the bar and ordered her a drink, one of many.

From there, he spouted a bunch of pathetic one-liners, which made her die a little inside. She played along, though, taking each contemptible quip with a fake grin and forced twinkle of interest in her eyes. He was dead drunk and reeked of whisky. But she needed blood, so she pretended interest.

Twenty minutes later, she had her tongue down his throat on the dance floor, swaying to the tunes of Johnny Cash's Ring of Fire. To keep from vomiting, she imagined it was Beelzebub's fingers gripping her ass, his mouth, his tongue.

An hour before dawn, they left the bar in her van. While his mind danced with images of them intertwined like mating snakes, Agrat contemplated the runes and hieroglyphs needed to open the gate to Hell. Blood was the oil, and his death was the key.

She eased on the accelerator a bit as she turned onto a side road cutting into the desert. With Brad lost in his thoughts (or possibly passed out), she navigated the barren landscape, down bumpy roads that turned into trails and then into nothingness.

Their destination was a small, black shack in the middle of nowhere. A type of waystation between worlds. And it was protected by a host of bloodthirsty monsters whose hunger knew no bounds. Meat was meat, and they devoured anything that wandered too close – which meant they ate a lot of stray dogs and more than a fair share of illegal aliens. Today, Brad was the meat.

In the early morning light, just behind an outcrop of massive boulders, the shack rose out of the ground like a gravestone. It leaned haphazardly to the left and looked ready to collapse. She pulled up and killed the engine. In front of them, the structure stood, its wooden orifice badly bleached from countless decades of rotting beneath an unforgiving sun. It was a basic wooden box with a pair of boarded-up windows. The door stood open.

"Where are we?" Brad asked dreamily.

"My play place."

"Your what?"

She looked at him. He was handsome for an Adam descendant, but when compared to the strength and majesty of Beelzebub, he was nothing more than a turd.

"You've heard of 50 Shades of Grey, right?"

He nodded.

"I have appetites. Dark ones. Naughty ones. I come out here to explore them in full."

"Jesus."

"He's not invited," she said with a wicked smile. "But you are."

"You want me to what, tie you up?"

"I want to be fucked. Hard."

"Jesus," he muttered again, his eyes wide.

"In there, I'll be your little slut, and you'll be my master. Nothing is off-limits. Nothing."

"Anal?"

"You can fill every hole."

"Cool," he said. He gave a big, hearty thumbs up.

She leaned over and kissed him hungrily on the mouth.

Agrat felt his body tremble as his cock swelled in his jeans to full mass. She felt one of his hands latch onto her left breast and squeeze hard. It hurt. Truth was, she liked S&M about as much as she did the Power Rangers, which was zilch.

"You want me?" she asked.

She threw open the door and darted for the shack's opening, hoping she had done enough to entice the dumb prick to follow.

Inside, Agrat leaned against the wall near the entrance with Misandry in hand. All around her, the shadows began to come alive and take phantom shapes as the monsters appeared, ready to feast. Somewhere nearby in the dark, she heard the steady snapping of mandibles.

Something grabbed her ankle, a slimy tendril covered with a thousand sucking, toothless mouths. It felt like someone put a cold, dead fish against her leg. Instead of plunging her sword into the feeding monster's bulbous body, she focused on Brad, who was just about to enter.

As soon as he crossed the threshold, she brought her sword down in a half arch, connecting right where the spine connected to the skull. The blade sliced through the bone and tissue without resistance, completely decapitating him. Brad's body slumped in the doorway while his head went rolling into the living shadows, where it was devoured by something resembling an enormous, pink-skinned toad with one lidless, segmented eye.

With Brad dead, her prize secured, she cleaved the thing attached to her leg in half with a mighty blow. She raised her sword with both hands as she watched the darkness around her stir and shift, their confidence fueled by their longing for sustenance.

"Keep back," she ordered.

The shack filled with angry hisses.

"Once I complete the ritual, you can have your meal, but not before. And if any of you step out of line to challenge me on this, I'll kill you like this lump of shit," she said. Agrat kicked the dead thing at her feet, which was already beginning to melt.

The shack filled with angry snarls so loud and fierce the walls trembled around her. And then came the voices, which were hideous perversions of speech that made her skin crawl.

"Be quick," one pleaded. "We are hungry."

"Ravenous," said another.

"We desire meat," another chimed in from a gloomy corner.

Inside the shack, the chatter of creatures mumbling and growling in their inhuman, deformed voices seemed to pick up on that one solidarity, that of meat. And that's when the chanting began. It was a twisted mantra, one reeking of depravity and malice, and it crippled her mind under its reverberation: meat, meat, meat, meat.

One of them emerged from the shadows.

It was a hairless blob, a walking tumor. It scurried along the wall on a pair of ill-formed human hands. It had six eyes, all bloodshot and swimming with madness. The foul thing stared at her with its bulbous orbs slick with pus and oozing a yellowish discharge. Beneath them was a mockery of a mouth, which opened to reveal several rows of jagged teeth.

"Stay back."

"Stay back," it mocked as it drew closer. "Why should we? What is stopping us from tearing you apart besides our own humble decorum?"

"I am Agrat bat Mahlat."

"And I'm Walter," the tumor said. "Who cares."

"I'm the Queen of Hell."

"Only makes the meat better," the thing said as it licked its lips.

"Come any closer, Walter, and I'll make you the appetizer."

The thing paused and blinked stupidly at her while the rest of the shack suddenly grew uncomfortably silent.

"Are you their Leader?"

"You could say that."

"Let me be your butcher. You give me a few minutes to complete my ritual, and I'll give you some delicious meat," she said with gusto. Agrat pointed at Brad's body and asked, "Do we have a deal?"

"We do."

Walter, if that was the thing's real name, gave her a bow as it retreated the way it came. A sense of normality began to fill the structure, but she knew she was on borrowed time. The maelstrom might have been over, but it was only a temporary reprieve.

Agrat dipped her sword in Brad's blood and started. She drew archaic ciphers into the dirt while chanting the words of the Eld, mystical, ancient, and of course, extraordinarily powerful. Like a computer needing a password, so did the gates of Hell. The process in and of itself was complicated, but under the watchful stares of the monsters, it was damn near impossible.

She knew if she screwed this up, she'd have to start the ritual all over again, which meant fresh blood. The thought of driving back to Rio Rico to track down another undesirable male made her stomach cramp. Focus, she told herself, and remember…don't mess this up.

For thirty back-breaking minutes, she focused entirely on her work as everything else faded into sweet oblivion. She didn't worry about what awaited her in Hell, her asshole ex or the bitch who saved him. Instead, she focused on the markings she was making on the earthen floor of the shack, making sure they were perfect.

"Almost finished, Mahlat?" one of the things asked.

"I'll finish faster if you shut your pie hole."

Finished, she rose up – her spine cracking loudly. She did a quick stretch but kept her focus on Misandry, which was leaning against the wall. It was at arm's length should one of the monsters wish to test their luck. So far, none had.

"Is it done?" another asked, its voice thick with desperation.

"You guys are worse than a car full of toddlers."

"Answer me, butcher, for promises were made, and promises were kept. Let us feed, let us feed!"

"Nobody moves until the gate opens."

"And if it doesn't?" Walter asked. The ugly beast had come out of his hiding place and now stood on the ceiling, his long tongue dangling almost to the floor.

She picked up her sword. A second later, the blade danced with black fire – hellfire.

"Then I guess we dance."

Just when she thought it might not open, the ground beneath her feet began to tremble. She watched gleefully as the blood trails crisscrossing the floor in patterns, and unknown runes started to glow with a greenish incandescence, which made her heart sing with relief.

It worked.

She smiled. The hail for meat from the monsters again filled the shack as the floor broke around her in large chunks. They drifted upwards on invisible currents towards the ceiling, where they remained suspended. A narrow staircase comprised of human skulls led down into the open earth.

"Feast," she told the monsters, "and be well fed. Protect my transport, and you will be well rewarded upon my return."

She headed down the twisting staircase as the creatures attacked Brad's corpse in a massive tsunami of teeth. She didn't look back as she hurried down the stairs, stretching before her like a madman's spiral. There was no railing, so she kept her body pressed against the wall as she progressed toward the gate, which glowed a dull red a few hundred feet below. And then, with a thunderous crash, she found herself entombed inside the earth. A quick glance skyward revealed a blackness so complete it terrified even Agrat.

She was buried alive.

She finally reached the door with her body aching and covered in sweat. It was round and composed of a dark red (almost purple) Garnet crystal. The face of the gate was smooth and barren, with a solid black crack running down its center. There were no markings on it, no instructions, nor strange demonic illustrations. It was, for lack of a better word, just a plain oval gemstone of extraordinary magnificence.

"Is that it?"

She spun around to see the tumor coming down the steps with its tongue dragging behind it like a third arm.

"What are you doing here?"

"Meat."

Walter paused on the last step with its sick eyes firmly locked on Agrat. Behind it, she saw two more monsters materialize out of the darkness. One was the size of a small child, while the other was a six-legged monstrosity resembling a spider. And she hated spiders.

"Is that the gate to Hell?"

"It is."

"How does it work?" Walter asked.

"Magic."

"Show me how it works because after I feast on your guts, me and my friends are going home."

"You got some balls creeping down here with me squirt, I'll give you that. Remember, you may have been the boss up there, but down here, you're nothing."

Walter snarled.

"You can growl all you want, you little bastard, but that isn't going to stop me from carving you up like a Thanksgiving turkey. You want to eat me? Well, come and get it."

She threw Misandry into the kiddie monster's face just as the six-legged freak jumped at her. Its front legs were raised, revealing a pair of large, black fangs. With a quick flick of her wrist, her sword reappeared in her hand. And she plunged it deep into the spider's body, which burst into flames as hellfire consumed it.

Tossing the dead spider aside, she found Walter still standing on the steps. He hadn't moved an inch.

"I thought you wanted to eat me?"

"I lost my appetite."

"I bet you did. So…what am I to do with you?"

"Spare me."

"I'll tell you what, you see that monster lying next to you?"

Walter looked down at him and his cleaved head. His brains were all over the steps, looking like spilled jelly.

"Eat him."

"Eat…him?"

"Don't play stupid. You heard me."

"I can't. He's my son."

"Correction – was your son," she said coldly. "Now he's nothing more than maggot cheese. Now start eating, or I'll start chopping."

Walter meandered over to his dead child and took a bite right out of his shoulder, causing a massive gush of blood to spray in his face.

"Taste good?"

"I hate you Agrat bat Mahlat."

"I'll be back this way soon. When I return, I expect to find nothing but the bones remaining."

Agrat approached the stone and placed her hands on its cold surface. She pictured where she wanted to go: the Crimson Keep located in Morana, Hell's capital city.

"See you soon, squirt," she said.

There was a loud crack as the door to Hell swung wide.

And she walked through.

CHAPTER 4

Passing through the gate, Agrat arrived in a portal room at the Keep. It was a small chamber, about the size of a couple of prison cells stitched together with a high ceiling. It was windowless and as cold as a meat locker. Agrat threw her arms around her chest as she stepped off a small platform in the center of the room, a Gate Stone. As she did, a half dozen poorly wired neon lights flickered to life, flooding the room with false light.

Freezing, she raced across the room towards the door on the far end. She reached for the handle, but the door suddenly swung open before she could grab it.

Standing in front of her, dressed in the ugliest purple suit in existence, was Belial. Unlike Beelzebub and her ex, who were well-built and strong, he was damn near anorexic. His head was frosted with white hair, and a gold prosthetic nose was in the center of his oblong face.

"My Queen," Belial said as he scratched his nose. He glanced past her, back into the dark interior of the portal room. "Is it…just you?"

"I'm not enough?"

He slammed his hand against his chest and clicked his heels together as Dorothy did in that distant hellscape known as Oz. "I'm sorry, majesty, I meant no disrespect."

"Get out of my way," she said. She shoved him aside. She rushed into the warmth of the courtyard, rubbing frantically at her shoulders and arms, which were covered with frost.

"Did I say something wrong?" Belial asked, racing after her.

"Not yet."

"So Orthon and Chemat…dead or delayed?"

"Dead. We were attacked."

"And Lucious?"

"Gone," Agrat said. "And you'd never guess who saved his ass either, a real blast from the bloody past."

"Someone…saved him?"

"Lilith."

"The first wife?" Belial asked as his eyebrows shot up in crazy, quizzical arches.

"The one and only."

"Impossible. I heard she died during the Crusades."

"You heard wrong. Not only is the bitch alive, she managed to take out both mine and Mastema's teams single-handedly."

"Is Mastema dead?"

"You're not that lucky," she said as she walked towards the Keep. "He got pretty messed up in the fray, though, and actually had to jump bodies. He's a she now."

That made Belial chuckle.

"He's useless to us for the time being. At least until he recharges his batteries."

"What will we do?"

"Wait. The only way to find them now is using Mastema's spy network."

Belial nodded.

The two made it across the courtyard, walking briskly. As part of their travel, they found themselves in the cold shadow of the Crooked Tower, a dilapidated watchtower that leaned in the sunlight and dust like a broken finger.

"I tell you what, Belial, we should have never trusted Mastema and those Nonentity twats with this execution. I should have done it myself once we got topside."

"Mastema would have never allowed it."

"Who cares."

"That would be everyone else," Belial said. "We had no choice. Lucious can't be killed here, and it isn't like we can just exile him beyond the Spine."

"I know that," she snarled miserably.

"What happened up there?"

Agrat stopped walking and looked at Belial, who was scratching along the outside of his nose.

"Mastema hesitated."

"What?"

"Instead of cutting the bastard's throat, the moron monologued. Because he did that, Lilith could spring her little trap and pluck Lucious right from under our noses."

"No way."

"Yes way," Agrat said as she shook her head. "His hesitation screwed us. And now Lucious is up there with Lilith doing who knows what, and that scares me."

"Mastema was never known for his brains."

"I was positive when we presented Lucious to him practically gift-wrapped, he'd jump right in with his blades. But he didn't."

"Do you think he knew?"

"About Lilith? No. But someone had to know."

"The only other person who knew was Abaddon. He chose both the time and location," Belial said.

"That's a dangerous allegation you're making."

"But not a far-fetched one."

"How about we keep this between us," Agrat said as she started walking again, "at least until we have evidence to support this accusation. We have enough enemies already; we don't need to make more."

"You got that right."

They walked silently for a while as thunder crashed somewhere in the distance. Looking skyward, Agrat saw a sky about to fall. The clouds were blood red and hung heavy and low in the sky. "Great," Agrat said, "and now we're about to get pissed on."

"We need a good rain."

"Hell needs a flood. And speaking of Hell, what news here?"

"Beelzebub has already taken care of some of Lucious's most loyal generals during the night. He ground them into hamburgers and scattered the meat across the Grey Wastes for the monstrosities."

"Who?"

With each name he said, Belial flipped a finger up on his right hand in steady session. "Balaam, Mormo, Dagon, Bile, and Mictian. As for their legions, they were broken up and reassigned to those loyal to Beelzebub. Those who refused were exiled beyond the Spine."

"What about the Lords?"

"The Council of Thirteen will meet tomorrow."

"Tomorrow?" she repeated. "So soon?"

"It's not like we can keep Lucious's disappearance secret, your Highness. Word will spread, and rumors will grow. Beelzebub wants to face this head-on rather than let it fester. As for the bloodletting, I fear it has only just begun."

"It's a small price to pay for revolution."

"I know."

"Don't tell me you're having second thoughts?" Agrat asked.

"Not at all."

"Good, because it's too late to change your heart."

He nodded as they passed a few of the Keep's handmaidens, who bowed their heads in respect as they approached and remained that way long after they passed. Their walk took them through a small garden and towards the Great Hall and the living area of the Crimson Keep, where she would no doubt find Beelzebub.

"Where is my daughter, Naamah?" she asked. "Did you do as instructed?"

"She was sent to Nysa right after you left my Queen. She is with Lord Leviathan. She'll be safe there."

Agrat shook her head. "Nobody is safe during an insurrection, especially not the children of former kings. I don't believe Beelzebub would do anything to Naamah, but I'm not taking any chances. I lost one daughter; I refuse to lose another."

"Understandable," he said. Belial scratched the side of his nose and asked, "Do you want me to arrange a meeting with her?"

"I still don't know where I stand with Beelzebub following this colossal botch. If heads roll, I'd rather Naamah's not be one of the ones in the tumble. For now, keep her presence hidden, and if anyone should inquire about her location, you should tell me immediately."

"Yes, my Queen."

"Where's Beelzebub?"

"He's taken residence in Lucious's former solar. Last I heard, he was holding council with Abaddon."

This didn't surprise her, seeing as Abaddon was Hell's key strategist. If anyone would be whispering in Beelzebub's ear, it would be him.

"Any word what they've been discussing?"

"Don't know," he said with a shrug. "It's been pretty hush-hush since after midnight. Seems the entire second floor of the Keep is off limits and currently under heavy guard."

She nodded.

In front of them was the Inner Wall of the Crimson Keep. The walls were enormous constructs crafted out of pure lonsdaleite, painted black. The only way through the impenetrable barrier was the Black Gate, which stood at its center. It was an onyx door inscribed with phantasmagorias of the Great Fall. Beyond that, the Royal

Gardens waited, which grew around the main living area of Hell's elite nobility.

A handful of soldiers were standing guard before its behemoth doors, all wearing the Lucifer insignia. She doubted any of them were actual members of his legion; they were probably impersonators sent to preserve the illusion of normality.

As they drew closer, she noticed a new addition to the wall that day, one Agrat didn't particularly appreciate. Hanging from its enormous walls were countless Keep domestics, all she knew. Some swung by their necks, others by their ankles. All their mouths were sown shut; their bodies expertly skinned.

"A new dawn in a new Hell," Belial said.

"When did this happen?"

"Right after Beelzebub moved in."

When the soldiers spotted their approach, they ordered the doors open. There was a deafening crack as the locks released, which caused a flock of carrion birds roosting along the wall to spook and take flight.

"It's not too late," Belial said.

"For what?"

"To Run."

With the Black Gate open, she saw a path of yellow cobblestones cutting through the garden like a sacrificial dagger. And running its full length were scores of severed heads mounted on pikes, their mouths stuffed with maggots and mango worms.

"Still so confident?"

"Less so," she admitted.

"It's okay to be afraid, my Queen."

Agrat slapped him so hard that his nose flew into a cluster of nearby weeds.

"What did I say?" he asked, clutching his cheek already branded with her handprint.

"You think we're on such good terms that you think you can make such wild assumptions about me? Afraid? Afraid my ass."

"I'm sorry."

"Damn right, you are. Now go find your stupid nose and piss off. Your presence annoys me."

Without protest, Belial ran over to the weeds and began searching for his nose as Agrat started the long walk to face her fate. Whatever that meant.

As she passed through the Black Gate and into the garden, she did her best to avoid the blood raining down from above. She didn't do well, as some landed in her hair and splashed her shoulders. Cleaning it off the best she could, she hurried along the path, feeling the bloated eyes of the decapitated following her every step.

Rounding the corner, she discovered the fresh horrors of Beelzebub's newly established wrath. All the Yew trees in the garden contained yet more victims hanging from their leafless branches. She saw men and women alike because, in death, all were equal.

She made it to the Great Hall, which opened before her like the belly of a prehistoric beast, vast and empty. With the drapes drawn and the lights off, the interior was dark and unwelcoming. A large trestle table was in front of her, still covered with the rotting remains of last night's meal, Lucious's own last supper.

The rest of the room was empty.

"Where is everyone?" she wondered. Hadn't Belial said the place was crawling with heavy guards?

Confused, she made her way over to the staircase leading to the second level and charged up the steps two at a time. She was near the top when she spotted a young girl approaching, carrying a tray cluttered with dirty dishes. She didn't recognize her, but her garb established her station as an ordinary house servant.

When the serving girl noticed Agrat, she quickly dropped to one knee, nearly spilling her tray's contents all over the floor.

"Girl?"

"Yes, my Queen," she replied, her voice a barely audible squeak.

"What happened to the guards?"

"Some were sent to the kitchens – others went home."

"Under whose orders?"

"Beelzebub."

"Outside, so much death. What happened here?"

"I…"

Her words tapered off as her face drew a whiter, paler shade. Considering the horrors she witnessed, Agrat understood her hesitation. The last thing she wanted was to say the wrong thing and end up like the others in the garden.

"Go on. You are safe," Agrat ensured delicately.

The girl took a deep, uneasy breath before answering. She said, "Beelzebub ordered this house cleansed my Queen. From what I've been told, this happened not long after the feast, but I can't say with absolute truth since I wasn't here. I know that when I arrived this morning, they were still at work with the purge."

"Who?"

The girl cleared her throat before continuing her tale. "Beelzebub's soldiers. They dragged people out of the Keep and butchered them in the courtyard while they screamed for leniency. We were ordered to watch. Beelzebub wanted us to know this would happen to us too if we failed to serve."

"Were any spared?"

She shook her head.

"I take it you are from Beelzebub's old estate?"

"Yes, my Queen. I have served him since my arrival."

She meant suicide, but Agrat understood the girl's reluctance in stating the sad, depressing fact of her damnation.

"Is Abaddon still with him?"

The girl nodded.

"How long have they been together?"

"All morning. I just served them a late breakfast, my Queen. Did you need anything collected from the kitchen? I can have the cook…"

"Wine. In a chilled chalice. No food."

"Of course, my Queen," the girl said as she whisked past Agrat and disappeared down the steps, her gray robes flowing around her thin frame like a death shroud.

Agrat headed down the familiar corridor to the room she once shared with Lucious. The closed doors never looked ominous before, but today, they looked like the doors of a sepulcher. She opened them and stepped inside.

"We do not want to be disturbed," Abaddon snarled hotly.

He stood at the far end of the room next to Beelzebub, dressed in his usual long, flowing red robes that covered the floor around him like a pool of blood. The creepiest thing about it was how they slithered about the floor as if alive. When he finally turned to look at her, she couldn't see his face beneath his oversized hood. All she could see was an abyss-like blackness with a pair of pinprick yellow flames at its center.

As for her love, he stood near the window – looking at a nearby mountain range known as the Spine. It worked as a barrier between Hell and the Grey Wastes, a wicked land controlled by the monstrosities. He was dressed in a black t-shirt and a pair of faded blue jeans tucked inside a pair of snake-skin boots. A pair of leathery, black wings was pulled up tight and snug against his back. There was a time in Heaven and under the Eld's grace when many worshipped them for their immense beauty. Regardless of their transformation in the great pit, Agrat still worshipped them.

"You don't want to be disturbed?" she repeated playfully. "Fine, maybe I should just fuck off back to Earth then."

"Pardon my insolence," Abaddon said with a dry laugh. "I did not know it was you, my Queen."

"You are most wise, but not even you can see through walls," Agrat replied, entering the room. "So, what you two gossiping about up here all alone? Girls?"

Snapping out of his silent contemplation, Beelzebub turned and looked at her with his eyes glimmering in gold.

Without restraint, Agrat raced across the room and leaped into his arms. He hugged her tightly, and she returned it with extra vigor. It felt good to do it so openly and freely after all the time sneaking around in the shadows.

"You've returned earlier than expected," he said. He kissed her gently on the forehead. "We thought after his execution you'd linger topside a bit to celebrate your liberation."

"She couldn't be kept from you, my lord," Abaddon said with a chuckle. "You are the perfect drug."

Though she didn't want to sabotage this wonderful moment, she knew she had to tell them the truth. With a heavy heart, she said, "As much as I love the lunkhead, that's not why I returned. I returned because there was nothing to celebrate. We failed."

"Failed?" Abaddon repeated, shocked. "How so?"

She told them about the night's chaotic happenings, leaving out none of the details. And as she spoke, she kept a close eye on Abaddon, reading his body language like a book. She watched his eyes, jaw, or for any exaggerated nodding that might signal stress. She saw none. If he knew something about the escape, he kept his dark secrets securely hidden.

Finished, she waited for Beelzebub's reaction with a terrible unease. She remembered all the skinned servants and the heads lining the path with their jaws slackened and their mouths overflowing with slimy, fat worms. Am I next? She wondered as she imagined her own head decorating a pike.

"Penny for your thoughts, my love," Agrat pressed gently, not liking the grave-like silence.

"I'm not sure I have any yet. Is Mastema sure it was Lilith? I heard she died during the Blitz."

"He swears to it."

They looked at Abaddon.

"I don't know about the Blitz," he stammered, "but I have it under good authority from a local Nonentity in Japan named Rabis, that he saw her eradicated in Nagasaki."

"How many times has she died?" Agrat asked. "Someone needs to tell her she's supposed to be dead."

"Why would Rabisu lie?"

"Because he's a gutless Nonentity, for starters," Agrat fired back. "We all know Nonentities can't be trusted, which is why I still find it perplexing we put so much faith in one."

A gentle rapping at the chamber door killed Abaddon's chance at an explanation. The door slowly creaked open as the serving girl from the stairwell poked her head inside.

"I'm sorry to intrude, but I have the Queen's wine."

She showed them the chalice.

"Bring it to me," Agrat ordered, her hand outstretched. The girl ran over, handed it to Agrat, and then bolted from the room.

To bar any further interruptions, Beelzebub stormed over and locked the door. With it secure, he looked back at Abaddon and ordered him to finish his thought.

"I was just going to remind everyone why we aligned ourselves with Mastema in the first place because, in the aftermath of failure, it seems we have forgotten. Earth is the only place Lucious is weak enough to be killed, and since Mastema governs the Earth realm, he demands payment for its usage. That payment was Lucious's soul."

Agrat hated to admit it, but Abaddon was right — as usual.

"But why would Lilith, if it was Lilith, risk her neck saving Lucious?" Agrat asked. She looked at Beelzebub and then at Abaddon as she drank her wine.

"The more important question, as I'm sure you've contemplated deeply, my Queen, is how. Someone had the foresight to know where Lucious would be and when, hence the assassin. Most of the conspirers to eliminate our dear, sweet Lord are in this room. I know I didn't do it. I doubt either of you had a hand in keeping Lucious alive because it is detrimental to our cause."

"Then who?" Beelzebub asked.

"That's the million-dollar question," Agrat replied.

"At this point," Abaddon said, "it doesn't serve us to weave pointless conspiracy theories about whom it may be because the conniver will eventually reveal themselves. I suggest you," he said as he pointed at Beelzebub with one wormy finger, "focus all your attention on the upcoming meeting with the Council. That is, without question, your most immediate threat."

"Speaking of the Council – why are you meeting them so soon?" Agrat asked Beelzebub. The Council of 13 was comprised of the ruling elite of Hell, most hand-selected by Lucious. It was madness to meet with them so soon, especially with him still alive and out there, capable of unleashing havoc.

Beelzebub took her hand and squeezed it. "I've been hiding in the shadows for far too long, and I hate it. I'm no schemer; I'm a warrior who prefers to look his enemies in the eye rather than stab them in the back. I'm not proud of the way we dethroned Lucious. Love him or not, he liberated us from the Eld's tyrannical rule. I plan on unmasking myself upon the morrow and fighting for my right to be King. And I want you by my side."

She smiled. "I'll be there, my love."

"If I may interject a moment," Abaddon said. "Since Mastema told you it was Lilith, does that mean he still lives?"

"Barely," she said. "His body was destroyed in the skirmish, so he possessed some poor waitress. So, he is now a she. He also told me he needed to rest before continuing the hunt. So, I guess until he's ready, I'll stick around. Assist where needed."

"Good to hear," Abaddon said, clapping. "You are greatly needed here."

She nodded.

"Once he's ready," Beelzebub said, "I want you topside so you can finish what you started. And when you come back, I want his head."

"Nothing would give me greater pleasure, my love."

They kissed.

That night, while Agrat and Beelzebub transformed Lucious's old bedroom into their personal pleasure palace, Mastema drove to Mesa, Arizona, sweating blood.

He wanted to keep going. Not only to put more distance between him and Ray's Diner but just to get the hell out of Arizona in general – he hated the damn state. And the last thing he wanted to do was die there. Battling against fever chills, body aches, and one big ass headache, Mastema reached out to one of his Lieutenants, a slimy toad named Zozo.

"My King?"

"Where are you?"

"I don't know. Some pathetic little graveyard in the middle of nowhere with a couple of dumb-ass teens. They're actually trying to summon the Devil with an Ouija board. I think I will possess one of them and then kill the rest."

"Well, stop with the games and come to me quick. I need your help," Mastema said, telling Zozo about the night's twisted events.

"Did you say…Lilith?"

"Yeah."

"Lilith saved Lucifer?"

"Yeah," Mastema repeated, annoyed. "Are you deaf? You got maggots in your ears or what? Lilith saved Lucifer."

"I thought she died during the Battle of Stalingrad?"

"Well, I don't know what to tell you – either she's been resur-fucking-rected, or your information is bogus. Besides, that's kind of missing the point, Zozo – I'm knocking on death's door and need your assistance. You going to come or murder a bunch of teens?"

"Can't I do both?"

"No."

"You buzz killer. Where you at?"

Up ahead, he saw a hotel with its Vacancy light blazing. He turned into the parking lot and parked near the office.

"Some dive in Mesa called Oyo. Did you see it?"

"As clear as day, my lord."

"How long will it take for you to get here?"

"I'm riding the winds of change as we speak."

"Good," he said. He grabbed a dirty shirt off the floor. "I want you to contact Tzit; bring him with you."

"Can't you call him?"

"Did you not hear what I said, you twat? I'm dying. If I don't get some rest, I'll be dead by dawn."

"As you wish, my lord. See you soon."

He turned off the car and checked his reflection in the mirror. The waitress, his latest meat suit, was kind of pretty. Once you washed away all the filth and terror. Using the shirt, he cleaned off the blood and sweat. Finished, he dropped it on the floor and drifted deep inside his head – searching for the trapped soul of the possessed woman.

"You in here, sweetheart?"

No answer.

"There's no use hiding – I can feel you. You can either step forward on your own, or I'll drag you out."

What…what are you?

"I'm Mastema, King of the Nonentities. But you can call me Master. What's your name?"

Fuck you.

"Tsk, tsk – is that any way to talk to your Master? If you want to survive this encounter, I'd check that temper because the only thing keeping you alive is the fact that I haven't killed you yet. Now tell me, what is your name?"

Linnea. Please Mastema…

"Master."

…Master, she corrected, I have kids.

"Sounds like a personal problem to me. Now look, I'll make a deal with you, Linnea. You help me book a room, and I'll give you a chance to call your brats. Deal?"

Yes.

"I'm going to give you back your body but remember everything you do…I see. If you do something stupid like call for help, I'll not only end you, but I'll end your family, too. Do you hear me, Linnea?"

Yes.

"Do you believe me?"

"I saw what you did at the diner."

"I'll take that as a yes," he said as he popped open the glovebox. Inside were a few bricks of cash — all nicely pressed and bound with rubber bands. He took one out and placed it on the seat next to him. "We don't have any ID, so we'll have to appeal to their greed. If that doesn't work, you'll either blow them, or I'll kill them. Any questions?"

What should I say if they ask why I don't have my ID?

"Whatever you think will work."

How much cash is that?

"10k."

How much can I use?

"As much as you need. Are you ready, or are we going to keep playing this round of 20 Questions?"

Ready.

He retreated into her subconscious like a traumatic memory, and like a freight train, she came rushing forward — taking back control of her body.

He watched.

The first thing Linnea did was stare at her hands, which shook uncontrollably. And then she touched her face, her hair, neck, and chest as she struggled against a tidal wave of shock.

Get a hold of yourself, woman. Take the money and get me a room before I lose my patience, Mastema snarled.

"I'm trying."

Try harder.

She took a deep breath, snatched the money off the passenger seat, and exited the car. She entered Oyo's small office on a pair of shaky legs. There was nothing inside, just a large counter cutting through the center of the room with an old, obese woman sitting behind it.

So much for the blow job, Mastema said.

The woman didn't look up at Linnea as she approached; she just continued typing on her computer. Mastema and Linnea knew she was faking her work because the computer screen was not reflecting in her wireframe glasses.

Linnea cleared her throat.

Without looking at her, the woman said, "We have a nonnegotiable $150 security deposit upfront. If you have a problem with that, you can find yourself another hotel."

"I'm fine with that."

The woman looked up at her, allowing Mastema to glimpse silver hairs growing above the whale's lip. It was without question the world's ugliest mustache – and he knew Hitler.

"Rough night?"

"You have no idea," she said. Mastema read the woman's name tag hanging above her sagging fun bags, a set of tits not looked upon favorably in decades, and said, "Look, I'm in a bit of trouble here, Miss Wray, but I don't have my ID or credit cards because I left a bad situation in a rush. I'm looking for a place to stay for a few days until things cool down. I have cash."

Miss Wray nodded and then asked, "Man trouble?"

"Isn't it always?"

"You should think about joining the other team, doll face," she said with a wink. "I'll help you out. You need me to call the police for ya?"

"No. I'm going to call my sister."

Miss Wray gave her some paperwork to fill out and took her money, double the regular amount, of course. Then she got her key to room 217. As they walked to the car, Mastema reclaimed control of the body.

He drove the car to the back of the hotel, finding his room on the second floor. He grabbed a bag from the trunk and charged up the steps barefoot, having abandoned the high heels in the car. He was almost to the room when Linnea called out to him. Are you still going to let me speak to my kids?

"I will if you stop asking me about it."

He unlocked the door and stepped inside, gagging temporarily on the room's musty stench. He slammed the door shut, flicked on the light, and turned on the air conditioner unit, cranking it up to full. The room was your average hotel with nothing of interest except for its lack of cockroaches.

He dropped his bag and walked over to the bed, which was lumpy and dirty. On the center of a badly cigarette-burned quilt was a pool of still-warm cum. Mastema didn't care about it or the rest of the filth in the room; he needed sleep, and he was going to get it. He jumped on the bed, which moaned bitterly beneath the weight. Not the weight of the waitress but the demonic spirit inhabiting her petite frame.

Mastema grabbed the phone off the nightstand and set it beside him. Before he drifted off, he allowed his host body a chance to call her children. He warned her he'd listen and watch, but he didn't. He could care less about her sweet words or empty promises whispered to a bunch of brats. He went to sleep dreaming of sweet, violent revenge on the bitch and Lucifer.

CHAPTER 5

Agrat rolled over, reaching for Beelzebub, but all she found was an empty, cold space. Sitting up, she glanced over at the displaced bedding and wondered how long he'd been gone and just how drunk she was not to notice him go.

With her head pounding, she grabbed a bottle of wine off the nightstand. With a groan, she uncorked it with her teeth and spit the sour stopper across the room as her blankets slipped away from her slender frame, exposing her breasts to the chill of the chamber. She didn't care as she finished the last of the wine in a few greedy gulps.

She belched.

Agrat closed her eyes as her body ached from a night of disgusting depravity. After Abaddon excused himself, Agrat and Beelzebub indulged themselves in absolute wickedness. They drank and then banged into the predawn hours while the souls of the condemned rained down from the sky.

The sex had been perfect, but she still wanted more. Her pussy ached for Beelzebub's throbbing manhood, which made Lucious resemble a broken pencil. She wanted to feel it inside her, wanted to feel the fullness of it as it rubbed and explored her womanhood until she reached climax. As great as his cock was, Agrat loved his mouth more – loving the way he devoured her. His mouth was magic, and she wanted to experience it again.

But she had to wait.

Annoyed, she shouted for a serving girl – her voice booming off the walls like a gunshot. A second later, she heard a knock at the door just before it slowly opened a few cautious inches. Peeking in was a young, brown-skinned girl with curly hair. If Agrat had to guess, the girl couldn't have been a day over 15.

"Ma'am?"

"Ma'am? Are you kidding me?"

"I'm sorry…I…"

"Call me ma'am again, and I'll have you boiled alive in the public square. What time is it?"

"A little after eight."

"Have you seen Beelzebub?"

"He's in the Grand Hall preparing to meet with the Council, my Queen. Did you want me to bring breakfast?" the girl asked.

"What I want is for you to piss off."

The servant girl didn't need to be told twice; she slammed the door and was instantly gone. Agrat sighed, longing for her old servant girls, who now resided outside as tree ornaments. She decided once a sense of normality returned to the kingdom; she'd convince Beelzebub to cut them down so they could return to work.

Speaking of returning to work, Agrat thought she better reach out to Mastema. Leaving him alone for too long, unchecked, was dangerous. Leaning back against the headboard, she closed her eyes and focused all her energy on the King of the Nonentities; she started drifting.

Making a connection from Hell to an earthbound spirit was typically difficult, but doing so while horribly hungover as Agrat was made it next to impossible. The first few tries, she failed so miserably that she nearly gave up on the foolish notion altogether and probably would have too if there wasn't so much on the line.

She closed her eyes and tried one last time.

And it worked.

She saw a light at the end of a long, dark tunnel – a vortex between worlds. She floated towards it until the light consumed every inch of her celestial being. It was like an old dial-up connection in the primitive digital age, minus all the annoying sounds and mind-numbing load times.

Agrat? You live?

"Surprised?"

Absolutely.

"Well, what can I say? I'm a survivor. Where are you?"

A hotel, he replied brazenly.

"Could you be more specific?"

A dumpy one. Why do you care? Are you coming back?

"Not yet."

Then don't ask. Once you're topside, I'll give you the details.

"How are you holding up?"

I'm falling apart faster than a cheap Chinese suit, but I'll live.

You hope, she thought. "You feel like you can track yet?" she asked, hoping he'd say yes. She was more than ready to start hunting again.

Soon.

"How soon?"

When I'm ready, you impatient cunt. Unlike you, I almost died last night. If it weren't for an emergency possession, I'd be dead, and your mission would be over and done with. Do not contact me again. When I'm ready, I'll reach out to you, and not a moment before. Understood?

The light vanished as Mastema closed himself off to her. Furious, she kicked off the blankets and snatched a dark gray robe off the back of a chair as she stormed across the chamber.

"That miserable…no good…arrogant dick," she said as she slipped into a robe. "Who does he think he's speaking to, one of his Nonentity fucks?"

She went to the window, unlatched the heavy shutters, and threw it open. Outside, beyond the Crimson Keep and its walls of red stone, she saw the capital city of Hell hidden behind a thick, dirty haze.

Morana.

Most of the city's dwellings were hidden from view due to the massive black ramparts coiling around the city like some great serpent, but the taller structures rose above it. The tallest of these glass beasts was as tall as the Empire State Building in New York but more phallic and apocalyptic in design.

There were a million twinkling lights from the city's business quarter and massive viewing screens the size of billboards broadcasting a steady stream of news and brainless entertainment in high-definition madness. The sky above the city was flooded with a hodgepodge of modern aircraft like helicopters and planes and demonic flying machines from steampunk nightmares and winged monsters. And at the heart of it were the spires of the Campanile of the Mourning reaching into high the sky like skeletal fingers.

"To hell with Mastema, King of nothing."

Agrat showered and then slipped into jeans, a pair of pink leather knee-high boots, and a red t-shirt with the words Stephen King Rules itched in yellow across her small chest. She ate a light breakfast as she waited for the Council to convene. She wanted quiet and a chance to collect her thoughts. But she didn't get it. Ten minutes before the meeting was to begin, Abaddon entered.

"My Queen," he said from beneath his massive, blood-red hood, "how did you sleep last night?"

"Didn't get much sleep."

"Stress?"

"Sex. Can I ask you a question?"

"About sex?"

"Did you plant this seed in Beelzebub?"

"What do you mean?"

"This stupid meeting, Abaddon," she said as she crossed her arms. "If you ask me, this damn thing isn't just stupid, it's damn near suicidal. Do I have to remind you of who sits on it? These aren't just some random Lords; these are some of the most loyal and beloved of all Lucious's Fallen. You think they'll just sit there and accept this regime change?"

"I don't know what to expect, but I did offer Beelzebub counsel."

"And?"

"He told me to go and fuck myself. In the end, the ultimate decision sits with the king, and he has made his choice. All we can do is stand with him and let the chips fall where they may. Are you ready? He is waiting for you."

"Would you be surprised if I said no?"

"I'd be more surprised if you said yes, my Queen."

He offered her his hand. It was a fleshless thing, all bone. She took it, and then they headed down the corridor leading to the staircase. They were about halfway down when she spotted her love standing at its base, looking suave in his new suit.

"He looks good."

"He looks like a King," Abaddon said.

Agrat raced over to him and kissed him firmly on the cheek. And then she punched him in the shoulder as he stepped back in surprise.

"What was that for?"

"Have you ever heard that song 'Wake Me Up Before You Go-Go'?"

"Do I look like the type who would?"

"Not really."

He kissed her forehead and then took her hands as they started walking. But they weren't going alone; a handful of his royal sentries followed behind them. They were dressed for war in their heavy battle armor. On their hips were large ass bastard swords forged in the furnaces of Hell, and in their hands, they carried triple-barreled shotguns.

"Abaddon and I have been talking," he whispered. "We believe when you return topside that a Lord should go with you. Someone we can trust."

"Oh, joy."

"Come on, Agrat, don't be like that. A Lord can offer you better protection than an imp and give you better counsel. If nothing else, at least consider it."

"I'll consider it after I find out who it is," she said. She glanced back at Abaddon, who trailed behind them like a ghostly specter. "Who did ya'll have in mind?"

"Belial," Abaddon said.

She stopped.

"Belial? Out of all the Lords..."

"We can trust him," Beelzebub concluded sternly.

"Are you guys ribbing me right now? Because if you are, this isn't funny, not even in the slightest."

"This is no joke," Abaddon added.

"Well, it should be. Let me remind you what happened the last time Mastema and Belial shared a room because you both forgot. Mastema bit his nose off! Can't we choose somebody else?"

"We both agree he is the best choice," Abaddon said.

"Hate to see your worst choice."

"How about we survive the meeting first," Abaddon said. "After that, should we survive, we can discuss it further."

"Fair enough," Beelzebub said with a nod. "How about you go ahead of us and clear out the hall? Especially any armed escorts. If the Council asks why, inform them their questions will be addressed once the meeting begins."

Abaddon raced off towards the main hall in a mad sprint, his robes trailing behind him like a wave of blood.

"Nervous?"

She looked up at Beelzebub, who loomed over her. She smiled at him and said, "I'm not if you're not."

"You think a meeting with a bunch of policymakers intimidates me? I swung my Warhammer at the Eld's face. This is nothing."

"Would you kill your brothers?" she asked.

"Those who revolt against me are not my brothers."

"You're vicious."

They kissed as the corridor filled with the thunder of angry shouts.

"Seems like things are off to a great start," Agrat said.

"Shall we?"

She nodded.

With their fingers tightly intertwined, they entered the main hall. There, they saw Lesser Lords and a handful of high-ranking human officials screaming as they were ushered unceremoniously out by Beelzebub's forces.

The hall for the meeting was a large chamber. It was a place Agrat knew well, having spent eons inside its cavernous space sitting beside Lucious. The thrones were on the far end, sitting on a small stage. These faced a long black marble table, where the Council of Thirteen sat in anticipation of today's surprise summoning.

Without a word or greeting, they headed directly towards the stage. As she walked, she cast a quick look at those in attendance. The chair Beelzebub typically occupied was empty, but the others were all full. Along the left side of the table were Paimon, Zagan, Xaphan, Volac, Uvall, and the sickly obese Stolas. On the right sat Sabnock, Murmur, Naberius, Shax, Rahvoret, and Belial at the far end.

It was the longest and most uncomfortable walk of her life. The worst part about it was the way the eyes felt; she literally felt them digging into her, borrowing deep like maggots on a rotten, bloated corpse. They were near their destination when Sabnock suddenly broke the peace.

"What is the meaning of this? Where is Lucious?"

"He's gone," Beelzebub said as he led Agrat with an iron-clad grip towards the thrones.

"What do you mean he's gone?" Paimon asked in his salsy lisp.

Instead of answering, Beelzebub and Agrat headed up a small flight of steps leading to the thrones. Agrat took her usual position as Beelzebub claimed dominance over Hell by taking Lucious's seat to the shock and gasps of the Council.

"Get out of that chair," Volac demanded. "That is reserved for our King, and you know it!"

"I know, that's why I'm sitting in it."

Agrat was amazed by Beelzebub's stoic calm under such calamitous circumstances as the one they faced. Before them sat the most powerful and influential demons in all of Hell, and he wasn't even sweating.

"Explain to us this madness," Zagan said in his nasally, high-pitched voice. "Where is our King?"

"Dead."

There was a round of shocked gasps from the council.

"And there will be no glorious resurrection for him, so you might as well bury the thought. He was taken topside, and after his execution, I had Mastema swallow his soul," Beelzebub said. He leaned back into the throne, arms crossed as he grinned manically. It was clear to Agrat that he was enjoying the moment, relishing it. "So, as you can see, brothers, nothing is left to save except yourselves."

Shax charged.

Agrat sprang to her feet with Misandry in hand as Shax charged up the steps like an enraged bull, his hands engulfed in flames. Agrat was about to bring her sword crashing down on the rogue Lord's neck when Beelzebub snatched him by the throat.

Shax tried to punch him, but Beelzebub slapped it away like he would an annoying fly. Holding him by the neck, the new King of Hell rose from his throne as Shax kicked and trashed wildly. Someone shouted for mercy, but Agrat couldn't pinpoint the advocate.

"I respect you, which is why I'm rewarding you with a quick death," Beelzebub said.

"You're a gutless bastard," Shax said breathlessly, "who rules Hell with a whore for a Queen."

"So much for the quick death," Beelzebub said. He jammed a dagger into Shax's abdomen, again and again in rapid succession. On the last thrust, the blade ignited in black flame. And he buried it deep, twisting and turning it as the Lord's guts roasted on the inside.

Beelzebub tossed him to the base of the stage as his guards ran over with their guns raised.

"Don't just stand there – shoot this dickhead."

They opened fire on him. At such a close range, the damage was massive. One shot took off his arm at the elbow, while another took off a leg. One guard managed to blow his head off, which burst like an overripe watermelon.

Beelzebub raised a hand, silencing the thunder. His guards quickly reloaded their boom sticks.

"Have his remains sent to the Feeding Pits. And just so he's not lonely, have his wife and children sent there as well."

"Beelzebub…"

"Choose your next words very carefully, Uvall."

"His family?" the Lord asked cautiously.

"What about them?"

Uvall looked at the others clustered around him for support, but nobody said anything. They just stared at him blankly. He carefully continued, "I just think you should show some compassion."

Beelzebub retook his seat. "I could do that, but I won't."

Agrat sat as house servants collected the remains of Shax and his scattered limbs, dropping them in a basket. She had assumptions about how this was going to go but never thought she'd witness outright butchery in these sacred halls. The look on the surviving council members seemed to reflect this chain of thought as well. Within 30 seconds, all of Shax was removed from the hall – the floor mopped.

"Let me propose a question to you, brothers: when was the last time we gathered here to celebrate a victory against our enemies?"

Nobody answered.

"We've lost so many times I've forgotten what victory tasted like. Under Lucious, we lost the Grey Wastes to the Nameless Thing and his army of monstrosities beyond the mountains. And what of our last attempt to invade Heaven?"

"Disaster," Belial grumbled.

"We lost more than half our strength in a single battle. When I returned to Hell afterward, I was covered in blood, not of my enemies, but of friends. It was then, on that accursed day, that I decided we needed a change. It wasn't because I hated Lucious or desired his position but because I grew exhausted from having my teeth kicked down my throat.

"Agrat and I decided to save Hell from a leader steering us towards oblivion. And though it pained me to do so, I did what none of you had the balls to do: I acted. Now, it's time for Hell to move into a new age with fresh leadership. And to taste sweet victory once more! So, what say you?"

Agrat watched as the Lords looked at each other nervously, with their eyes bulging in their sockets. Beelzebub reached out towards her hand, and she took it. It was cold and clammy, a corpse's hand.

"How can we trust you?" Stolas asked as he rose from his seat, his obese belly knocking the table as he stood. "You stabbed our King in the back, slaughtered the servants of his house, and killed one of your own brothers."

"The outside doors are locked and will remain so until you declare allegiance to me or die. It's that simple. And since you are standing, we'll start with you, Stolas."

Say yes, Agrat thought desperately. Please say yes.

"I'm in," he said and sat back down.

"Wise decision. Paimon, what about you?"

Everyone stared at the Lord as he reluctantly rose to his feet. Agrat knew if Paimon pledged to follow, then others would likely too because he was the Chief Counselor to Lucious and one of his closest friends. Winning him would be a decisive and highly favorable turn of events. She crossed her fingers.

"Stolas was never known for having much of a spine, but I do, and I don't bend the knee so easily. You are a dishonest, treacherous bastard unworthy of the crown and the responsibilities that come with it. If you were angry at Lucious, as a member of this council, you had every right to express it. But you never did. Instead, you plotted secretly behind his back while you banged his wife."

"You…"

"I'm not finished," Paimon shouted, cutting off Beelzebub. "I will not be interrupted, not by you or anyone else."

Agrat couldn't believe her eyes when her lover did nothing to Paimon's outburst. She wanted him to lash out vehemently against the Lord; she wanted dismemberment, but instead, she got a docile reaction as her love did nothing.

"You are a coward, not a King. And if you are the future of Hell, I want no part of it. As for the rest of you," he said as he looked at the other members of the council, "do what you want. Save your worthless hides by getting on your knees and sucking this maggot's grotesque cock, but I will not be joining you. If any of you ever loved, truly loved, Lucious like he loved us, you wouldn't do it either."

Agrat watched in horror as Murmur stood.

And then Xaphan.

"You brothers feel the same?" Beelzebub asked indifferently.

"You are not my King," Xaphan answered.

"Nor mine," agreed Murmur.

"Anyone else wish to throw it all away?"

Agrat looked at the other council members as her heart thudded like a bass drum in her chest. Then Belial stood, putting one of his hands on Paimon's shoulder. With the other, he cut his throat, so deep and intense the Lord's head flipped backward like a Piz dispenser, spewing blood all over the table, floor, and Belial's suit.

"Now you know where I stand," he said, shoving Paimon aside.

Agrat knew the display was meant for her, not the council or the new King. Belial wanted to demonstrate he was a man of action, strength, and resolve. More importantly, it was to entice her should she grow tired of Beelzebub. She knew this because she could sense his carnal desires oozing out of every pour.

"Do you wish me to apply my trade to the rest of these traitors?" Belial asked.

"I'm no traitor," Xaphan protested.

"You are a traitor…a traitor to our new King!" Belial shouted, pointing his knife at the Lord.

"Guards," Beelzebub shouted. "Crucify them in the public square. As for Paimon, send him and his family to the Feeding Pits."

She expected to see the former council members fight back, but instead, they went willingly. As for Paimon, his carcass was punctured by meat hooks and dragged away like dead cattle. What transpired next was nothing shy of a black miracle. The remaining members of the Council of Thirteen, the surviving few, declared their loyalty to Beelzebub.

To ensure nobody saved their necks long enough to revolt later, Agrat recommended everyone sign their names in the Book of Shadows, an ancient ledger created by the Kernunno. If they broke their blood oath of fidelity, whoever signed it would be banished to limbo.

Nobody objected when Abaddon presented it for them to sign. Afterward, they all reclaimed their seats and drank goblets of spiced wine in celebration as the mood of the council went from dire to one of fanaticism as legions were divided and the wealth of the dead, exiled Lords was redistributed.

Beelzebub had won.

Into the Void

CHAPTER 1

"How are you holding up, big guy?"

"Considering I haven't showered or changed my underwear in two days, I think I'm holding up pretty well," Lucious said. He was sitting Indian style in the center of the cell and, up to Lilith's arrival, was busy passing the time by counting the crosses on the wall. Ironically, he just reached 666. Brushing his bangs out of his eyes, he asked, "Is our mutual acquaintance back?"

"Nervous?"

"Hell no. Try bored. It isn't like you're the Queen of conversation, is it? And the food…Jesus…you should be locked up for human rights violations on that alone."

"Oh. My. God. Half the world survives on fast food these days, Lucifer. Get with the times and live in the now. Besides, it's not like I'm going to bust my ass cooking for you. I got better things to do with my time, like watching paint dry."

"I doubt you have the skill outside of putting a few cold cuts on bread and slathering it with mayonnaise."

"Mustard," she corrected.

"Eating fast food is equivalent to ingesting excrement."

"Fair enough observation, I guess, but it's better than eating dirt."

"Is it?"

She shrugged.

"Would you be surprised to learn the Father of Fast Food is a demon?"

"Not really."

"His name is Gressil, and he's directly responsible for over 40 of the most popular fast-food chains."

"No shit?"

"His proudest accomplishment was the creation of Popeyes."

"The chicken place?"

"You ever been there? It's like being in Hell."

"You must be so proud."

"I gave him a plaque," he said as he got up.

"This demon…"

"Gressil."

"Yeah, whatever. Is he one of the keepers of this Shroud thingy?"

"One of many," Lucious said nonchalantly.

"Why don't you tell me where he is so I can kill him."

"Sorry babe, no freebies."

"Oh. My. God. Did you just call me babe?"

"Better than bitch."

"I could torture it out of you," Lilith said.

"You're welcome to try," he said. He leaned against the door and said, "I must warn you, I have some pretty kinky turn-ons. Let me ask you something…did they take this long when considering your terms?"

"Does it matter?" she asked.

"I wanted to calculate my odds."

"Calculate this," she said. She gave him the finger. "I'm not going to tell you anything. Besides, I like watching you squirm on your hook."

Talking to Lilith was really weighing on Lucious in a horrible, no good, very bad way. One day of this sort of slow torture was one thing, but two days of it was beyond excruciating. If Gabriel didn't return soon, he'd sacrifice himself to the crosses on the walls.

"What did you ask for?" Lucious asked.

"Why are you so interested in my arrangement?"

"Curiosity."

"Well, we both know what curiosity did to the cat."

"Do I look like a cat?" he asked with a smirk.

She looked him up and down, her eyes full of judgment. "You really don't want to know what I think you look like. Anyway," she said as she fished out a set of keys from her pocket. "I'm going to open the door, but if you do anything stupid…"

"You'll kick my ass," he said as he finished her sentence. "I've heard all this before, multiple times. Trust me, I know."

She unlocked the door.

When he opened it, she did a wild back flip, landed, and raised both her arms in front of her face in some self-defenses pose. He thought she looked stupid. Raising his arms in peace, he said, "Relax, I'm not going to do anything."

To demonstrate his innocent intentions, he offered her his best smile. It only made her cringe.

"Don't do that…you smile like a shark."

"At least I smile."

"Oh. My. God. Do you ever shut up?"

"Not really."

"I can see why your wife left you," she said as she stormed down the hallway. "Gabriel is waiting for you in the waiting room."

Lucious followed her. Sure enough, the angelic prick was waiting for him, dressed in the same robes as their last encounter. Tucked under his left arm was a folder, which no doubt contained his fate. Deal or no deal, he thought; the hammer was about to fall.

"You're looking good," Gabriel said. He waved at Lucious as he entered the room. "I see Lilith has been treating you well."

"If you consider being forced fed toxic waste being treated well, then I've been living like a king."

Confused, Gabriel looked at Lilith and asked, "Toxic waste?"

"The Prima Donna ate fast food."

"Let's cut the crap," Lucious said as he pointed at the folder. "Is that His decree?"

"It is."

"Great! Can we get on with it, please? I mean, if I'm about to die, I'd rather get it over and done with than stand around all day listening to you retards jibber-jabber."

"No need to be rude, Lucifer," Gabriel replied, opening the folder. He flipped through it until he stumbled on a pink paper. He pulled it out and set the folder on a dust-covered chair.

"Pink?"

"Michael picked it."

"Of course he did," Lucious said. "What's the verdict?"

"He said no."

"To what?"

"To everything."

"So, does that mean I get to kill him?" Lilith asked, sounding too excited – like a girl being asked to prom by the school's hottest stud muffin.

"Yes," Gabriel said with a smile.

"Fine," Lucious said with a shrug. "Get it over with. I've heard there are other worlds than these."

"I need to get my chainsaw, just a second," Lilith said as she ran towards the nurse's station. She was nearly there when Gabriel called after her. She stopped and looked back, confused. "Too messy?"

"I was kidding."

"Kidding?" Lucious and Lilith said in unison.

"What, I can't have a little fun?"

"You asshole," Lucious snarled.

"Guilty," the angelic douche said with a laugh. He looked down at the paper in his hand and said, "As far as Hell is concerned, the Eld agrees with your terms. After the Shroud has been removed, He'll work to have you regain your status as the King of the Pit."

Lucious looked at Lilith, who was sulking at the nurse's station. "I told you He'd agree to my terms. Desperation breaks the strongest of resolves, dear one. Remember that."

She flipped him off.

"But there are two conditions to this, Lucifer," Gabriel said gravely. "The first condition is that you'll be 100% responsible for keeping your kingship. Do not ask or even consider additional support from Him in any way, shape, or form post-recouping your sovereignty."

"Fair enough," Lucious said.

"Secondly, once you begin your new rule, there will be no attempt to reestablish a second Shroud. Any attempt to do so will result in your immediate perdition. Do you agree to these two conditions?"

"Absolutely."

Gabriel's finger burned a bright gold as he made a few check marks on the paper. Then he said, "As for the fate of Eisheth. I'm afraid this condition was rejected."

"What? Why?"

"The Eld cannot risk having her return to Hell knowing what she knows. I'm sorry."

"Fuck your sorry."

"Considering the current state of your former kingdom," Gabriel fired back angrily, "this decree may have very well just saved her life. Shall I continue, or should I stop here?"

Biting his bottom lip, Lucious gestured for him to continue.

"During your conquest to remove the Shroud, lives of the innocent shall be spared at all costs. This rule also extends to the rest of your team. Failure to comply with this will result in your immediate execution."

Lucious nodded.

"Michael has been delegated with the task."

"Michael?" Lucious said with a laugh. "I bet he volunteered."

"He did. Do you agree to this term?"

"Sure. Whatever."

Gabriel's finger glowed as he made some additional zippy doodles on the paper. Finished, he looked back up at him and continued. "About the army…"

"Please tell me He said no," Lilith said, adding her own two cents.

"I'm sorry, Lilith, but He agrees."

"Oh. My. God. Seriously?"

"Please, Lilith," Gabriel said, "don't interrupt."

"Yeah," Lucious said, "don't spoil this for me. Listening to the Eld concede to my commands gives me a chubby."

"Concede? Tell me again what He said about Eisheth?"

"Enough with these childish insults," Gabriel commanded. "You two are aligned now, fighting for the same righteous cause. Somehow, someway, bury the hatchet."

Annoyed, Lilith threw her arms up in frustration and disappeared behind the nurse's counter. Lucious hoped she wasn't getting that chainsaw of hers.

"What about the army?" Lucious asked.

"The Eld says you can only conscript those bound to the pit. In addition, hell-bound offenses cannot be indulged by anyone in your ragtag militia. Doing so will result in immediate dispatch to the deepest, darkest part of Hell – the Grey Wastes."

"Hell-bound offenses. How will they know?"

"Let them figure it out. God forbid they actually pray for answers or crack open the Bible. Do you agree to this term?"

"What do you think, man?"

"You have to say it," Gabriel said, his finger glowing with divine energy. "I don't make the rules. I just enforce them."

"Yes, I agree. Damn."

Gabriel's stupid glowing finger flared brightly once more as he did some masturbatory writing on the paper. Finished, he offered it to Lucious.

"Is this the contract?"

"Hold the phone," Lilith said as she joined them. "Why are we giving him access to an army? Look at him, Gabe; he's broke and powerless; let's keep him that way."

"Lilith…"

"Don't you think killing this turd would improve the Eld's health woes better than slaughtering a bunch of lesser demons? This dude is the root of His cancer!"

"We went over every viable option long before we put this plan into action, Lilith. This wasn't our first choice nor second," Gabriel said gently.

"What number was it?" Lucious asked.

"It was in the high thousands."

"This is so fucked up," Lilith said. "We plan to go to war against the forces of darkness working with its architect! He's the Great Deceiver, the Mourning Star, and we're letting him lead the assault. This is madness."

"You can always opt out of your contract," Gabriel said. "This is how the Eld wants to proceed, so you can either be part of the solution or you can hit the road."

She sighed.

"Do you wish to continue Lilith?" Gabriel asked.

"Fine. I'm in."

"Until death do us part," Lucious mocked with a laugh.

"Eat a dick," she said as she rushed off.

Lucious took the contract, which was several pages long, and began reading through the legal mumbo jumbo. It would no doubt confuse most novices, but as a master scribe of befuddling pacts, he found it to be light in content with absolute zero pitfalls. This didn't surprise Lucious much since the writer was the epitome of a goody two shoes.

"Is this it?" he asked Gabriel, still skimming.

"It is. Everything to your liking?"

"I believe it is."

"Then sign it, and I'll be on my way."

Lucious raised his right middle finger to his lips and bit into it with a meaty crunch.

"I had a pen," Gabriel said.

"Don't need it," he said, signing the contract with his own blood. With it still wet, he tossed it back at Gabriel, who tried to snatch it from the air without touching the crimson signature.

"Looks like we're partners," Lucious said.

"Joy," Gabriel replied as he placed the contract in the folder, doing his best not to touch Lucious's blood, which oozed from between the pages. "With that out of the way, we can officially start your first mission."

"First mission?" Lucious repeated.

"You will need to head to Phoenix to pick up your weapon's expert; he's expecting you."

"Does this expert have a name?" Lilith asked.

Lucious spun around, spotting her standing in the shadowy interior of the hall leading back to his cell.

"Sorry," Gabriel said as he patted himself down, "but I think I left the name in my other robes. Anyway, once you pick him up, you'll need to start recruiting your army."

"That will take some careful consideration," Lucious said. "Tearing down the Shroud won't be easy. It will take an elite lot, Heaven's own Dirty Dozen."

"Well, don't take too long to generate a list because time is not on our side. In the meantime, just to get the ball rolling, we have received word someone you might find useful is about to die in a mob hit in the next six hours, give or take traffic."

"I don't suppose you have their name in your robes someplace," Lilith asked, annoyed.

"The Nigerian Cannibal," Gabriel replied proudly.

"The who?" Lucious asked.

"Shouldn't you know him?" Lilith asked. "I mean, aren't you supposed to know all the names of the wicked running amuck here?"

"Do I look like Santa Claus?"

"You are wearing a red suit," Gabriel pointed out.

Lucious ignored his quip and asked, "Who is he, and why is he worth our time?"

"He's the former enforcer for the Pulizzi family in Boston. He recently tried to hang up his guns and ride off into the sunset and retire," Gabriel said. "But the new Don, Angelo Genovese, doesn't want the Cannibal turning snitch, so he sent some people to take him out. As we speak, the wolves are closing in on their prey. Once he dies, we want you to venture into the Grey Wastes to obtain his soul. The weapon's tech in Phoenix has all the details and the means to achieve this."

The Grey Wastes? Jesus. He could tell by the blank expression on Lilith's face that she had no clue what Gabriel was talking about. And she was lucky, too, because the Grey Wastes was the nightmare fuel for demons and all that inhabited Hell. His working knowledge of the place was limited, but he knew everything beyond the Spine mountains belonged to the Nameless Thing and the monstrosities dwelling there.

"Nope, not interested," Lucious said finally. "Tell the Eld to forget him. I'll come up with a list in a few hours."

Lilith and Gabriel stared at him.

"Don't look at me like that, I said no. Hell no. We can find somebody else."

"Who?" Lilith asked. "This is one lead we should follow through on. The Cannibal is a beast, an expert killing machine. We need him."

"If he's heading to the Grey Wastes, you can forget him. Let me break it down for you because you clearly have no idea what I'm talking about. The Grey Wastes is where the truly wicked are cast after shuffling off their mortal coils. We also use it to send undesirables and political adversaries for eternal damnation. Have you ever read Dante's Inferno? Well, that's the Inferno. No soul is worth it. None."

"Oh. My. God. You're afraid. Imagine that," Lilith said. She looked at Gabriel, "Lucifer is afraid of something. I always thought the legendary rebel angel feared nothing."

"I'm afraid of spiders, too," Lucious said. "But if you want that soul so badly, Lilith, how about you go and claim it? I'm not going."

"I'm game."

"If that's settled, then here," Gabriel said as he handed Lilith a piece of paper. "It's the address for your tech in Phoenix. Pick him up and then return here to start planning. This is going to be your base of operations moving forward.

"This dump?" Lucious said as he looked around.

"While you're away, I'll have some angels come and fix it up - make it a bit more livable."

Livable, somehow Lucious doubted that.

CHAPTER 2

Lucious was bored out of his mind heading to Phoenix. He tried to engage in some light conversation with Lilith to help pass the time, but that ended with a quick death. And there was no music either to help alleviate the crippling silence inside that death trap because the stereo had committed suicide the night before. He didn't mind that so much since he wasn't in the mood to listen to demonically influenced tunes anyway.

Gnawing on the bottom of his lip, Lucious watched the desert landscape pass by until his eyelids grew leaden, and he eventually drifted off to sleep. When he awoke later, they were parked outside a long, single-story building with a perfectly manicured lawn.

"We there?"

"Yup."

"What is this place?"

"Grimshaw Mortuary," Lilith said, bored.

"Mortuary?"

"It's the address Gabriel gave us," she said. She passed him the note.

The paper was yellow, and when he unfolded it, he saw elegantly crafted cursive scribbled across it in sparkly gold. It seemed like a lot of work for a simple address, Lucious thought, crumbling it up and dropping it on the floor with the rest of the trash.

"Did you have to do that?"

"Is that a rhetorical question?" Lucious asked.

She sighed.

"You ever met this tech before?"

"Can't say that I have."

"Then how are we supposed to know who they are?"

"I guess we'll just know," she said with a shrug.

"This is bullshit."

"I won't argue with that."

Lucious unsnapped his seatbelt and opened the door, which resulted in a blast of afternoon heat to punch him in the face. He didn't mind it so much because it was better than the artificial cold of the Ford's interior.

"Where you going?" Lilith asked.

"Inside."

"Inside? Get your ass back in here."

"Uh…no."

"That's an order," Lilith fired back hotly.

"That's cute," he said as he slammed the door in her face. He stretched his back and then headed towards the entrance. He was almost there when he heard Lilith racing after him.

"I thought you were going to stay in the car?"

"Sorry, sunshine, but I'm not letting you out of my sight."

They reached the door. As the gentlemen he sometimes pretends to be, Lucious opened it for Lilith and stepped aside so she could go in first. She shoved him inside instead.

"What was that for?" he asked, stumbling in.

"No reason. I just think you suck."

The interior was dimly lit and had a gloomy, depressed atmosphere with all the dark leather sofas and dark gray walls. To their immediate right was a small office, where a young woman with curly blond hair sat speaking on a phone. When she spotted them, she waved, and they waved back.

"Do you think that's the tech?" Lucious asked in a hushed voice.

"I don't know."

To the phone, the woman said, "No excuses! Be here, or you can find another job. Look, I've got to go; potential clients just strolled through the door."

She hung up and exited the office, her lips pulled into a salesman's slimy smile. She shook Lilith's hand and then turned towards Lucious, saying, "Welcome to Grimshaw. My name is Mandy Torrance. How can I assist you today?"

"Were you by chance…expecting us?" Lucious inquired cautiously.

Mandy stared at him for a long, uncomfortable moment before eventually saying, "I'm sorry, did you have an appointment? I don't have anyone scheduled. Maybe you spoke with one of my assistants, Stephen or Clive?"

The woman standing before them in her ugly, charcoal gray business suit with the fake shoulder pads wasn't the tech; Lucious was pretty confident of that. Not wanting to draw any unwanted attention, he said, "I can't remember who I spoke with. As you can imagine, this has been a tough time for our family."

"Absolutely. And I'm sorry to hear that," Mandy said, not sounding at all sorry.

"Our momma," Lucious continued, "has the cancer. Doctors don't think she has much time left, so we thought it best to prepare."

"I understand," Mandy said. "First, let me just say thank you for thinking of us during this difficult time. Here at Grimshaw, we pride ourselves in working with our customers to ensure a painless transition for their loved ones and have been doing so for the community for over fifty years."

What a grief mop, Lucious thought as he followed the uncaring cow through the mortuary on a quick tour. The place turned out to be a dreary, lifeless building lacking any warmth or comfort. He couldn't imagine how someone in the heavy throngs of grief would find the damn place at all consoling.

Mandy showed them the coffin room, where he nonchalantly checked the prices of coffins with little interest. They ran into Stephen, who turned out to be a tall, skinny man with scruffy hair and thick glasses. Like Mandy, Lucious felt that he wasn't the tech either. After more useless chatter, Mandy gave them her business card, and they returned to their car.

"Are you sure this is the right place?" Lucious asked, going inside.

"You read the note."

"I hate to break it to you, but I didn't sense anything divine in that place. It's dead."

"Just because we're supposed to pick them up here doesn't mean their gear is on the premises. Maybe they live nearby or something, I don't know."

"Do you actually know anything?" Lucious asked.

"Oh. My. God. Listen, when I got my orders to head to butt-fuck nowhere, to some Godforsaken Podunk called Elephant Head – I did so without hesitation. Hunkered down behind a tall hedge, getting eaten alive by mosquitoes, I waited with all the patience of Job for my target to arrive. Like now, all I had was an address. That's it. Seeing as I didn't want to fail the Eld in his time of need, I endured it all with a smile on my face. And you should thank your lucky stars I did, too, because you wouldn't be here to bitch and moan about your current predicament if I hadn't."

"You smiled?"

"Grinned."

"And I suppose you want a thank you or something like that?"

Lilith shrugged as she cranked the much-needed air conditioner to full. "Do whatever you want. Just stop acting like such a damn emo."

"What does that mean?"

"Forget it, Lucifer."

He sighed as he leaned back in his seat, adjusting his sticky collar. "I can't believe this. You, me – on a stakeout, waiting for some heavenly tech to arrive so we can wage war on the forces of evil. My forces. My friends."

"And to think it's only Tuesday," Lilith said with a chuckle. "You think I like this – being stuck in a car with a piece of shit like you? I don't know what Hell is like, but I think I just discovered what mine would be."

"What's that?"

"An eternity trapped in a car with you."

"It could be worse."

"How?"

"We could be listening to 'We Built This City,' by Starship."

She laughed only momentarily because once she realized what she had done, she aborted it like a sixteen-year-old does an unwanted pregnancy.

"It's okay to laugh, Lilith; I'm not a complete and total monster. Remember, we're teammates now. As Gabriel said, we have to find a way to work together. To coexist," he said as he fanned himself. "Man, it's hot in here. Can you turn the AC up in this metal coffin? Geeze, people who say Hell is hot clearly have never been to Phoenix."

"It's as high as it'll go, Lucifer. I guess you better get ready to sweat."

"Well, I hope that tech shows up soon because I'm melting like the Wicked Witch in The Wizard of Oz."

The afternoon hours drifted by unceremoniously while the two baked inside the car with no conversation between them. During that time, only three people arrived at the mortuary, none of them proving to be the tech.

The first two were just some random old couple who shuffled towards the building with their hands intertwined and an oxygen tank trailing behind them on a small trolley. The second was a greasy delivery guy from Domino's Pizza.

Unable to take the heat or the agony of the wait a second longer, Lucious punched the dashboard and shouted, "This is unbearable!"

"Oh. My. God. Unbearable? We've only been here," she paused to check her watch, which was a small, pink, dainty thing on her wrist. "Three hours. Relax."

"Waiting is not something we demons do well."

"No shit."

He opened the door and started to climb out when she suddenly grabbed his arm.

"Where the hell are you going this time?"

"To stretch my damn legs. My left is asleep. And so is my ass."

"Someone might see you."

"Good. Let them take a picture of me for all I care," he said, freeing his arm. "Besides, it's not like someone will recognize me; I'm not Justin Bieber."

He exited the car while she complained behind him like an overbearing mother-in-law. He slammed the door in her face and leaned against the car, melting in the unforgiving heat. He felt repulsive. His entire body was slick with two days' worth of funk, and his clothes were corpse stiff. Bored, he looked across the street. There was a salon called Glam Nails, a generic bank, and a Chinese fast-food joint called San Kitty of the Orient. Behind a Taco Bell on the corner was the rest of Phoenix.

"Did you hear me? I told you to stay in the car."

"And look how well that turned out for you."

She strutted right up to him and punched him in the shoulder. It didn't hurt him, but it did her. She stepped back, clutching her hand as tears flooded her eyes.

"Break something?" he asked, not really giving a damn.

"What are you made of, adamantium?" she asked, examining her throbbing hand. Nothing was broken, but her wrist hurt badly.

"What's the date?" he asked.

"I don't know, does it matter? Do you even care about my hand? You could have broken it."

He chuckled. "I'm not the one who hit you."

She rolled her hand, listening to the joints crack in her wrist. "Why do you care about the date? It's not like you have plans or anything."

"Just trying to extend the olive branch, man. You know, find some common ground for us to work from."

"There is no common ground between us, and there never will be. If you die during this mission, I won't shed a tear. Not one."

Just then, a '73 Ford Gran Torino turned into the mortuary parking lot, followed by a thick cloud of cancerous black smoke. It pulled into a spot a few rows down from where they were, blasting a bit of Stairway to Heaven from its high-tech sound system.

A second later, the driver climbed out. He was a slender man dressed in jeans and wearing a Pink Floyd t-shirt half tucked in. He had a thick, frazzled beard and long, shaggy brown hair that came down just past his shoulders.

"Oh. My. God."

"What?"

"It…it can't be."

Lucious could tell she recognized him; judging from her shocked expression, it wasn't a good thing. "You know him?"

"That's Adam."

It couldn't be. He stared at the man, trying to see past the greasy hair and beard, searching for a glimmer of the face that stole the Eld's love from the angels. But couldn't. The man was unimpressive, a scruffy nobody who wouldn't get a second glance from a disease-infested hooker desperate for cash.

"How can you tell?" he asked.

"Some faces you never forget," she replied, coming around the car. And then she called out to the hippie, "Hey Adam!"

When he spotted her, he stopped dead in his tracks.

"You remember me?"

Even though he shook his head, Lucious could tell in his bloodshot eyes that he did. He remembered her very well.

"Seriously? It's me, your first wife. You know, the one you tried to objectify in the Garden. Does that ring any bells?"

"Like totally."

And then he bolted.

"Yeah, I'd say he remembers you."

"Shut up," she said. She watched Adam dash across the yard and disappear behind the building.

"Well, I better go get him."

"You do that," Lucious said.

Lilith tore across the yard as Lucious nonchalantly followed. When he came around the building, he saw Lilith tackling Adam. It was a good hit, a vicious takedown that would make any NFL lineman proud. She rolled him over, pinning him down with her knees on his chest.

"Get off me," Adam said with a grunt.

"Why'd you run?"

"I can't breathe, man. You… you're crushing my chest."

"Then answer my question, little jackrabbit."

"I thought you were here to kill me," Adam said.

"Kill you? I should, shouldn't I."

Lucious strolled up to them and put his hand on her shoulder. "You'd only be killing our tech. I don't think the Eld would like that."

Lilith got off him as Lucious helped him up.

"You are the tech, right?"

"Yeah," he said with a nod. "Gabriel mentioned the Eld's champions would arrive today, but I never suspected one of them would be her dude."

"I'm starting to see a pattern of Gabriel's selective memory," Lucious said. "Did he mention anything about us needing to go to the Grey Wastes?"

"He did. But, like, why do you want to go there, man?"

"Soul collecting," Lilith said.

"There are safer and easier ways to do that than traveling there. You go trekking around the Wastes; you're more likely to have your soul devoured than like collecting one man."

"I tried to tell them that," Lucious said, "but these butthole surfers don't want to listen."

Adam looked at Lucious, studying his face. "And who are you? Are you like her boyfriend or something?"

"You don't recognize him?" Lilith asked, shocked.

He stared at Lucious for a long, concentrated moment before saying, "Am I supposed to or something, dude?"

"He's Lucifer!"

Adam stared at him again with his mouth agape, eyes wide in disbelief.

"How's it going," Lucious said with a wave. "Long time no see. How you doing?"

"You're like, really, Lucifer?"

"The one and only," Lucious said. He offered him his hand.

Adam looked at it.

"I'm not going to bite Adam. In fact, I'm one of the good guys now. I'm working for the Eld."

"Really?"

"Yup."

"Cool," Adam said as he shook his hand. "This is beyond crazy, dude. When he said champions, I suspected angels or something. Not you two. If anything, I thought you'd be like on the other side trying to stop us, dude, not helping. This is insane."

"It's been a strange week," Lucious said.

Lilith slapped their hands apart and got right up in Adam's face. "How can you shake his hand? Did you not hear who he is? This is Lucifer, Adam, the guy who tricked Eve in the Garden and condemned all mankind to death."

"But he's here now, man, doing the right thing."

"Oh. My. God. I'm surrounded by retards."

Lilith stormed away, stomping her feet like a child mid-tantrum.

Lucious thought it was cute.

CHAPTER 3

Lucious stood behind the mortuary with Lilith, doing his best to appear inconspicuous as they waited for Adam to let them inside. To pass the time, he repeatedly read a billboard staked in a nearby vacant lot. It wasn't Shakespeare, hell, it wasn't even Stephenie Meyer, but at least it was something to kill the boredom. On it was a giant floating head of a middle-aged woman with a hideous smile and blank, black eyes. Clearly, a woman past her prime, Lucious thought, and probably hadn't had a good fuck in a decade. Beneath it, written in big, bold yellow letters, it said: for the best land prices in the valley, call 408-634-2806. Ask for Jenny Carlson. What are you waiting for?

"The apocalypse," Lucious murmured to himself.

"What?"

"I was just talking to myself."

"Whatever," she said with a sigh. She leaned against the wall beside the mortuary's rear exit, where Adam told them to wait.

"You happy to see him?"

"Adam? Yeah. Thrilled," she said as she rolled her eyes.

"How's he look?"

"Exactly how I feel," she said with a chuckle, "like absolute shit."

"Don't hold anything back."

"Why should I? He's an asshole. And Eve's no better."

"What do you have against Eve? I found her lovely."

"You would."

"Is it the apple?"

"Yes, it's the apple you dolt. She screwed everything up – and what she didn't screw up, you came along and destroyed. It wasn't so bad when I first entered the primordial Earth after leaving Eden. I mean, it was quiet, untouched, and stunningly beautiful in its own way. I found it therapeutic after enduring so much misery in the Garden with that twat waffle Adam. And then one morning, I spotted him and his bitch walking through the morning fog, naked and looking horrifically confused."

"Did you help them?"

"Hell no. I hid. I was sure they'd die in the wilderness, but the Eld had different plans. Exiled, yes, but not forgotten. He took pity on them; soon enough, their spawn began spreading across the planet like a plague. Eve didn't just destroy the Garden; she destroyed the Earth too."

The door suddenly swung open. It would have struck Lilith in the face if she hadn't had ninja-like quickness and caught it. Lucious thought she might swing it back in Adam's face, but she showed something he didn't know she had – restraint. As for the First Man, he stood just inside the threshold dressed in a white shirt and black slacks. His sleeves were rolled up, which revealed a tattoo on his left arm. A raven perched on a skull, done in all black.

"What the hell took you so long? Have to change your diapers or something?"

"Nah, man," he said, "but I did have to change into my work clothes. Dig the threads?"

"No. You look like a dork."

"Don't hate on me, man; it's not like I can just let people in off the streets. This is like a house of mourning and stuff. Precautions had to be made, man, precautions. Got to play it safe, if you know what I mean."

Standing downwind from Adam, the stench of marijuana was unmistakable. Lucious guesstimated Adam and probably smoked a quick J after encountering the she-wolf to calm his shattered nerves. He didn't blame him. In fact, he hoped he had some more.

"Are you high?" Lilith asked.

"Nah, man."

"You smell like a Bob Marley concert."

"Cool," he said with a smile.

"So, uh, what's next?" Lucious asked.

"Gabriel told me you need fresh meat for a soul, so I made sure to keep some on ice," he said as he gestured inside. "I have like three. I'll warn you upfront: these aren't the best stock. But I guess under current circumstances, beggars can't be choosers."

"Why three?" Lucious inquired.

"Better to have than have not, dude."

Lilith started to go inside, but Adam quickly blocked her way.

"You got a death wish?"

"Before entering," Adam stammered, "I, huh, wanted to throw down, like, a rule."

"Are you serious?"

"This is like a house of mourning and stuff, so like, I won't tolerate any negativity."

"Fuck you, Adam," Lilith said. She shoved him aside.

Lucious watched as she stormed inside like she owned the place. And on some level, Lucious suspected she did. Feeling bad for the First Man, he patted him on the shoulder as he entered the frosty interior of the mortuary, hating it instantly. Behind him, Adam quickly closed and locked the door.

"Remember, let's keep our voices down," Adam said as he maneuvered to the front of their pathetic queue.

"You're the only one talking genius," Lilith said.

Instead of snapping back at the always quick-lipped she-bitch, Adam simply gestured for them to follow. They rounded a corner and found a connecting hallway leading to a large metal door. An electronic lock was next to it, filling the hallway with a phantom green glow. Adam raced to it, punched a few buttons, and the door's locking system disengaged with a loud click.

He opened it and stepped aside, allowing Lucious and Lilith to get a clear look inside the embalming room with its milky white fluorescents and dark grey walls. Here the aroma of cinnamon was so overbearing it was damn near suffocating.

"You use that to cover up your pot stink?" Lilith asked.

"Nah, man, that's to cover up the stench of decay. No matter how fresh the body, the dead tend to stink a certain kind of awful. I don't know about you, but I'd rather, like, smell cinnamon than that stuff."

They walked into the embalming room single file, with Lilith at the front. It was a small, sterile place with a single autopsy table at its center, covered with a white sheet. Along one wall was a counter with a couple of sinks, and at the back was what they came for a large body freezer. There was a lot of other equipment scattered throughout the place, odd gizmos for preserving the dead for entombment, but nothing they needed. The only other thing of interest in the place was under the table, which was an ugly, snot-green floor mat.

"Where's Eve?" Lucious asked. "She works here too?"

"Nah, dude. I haven't seen her for a long time."

Lilith laughed at that. And then asked, "Have a problem keeping wives?"

"I don't have a problem keeping wives' man. The only problem I ever had with a 'wife' was you," he said as he pointed at her. "Eve and I were like two peas in a pod, man; not even our expulsion from Eden affected our love. What we had was beautiful."

"But was it consensual?" Lilith probed; her voice ripe with rattlesnake venom.

Realizing things might get ugly, Lucious decided to step between them. "Guys, can we focus here? It seems we're getting a little sidetracked. Remember, we're all on the same team."

"I just want to know if Eve had a voice or was she just some mute designed to obey and serve her man. It's not a hard question."

"You're sick, dude, like totally off your rocker. I loved Eve. Believe it or not, I loved you too at one point."

She laughed. It was a contemptuous laugh intended to rip and tear like the teeth of a broken machine. Then Lucious seriously wondered if Lilith had a soul or was just all fire and rage.

"It's true," Adam said defensively. "I wasn't the one who left, remember? That was you. What can I say, man? You ripped my heart out, Lily, and left me to rot."

Something about being called Lily sent her into a fury. Lucious watched, stunned, as she grabbed a metal tray off the counter and hurled it at Adam's head. He would have eaten it if the stoner had been half a second slower. Instead, it bounced off the wall behind him with a loud clang.

"Dude?!"

"Lilith," Lucious shouted, "calm down!"

"The only thing stopping me from beating your ass unrecognizable is the fact you serve a purpose. Once that purpose ends, all bets are off. You hear me?"

"Anyone ever tells you you've, like, got some real anger management issues?"

"Yeah," she said. "Everyone."

"Okay, Okay," Lucious interjected, "that's enough. I'm not typically considered the voice of reason, but I think both of you would agree it's time for us to get back to the task at hand…like securing the bodies for transport and getting out of dodge before we're discovered."

"Fine," Lilith said, exhausted.

"Totally," Adam agreed as he walked over to the six-door corpse refrigerator and popped one open. Lucious expected to see a human popsicle lying on the slab, but instead, there was a government-issued green storage footlocker, one commonly found in military training barracks.

"What's in there?" Lilith asked.

"Everything you'll need to fetch that soul of yours."

"You keep weapons here?"

"Nah, man, not usually," he said. He struggled to unlock one of the many padlocks on it. "I brought it in the day before once I knew you were coming."

"Give me the keys, Adam," Lilith said, stepping forward with her hand open.

"I got it."

"The hell you do," she said as she snatched his keys from his hand. She had all the padlocks unlocked and lying on the slab in five seconds. Smugly, she said, "Stay off the drugs, Adam. You've nearly smoked yourself stupid."

"That's like kind of the point," he said as he opened the box.

Inside it, Lucious saw a handful of gadgets straight out of a sci-fi pulp magazine from the 50's. It was all manmade gear, crafted from everyday items with a touch of high-tech insanity. He saw weapons amalgamated with tubes, wires, and things beyond his intelligence. He was impressed with Adam's craftmanship and the man's madman creativity.

"I can't believe you're like going to the Grey Wastes," he said as he handed Lilith the rifle.

She tested the weight against her shoulder as she peered down the barrel, checking its sight. To Lucious, it looked awfully like the one she used to save him at the diner, with some slight modifications. What caught his interest most, of course, was its humming magazine.

"What's its fire?" Lucious asked.

"Bullets, man."

"I know that, Adam; what kind?"

Adam pulled a plastic baggy from his rear pocket, packed full of tightly rolled joints. He took one out, lit it with a Spider-man zippo, and then took one long, happy toke. With his lungs full of sweet bliss, he said, "Dude…the logistics are beyond your comprehension. Just know it can like, kill demonic and otherworldly deities, you know like the ones our precious here is about to encounter in the Wastes."

"Oh. My. God. Is this really the best time to be doing that?"

"Can you think of a time not to do it?" he asked, blowing perfectly constructed spherical rings in her face. "Because I sure can't, man."

While they talked, Lucious reached into the locker and grabbed a strange, small sphere with a red button. It reminded him of the thermal detonator from Star Wars, the one Leia used to threaten Jabba the Hut. Looking at Adam, he asked, "What's this thing – a movie prop?"

"Be careful with that thing, man; that's a grenade."

He quickly put it down before he accidentally blew off his genitals.

"You could have warned me, Adam."

"I just did," he said. He took another puff.

Lilith began to gear up for the mission by grabbing some of this and that from inside the locker. When she was finished, she looked a bit ridiculous. She had two handguns holstered across her hips and a rifle strapped behind her back. In her hand, she held a device Adam explained to be some soul tracker. To Lucious, it looked like an electric mixer minus its attachments.

"Lilith," Lucious said, "this mission…"

"Is going to happen," she said curtly. "I don't know why you're so against it. The Eld has hand-picked a warrior for us, and we'd be stupid not to follow up on it."

"And what does the Eld know about warriors? The guy is a pacifist."

"He kicked your ass enough times, didn't He?"

"Technically, no."

"Technically?"

"Whatever. You want to go, go. Nobody's stopping you."

"Damn straight nobody is," Lilith said as she turned her attention to Adam. "So, how do we do this? Is there a gate or something?"

"You should listen to Lucifer on this one, Lilith. The Grey Wastes are no joke. It's a wicked place. It's worse than Hell."

"Yeah? Well, so is Tampa."

"What do you know about it," Lucious asked.

Adam pointed at his temple and said, "The apple, dude. It's the same reason I can make all this sweet stuff. I have Godlike knowledge."

"Fine," Lilith said as she stuffed a few extra magazines into her satchel, "tell me about this supposed wicked place, Adam."

Lucious was curious, too. He didn't know much about the monstrosities living beyond the Spine. He had never met the Nameless Thing, but he had the misfortune of speaking with one of its intermediaries when the peace treaty was signed. The thing had all the ligaments of a human but in all the wrong places. It was like something got decimated by a landmine and then reconstructed by an alien who had no idea how a human was supposed to look. The thing called itself Nalusa. It stood well over five feet and had thick, scaly skin swathed with bristly black hairs and large, pulsating tumors. The most revolting part wasn't its squashed head with its half dozen bulbous eyes but how it communicated. It spoke from its enormous, shit-encrusted asshole, its voice constructed by taco farts.

"Anyone want a hit first?" Adam asked, offering them both the joint.

They both refused.

"Well, with our time being so limited and stuff, I'll give you guys the Cliff Notes version if that's cool. First, I suppose you both should know it has two names. In Hell, it's known as the Grey Wastes, while in Heaven, it's called the Deadlands," he said. He took a quick hit of his sweet leaf before continuing. "It is inhabited by vicious beasts, things you better pray you to avoid at all costs, Lilith, because these things are like nothing you've ever encountered before. They're called the Cimmerian, and they eat demons."

"And the Nameless Thing?" Lucious inquired.

"Not so nameless dude. He is Oggoth. And he is the brother of the Eld."

"Impossible," Lilith protested. "The Eld has no brother."

"That's what the Eld wants everyone to think, man. The dude is like a total dick weasel, a being crafted from the same stellar dust the Eld was born from. Instead of being born from the light, he was spawned from the dark of the interstellar void, pure dark matter. And dig this, he came first."

The information blew Lucious's mind like a sniper's bullet. To think, after all the time he spent with the Eld, he never mentioned having a brother. This was amazing.

"His brother man," Adam continued, "was a true Dr. Frankenstein. He created monsters, those Cimmerian, and they ruled the primal universe with tooth and claw. For thousands of years, they presided over the dark, unchallenged. That is until the Eld revolted against

Oggoth and his army of freaks. At first, the Eld lost big time. The poor dude was no match for His older brother, and His creations died in droves. But then, just when He felt like all hope was lost, the Eld stumbled upon their weakness and managed to defeat them. We're lucky He did to man because had He failed, none of this," he said as he gestured around the room with one grand motion, "would exist."

"What was the weakness?" Lilith asked.

"Light. The precursor to the Seraphim, an ancient order of angels known as the Atziluth, came into being composed of pure light and wielding swords of fire. They turned the tide, man. And Oggoth and his creations were eventually banished to the outer reaches of Hell, the Grey Wastes."

"That's insane," Lucious said. "I've never heard of any of this. He never spoke…"

"He never will," Adam said.

"You know that was all well and good, but I could give a rat's ass. What I want to do is get in, grab the soul, and get out. You got any knowledge in that melon of yours to do that?"

"Dude, language!"

"I'd be more concerned with my boot Adam because it's going right up your ass if you don't get that gate opened in the next five minutes."

"You better do what she says," Lucious said, "she's got some big feet."

"You got to work on your patience, man," Adam said. He passed the last of the joint to Lucious. He walked over to the embalming table and pushed it to the far side of the room, its wheels screeching angrily. Finished, he returned, kicked the green mat out of the way, and squatted down, hovering above a metal door.

"Does that lead to the Grey Wastes?" Lilith asked.

"Nah, man, the storage cellar. It's like where we keep all our cleaning supplies and fluids. Nothing special. At least not yet, anyway," he said with a wink.

"How does it work?" Lilith asked.

"Magic."

"Oh. My. God. You truly are dumb, Adam."

"You don't believe in magic, Lilith?"

"No, Adam, I don't believe in magic. I'm not 12."

"Shame," Adam said as he popped open the door. What lay beneath was a simple, narrow staircase leading into a cramped storage space with shelves packed with large plastic bottles. He slammed it shut and then glanced over at Lilith. "I would have thought at some point you would have come across someone who dabbled in the Secret Art. No? Never?"

"No," she said with a groan, "never. Let me guess: you're a wizard, right? Some real-life Harry Potter. Where's your wand? Your stupid flying broom?"

"Who said anything about wizards' man? People who could tap into it were known as Artists or Practitioners of the Art. Wizards are fictitious constructs created by fantasy authors and nerds. But yeah, man, I am a Practitioner."

Adam reached inside his shirt and pulled out a silver key attached to a fray, leather band around his neck. He held it up so she could view it better in the light and then showed it to Lucious, who peered at it curiously through a vale of pot smoke.

"This is a magic key. You see it like bends reality, allowing its owner to create pathways wherever they want, even other worlds."

"Give me a break," Lilith said.

"It might sound like a lot of hot air, but he's right," Lucious said as he crushed the remains of the joint beneath his foot. "The Art is basically residue from the creation…remnants of the Eld's earthbound energies."

"Oh. My. God. This is literally the dumbest crap I've ever heard in my life."

"Doesn't matter how it sounds, man, it's still the truth."

"This is why you don't need to risk your neck trying to save the soul in the Grey Wastes. We don't need it," Lucious said. "We have other options. Better options here."

"Oh really? Like who?"

Though he wasn't exactly sure who he wanted to recruit yet, one name instantly sprang to mind. It was a solid pick but a complex sale. Lucious wasn't sure if she'd even be willing to join the team, but he suspected a shot at redemption might be hard to resist for the immortal Queen of the Undead, Neva Rios. Lilith didn't believe in the Art, so he wondered if she'd even believe in vampires.

"Neva Rios. She's a Nosferatu."

"A vampire?"

Lucious nodded.

"This just keeps getting better," Lilith said with a laugh. "First magic, and now we got sparkly vampires. What's next, werewolves? Leprechauns? Hell, why stop there…the tooth fairy? Let me ask you something, Lucifer, what makes you so nervous about this soul? Is it because the Eld selected it?"

"I just don't think it's worth the risk."

"If the Eld wants this soul for His war effort, He will get it. For Him, no risk is too great. You got that, Lucifer? Adam, open the gateway to the Grey Wastes; I've got a soul to collect."

CHAPTER 4

"He's not looking so good."

"Yeah, tell me something I don't know," Tzit said as he turned their stolen car into a Taco Bell drive thru. They arrived in Arizona just a few hours ago to find their King in a wretched state. When Zozo reached out to him, saying that Mastema needed his services after a battle, he thought he might just be banged up a bit, needing some stitch work, bandages, or some minor healing. But what he found was a King - knock, knock, knocking on Heaven's door, lying in a sagging motel bed sweating black blood. With a groan, he said to Zozo somberly, "I think he might be dying."

"You serious?"

"Absolutely."

"But he's immortal."

"Correction. Was immortal."

"Come on, stop being so gloomy and doomy. He's just weak. Hungry. We get him something good, something young, and he'll snap out of his temporary funk, good as new. Dying? Give me a break, man."

"Maybe we should talk to Shedim. She'd know what to do."

"You have a death wish? Then go on ahead, call her. See what happens."

Tzit pulled up behind a Jeep and rolled down the window of his '71 Plymouth Cuda, ready to place their dinner order. The food wasn't for Mastema or them but for their possessed bodies. They really didn't need nourishment, but the meat suits they wore needed it to stay alive, so they fed them a steady diet of trash and hot crap. Zozo wore a young woman, some goth chick in her early twenties. He snagged her not long after arriving in Arizona. Neither knew her name because her soul was consumed the moment Zozo flew up her nostril's unseen, like an invading virus. Tzit hated women, so he snatched the body of a traveling rancher – an excellent old cowboy sporting a shoulder-length mullet.

In front of them, the Jeep blasted overproduced rap to high heavens as its occupants laughed and passed around a joint. Amongst the smoke, sitting almost angelic-like in the back between a couple of colored dudes was a young lady with short blond hair and a nice, succulent figure.

Meat for the beast.

"You see what I see?"

"Yeah, that new Grilled Cheese Burrito looks pretty yummy."

"Not that," Tzit said as he slapped Zozo in the tits. "The girl in the Jeep."

"The one in the back?"

"Exactly."

"Looks tasty. Let's nab her and one of those new Taco and Burrito Cravings packs. That's a lot of food for just ten bucks," Zozo said. He licked his lips.

"Can you stay focused for five minutes, you moron," Tzit said, annoyed. "We'll feed these pus bags after we take care of Mastema. That girl will do him some good."

"What's your plan?"

"Don't know yet, but it'll be ripe with ultra-violence."

"My favorite kind," Zozo said as he clapped childishly.

Tzit pulled out of the drive-thru lane and parked the car in a nearby space, keeping the Jeep in their line of sight. Tzit counted five occupants, including their target.

"Do you believe Mastema?"

"About what?" Tzit asked, keeping his eyes on their prize.

"Lilith."

"Of course not. He's sick, seeing ghosts. Whoever messed him up back at the diner might have looked like her, but Lilith is long dead – nothing more than dust. Everyone knows she died during the fall of Haifa."

"But…"

"But what if it was her?"

Zozo nodded.

"I guess we'll just have to kill the bitch."

"But if she could do that to Mastema, imagine what she'd do to a couple of shlubs like us."

"Still think we shouldn't reach out to Shedim?"

Zozo shrugged.

"We'll cross that road when we get to it. For now, let's focus on saving the boss."

The Jeep pulled away from the window, and Tzit gave chase, following them along E. Baseline Road. Traffic was light in the late afternoon, so tracking their unsuspecting targets was not difficult. It also helped they didn't seem to be in a rush, for they drove leisurely towards their destination – wherever the hell that was. Tzit kind of felt bad for them, seeing as their last meal was going to be Taco Bell.

"You ever meet Lucifer?" Zozo asked.

"Once."

"Really?"

"It was nothing special, just a random encounter lasting twenty seconds. If that."

"Twenty seconds more than I had with him," Zozo said. "Most famous person I ever met wasn't even divine; he was some Hollywood pedophile."

"Got to be more specific than that because you just described most of them."

"Have you ever heard of Charlie Pitman?"

"The guy who directed all those superhero movies?" Tzit asked.

"Bingo. But to hell with that joker, tell me more about meeting the Mourning Star."

"Like I said, not much to tell. He was topside meeting Mastema, and I just happened to be there. We shook hands, exchanged a few pleasantries, and then he was gone."

"That's it?"

"That's it."

"At least I fucked my Hollywood pedo," Zozo said. "We were at one of those After Party parties up in the Hollywood Hills. I can't remember whose house it was, but this was before Charlie made it big. It was his initiation night, and Timothy Stone, the producer, supplied the sacrifice – some illegal immigrants brat snagged by the Border Patrol. Cute kid, maybe 7 or 8. The boy didn't speak English, but that didn't stop Stone or Pitman from banging him in the ass so hard it ruptured his spleen. They cut his throat before he bled out, and Pitman drank his blood. Later that night, they cleaned up the corpse and cooked it on a spit."

"What were you doing?"

"Watching from the shadows, bodiless. When everything was over and done with, the body taken away, I slipped into his bed and rocked that mother like a hurricane. It was fun. He thought it was a dream until he woke up bleeding from the asshole. I punctured his colon," he said as rubbed the back of his neck. "You do realize once we find them, we'll probably have to fight Lucifer."

"We'll be good if we can get Mastema back to his old nasty self. Besides, once we pinpoint their location, we can always summon more Nonentities. Hell, we might even reach out to Shedim."

Zozo nodded.

The Jeep turned on Greenfield Road and then gunned it as they passed beneath an overpass. This wasn't Tzit's first stalk and kill, so he didn't panic. He kept his eyes on the Jeep as it weaved around a few slower cars and then gunned it through a yellow light.

Tzit ran the red.

"I wonder where they're going," Zozo said. "I'll bet a hundred bucks they're going to some rundown apartment to get fucked up."

"Probably."

Up ahead, the Jeep got into a turn lane across from some park called Holmes. At least, Tzit thought it was supposed to be a park, but it was more grass than anything else.

"Looks like they're going on a picnic," Tzit said.

"Could have picked better food."

"Yeah," Tzit laughed. "If we weren't going to kill them, they'd be praying for death soon enough after eating that garbage. Hell, we might even be doing them a favor by killing them."

Tzit turned into the parking area and found a spot next to the Jeep, which was already deserted. As for its occupants, they were on their way to claim a vacant picnic table not too far from the road. Climbing out of the car, Tzit noticed the place was practically empty outside of a father and son playing at a small play area.

"You got a plan?"

"Mayhem," Tzit said as he walked towards them. He noticed they were watching them as they approached, probably trying to figure out what the hell they wanted. Drawing closer, Tzit noticed a delicious smell hanging in the air — the scent of cold steel. They were armed. Judging by the words and symbols tattooed all over their arms and faces, they were clearly gang affiliated. Which gang Tzit didn't know, but what he did know was a gang was about to find itself 5 members short.

He locked eyes with a big, burly Mexican-looking bandit and invaded his mind. Like a spider injecting its prey with a shot of lethal venom, he poisoned it with dark, murderous thoughts. The bandito drew his Glock and shot the man next to him point blank in the head, blowing his brains all over the picnic table in a wild strawberry gush. Tzit then forced him to turn the gun on himself and end his own life.

The girl screamed.

Tzit quickly put her to sleep as the two-colored guys jumped to their feet with their shirts blood splattered. They were confused. Mortified by the sudden violent outburst of their friends. So much so that they failed to notice the goth chick approaching with a pair of carving knives in her hands, their blades midnight black.

Zozo decapitated one of them while the other went for his gun. It got stuck on his belt and accidentally fired prematurely in his pants, blowing off the man's own dick. Staggering back, the front of his white khakis bright red, Zozo jammed a knife in his eye – ending his pathetic life.

Tzit scooped up the girl and scrambled back to the car while Zozo grabbed the Taco Bell. The Nonentity didn't care that some of the food was covered in blood and brain because it added to the flavor. Improved it. Zozo got in the passenger seat while Tzit secured the girl in the back. They were on the road again a minute later, heading back to motel hell.

Adam stuck his enchanted key into the small door's lock and turned it. Suddenly, the lights in the embalming room dimmed as the temperature plummeted drastically by the second.

"Is this normal?" Lilith asked.

"It is when you're opening portals to Hell, man."

"How long does it take?"

"Already done."

"That's it?"

"Yup," Adam said as he rose to his feet. "And if you're, like, serious about this trip, man, I'd advise you to keep your goodbyes short because it won't remain open for long."

"How do I get back?" she asked.

"Click your heels three times."

Lilith stabbed him hard in the chest with her finger and said, "Stop messing around, Adam, before I slap you back to the 80s. Now tell me, how do I get back?"

"Use the key, dude," he said as he handed it over. "All you've got to do is focus your thoughts on me, and you'll return."

"You?" she said disgusted. "Why does it have to be you?"

"You could, like, focus on him if you wanted," he said. He pointed at Lucifer. "It's up to you in the end, man, but that's what you've got to do."

"What if there's no door?"

"Dude, you don't, like, need one. You can put it against a tree or a wall or even stab it into the earth. A portal will open, and then, like, all you've got to do is jump through."

"That's it?"

He nodded.

"You better not be trolling me," Lilith said as she hung the key around her neck.

"Why would I do that?"

"Revenge."

Adam laughed.

"Before you go, you need to know there are more things to fear in the Grey Wastes than just the Cimmerian," Lucious said. He was standing on the far side of the room with his back against the wall. "There are also the damned. Watch out for them. And remember, trust no one."

Adam grabbed a couple of grenades from the foot locker and returned to the door. Releasing one of their pins, he dropped down and opened it. Not very wide, just a couple of inches – just enough to pass the explosive through and then shut it with a loud slam. A second later, they heard the muffled sound of a detonation somewhere distant.

"You guys hungry? I've got this major craving for some pizza," Adam said as he prepared another grenade. "Maybe we should order something – maybe get some Dominos."

He dropped another grenade through.

Another boom.

"You've got some balls, man," Adam said to Lilith. "Going over there, alone. I wouldn't do it. No way, no how, dude. I glimpsed it once in a vision. And it was terrifying."

"It seems I've got the biggest pair in the room."

"Yeah, all balls and no brains," Lucious corrected. "A combination like that is going to get you killed."

"You'd like that, wouldn't you?"

Lucious shrugged.

Lilith looked at Adam, "Can I go yet or what?"

"You should be safe…at least temporarily. If anything were slithering around the door, it'd be deep-fried like a piece of Kentucky Fried Chicken. Speaking of which, that, like, sounds good too. Hey, Lucifer, how about we get a bucket of chicken instead? A side of slaw? Mashed potatoes?"

"Whatever," Lucious replied with a shrug.

Lilith opened the door to Hell.

What awaited her on the other side paralyzed her instantly, as if she had mistakenly looked into Medusa's eyes and turned to stone.

Mastema lay on the bed inside a stuffy motel room, reeking of excrement as he melted into a mattress. He could literally feel himself rot. And it wasn't pleasant.

As for the waitress, she died days ago.

While waiting for his henchmen to return, his only companion was the room's small TV mounted to the wall. It had three channels. One was some local station that showed a bunch of reruns from the 70's and 80's; crap like cheesy Kung Fu, Little House on the Prairie, Mash, Cheers, Happy Days, and Alf of all things – plus a bunch of other dated nightmares. The second channel was news, and the third was just straight-up porn.

He watched porn.

The current one told the story of a so-called virgin actress arriving in Hollywood to make it big, but instead ended up taking it big – right up the poop shoot. The story was crap, the acting atrocious, but it was still better than Little House on the Prairie.

Through the wall of the adjoining room, Mastema felt the lifeforce draining away from the room's occupant, some dumbass junkie overdosing. Mankind was such a waste of God's love, Mastema thought, licking his lips. They lived their pathetic lives completely lost as they squandered what little time they had glued to electric screens.

Or worse, killing themselves by poisoning their bodies with drugs, booze, and cheap food. Humans were morons – all of them.

Knowing a Psychopomp would come soon to claim the occupant's soul, Mastema snagged it through the wall and devoured it. The thing was tainted, the shine all but gone – so it tasted like hot ass and gave him little in the way of actual nourishment. He needed something pure, something young and fresh. He hoped Tzit and Zozo would find him something soon because he wasn't sure if he'd last much longer. He had just started to doze when he heard a voice crackling like thunder in the dead man's room.

"What the fuck!"

It was a Psychopomp, one of the Dead Wranglers. It was their job to collect souls for judgment – at least the ones that weren't already claimed or eaten. It was a constant struggle between the damned and dying, the Wranglers and the Nonentities, for souls were extraordinarily valuable, especially those with remarkable shines.

Those souls were rare.

And tasted the best.

Mastema watched as a dark figure took shape at the base of the bed. It was a tall, lanky figure dressed in a dirty black suit. Its face was pale, topped with a wild fro of stringy, dark hair, and its eyes raged with fire.

"I should have known it'd be one of you Nonentity dicks stealing my soul. Are you trying to ruin me? I got a damn quota. Did you know we Dead Wranglers are trying to pay off a damn debt so we can get into Heaven, and you Nonentity schmucks keep screwing it up for us by eating our damn bounties."

"Cry me a river."

"So, which one are you?" the Psychopomp asked, hopping on the back of a nearby chair and sitting on it like an inquisitive bird. "Judging by your award-winning demeanor, I'm going to guess Bukavac. No wait, I got it, Suanggi."

"I'm their King."

"Mastema?"

"Damn straight. Now get out of my room before I pop your head like an overripe zit."

"You're melting."

"Thanks for the newsflash asshole."

"How do you expect to kill me when you can't even get out of bed."

"I can…"

"No. No, you can't. Do you smell that Mastema?"

"Smell what?" he asked, annoyed.

"The sweet smell of death," the Psychopomp said with a smile. "You're dying."

"I can't die," Mastema snarled before breaking off into a series of vicious, mucus-heavy coughs. They were so violent and intense that each cough rocked his body like a bullet.

"You keep telling yourself that. You want some water?"

Mastema nodded.

The Psychopomp jumped off the chair and went to the bathroom. Sitting on the edge of the dirty sink was a plastic cup with a giant cockroach perched on the rim. He flicked it off, filled the cup with lukewarm water, and then returned to the King of the Nonentities.

"Are you scared?"

"About what?"

"Dying," the Psychopomp said as he handed him the water. "You've done a lot of evil things, which means there is only one place for a soul as heavy and wicked as yours. And I'm not talking about Hell; I'm talking about the Deadlands."

Mastema took the water and drank as the douchebag's words moshed around inside his head like a bunch of metalheads at a Suicidal Tendencies concert. He was correct; if he did cast off his mortal coil, he'd be bound to the darkest part of Hell – a place where even demons feared to tread.

"I'll be fine after I eat. I'm just a little weak."

"Weak? Your body is leaking more oil than a freshly tapped oil well."

"What's it to you?"

The Psychopomp shrugged.

"Thanks for the water," Mastema said as he tossed the cup aside. "We done being friendly now?"

"I guess. Good luck," the Psychopomp said as he headed towards the door. Before leaving, he glanced back at the King and said, "You better hope your soul doesn't meet the same fate as the countless ones you've consumed over the centuries. The Deadlands might suck, but it's better than the absolute nothingness of oblivion."

The door to the motel room flew open, causing the Psychopomp to vanish in a puff of dust as Tzit and Zozo stormed in. He was happy to see them, but he was absolutely euphoric when he saw what they brought him, and it wasn't the Taco Bell.

It was the girl.

Judging by her scent, she had a lot of delicious shine left.

Mastema instantly perked up as he watched them place the unconscious girl in a chair next to the bed. Zozo plopped down in the other chair, slamming his bag of stolen food on a table – spilling lettuce and cheese everywhere.

"Can you not make a mess?" Tzit grumbled, slamming the door. He quickly locked it and turned to look at Mastema. "How you doing, my Lord?"

"I had a visitor."

"Who?"

"A bastard Psychopomp. A guy in the room next door is dead, so I ate his soul."

"That's good," Zozo said as he unwrapped a burrito.

"It was a damn druggy. His soul tasted like a greasy asshole."

"Do you feel any better?" Tzit asked.

"A little, but it's already starting to fade. But she'll do me wonders," Mastema said. He pointed at the girl. "She looks exquisite. You guys did good. Real good."

Tzit bowed.

"Get her ready."

"Of course," Tzit said as he walked over to the girl. Scooping her up on his shoulder, he looked down at Zozo, who was busy stuffing his face with a Beefy 5-layer burrito, and asked, "You going to help prep this cow for slaughter or just sit there shoveling garbage into your stupid mouth?"

"I'll help."

Mastema watched them disappear into the bathroom. Though he didn't want to get up, he peeled himself off the bed and shuffled, zombie-like, after his henchmen. It was a challenging walk, one ripe with pain as the waitress's joints popped and ankles cracked. When he reached the bathroom, Tzit, and Zozo were already stripping the clothing off the girl like a butcher does a cowhide. And the girl slept through it all, trapped in a dreamless prison.

Zozo ripped off her shirt and bra, exposing her firm breasts. As beautiful as they were, Mastema was pleased to see her skin unblemished by tattoos or heavy scarring. Tzit worked her legs, ripping off her pants with little care. While they worked, Mastema knelt, picked up her discarded clothes, and fished out her wallet. Inside were a few credit cards, a Kroger card, and her driver's license.

"Michelle Curtis," Mastema said bemused. "Dig this, she's a Christmas baby."

"Almost like eating Jesus," Zozo said with a laugh.

"How old is she, my Lord?" Tzit asked.

"18," he said. He tossed her license in the toilet. "And that's not the best part about this prize catch either. Look at her belly. She's ripe with child."

"Two for the price of one," Zozo said and clapped.

"Wash her. And then bring her to me."

Tzit and Zozo bowed and got to work while Mastema returned to his bed smiling. Her soul would heal him well, but the developing fetus would do him even better. After his feast, he felt very positive about renewing the hunt for Lucifer and that bitch.

CHAPTER 5

Looks like I'm rolling solo, Lilith thought, approaching the trap door sluggishly, with all her usual pip and zing depleted. She wanted to put all the blame on the gear for her lethargic approach, but deep down, she knew better. The strictness of her throat, the dry mouth, and the heavy pounding of her heart told her, loud and clear, she was terrified. It wasn't just the monsters waiting for her in the Wastes that frightened her. It was the thought she might actually fail. It was this monkey she wanted to shake, but the little prick refused to get off her back.

Reaching the door, Lilith took one last deep breath before opening it. A sudden flash of vertigo struck her like a brick after seeing the twisted world lying south of Heaven open before her.

"Oh. My. God."

She clenched her eyes shut as she waited for the wave of nausea to pass and to come to terms with what she had just seen beyond the door.

An ocean.

The stench of sea salt flooded her nostrils, burning them.

"You okay, Lilith?" Adam asked gently.

"I'm fine. Just need a second, is all."

She slowly reopened her eyes. In front of her, stretching towards an unknown horizon was a beach of ashen sand riddled with bone. And beyond it, just a speck, she glimpsed a brand-new ocean beneath an inky black sky.

Cautiously, she poked her head in and looked around. Off to the right, on an outcrop of jagged black rocks, was a tower surrounded by enormous bat-like creatures flying on invisible updrafts. To the left, bathed in heavy fog, was a dead forest. And in its branches, she glimpsed humans wrapped in thick webbing.

"We won't think less of you if you turn back," Lucious said. "Be smart. Close the door. The Grey Wastes is no place you want to go parading around in. And I would know I fought my fair share of battles against things beyond your imagination. It's madness to cross over, especially for something as mundane as a soul. We can get more."

Lucifer actually sounded genuinely concerned for her, but she doubted his veracity. He was a master manipulator, after all, who preyed on human emotions like pedophiles did children.

"Yeah, man," Adam agreed, "let's close that thing and, like, get some Chinese food. I know this really killer noodle joint a couple blocks from here."

"You guys really are pathetic," she said.

"But we'll live. You go over there. I can't make such claims," Lucifer said.

She gave them both the finger and jumped through. When she hit the beach, the door vanished behind her. Scrambling to her feet, she heard some wicked thing scream tear through the silence like a pissed-off chainsaw. Behind a nearby pair of sand dunes, she saw the sky fill with dust and ash as something big headed her way.

"That was fast," she said. She turned towards the wood, ready to bolt like an Olympic sprinter. But before she could even take one step, she saw a man walking towards her dressed in a raggedy black trench coat and ripped-up jeans. In his left hand, he carried a long staff topped with a severed head. Not taking any chances, she dropped to a knee and prepared her rifle.

The man stopped.

"Stay back," she commanded.

She wasn't sure if he'd understood her, seeing as this was Hell and it was comprised of sinners from not only across the globe but from different eras. For all she knew, the dude could only speak Finnish. But the man surprised her, raising his free hand high into the air.

"You angel? I saw the God bombs. Saw them driveway monsters. You did it. You."

"What are you blathering about?"

"You angel?" the man repeated.

"Who are you?"

"Me? Bloat. My home there," he said. He pointed at the dead forest. "We must go, angel; they will return soon. Return to eat. The wood. Wood safe."

Lilith stared at the rotten head mounted atop Bloat's staff. Most of the flesh was gone, but where it remained, she saw fat, pink worms squirming. It had no lips, and she could see its yellow teeth and putrid black gums even in the poor light. The oddest thing about it was its eyes, which showed no signs of decay.

"Who's your friend?"

"Mr. Nielson. Saved what I could from monsters – they ate rest. Now come. Dally not."

She slowly got back to her feet but kept the gun pointed at the strange man and his head. Confused, she asked, "Why bother keeping that damn thing?"

"He friend."

"He's dead."

"Death here be temporal," Bloat said with a sigh. "Only thing eternal here be suffering."

"What's in the woods?"

"Death."

Damn, she thought, at least he's honest.

"Up the beach?"

"Death, too. Death everywhere. Stay long; you'll find that out yourself. But at least in the woods, you can hide. Beach not safe. To open. They'll see you."

"You know this place good?"

"Good enough not to be dead. Come," he said as he fled towards the woods.

Though something was very off about Bloat, Lilith knew she needed a guide. Lowering her weapon, she followed the strange man as another wretched scream filled the sky so loud it actually shook the ground. She found a small path leading to the wood, which was covered with mounds of discarded bone and bloated corpses ripe with maggots. When trying to pass near one, it reached out towards her with its mangled, broken fingers.

"Save me," the corpse groaned through a mouthful of cracked teeth.

It grabbed her ankle.

She bashed in its brains with the stock of her rifle. When the grip slackened, she bolted down a narrow ravine and jumped a stream of boiling black water before reaching the wood. Here, she paused. Bloat stood just inside the tree line, resting against his staff. If there was going to be an ambush, she figured it would happen here.

"You alone?"

"You here," Bloat answered.

"That's not what I mean, and I think you know it."

"Yes. Yes. Alone."

Behind came another scream, rich with rage. Back at the dunes, a pink fleshy pillar rose into the air like an erect penis. All along its body were deep blue veins and folds of fat meat covered in pustules and tumors. Its mushroom-like peek tilted down, revealing a small slit in its fleshy center. White lumps of foam oozed out in thick globules, and when the folds pulled back, she saw half a dozen rows of teeth.

"Come while you still can," Bloat called.

She had no choice; she could die here or in the woods. Both made little difference since the outcome was exactly the same. Dead was dead. With a sigh, she entered the forest with her rifle ready. Almost at once, she noticed the temperature drop sharply. Her entire body broke out in gooseflesh as she entered its foggy interior. Here, the scent was a complex fragrance of moss, fungus, and putrefaction. She quickly scanned the shadows, searching for movement or to catch a glimpse of a retreating figure – but she saw nothing.

"Hide," Bloat shouted. "It comes."

Bloat disappeared behind a nearby tree like a ninja, disappearing entirely from view. Lilith crutched low as she scuttled along tall grasses and thick underbrush for safety. Beneath her feet, the ground danced as if alive. Whatever that thing was, it was coming hard and fast. She found a tree and got behind it, offering a quick prayer to the Eld for strength, vigilance, and for a much-needed break.

There was another cry, closer this time. Close enough for her to smell its rancid stench pour into the wood like a toxic cloud. It reeked of sulfur. She wanted to look, to witness the strange oddity in all its twisted glory, but knew in doing so, she'd just be giving up her position. With a deep breath, she shouldered her rifle and took out one of Adam's grenades. Once that monster breached the woods, she'd throw it right into the damn thing's meatus and blow it to shit.

Minutes ticked past, each one slower than the last until the minutes felt swollen and distorted. It wasn't long before she lost track of time entirely and the weight of eternity began to weigh heavy on her shoulders. And then her muscles began to cramp. At first, it was just a dull ache in her left thigh, but soon, it transformed into a hot pulsation in both legs and ankles. She wanted to move, but every time she thought about risking a step, the thing beyond the wood moved.

It was trying to wait them out.

Above her head, the leaves of the dead tree rattled. Through her back, she felt the gentle vibrations of movement echoing along the trunk as something crept down, down, down. Glancing up, she saw a spider-like creature the size of a softball. Its body was slick black with dark gray hair follicles running along its legs. It had six large, red-tinted eyes hovering above a pair of mammoth fangs, which dribbled a bright, green, liquescent substance.

She dropped her grenade and went for her rifle as the bastard charged down the last few inches, screaming as it came. She slammed the barrel of her gun into its open maw, stepped out from behind the tree, and flung it at the dick monster. She watched the spider spread its legs wide and attach itself to the thing's head like one of those xenomorphs from the Alien movies. She didn't bother watching the battle. Instead, she bolted for the darker interior of the wood.

Bloat followed.

"Most wise angel," Bloat said as they jogged deeper in. "Highly poisonous are the Death Spinners. I doubt pink worm follow. If not already dead."

"Thanks."

"How you come, angel?"

"A door."

"Does it swing both ways?"

"What do you mean?" she asked as their run transformed into a brisk walk as they cautiously maneuvered around trees and streams of boiling goo.

"You can come, which means you can go. Right?"

"Damn straight Bloat," she said, irritated. "You think I'm sticking around this dump? You can forget it. This is a temporary visit."

"You can take passenger, yes?"

She could tell where this was going. She stopped walking so she could look the strange man in the eyes. Brushing her bangs out of her face, she asked him to get to the damn point.

"You take me?"

"I'll tell you what, Bloat, you help me get what I came for, and I'll consider it. How's that?"

"What you come for?"

She reached into her front pocket and pulled out the soul tracker. It was a small device, about the size of a pack of cigarettes. She pressed a button on it, causing the screen to light up and spook poor Bloat, who went staggering backward.

"Relax. This is going to show where we need to go."

"Like map?"

"Oh. My. God, yes, like a fucking map."

She stared at the pixelated images on the screen, which looked like a GPS crafted in the early 90's. It took her a moment to figure out that the blue dot at the bottom of the screen was them, and the red dot flashing on the opposite end was the soul. There was a distance counter on the upper-left corner, which read 10 miles.

"Which way it say go?"

"That way," she said and pointed.

Bloat shook his head and said, "No. Go another way."

"Why? What's over there?"

"Abyzou."

"What the hell is an Abyzou?"

He lowered his voice when he said, "The Blood Witch."

"I hate to break it to you, witch or no witch. Your salvation lies in that direction, too. So, are you in or out? Make your decision quick because I don't have all damn day."

He leaned against his staff and said, "I lead for a ticket out. That be my price."

It was her turn to mull.

Like Lucifer, she also signed a contract with similar terms and conditions. She didn't want to lie or mislead Bloat, but she knew she couldn't navigate the terrors of this world without him, but there was no way she was going to take him with her. She licked her lips and stared at Bloat, who stared back at her impatiently.

"Well? How you say – in or out? Don't have all damn day."

"Don't be a jerk. But yeah, we got a deal."

"Excellent," he said with a smile. "Which way again, angel?"

She pointed in the general direction once again, and Bloat nodded. He told her to follow, and she did. Together, they walked through the dark interior of the wood, keeping their guard up because death lurked everywhere.

"You think we'll ever see her again, dude?"

"Good question. I don't know, I guess we'll have to wait and see," Lucious said. He walked beside Adam with two thawing corpses draped across his shoulders. "I'll say this much, if anyone can do it, it's her."

"You can say that again."

"You worried about her?"

"Nah, dude, I'm worried like for the Cimmerian. After her trip, we must add them to the endangered species list."

They came around a corner and stopped just outside a plain wooden door with an Employee Only sign nailed to it. Adam fished out a set of keys and unlocked it. Together, they stepped inside the shadowy interior of a garage. It would have been completely pitch-black inside without the streetlight cascading through the garage door windows. Inside were a pair of black hearses.

"You smoke the leaf, dude?" Adam asked, opening the rear loading door.

"Sometimes."

"You got to try my stuff, man. I grow it. I've been doing it for decades…mixing a bit of this and that until I, like, created the perfect child, my own herbal Frankenstein, if you will, dude. I call it Tangerine Dream."

"That's cool," Lucious said, body-slamming the bodies into the back of the hearse. He was relieved to have the dead, empty husks off his shoulders. Just carrying them around gave him a bit of the heebie-jeebies. Leaning against the car, he rubbed the stiffness out of his neck as Adam produced another joint.

"Looks like you need to take a load off, dude."

"Is that Tangerine Dream?"

"My baby," he said with a smile.

Adam lit it and passed it to Lucious.

"You know, I'm the one supposed to be tempting you to do stuff."

They both laughed as Lucious took a drag. Adam was right; it tasted damn near perfect and instantly worked to ease his stressed-out mind instantaneously. It was the perfect drug. He took another quick hit before passing it to Adam.

"I don't know about you, dude, but I'm like glad she isn't here right now," Adam said. He took a hit. "Don't get me wrong, I like totally hope she comes back in one piece and all that jazz, but dude…talk about a buzz kill."

"Was she always such a killjoy?" Lucious asked.

"As far back as I can remember – yeah. I don't know what it was about her, dude; blame her programming or something, but she was always a bit of a drama queen. Never happy. Nothing I did ever pleased her. It got so bad, man, that animals in the Garden began leaving in droves to escape her constant nagging."

"I can believe it. Was Eve that way, too?"

"Nah, man. Eve was a peach. She had this heart that just…"

Lucious saw the grief flash across Adam's face as his head swam with memories of his lost love. He reached out and squeezed him on the shoulder and said, "If you don't want to talk about it, it's cool. I won't push."

"It's fine, Lucifer. I just…I just miss her, is all dude. She was like my everything."

"I understand. I know how you feel."

Adam nodded as he smoked thoughtfully for a long while, no doubt lost in memories as deep and hungry as quicksand. Eventually, he found his mental footing, looked at Lucious, and asked, "How do you know how I feel, dude? I mean, like, no offense or nothing, but you're like the Devil and stuff."

"So."

"So? I mean, aren't you supposed to be like this big bad voodoo daddy or something?"

"Well, even monsters can love. Even one as big and bad as me."

"Come on, dude – don't mess with me."

"I'm not messing with you, man, I was married."

"Was? Oh man, sorry, did she, like, pass or something?"

"Not yet."

"That's good."

"It's only because I haven't killed her yet," Lucious said with a laugh. "She's the reason I'm stuck here in this fucked up predicament working with that asshole, the Eld. She had me drugged and then dragged my unconscious ass up here so Mastema could swallow my soul."

"The King of the Nonentities?"

"Yup."

"That sucks, dude."

"Tell me about it."

"Can I ask you something?" Adam asked.

"Shoot."

"Back in Eden…the snake, was that, like, you?"

Lucious smiled as his mind drifted back through the sands of time to the grandiose Garden of Eden, which now lay hidden beneath the sands of the Sahara. Time eroded most of his memories of the place, but he remembered the damn tree. It stood alone on top of a hill silhouetted in gold, heavenly light – even at night when the stars and moon were still learning to shine. Lucious would stand there, eyes transfixed on it and its dangling fruits – dripping with sweet, divine knowledge. And he wanted it. Needed it.

But he knew he couldn't just walk up to it and snag one. Everyone in Eden knew it was forbidden. Knowing the Eld's temper, he didn't dare risk the wrath of a pissed-off God, so he needed some rube he could manipulate - someone like Eve. And though he never took the form of a serpent, Lucious used his sweet tongue to poison a simpleton's mind. He started grooming Eve on a Monday evening, and by that Sunday, the Garden burned. He remembered watching all the glorious fruits in the tree instantly rot after Eve took her first bite and then, moments later, offered it to Adam.

"You alright, dude?" Adam asked. "I thought I lost you for a moment."

"I'm good."

"Remembering the Garden?"

"The little I still remember of it, yeah. There's not much left. Ghosts of ghosts."

"And the snake?"

"What snake?"

"Dude, the one that spoke to Eve."

"I hate to tell you this, but there was never any snake. Eve was worried you'd get jealous running off every night to talk to me, so she told you about the serpent. And before your mind goes to dark, unhealthy places – we never did anything sexual. Just talked. Trust me, I tried to slither my way between those sweet thighs of hers, but she kept her entrance securely locked. She loved you."

"That's deep," Adam said. He shook his head.

"You, okay?"

"It's cool, man. That was like a super long time ago and stuff, you've probably changed a lot since then – matured and whatever."

"Actually, I haven't changed at all. In fact, if I had a chance, I'd probably do it again."

"Dude!"

"What?"

"I'm trying to forgive you."

"Seriously?" Lucious asked, confused.

"Yeah, man, snake or no snake, Eve and I still had free will, man. We could have resisted. Refused. But to tell you the truth, we were kind of curious about the apple, too. I suppose what we needed then was like a little push or something to do it. That's why we didn't blame you when the Eld appeared to us later. We took full responsibility for our actions and, like, left."

"Wow," Lucious said in surprise, "I don't know what to say?"

"Don't worry about it, dude. You could just pass me the last of the joint."

Lucious passed it back.

"What happened to Mastema?" Adam asked.

"Dead, I think. Lilith messed him up pretty well. With that said," Lucious said as he slapped his hands together, "we better get back to work before we get caught out here."

"Yeah, good idea, dude."

They put out the joint and returned to the embalming room to collect the last body. Once Lucious secured it like a caveman would a bludgeoned bride, they started back towards the car, with Adam struggling to carry his footlocker.

"Need help with that?"

"Nah, man, I got it."

"What's next?"

"I've got a U-Haul packed and ready to go a few blocks from here. We'll swing by, pick it up, and head back to your safe house."

"Do you know where it is?" Lucious asked.

They both froze just outside the garage.

"You don't know?" Adam asked.

"No. You?"

"This is not good."

"Are there settlements here?" Lilith asked.

"Some. There is one just a few miles that way," he said. He pointed his staff in an easterly direction. "Called Ommadawn, it is, and is, the largest of all the cities in the Wastes. Great place. If you can get there."

"The monsters?"

"More than monsters lurk the wood angel. There are nomadic tribes of freaks we call Skinners. You see a monster will eat you, but then move on. A Skinner will keep you around, harvesting the good parts. Then, they let you heal before taking them all over again. And again."

"Is that what happened to you?"

"Aye."

"How did you escape?"

"A worm broke camp. Slaughtered Skinners. I ran."

They walked silently for a few minutes as the terrain changed slightly. Towards the entrance of the wood, the trees were spread out, but here they grew huddled together with their thorn-coated roots poking up out of the ground, looking like pissed-off snakes.

"These trees…"

"Feed on flesh, not sunshine. Don't touch."

They moved as quickly as Bloat's leg allowed, which was driving her crazy to move at such a slow pace. She would have left him behind but didn't dare leave him. Not here in this post-apocalyptic nightmare, where even trees ate you.

"May I ask question?"

"If you're feeling lucky," Lilith replied, annoyed.

"Lucky? I don't…"

"Oh. My. God - just ask already."

"Why you here?"

"Business," she answered bluntly as she pulled out her tracker. They were close to the Cannibal, about five miles out. "What about you, Bloat?"

"Wicked man deserves a wicked place."

"At least you don't deny it."

"How deny, I'm in Hell."

"When did you die?"

"Hard to say in a place where time has no meaning. My memories of my former life, no see. Mind dark. Empty. I try not to think about it much. Maybe better that way, no?"

"You'll have to face those demons at some point, Bloat. You can't run forever."

"I run fast."

"Sure, you do, but sure don't walk it, though, do you?" she said.

"I have more than paid for my sins."

"Is that right?"

"Aye."

"But how can you pay for something you can't remember?"

Somewhere, deep in the woods, a series of loud screams filled the air. It wasn't a single voice but many – all full of pain and terror.

"What the hell is that?" Lilith asked, unshouldering her rifle. Getting ready.

"People paying for their sins," Bloat said soberly. "You get used to it. Like rain on Sunday. If I may suggest, find new route for your business."

She checked the soul tracker and found the fastest way to the target was dead ahead. Not sure how time worked in Hell, she didn't want to linger here any longer than she had to, even if their route put them dangerously close to whatever made those people scream.

"No," she replied sternly, "we stay the course."

"Course, no good if we die."

"What do you care, Bloat? You're already dead."

"You not," he said. He grabbed her arm with one of his gnarled hands. "Come, angel, I beg. We will find a new way. Safe way."

She yanked her arm free and fought back the temptation to knock the asshole cold as the swelling of cries reached an ear-shattering apex. One that chilled Lilith to the core. Staring at her guide, she asked, "You want to get out of here, right?"

"Aye."

"My target is that way. If you want to go, fine, get – I won't stop you. As for me, I'm going that way, and once I get my target, I'm gone like Donkey Kong. You get me?"

"Most of what you said, aye."

"You in or out?"

"In."

"Then let's go."

They walked through the woods, doing their best to keep their distance from the trees. A couple of times, the path they took got swallowed by a thick fog – and they'd have to stop and wait for it to clear. The only real high point, if one could be had in the deadly wood, was the screaming stopped. To keep her sanity, Lilith imagined she was walking in a foggy Irish moor.

"Is it always foggy like this?"

"Most days."

The fog dissipated finally, revealing an old, rutty road cutting through the wood. Lilith and Bloat raced to it before losing sight in the ever-changing fog. A few hungry trees made last-ditch efforts to capture their fleeing prey but failed. Reaching the road, Lilith made a horrifying discovery – beneath her feet wasn't a road at all – it was a mound of discarded carcasses half frozen in the mud. It stood about a foot off the ground and about eight feet wide. She didn't know how many dead it would take to make such a thing, but it had to be a lot.

"We…take this?" Bloat asked.

"Better than walking blindly out there," she said as he stepped on it. "Any idea what caused this?"

"A lifetime of mistakes."

Truer words had never been spoken.

The two started walking again through the rolling mist as the trees screamed in rage. On a few occasions, where the trees grew near their makeshift road, roots shot at them in a vain attempt to snag them. After a couple of lonesome miles, the trees along the bone road began to thin out until they fell away altogether. By the third mile, even the fog seemed to lose interest in them, and actual sunshine began snaking through the wood, filling it with broken shards of sunlight.

And, of course, what lay ahead.

They stopped.

"Oh. My. God. What the fuck is that?"

"Abyzou. The Blood Witch."

"Great," she said as she shook her head.

Up ahead was a clearing with a black marble throne at its center. Dressed in long, blood-red robes sat a tall, thin figure. In its fisted hand was a rusty chain interconnected to several dozen people standing naked in the field. The poor bastards looked like zombies more than anything else because most of them were not completely whole. Most were missing limbs or were skinless husks covered with squirming, fat maggots.

"It sleeps," someone said.

At first, Lilith didn't know where the disembodied voice was coming from – then she looked up. The severed head on Bloat's stick had its eyes open – and they weren't the dull color of a cadaver but the deep green of a living man.

It was alive.

"Holy crap!"

"Howdy, ma'am," Neilson said pleasantly. "Name's Charlie D. Neilson the third. Nice to make your acquaintance. You're the first angel I've ever met. You sure are pretty."

"Uh, thanks."

"So, if I understand this correctly, ma'am – Bloat is getting a ticket to Heaven, correct?"

"He is."

"Am I included on this here ticket too?"

She didn't know what to say; she was, after all, negotiating with a severed head, so she simply nodded as her brain melted in its skull.

"Excellent," Neilson said with a devilish grin. "Well, then, it should please you both to know Abyzou is snoozing like the dead."

"How do you know?" Lilith asked.

"I can sense it. If I were you two long-horns, I'd across lots before Abyzou wakes up. She's hungry enough to eat a saddle blanket."

It was clear to Lilith that Bloat and Neilson were clearly from two different times and places in the human timeline, with Neilson sounding like a cowboy straight off some 50's soap opera.

"Any suggestions on how we can sneak past?" Lilith asked.

"What do you want from me? I'm just a head on a stick," Mr. Nielson said. He closed his eyes.

"Is that seriously it?"

Bloat looked up at Nielsen as he shook his staff. The eyes remained shut. Looking back at Lilith, he said, "It would appear."

"Can he be trusted?"

"I trust."

Lilith checked the tracker to find the location of the soul once again. The damn thing was on the opposite side of the clearing, maybe two miles as the crow flies. Putting the tracker in her pocket, she raised her rifle, wondering if the thing was powerful enough to kill a witch.

"What's beyond this?" Lilith asked.

"The Razor Fields."

"Who names these damn places," she said. She shook her head. "Wonderful, the Razor Fields. What's there?"

"Nothing much. An old settlement."

"That's probably where he is."

"Who?" Bloat asked.

"None of your business is who, Bloat. Is there a way around this place, or must we go through it?"

Bloat pointed East.

Leaving the road, they took their time navigating the terrain, trying to avoid the nightmare trees. About a half mile in, they hit a roadblock. Spun between the trees was thick webbing. In a few of them, wrapped up like burritos, were people.

"You know what this means, right, Bloat?"

"Abyzou?"

"We've got no choice. We can only hope the bitch still sleeps."

Adam drove behind the skeletal remains of a once prosperous strip mall. Two days ago, during a mostly peaceful protest, stores were ransacked. Some had their windows smashed, a liquor store got looted, and a corner mattress shop was set ablaze. Behind it, parked between a couple of large dumpsters – was a 17' footer U-Haul truck. Someone, during the time Adam was gone, had tagged it along its side. In big black letters, it read, "Cock Suckers."

The two got out, moving quickly in the deepening shadows. Adam unlocked the back and lifted its massive door while Lucious grabbed a couple of bodies. As he walked towards the U-Haul, Lucious felt a cosmic vibration radiating from inside it. It was powerful and undoubtedly belonged to the Eld. He froze momentarily, fearing his old nemesis might actually be in there like a crouching tiger, hidden dragon – ready to pounce on him.

"You alright, dude?" Adam asked, sticking his head out. "You feel it, huh?"

"Kind of hard not to."

"Divine energy, man, a lot of it too. The Eld sent it to me so I could work on, like, my demon-killing gear for the upcoming war and stuff. You should be fine."

"Should be?"

"I make no promises, dude. Now load up those bodies before someone sees us."

"Thanks, Adam."

The First Man gave him a thumbs-up before disappearing into the truck.

Lucious took a deep breath before approaching it as police sirens screamed in the distance. Reaching the U-Haul, he tossed the bodies on the floor before quickly retreating to the hearse. He walked quick, almost a slow jog.

That's when he saw a man standing at the back of the hearse, dressed in a suit straight out of the 1970s. The fashion victim was clearly an angel, a member of one of the lower orders – one of the Principalities, which was basically the blue-collar level of the angelic order. The man dressed in an ugly Groovy Plaid suit took a moment to place, but his identity eventually crawled back to Lucious like a starved dog.

"Netzach?"

"If it isn't the man, the myth," Netzach said. He turned to face him. "When I heard the news, I didn't believe it – Lucifer coming back to the flock to serve the Lord, our God? But here you are. Working alongside the First Man to win back this world."

"I'm not back. And please, don't call me Lucifer – call me Lucious."

"Lucious?" Netzach asked, confused.

"It's my free name."

"Sorry to hear that," Netzach said with a weaselly laugh. "Sounds like a punishment, a name one gives oneself as a form of repentance."

"At least I'm not dressed like one of the Bee Gees. Why are you here? More importantly, why are you dressed like that?"

"What's wrong with my threads?"

"Everything."

"Whatever. As far as why I'm here – I was dispatched."

"By who?"

"Gabriel."

"Why couldn't he come himself?"

"He's got better things to do than babysit you clowns."

"Yeah right," Lucious said with a laugh.

"He asked me to give you this," Netzach said. He offered Lucious a folded piece of paper.

"What is it? A love note?"

"You wish. It's the address to the safe house you so eloquently forgot."

"Thanks," Lucious said as he quickly snatched it from his hand, giving the angel a paper cut.

While Netzach sucked on his finger, Adam came strolling around the hearse whistling to himself – clearly lost in his own head. But when he saw the glowing guy, he froze.

"It's cool, Adam; this John Travolta-looking asshole is an angel, one of the Principalities. I know it's hard to believe with him looking like he just wandered off the set of Staying Alive, but it's true," Lucious said.

"Thanks, man," Netzach said, "you really think I look like Travolta?"

"No."

Adam crept closer to the strange glowing dude, who looked like someone suffering from radiation sickness, and asked, "So, like, what can we do for you, dude?"

Before the angel could answer, Lucious answered him.

"He's running errands for Gabriel. He brought us this," he said, offering the paper to Adam. "It's the address to the safe house."

"Cool," Adam said as he took it. He flashed them both a big smile as he reached inside the hearse to grab his footlocker.

"You need help with that?" Netzach asked.

"Nah, man, I got it."

Still smiling, he returned his footlocker to the U-Haul, leaving them alone. Somewhere in the distance, they could hear the annoying chants of the returning protestors as they came back to do more damage in the name of so-called justice and progressivism when, in truth, they were really back to pillage and burn.

"The world is falling apart," Netzach said.

"It's been falling apart since the day it was created. It's just sped up," Lucious said. When he turned to look at Netzach, the angel was already gone.

When they reached the clearing, Abyzou was awake.

And eating.

Lilith and Bloat watched in horrific silence as she feasted on a young woman, burying her head deep inside her victim's midsection as she ate greedily. All around the girl's feet were chunks of discarded flesh and entrails.

"Holy moly."

"She eats the babies."

"What?"

"She breeds women," Bloat explained, "and then devours unborn."

Lilith hadn't liked the witch before, but she hated her now. She would have shot her dead right then and there, but that wasn't the mission. Cursing beneath her breath, she surveyed the area, trying to figure out what the hell they were going to do. The way around the clearing on the left side of the road was packed to the brim with those man-eating trees, with their roots sticking up out of the mud like a pedophile's dirty erection.

"I hate to break it to you, Bloat, but it appears we have to enter the clearing."

"We can't," Bloat whispered, his voice riddled with panic. "We do, we die."

"There's no other way, man."

He nodded.

Together, they approached the clearing – slowly. She had her rifle ready and pointed at one of the nearest of Abyzou's zombies. If it moved towards her, she'd blow its head off without a single ounce of regret. Like everyone trapped there with the monster, it had a collar around its neck connected to a long, rusty chain.

"This is madness," Bloat hissed as they drew closer. "We step in there; we won't step out."

"Salvation has a price. You ready to pay it?" she asked, stepping into the clearing.

Together, they crept along its outer rim, trying to avoid the zombies standing in a morbid state of eternal attention. It seemed to Lilith the things were locked in some sort of trance, no doubt under a spell cast by the evil cow sitting on her throne.

They were making significant progress as they maneuvered around its circumference. A sudden movement in the wood caught her attention as hungry predators stalked them from the shadows of the dead trees. It seemed even the monsters of the Grey Wastes were terrified of entering the domain of the Blood Witch.

And then it happened.

Behind her, she heard a loud crack as the idiot Bloat stepped on a dry twig. Almost instantly, the mindless slaves activated and attacked as one rotten unit. They swarmed at them, growling and spitting as they gave chase with their hands reaching. Though badly outnumbered, the horde struggled to reach them. Part of it was their own decrepit state, but the other was the chains connecting them to Abyzou's venomous network.

Looking back, she saw Bloat struggling to keep up thanks to his bad leg. Though slow, he was still well enough ahead of the pack to avoid their hungry hands, but only by a smattering of inches. One slip-up and he was a goner.

Turning around, Lilith saw one of the things stumble in front of her, blocking her escape route. She tried to stop, but her own momentum sent her plunging into the thing's foul embrace. She attempted to raise her rifle, knowing she only had seconds to spare, but the thing latched onto the barrel and kept it pointed at the ground.

"Save me," the thing pleaded in a raspy voice.

Knowing she didn't have much time, she fished the soul collector out of her pocket, which was a small cylindrical object about the size of a woman's lipstick. Before leaving, Adam explained how it worked. All she had to do was point and click, and presto, the soul would be magically transported into the storage unit for safe and easy transport.

She fired.

The skinless twat in front of her burst into a ball of red-tinted flame and then vanished in an instant. Pocketing the device, Lilith bolted towards the far side of the clearing as the Blood Witch began to speak in a putrid, guttural voice. At first, the words were unrecognizable gibberish but soon morphed into more modern languages as she jumped from Chinese to French to German to Spanish. Being fluent in 42 languages, Lilith understood all too well what she was saying in her frenzied repetition. She was saying, thief. Abyzou's tour-de-force in universal languages continued in her rage until she screamed thief in perfect English – and Bloat gasped.

"English, is it?" The Blood Witch called as the dead stopped their mad pursuit. "I should have suspected a thief's language of choice would be as primitive and uninspired as English. And a male, no less."

She thinks there is only one Lilith thought. This gave her a dangerous idea, one she hoped the Eld would approve of because if He didn't, this short trip would become more permanent. Lilith ran over to Bloat and grabbed him by the arm, dragging him towards the far side of the wood, their nearest escape. Above the shocked moans of the collective and the rustling of their chains, Abyzou shouted, "Freedom to the one who brings me the thief!"

The words seemed to stir fresh passion and mobility into the collective because they ascended upon them like a crashing wave of depravity. They came from all sides, swallowing up the narrow opening between them, and escaped. Doing their best, they hustled across the uneven terrain, tripping over discarded bones and slipping in rotten viscera.

"We won't make it," Bloat croaked.

"No, we won't, but I will."

"Angel?" Bloat called, confused.

"Never said I was an angel," she said. Lilith shoved him into a throng of outstretched arms. As they surged around him, she put everything she had left in her reserve and darted for the tree line.

Behind her, Bloat screamed.

Bursting into the wood on the far side, she continued her sprint, weaving this way and that as she slipped past webs and the always-hungry trees. Something popped up in front of her, a black shape with burning yellow eyes. She introduced the thing to her rifle and shot the brute between the eyes with a bit of divinity.

Exhausted, she staggered through the tree line and into a field covered in tall, sharp grass the color of blood. And she wasn't alone. Scattered throughout the field were a half dozen strange monsters of various shapes and sizes, hideous things, morbid mutations of humanity. There were people, too, dressed in suits of human flesh and armed with spears and other primitive weapons. Nobody was fighting; they just stood there with their eyes transfixed on the sky above the remains of a black cathedral, where a spiraling vortex of comprised, Divine Light spun.

With a deep breath, Lilith bolted into the Razor Fields and the final stretch of her journey through Hell. With her muscles and lungs on fire, she battled against exhaustion with nothing more than her stubborn will. To her, nothing else mattered but the cathedral and the spiral of light rising out of it, the promise of the awaiting soul.

With her legs burning, she burst into the shadowy, rich antechamber absolutely wrecked. She collapsed against the wall as she struggled to catch her breath. She raised her gun and pointed towards the open archway, just in case anything outside decided to get cute.

"Calm down," she muttered to herself between gasps of air.

Her body was drenched with sweat while her arms bled from a half dozen cuts, a gift from the blade-like grass of the Razor Fields. She felt dizzy as her stomach lurched, threatening to spew the remnants of her lunch all over the cobblestone floor of the cathedral.

Outside, something howled in fury – causing the structure to shake beneath the weight of its enormous roar. Though beyond exhausted, Lilith took that as her cue to get off her ass and finish what she came to do. Pushing off the wall, she headed into the nave, which was in total disarray. Large chunks of collapsed ceiling filled most of it, surrounded by broken pillars that looked like dead things excavated ribcage. Bones and enormous piles of crap were everywhere, filling the place with the repugnant stench of excrement and decay. Lilith, during her long life, never smelled anything as foul as this place.

Coming around a large rock mound, she saw the transept, which was cluttered by four massive black crosses. Nailed to them, with the stomachs split from chest to navel, were pregnant women who had their babies dangling between their legs on slimy umbilical cords. Behind them, in the bombed-out ambulatory, was the base of the spiraling vortex. Inside it, engulfed in the light, was a naked black man – the Nigerian Cannibal.

With a loud thunder crack, the vortex vanished. The Cannibal slowly got to his feet, clearly dazed and confused. She watched him look around the place as he scratched his nuts, trying to get his bearings. He was in good shape for being dead, all muscle. She suspected he was one of those gym guys who spent hours pumping iron and drinking gallons of protein. He was handsome, too, for an older dude. And had a big, thick cock.

She cleared her throat and called out to him.

He turned to look at her, his gaze cold and calculated – a killer's stare. When he spoke, his voice was deep and riddled with malice.

"Who the hell are you?"

"Name's Lilith."

"Well, Lilith, do you mind telling me where the fuck I am?"

"Hell."

He laughed dryly.

"That wasn't a joke."

"My grandma always told me I'd end up here if I didn't change my ways. I guess the old Betty was right," he said as he walked towards her.

He was tall, well over six feet. On his right arm, she noticed the tattoo of a naked woman impaled on a stake, which seemed strangely normal in their nightmarish surroundings. When he reached the crucified woman, he stopped.

"Friends of yours?"

Lilith shook her head.

He leaned against the cross and began fondling one of their breasts. When the dangling fetus reached out and touched his leg, the Cannibal punted it through a nearby window.

"So, Lilith, what can I do for you?"

"I'm here to take you back."

"To Earth?"

She nodded. Somewhere outside the cathedral, she heard the waling of the baby. Her heart immediately began to sink.

"Look, I've been around the block enough to know nothing in this life is free, bro. And I'm guessing a ticket out of Hell is going to be mighty damn costly. Am I right?"

"It is."

"Hit me with it."

"A job."

"A job," the Cannibal repeated with a snicker. "You ventured to the abyss to hire yourself a hitman? You must be desperate."

"We wanted the best."

"The best, huh? Well, you ain't wrong! Who's the target?"

"Heads of the Satanic State."

"The heads of what?"

"It's a long story, better told elsewhere. If you take this job, I can tell you that you will not only escape Hell but actually get a shot at Heaven."

"Oh yeah? I've got a lot of blood on my hands, girl – you think you can absolve all of it?"

"I can't," she said, "but I know who can."

"Who?"

"God."

CHAPTER 6

Lucious sat on the dusty nurse's station with a half-eaten bag of Doritos between his legs and one of Adam's fantastic blunts wedged between his lips. A stone-cold Papa John's pizza was next to him, lying open in a pool of congealed grease.

Somewhere inside the bowels of the dead hospital came a steady metallic pounding as Adam worked on…something. Lucious was certain Adam told him what he was up to, but he couldn't remember, thanks to the mind-numbing effects of his modified sweet leaf, the man's beautiful Tangerine Dream. He wasn't smoking it for its smooth taste or the cool calm it produced but because it helped him repress the heartache and a score of unwanted memories of dead life.

As for the hospital, its resurrection was one of extraordinary magnificence. After their departure, the angels worked seriously on the dead relic. All the wiring had been replaced, the bulbs had been changed, and a brand-new air-conditioning unit had been installed. In the old storage room behind the nurse's station was a makeshift pantry packed with food and two small refrigerators filled with water and pop bottles. New furniture was installed inside all the rooms, and the once empty main entrance now had a pair of lazy boy recliners, a huge sofa, and a large dining room table. The best part for him had to be the addition of running water. After discovering fresh clothes in his old cell, Lucious rushed to the showers and scrubbed his body raw for two solid hours. As much as he liked Adam's glorious weed, he loved his clean underwear even more.

A minute later, an Exhausted Adam strolled into the room shirtless and covered in black muck. He plopped down next to Lucious, grabbed a slice of pizza, and began munching.

"How goes the efforts?"

"Not bad, dude. Still, there is a lot of work to get the lab up and running, but it's getting there. You know what, though? That basement is one scary place, man. I'm talking, like, Nightmare on Elm Street sort of terror down there. You ever see that film?"

"Of course."

"And if that wasn't bad enough, dude, I'm pretty sure it's haunted."

"What?" Lucious asked in disbelief.

"After you helped with the bodies, I went to work setting up the lab right. And I swear, man, someone—or something—started messing with me. First, they started throwing rocks. Then they started moving my stuff around. I still can't find my screwdriver, dude. I keep imagining Freddy messing with me before he comes after me with his knife fingers."

"Well, I doubt it's Freddy. So, this place has ghosts – big deal."

"It might be more than that. I think all the noise we've been making, plus a bit of divine residue from the angels, has resurrected more than just this old building. You see anything out of the unordinary up here?"

"Nope."

Adam took the joint from Lucious and took a quick hit, then asked, "How much have you smoked, man? You look totally gassed."

Lucious reached into his front pocket and removed the little baggy Adam gave him with pre-made joints. There were ten when they arrived; now there was one.

"Dude! Take it easy on this stuff, man."

"I am, dude."

"Yeah, I can see that, man," Adam laughed. After scarfing down some pizza, he said, "A ghost could have walked right in front of you, waved, and you still wouldn't have seen it."

"A spirit wouldn't have the balls to walk up on me. Too afraid I'd cast them to Hell."

Adam nodded thoughtfully.

"Can I ask you a question? Something serious?"

"Does it have to be serious, dude?"

"I suppose it doesn't have to be, but it's been nagging at me for a while."

"Fine," Adam said as he took a long hit. "Go on, dude, ask me."

"What happened to Eve?"

"Going back to her, again, are we?"

Lucious shrugged.

"Look, I won't tell you the whole story, man, but she likes dead and stuff. A long time ago."

"Died? How is that possible – she was an immortal."

"Jesus."

"Sorry, Adam, I didn't mean…"

"No man – it was literally Jesus. He forgave her down in Galilee just before the Romans nailed him to a couple of boards. I could have died right along with her, dude, but back then, prophets were like a dime a dozen, and she dragged me to meet all of them. I got burned out, man, got tired of the lies and the deceit, so I didn't go see the latest flavor of the week – this dude called Jesus. Back then, I gave up on everything pretty much and just focused on oppressing that apple's effects."

"How did you do that?"

"Drugs mainly. Beer helped, too."

"Did you invent that?"

"I did, dude," Adam said with a laugh. "Wine too. Anyway, at some point, Eve heard about this man called Jesus running around healing the sick and walking on water – you know – all that stuff. I didn't believe it and told her as much, so she sought him out alone. And the rest is history; she got to find peace while I got stuck on this rock for an eternity, dude. I tried to find him, but by then, it was already too late. He was already dead and gone."

"That's insane."

"Yeah, man. There hasn't been a solitary day from then until now that I don't grieve for my sweet Eve. I miss her, dude, miss her big time."

"At least you're finally getting your second chance. Do this right, and you'll be reunited."

"I guess, man."

The ceiling above their heads suddenly opened with a flash of brilliant flame. A second later, Lilith crashed to the floor, knocking over chairs and a few tables.

"Dude," Lucious said, shocked. "I was not expecting that."

PART FOUR

War Ensemble

CHAPTER 1

Three body bags sat on metal slabs in the basement, which reeked of mold and dust. Adam did his best to tidy it up, but the state of the hospital's bowels was that of an old man dying of colon cancer. Somewhere above them, Lilith washed the filth and blood from her journey to the Wastes while the pipes gurgled and clanged.

"Good thing we took extra," Adam said, scratching his chin.

"I guess. What do we do with the one we don't use, dump it somewhere?"

"Dude, we can't just dump a body…that was like someone's loved one."

"Not mine."

"I'll bury it on the grounds, man, and make sure to give it, like, it's last rites."

"You do that. In the meantime," Lucious said with a clap. "Tell me what we got? Show me the merch."

"Before I do, I want you to remember something…we're like beggars and stuff, which totally means we can't be like choosers. Okay? So," Adam said as he walked towards the slab, "we got two males and a female to work with. This one here is the former Thomas Hornsby, who died of a massive coronary at the tender age of 48. The one in front of you," Adam said as he pointed, "is Janet Corwin Barbeau; she died of natural causes at 99. The one in the middle is William Taggert Parker, 35."

"How did he die?"

"Got stabbed to death during an alleged burglary."

"Alleged?" Lucious asked.

"Everything is alleged these days, even when the crime is caught on video. Truth has become subjective to those covering it. You get used to it around here."

Lucious didn't care about the Earth and its current long list of problems. The sooner it burned, the better – all he wanted to do was get back to Hell. Looking at the body bags, he asked, "Do you have any suggestions?"

"I think William would be the best host for the Cannibal."

"Why?"

"He's black."

"How is that important?"

"Resurrection is scary enough, dude, in its own right, but to like to wake up as another race just might kill him all over again."

"Seriously?"

Adam shrugged.

"Didn't realize that would be an issue. I'd just be happy to be alive again. Oh well," he said. He approached the bodies. "I'd still like to peek at Horny before making our final decision; race be damned."

"It's Hornby, Lucious."

"Whatever – tomahto, tomato. Open the bag."

"Fair enough," Adam replied, unzipping the bag. Inside was a middle-aged man with the purple tint of the dead. He had long, stringy blond hair, a goatee, and a pair of yellow teeth poking out between wormy lips.

"Guy has a face only a mother could love – if the mother was a blind crackhead. Bury that guy and bury him deep. We'll use the old hag for our mystery guest and Taggert for the Cannibal."

"Dude," Adam said in disgust, "show some respect. Janet was someone's mother, someone's grandmother. Out there, right now, a family weeps for her."

"Yeah, at an empty grave because you stole the body."

"I didn't steal it."

"No?"

"Borrowed."

"You going to give it back, Adam?"

Adam didn't say anything.

"That family you speak so eloquently about weeps for the soul, not the vessel. And for that, they can continue to weep. We are preparing for war, and, for all intended purposes, I couldn't stomach looking at that Thomas dude for its duration."

Adam zipped the bag.

They spent the next few minutes examining the other corpses. Neither of them looked as bad as the first, but death gives horrible makeovers to everyone it touches. Adam and Lucious spent the next few minutes preparing the bodies for their upcoming resurrection. Adam dressed Taggert while Lucious took care of Grandma Barbeau. While attempting to slip on a pair of panties on the cold, wrinkly remains of the crone, Lilith strolled over decked out in a pair of shorts, cowboy boots, and a Rock Bottom Remainders concert shirt from their '95 tour. Both of her arms were also heavily bandaged from the cuts inflicted by the Razor Fields.

"Oh. My. God. What are you two morons doing?"

"What's it look like?" Lucious asked with Barbeau's legs resting on his shoulders and her panties dangling halfway up her varicose veiny ass.

"Looks like you're trying to rape a corpse," Lilith said.

"Ha. Ha. Very funny. We're actually trying to dress our newfound friends here, but they're proving to be difficult. Who would have thought dressing a dead body would be so damn challenging."

"You should try soul collecting."

"No thanks," Lucious replied, finally getting the undergarments where they needed to be, which was covering a long-neglected vagina peppered with thick, gray pubes.

Just then, a small rock pinged off the wall next to Lilith, missing her head by a few inches. She looked around the room in surprise. Confused, she asked, "What was that?"

"Our resident ghost," Lucious said.

"What do you mean, our resident ghost? I've been here for days and never witnessed anything paranormal, let alone a ghost."

"Dude, do you have to be so crass?"

"Shut up, Adam."

A second later, a stone struck her in the temple. It wasn't a brutal hit, nothing that would cause any real damage, but it was enough to piss her off. She spun around in the general direction of the projectile and shouted, "Throw another one, asshole, and I'll find a way to unleash unholy hell on you, ghost or not. I'll mess you up so badly you'll be practically begging for the Ghostbusters to come here to bust your ass. You get me?"

"You tell him," Lucious said with a laugh.

"You can shut up too, Lucifer," Lilith replied angrily. "Great, so this place is full of ghosts now. What's next…stigmata?"

Lucious and Adam finished the soul-numbing task of dressing the bodies while Lilith coached them through it by basically complaining to them the entire time. When the task was completed, it was already dark outside. Though a few lights were in the hospital's basement to illuminate Adam's makeshift workstation, the rest was pitch black.

"Where's the soul collector thingy," Lucious asked Lilith.

"What…no, please?"

Lucious held out his hand.

"You need to learn to relax," Lilith said. He handed it over. "Do you know how to work it?"

"I'm not stupid."

"You sure about that?"

"Ha. Ha," he said. He pointed the device at Taggert. He pressed a few buttons on it, but nothing happened – the dead remained unanimated.

"You've got to…"

"I got it, Adam," Lucious snapped. He started to click random buttons in frustration. The only thing he managed to do was make the damn thing beep.

"Can you give it back to Adam already? I'm in no mood to spend the rest of our pathetic lives trapped down here with you two jackasses."

"You don't have to be here," Lucious said.

"Oh yes, I do. I've got to make sure a couple of stoners don't screw this up. That soul ends up back in Hell. It'll be you two assholes going to collect – not me."

Lucious handed the device to Adam.

The First Man made them step back as he placed the device against Taggert's temple and blasted him with a shot of alien soul. The body on the table began thumping and bouncing around as life invaded the dead flesh. And while it did its dance, Adam pumped the body of the late Barbeau with the other.

"How long will this take?" Lilith asked.

Taggert sat up with a jolt, his eyes wide and his mouth slacked and drooling. He looked around the room, soaking in his surroundings as his neck muscles worked out the rigor mortis.

"Mr. Cannibal?" Adam asked gently. "Can you hear me?"

Barbeau's body came alive in mad, agonizing spasms. Lucious tried to grab her, but the old woman's body rolled off the table and hit the floor with a bone-crunching smack. This seemed to make something click for the Cannibal, who focused his attention on Lilith.

"You?"

"Hello," she said with a wave.

"Where are we now?"

"Arizona."

"Never liked this state," the Cannibal said. "You guys got anything to drink? My mouth tastes like a hot rectum."

"We got coke upstairs," Adam said.

"Who are you supposed to be, bro?" the Cannibal asked.

"Adam," he said. He offered him his hand.

The Cannibal didn't take it.

"When I said drink, bro, I'm talking about a proper drink. Whiskey. Got any?"

"Sorry, dude, there's no liquor here."

Popping up on the far side of the last slab, Lucious helped the old woman to her feet. Though the vessel was female, nobody in the room knew what lurked inside it. Holding the strange, unwanted guest, he asked them if they were okay and then waited for a clue inside the mystery meat.

"I'm fine. Just a little woozy," they said, their voice clearly female. The old woman looked over at Lilith, grinning mostly toothlessly at her. "Thank you, sweet child…for saving me."

"It's not like I had a choice, is it."

"Nor I."

"We should take this little party upstairs," Lucious said. "I have the feeling they're going to have a lot of questions, and if I'm answering them, I want to be sitting in the air-conditioning drinking an ice-cold Coke then down here in this filthy, ghost-infested basement."

That's when Lucious got struck in the head with a pebble. And somewhere in the twilight shadows of the basement, everyone thought they heard laughter.

Lucious stared at the newest editions of his squad of so-called righteous defenders and his army and shook his head in disgust. The Nigerian in his new meat suit was a mangled mess with a badly scarred face. As far as the rest of his horribly mutilated body was concerned, it was thankfully hidden beneath his dark suit. Next to him sat the old hag. She was thin, with her head topped with silver curly hair and more facial hair than a pro-wrestler. They were seated at a table, stuffing their faces like rats, while Adam and Lilith sat over at the nurse's station, being completely useless as always.

"Let's start simple," Lucious said, "introductions. That woman sitting over there is Lilith, she's a bit of a bitch. Sitting next to her is our weapon's expert, the First Man, Adam. As for me, I'm Lucious, and I'm running this monkey farm."

"Excuse me, bro," the Cannibal interjected, "but what the fuck do you mean by First Man?"

"Read Genesis," Lucious said.

"You talking about the dude from the Bible?"

Lucious nodded.

"The mother who ate the apple?"

"The one and the same."

Both the Cannibal and the old crone looked at Adam, who smiled back at them before taking a big bite out of a juicy, ripe Gala apple.

"And you said her name was Lilith? I don't remember her from the Bible. Do you, Grandma?"

She shook her head and went back to eating. The old cow guzzled down cola like it was going out of style. In the last ten minutes, she already finished off three cans and was well on her way to finishing her fourth.

"Never heard of her. I've never heard of you either," the Cannibal said. He pointed at Lucious. "What did you say your name was again, bro, Luscious?"

"Lucious."

"Sounds like a gay pornstar, bro."

"I'm a lot of things to a lot of different people, but a gay pornstar isn't one of them."

"You in the Bible bro?"

"Oh yes. You might say I'm one of the key players."

"If I may," the old lady interjected politely. "I just wanted to thank the young lady for saving me from my hellish predicament. I'm unsure what this is, but I'm happy to be here and will contribute any way I can."

"What is your name?" Lucious asked.

"Moragon Cuttleback. And seeing as the next question will probably be about how I came to be in the pit, I'll go ahead and answer that now. I was apprehended for witchcraft after refusing the advances of an Archbishop. I was twenty. Before being dragged to the stake, through the mud and the shit, I was raped and beaten so badly I couldn't even scream as my flesh melted."

"Damn, bro, that's messed up."

"You don't end up in the Grey Wastes as an innocent," Lucious said, "so you can stop playing the pity cards. Are you a witch? Before you answer…rest easy knowing the days of the witch hunts are long gone. You are safe here."

"You believe her, bro?"

"Why wouldn't I? I respect all the Night Mothers."

Her eyebrows shot up after she heard the name of the witch's secret order, a term few knew outside of its unholy networks. It was then that, no matter how she answered, Lucious knew what he had in his midst. Sitting before him, trapped in the reanimated body of an elderly woman, was a genuine witch, a Night Mother.

"Man, this just keeps getting weirder and weirder," the Cannibal said as he shook his head. We've got witches and biblical characters coming to life—what the hell is next, stigmata?"

"That's what I said," Lilith grumbled with a laugh.

Lucious ignored the Cannibal's outburst and remained focused on the old lady, the supposed witch. Moragon would be an excellent addition to his army if she were what she claimed she was. He stepped forward, putting his hands on the table, and leaned close to the woman. He asked her again, his voice commanding, "Are you a witch?"

"I am."

"Oh. My. God. Hold the damn phone – you mean to tell me I saved a witch?"

"That's exactly what you did," Lucious said. "And I couldn't be more thankful. No offense, Mr. Cannibal, but I would happily trade a thousand of you for a single Night Mother."

The Cannibal shrugged as he continued eating.

"How long have you been dabbling in the Arts?"

"Long enough to know a thing or two."

"Who was your Mistress?"

"Madam Martiale Esparzi."

"You don't say," he said impressed.

"Do you recognize the name?" Adam asked.

"I do. She was an extremely powerful Night Mother."

"And evil, no doubt," Lilith murmured.

"Very," Lucious said, his eyes trained on Moragon. "One of the worst, which no doubt means you have some nasty potency to offer us, Moragon Cuttleback, am I correct?"

She smiled at him with her milky gray eyes in their sunken sockets. Though the true Moragon was hidden inside the meat, he could still sense her maliciousness. There was no doubt a devil lurking there, and he couldn't wait to unleash it.

"You never really introduced yourself," the Cannibal said. "Care to explain who you are, bro? You said you were in the Bible, but I don't remember learning about some asshole named Lucious in my Sunday School."

"I'm Lucifer."

Moragon gasped as she dropped to the floor at his feet, kissing his shoes again and again. Lucious knelt down, gingerly took her by the hands, and escorted her back to her seat. After kissing her gently on the head, he said, "No need for that Night Mother, Moragon Cuttleback. We are all equals in this house."

"Yeah," Lilith said, "we're all equally fucked."

"Yo," the Cannibal shouted to Lilith as he jumped out of his seat. Staggering away from Lucious and the witch, he asked, "Back in Hell, didn't you say something about us taking out the Satanic State?"

"We are."

"Then why is he here? No offense Lucifer, but shouldn't we be killing your ass."

"You know," Lilith said, "I think we're going to get along just fine because that's exactly the argument I made after I learned we were bringing him onboard for this fight. But the forces that be told me we needed him."

"For what, bro?"

"We don't know where the Satanic State resides, but he does."

"So, I'm what…going to be working with Satan?"

"You've worked with worse," Lucious said. "How about you sit back down so I can explain everything to you."

The Nigerian studied Lucious closer now, his coffee-brown eyes searching for answers to questions he'd never find. Considering the brevity of the situation, Lucious found the Cannibal taking it pretty well. Most people who find themselves before the Mourning Star scream until their throats bleed and the last of their sanity oozed out of their ears. Maybe this collective cool made the Eld interested in acquiring his services.

"So, what's the deal, bro?" the Cannibal asked, retaking his seat.

Lucious explained the Shroud and how they were conscripted to save a dying God. When he finished, he saw the primates struggling with a mind rape of biblical proportions. While waiting for the shock wave to recede, he sat at their table, kicked up his dirty boots, and asked them if they had any questions.

"Not a question, bro, but I want to understand this insanity. So, we're working with you to hunt down demons to save God? Is that about, right?"

"You got it."

"Man, this is insane, yo," the Cannibal said as he shook his head. "You drop bombs like this on someone, bro; you need to offer something stiffer to drink besides cola."

"We've got Dr. Pepper."

"That's not what I meant."

"During your quest for redemption," Lilith said as she came over, "you are to avoid falling back into your sinful lifestyles. You do that, and the deal goes up in smoke."

"My life was nothing but sin, lady – I was a goddamn hitman!"

"Learn to pray, Cannibal."

"Yeah, no shit," he said with a snicker. "And can y'all do me a small favor – stop calling me the Cannibal? It's getting real fucking annoying at this point. I have a name, surprised you guys don't know it…it's Sage. Sage Williams. As for this show, is that it, or do y'all have more rules to follow?"

"Just one. No killing the innocent," Lilith said.

"You and Moragon," Lucious said, "have time to weigh your options, seeing as God blessed you monkeys with free will. You have until morning. In the meantime, Adam will take you to your rooms so you can clean yourselves up and get more acquainted with your new bodies."

The Cannibal got up, but Moragon didn't move.

"You have something you wish to say?" Lucious asked the witch, his precious Night Mother.

"I will serve. Not for Him, but for you."

Lucious smiled as he held out his hand — they shook. With a big, toothless grin, she got up and followed Adam to her room. She didn't walk on sunshine but on the penumbra of an eclipse.

Lucious had just laid down to catch some much-needed shuteye when someone knocked on his chamber door—not so much a knock as a thunderous pound. With a groan, he sat up on his cot and rubbed at his throbbing temples.

"For the love of God, can you stop with the banging? I hear you!"

"You decent?"

It was Gabriel.

"What are you doing here?"

"Came to talk."

"Surprised you found the time to speak to us lowly peasants."

"Can you open the door?"

Confused, Lucious slipped on a pair of pants and opened the door. In the hall, engulfed in his own faggoty illumination, stood the Archangel Gabriel. And he wasn't alone — standing next to him, dressed in heavy plate mail, was Michael.

"Hey, Lucy," Michael said smugly. "Been a while."

"Should have been longer."

"May we come in?" Gabriel asked.

"If I say no, will you two dicks piss off?"

"This is urgent," Michael said.

"Is that why you didn't send a Principality this time?"

"I'm sorry about that," Gabriel said. "I would have come myself to deliver the address, but something incredibly urgent required my attention. And it affects everything, including this endeavor."

"What?"

"Let us in already, and we'll tell you," Michael said, annoyed.

Lucious shrugged as he side-stepped, allowing the angelic assholes access to his room. Once they were inside, he shut the door. He would have turned on the light, but the room was already perfectly illuminated by the divine entities, so he decided to save on electricity.

"It's the Eld," Gabriel said as tears streamed down his cheeks in golden streaks. "He's taken a turn for the worse. If something isn't done soon, He'll…"

"Die a much-deserved death? Good," Lucious said as he grabbed a roll of toilet paper from the back of his commode. He tore off a few sheets and handed them over to Gabriel as Michael watched maliciously at his every move like a murder hawk.

"If He dies, the deal is off," Michael said with all the grace and love of a lawyer. "You know what that means for you and the rest of the scum in this building, right?"

"Yeah, we're fucked. Is that why you're here?"

"Someone has to carry out the executions."

"Bet you jumped at the opportunity."

"Damn straight, I did," Michael said with a mocking grin. "You think I'd miss a chance to introduce your neck to my axe, Lucy? I've been dreaming about it since the day you revolted."

"That's enough, Michael," Gabriel said as he stepped between them. We are not here to resurrect old feuds but to save our beloved Lord."

"So, what's the time frame we're discussing, Gabe? Hours? Days? What?"

"I wish I knew. Things are not looking good, so you must do something. Now."

"Now? We're not ready."

"Then get ready, Lucy," Michael snapped angrily.

"Element of surprise is our greatest asset against them. Once that's gone, once our plans are exposed, they'll come for us. How do you expect us to wage a war against the demonic hordes with five people, Michael? I need time to recruit and train."

"Too bad," Michael snarled.

"Michael, please," Gabriel said as he put his hand on his shoulder. "You are not helping with these violent outbursts."

"Next time you visit G, how about you leave your dog at home," Lucious said.

Michael lunged forward, hungry to unleash damage.

"Our greatest assist is the element of surprise. Once that's gone, we're…"

"It's a risk we're going to have to take," Gabriel said.

"Why don't you summon the rest of the Seraphim and fight this war yourselves?"

"If it were up to me," Michael said, "I would. First, I'd take your sorry ass back to Heaven bound in chains and then have Raphael crack open your skull and rip out all your dark secrets. But sadly, that's not the way He wants it. This battle is yours, so you need to figure out a way to make this initial strike one of legend. He has given you three days."

"And if we fail?"

"Then I'll come and collect," Michael said. He got right in his face, their noses touching.

Lucious tried to shove Michael, but the Arch-asshole didn't budge an inch, not even half an inch. But when he shoved Lucious, the result was quite different. He went soaring. After bouncing off a wall, leaving a slight indentation with his ass, he hit the floor with a thud.

"That's enough," Gabriel shouted. "We are no longer at war with each other, brothers. What was is no more. If we are going to be successful, we must bury our discord and learn to work for the greater good. The Eld is depending on us."

"Gabriel just saved your life," Michael said, his eyes blazing. "You've got three days, three! After that, nobody will save you from me – not even the Eld. Come on, Gabe, let's get out of this crypt so this ghoul can rot."

Without another word, the two angels ascended back to Heaven, leaving Lucious to spend the rest of the night trying to figure out what he would do.

CHAPTER 2

By morning, a vicious storm blew into Tucson. Heavy rain and hail pelted the hospital while thunder rocked the foundation and rattled windows. Walking in a sort of zombie-like daze, Lucious headed to the waiting room dressed in fresh jeans and a *Twisted Sister* t-shirt left behind by the angels. Inside his room were a couple of suitcases packed with random clothes. Though most of them sucked major balls, Lucious was happy to have something fresh to change into after wearing the same stuff for a few days.

In the waiting room, he found Adam seated at the table, eating a bowl of cereal. Next to him was a small radio playing today's horrid music, a ragtag of over-synthesized beats and voices. He recognized the singer as he strolled over because it belonged to the Archdemon Druji – Hell's prostitute. Using oversexualized lyrics and raunchy videos to corrupt young girls, she ruined lives like sugar did teeth.

"Morning sunshine," Adam said with a mouthful of Fruit Loops.

"Whatever," Lucious said as he plopped down next to him.

"Ghosts keep you up?"

"Yeah, ghosts from the past. Angels."

"Which ones?" Adam asked.

"The worst ones - Gabriel and that douchebag Michael."

Adam nodded as he munched and crunched.

Lucious told him everything, about the three days and the Eld's failing health, while the storm intensified outside. Somewhere above them, something heavy crashed to the floor, causing the lights in the waiting room to flicker like artificial lightning.

"Dude, that's a real Debbie Downer, man," Adam said. I suppose there are only two things we can do about this—we can give up and spend whatever time we have left being disgusting hedonists, or we can fight. That's it."

"What, no third option?"

Adam shook his head.

"What do you want to do?"

"For a chance to be reunited with my beloved Eve, I'll fight all the way down to Hell's gates. But that's just me, dude; I can't speak for anybody else. What about you?"

"I've got no choice. I either die fighting, or I die. I'm fucked either way Adam."

"We all are. Just some more than others," Adam said as he shoveled more food into his mouth.

"Well crap," Lucious said with a sigh, "this was not how this thing was supposed to go."

"Remember 2 Chronicles 20:17, which says, 'Do not be afraid and do not be dismayed. Tomorrow, go out against them, and the Lord will be with you.'"

"Not if He's sick."

"I'm just trying to cheer you up, dude."

"It's going to take more than some bull crap quote from the Bible to cheer me up. You got any more of that Tangerine Dream?"

"Dude, it's like 8 in the morning."

"Has that ever stopped you?"

"No. But if you keep smoking it, I'll have none left, man. We need to ration it out or something," he said as he spooned cereal into his mouth. You think those two will be ready?"

"Sage and Moragon?"

Adam nodded.

"Moragon might be, but there is no way Sage is. I mean, the guy has never encountered a real-life demon before. We aren't even sure his fragile little monkey brain could handle such an encounter. He might be able to kill other people, but this is a whole other ball game. What about you, Adam? Are you ready?"

"Dude, I'm a lover, not a fighter. I'll make your gear and stuff, but battling demonic forces is their bag, not mine."

"You ever met a demon before?"

"Nah, man, and I'd like to keep it that way too, dude."

"I need to come up with a plan," Lucious said. He ran his fingers through his hair. He looked over at the radio and asked, "You mind if I turn this damn pollution off? I need to think."

"No way!"

"You like this?"

"I don't like it, dude; I love it. Do you know who that is? It's the Queen of Pop, Tiffany Swan. She's a creative juggernaut, producing some of the most mind-blowing songs I've ever heard."

"You do realize she's a demon, right?"

"What? No way, dude, she's like an innocent and stuff."

"That's what she wants you to believe. Her real name isn't Tiffany Duck or whatever; it's Durji – and she's using all those gummy jingles to corrupt the masses, including your dumb ass, apparently. You know, I'd figure someone with godlike knowledge would be smarter than the rest of humanity when coming to false idols like this little sour tart. At least smarter than a bunch of teenage girls."

"How do you know?"

"I sent her here to troll the world. And she didn't come alone either; I sent her with the demon of musical discord, Hornblas. And judging by your response, it clearly worked."

"They part of the Shroud?"

"Absolutely. Hornblas is the President of Global Music Group – one of the largest music producers in the world. Those in his service, those who aren't demons or Weavers, are humans under his direct control. You name a top global superstar, and there's a good chance they work for him in some capacity. Some don't know they serve a demonic piece of shit, but most do, and most don't care so long as they keep getting fat checks. Haven't you ever heard of a horrible singer and wondered how they got so popular?"

"All the time, man."

"It's because they sold their souls for Rock n' Roll baby."

"This is heavy, man," Adam said. He walked over to the nurse's station, setting his bowl down. He stood there momentarily before asking Lucious, "Do you think if we kill this Durji, that might help the Eld?"

"It might. Why?"

"She's like coming here, dude. Two days."

"To Tucson?"

"It was on the radio like five minutes before you got here. She's coming here for like an album release party or something."

"Are you suggesting we crash it?"

Adam smiled.

"I like the way you think."

"I'll be right back," Adam said. He headed towards a nearby exit.

"Wait, where you going?"

Adam paused in the doorway and glanced back at Lucious, grinning mischievously. "I'm going to get high, dude."

"Didn't you tell me it's too early for that?"

"Yeah, I did."

And then he was gone.

Lilith was closing in on her 200th pushup when she saw a girl standing in the doorway just outside her cell, clutching a dirty Raggedy Ann doll. The girl, who appeared no more than ten, wore a white dress, knee-high socks, and black shoes. Her blond hair was pulled back into a ponytail, which hung lifelessly across her slender shoulder.

"Hi there," Lilith said gently, not wanting to spook the child.

The girl smiled.

Lilith got off the floor and cleaned the dust off her sweaty palms on the cuff of her jeans. The girl was cute, with a beautiful frosting of brown freckles across her cheeks and nose. Lilith loved the girl's lips, which were arched into a permanent frown.

"Where did you come from?"

"Down there," the girl said softly. He pointed back down the hall just as lightning spilled in through a half dozen hospital windows. A second later, thunder filled the hospital with an ear-shattering boom.

"You live near here?"

The girl shook her head.

"What's your name?"

"Valerie," she said as she stared down at her feet, "but friends call me Val."

"Well, this isn't a very safe place for a little girl, Val, especially on a day like this," Lilith said brightly. Give me your mom's number, and I'll call her. She's probably worried sick about you."

Lilith walked over to the bed and grabbed her phone. When she turned around, Val was replaced by the witch, Moragon Cuttleback. She stood in the doorway wearing a flower-printed sundress, which showed off too much of her prune-like body.

Confused, Lilith asked, "Where did the girl go?"

"What, girl?"

"The girl who was just standing there…Valerie."

"Afraid you've been speaking with the dead," Moragon said with a wet cackle. "This place be full of them. I should know, I spent most of the night conversing with them. And you would not believe the tales they told, full of wicked delights."

"What are you talking about, you loon?" Lilith said as she stormed out into the hall, the lights blinked overhead. Standing in the corridor, Lilith listened to the sound of fading footsteps, but besides the rain, she heard nothing.

"First time speaking with a spirit?" Moragon asked with a big toothless grin.

"Yeah. She seemed so real, so alive. I thought she was lost."

"She is. Heaven's door is closed to her, which is why she roams these decrypted halls until God trumpets signal his return."

"The poor thing."

"She likes you," Moragon said. "You remind her of someone important. That's why she revealed herself to you so clearly. You should feel honored."

"You said you spent the night speaking to the dead – are there really that many roaming the halls? I was here for weeks getting things ready and never saw or heard anything."

"Activity has increased thanks to all the angelic activity. They fed. They grew fat and strong – and after that happened, they've grown confident - kind of like your precious Valerie, who's probably watched you from afar since you arrived. Last night, I spoke with a nurse named Mollie, a car accident victim, a woman who died during labor, and a janitor named Joe. I must warn you that not all spirits are good. Take, for instance, the Top Hat Man; he's the violent entity dwelling in the basement. And he doesn't like us being down there."

"The rock thrower."

The witch pointed at her nose.

"It'll get worse as his power grows."

That wasn't good to hear, especially considering Adam's lab and makeshift weapon shop for the upcoming conflict were located deep in the hospital's bowels. And now, to make matters more difficult, there's a powerful entity down there dangerous and violent.

"I'll talk to Adam," Lilith said.

"You do that. I'll talk to the Top Hat Man and see if I can defuse some of the tension."

Lilith noticed something lying on the floor behind Moragon. It was a bloated heap of fur and maggots. The stench of it was repugnant and made her stomach twist in violent knots. Gagging, she cupped her hand over her mouth, fighting back the vomit.

"Smells delicious, doesn't it," Moragon said with a cackle.

"What is it?"

"A dead cat."

"Why do you have it?"

"I'm going to resurrect it."

"I'm sorry…you're doing what?" Lilith asked, not believing what she just heard.

"Witches need a familiar," Moragon said.

More magic nonsense, Lilith thought, staring into the witch's cold, milky gaze. For the first time that morning, she regretted crawling out of bed. First came the child's ghost, and now the witch with her dead cat. She needed a drink—a lot of drinks. She wished whoever stocked their makeshift kitchen had included a bar.

"I sense you do not believe. You want to watch?"

"Sure. I have nothing else to do. Wow, me."

Outside, the wind howled as the storm's intensity swelled. Rain pelted the windows as lightning forked through the low-hanging clouds. Lilith ran her fingers through her hair as Moragon plopped down on the floor and pulled the dead thing into her lap. The entire time she did this, her eyes never left hers.

"Sit."

"Oh. My. God. I can't believe I'm actually doing this," she said. She sat across from Moragon. It was out of pure morbid curiosity that she sat down in the dust and dirt instead of running, which is what her rational mind begged her to do.

"Do you use the Art too?" Lilith asked.

"For our craft, the Night Mothers do not touch it directly. We use its taint," she said, "as you will no doubt witness."

The lights dimmed overhead as Moragon began speaking in a hellish tongue as she stroked the dead thing in her lap. Lifting its head up, she proceeded to spit in its face, eyes, and mouth.

"Did you want to kiss it?" Moragon asked, twisting its dead neck around so it faced Lilith.

"Hell no."

Moragon shrugged as she lifted the disintegrating folds of the cat's belly, where some demented asshole had acted as a butcher on the poor animal just days before. When she raised the fatty flaps, a swarm of feasting worms spewed out, dousing her legs beneath their writhing corpora. There were maggots, red worms, and giant, black spiders. Moragon bit her free hand hard enough to draw blood and then jammed it into the putrefied innards.

There was a wicked crash outside as the lights in the hall went out. It would have been pitch black in the hall if not for the gray beams of light cascading through the windows along the wall. And then, just as Lilith was about to get the hell out of dodge, the cat, lying in its own putrid juices, began to breathe.

"You see," Moragon croaked. "It lives *again.*"

"Oh. My. God."

The cat sat up; its midsection opened like a book flipped to a middle chapter. Its eyes blazed in the limited light a bright emerald green. It looked at Lilith for a second and then over at Moragon, who was busy stuffing a fist full of insects into her mouth.

"It needs a name. Something sweet. Something worthy of its station," Moragon said as she licked her lips.

"I have no idea."

"I got it," the witch said, snapping her fingers excitedly. "We'll call it Dead Meat."

Moragon must have thought the name was the punchline to the world's funniest joke because she guffawed hard enough to blow some serious snot rockets.

"She's off her rocker," Dead Meat said to Lilith.

"Holy moly," she gasped, "you can talk!"

"I can also sing," Dead Meat said, "but I'll spare you the headache."

"But…"

"I know, I'm a cat. How can any of this be possible, right?"

Lilith nodded.

"I think, therefore I am," Dead Meat replied. The cat then did a quick take of its body and said, "Man, I'm fucked up. I hope someone finds the one responsible and returns the favor."

Lilith looked at Moragon, who had finally stopped laughing. The witch's chin was covered in salvia, dirt, and a few spider legs. "I didn't know it would talk."

"Don't forget to sing," Dead Meat added.

"Of course, they can speak. What did you think a Night Mother's familiar did all day, chase rats and lick their own genitals? They serve a purpose."

"I'm special," Dead Meat said as he hopped out of Moragon's lap. It sniffed around in its own guts before looking back over at Lilith and asked, "You going to eat this?"

She was so stunned that all she could do was shake her head.

"Cool, I'm calling dibs."

"Eat my sweet pet," Moragon said as she got to her feet. "Get your fill because we've got wicked work to do."

CHAPTER 3

The doors opened, and in came the Cannibal, dressed in the same wrinkled suit as the day before. To say he looked like crap would be an insult to excrement. Lucious figured he'd be cordial and said good morning to the hitman, but Sage only grumbled in return as he marched over to the nurse's station and disappeared behind it.

When he reappeared a few seconds later, he was holding the Breakfast of Champions, a package of Pop-Tarts. Instead of coming over to join him, he sat down at the counter and ripped open the package with his teeth like a dog.

"Couldn't sleep?" Lucious asked, trying one last time to break the ice with the man.

"Nah, bro. Been thinking."

"Overthinking can be dangerous."

"Ain't that the truth," Sage said, biting into his tart. "You got to admit this be some heavy shit to lay on someone who just died. My last twenty-four hours have been messed up with a trip to Hell, a resurrection, and learning God has recruited me to fight for the Light but work with the Lord of the Dark."

"I know how you feel."

"The hell you do," Sage snapped, spitting chunks of breakfast across the room.

"You think I'm without a soul?"

"Nah bro, you got one alright – but it be black as tar."

"And what color is yours? You didn't end up in Hell by accident."

The hitman didn't reply, he just chewed angrily. Lucious was pretty sure if he wasn't the Mourning Star, Sage would have stormed over and beat the living crap out of him.

"How many people have you killed?" Lucious asked.

"How many have you killed, bro?"

"None."

Sage laughed.

"My hands are soaked in the blood of angels, not man. I don't care about you or the other people on this godforsaken rock enough to come up and get my hands dirty. Besides, you monkeys do a good enough job killing each other that you don't even need my help."

"What about this Shroud bro?"

"It punishes Him, not humanity."

"Obsess much?" Sage asked. "Do you know what you sound like, Lucious? A disgruntled hoe seeking vengeance on their ex after a sloppy break-up. Is that where all this rage comes from, bro…getting rejected? Face facts, the creation of mankind seriously messed you up."

"And what fucked you up, I wonder? Most mass murderers come from broken homes. Let me guess, I bet your mother was probably some cracked-out prostitute who didn't even know who your old man was after knocking boots with so many johns."

"You better…"

"I must be on the right track…look at you, already getting hot under the collar. I bet someone probably twiddled your dinky as a kid. Probably tossed your salad, too. So, tell me, Sage, how old were you when you sucked your first dick?"

He was so embroiled with rage Lucious felt its heat from across the room. Laughing, he watched Sage throw his breakfast to the floor and hop off the nurse's station, ready to knock heads.

"I'd think twice before stomping over here, especially if you think you're going to beat my ass. I'm not weak like your other victims. I'll rip you to shreds and then devour that pathetic soul of yours."

Sage glared at him.

"Did you make your decision?"

"About what, beating your ass?"

"I can see the Eld didn't select you for your intelligence, Sage," Lucious said with a laugh. "Are you joining the team or are you about to piss off back to Hell. I'm happy either way."

"I want to make it perfectly clear to you and whoever's listening I'm not doing this for you, bro. I'm doing it for my Grand-Grand."

"Your what?"

"Grandma," Sage corrected, speaking cracker. "She was the only person in this world who gave any fucks 'bout me. She was a beautiful woman and about as devoted a Christian as you'd ever meet. She tried to keep me on the righteous path, but I was too stubborn and dumb to listen. If killing demons is going to help reunite me with her, I'm down."

"Does down mean yes?"

"Looks like we're partners until we either die or win," Sage said.

"Or die," Lucious corrected. "Sounds like I wasn't far off about your family's crooked history."

"Good job, you miserable turd – what do you want a cookie? My life was no fairy tale, and I made the world pay for it in blood. And now it looks like I'm going to be doing it again, but this time, it's going to be with the blood of demons. Tell me one thing, Lucious, what color of blood do they have?"

"You'll see it soon enough."

"Damn straight, I will."

The doors swung wide as Lilith and Moragon strolled in like they owned the place. Lucious figured on some level all women probably felt a similar sense of empowerment. This was their world, as the third-wave feminists proclaimed, and men just inhabited it until they needed something fixed, or a jar of pickles opened. Lucious couldn't wait for Lilith to finally get that reality bitch slap she so deliciously deserved. He just wanted to make sure he was there when it happened so he could relish it.

Focusing on Moragon, he saw the witch cradling a black cat. Confused, he watched her whisper something into its ear and set it down. Running across the floor with pieces of shredded skin dragging on the floor beneath it, the cat jumped into his arms, purring loudly. Though it stank of death, he scratched the cat behind its ears as he asked her, "Where did you find this thing?"

"On the third floor," Moragon answered, approaching. You might be happy to learn I found it in the center of a pentagram. It seems some of your followers use this place for their dark rituals."

"Or for their cosplays," Lucious said. "Most of my so-called followers here are a bunch of idiots who dress in leather and engage in orgies in my name."

On the other side of the room, Lucious saw Sage grab Lilith by the arm and pull her aside for some secret talky-talky. For most humans, the distance and their low voices would prevent them from being heard, but he heard them loud and clear – and he feasted on their every word.

"Yo, can I talk to you right quick?" Sage asked.

"Sure."

They walked over to the nurses' counter.

"Look, I just wanted to say thank you. You know, for saving my life and all that."

"Don't make it all for nothing," she replied, pulling her arm free. "Tell me you're in."

"Oh, I'm in, baby," Sage said enthusiastically. "Ready to kick some demonic ass in the name of the Lord."

Sage offered her his hand. She shook it. Across the room, Lucious thought how sweet the moment was, sweet enough to give him damn cavities.

"Is everything okay, my Lord?" Moragon asked. She gestured to Dead Meat, who jumped into her outstretched arms.

"I want to know who stabbed me in the back," Lucious said. "Tell me, what do you know about divination?"

"I can do it," she said confidently. "But under our current contractual constraints, I'm not so sure I can cast the Nightmare Eye without being immediately banished back to Hell."

"What ingredients do you need?"

"Goat ejaculate."

"That's not so bad. Not sure where we can get a goat, but I'm pretty sure I can convince Lilith to do it."

"I also need the menstrual blood of a virgin and the ring finger of a dead nun."

He sighed.

"I can try a lesser divination, but the results might not be what you seek. You're asking for a look into the one place where peering eyes tend to get gouged. I do pray pardon, my Lord, for the last thing I want is to disappoint you."

"It's fine," he lied. The truth was, Lucious was furious he couldn't get the hag to peek inside the inner workings of Hell because if she could, he was certain he'd find out who sold him out. Agrat was one of the pawns in the revolt, but he doubted she acted independently.

"These stupid divine mandates are castrating us. How does the Eld expect me to win this war for His dumb ass if he ties my hands behind my back?"

"We will find a way," Moragon said.

"I hope so. Last night, I found out we have three days to puncture a hole in the Shroud, or this little venture we got going gets canceled."

"What happens then?"

"We literally get the axe."

"That's not good."

"No," Lucious said with a nervous chuckle.

"Where's Adam?" Lilith asked, joining them. "I haven't seen his dumb ass all morning. I bet he's off someplace getting high."

"He is," Lucious said.

"What a cock smoker."

"He's got his reasons this morning Lilith, so try not to be a total bitch. Gabe and Michael stopped by last night to inform us that the Eld has turned for the worse. We now have three days to accomplish the impossible – we have to puncture a hole in the Shroud. Adam thinks he has an idea."

"And he needs weed to help him concoct one?" Lilith asked.

"I usually masturbate when stumped."

"Oh. My. God. I did not need to know that."

THE WRETCHED

PART FIVE:
When the Stillness Comes

CHAPTER 1

The transition from one King to the next proved much simpler than Agrat ever expected. Instead of blood flowing in the streets from a massive civil war, the cities of Hell remained peaceful, and the armies were left unused.

And it was absolute crap.

Yesterday morning, Beelzebub transmitted news of his ascension through all major networks and communication channels throughout the abyss, and not one brick was thrown, or head bashed.

This total lack of anarchy and bloodshed infuriated Agrat, who was desperate for an outlet for her accumulating rage. With the battlefields left empty, she started slaughtering the Keep's staff, which resulted in the beheading of 5 serving girls and one cook.

When she wasn't sending servants to the block for decapitation, she spent most of the days in the throne room with Beelzebub, listening to the council members give daily reports of peace and civility throughout the realm. She didn't understand it – did nobody care Lucious was overthrown?

This bugged her.

Thankfully, the tedium died the following day.

While still drifting in the deep black of dreamless sleep, Agrat began to feel something gnawing at the back of her mind. It felt like something was trying to eat its way into her subconscious. With a jolt, she sat upright, breathing heavily. She looked around frantically, letting her eyes adjust to predawn gloom as the chomping intensified. Someone was trying to contact her…but who?

There was only one way to find out. Agrat took a deep breath and let the presence come forward. And it did, with all the gentleness of a Category 5 hurricane.

I FOUND THEM!

The last bit of lingering sleep was instantly dissolved by Mastema's screaming. It had been days since they last spoke, and his voice had somehow returned to its usual intensity. Was he healed? Was he finally ready to finish what they started? She hoped so because she sure as shit was. All this waiting-around crap was driving her insane.

"Mastema?"

In the flesh, he said, his voice echoing around inside her skull. *How's my favorite hell-bitch?*

"Don't call me that."

How about…conspirator? Does that sound better? Wouldn't want you to hurt your feelings.

"Get to the point," she snarled as she slipped into a robe. Even though he couldn't see her, the thought of her being naked in his presence was an unwanted feeling.

The hunt continues, he professed proudly. *My spies have found our prey.*

"Where?" she asked, unable to contain her excitement – which bubbled out of her like hot magma. She needed this. She needed to get out of the Keep to do some much-needed slaughter.

I'll tell you once you get your little ass over here and not a moment before, my sweet conniver. I wouldn't want you to go hunting without yours truly.

"I wouldn't…"

You would, he growled – aborting her thoughts like a teenager does an inconvenient pregnancy. *I'm not stupid, Agrat, nor am I some lesser demon who can be tricked or intimidated by some hell-bitch like you, a damn false Queen. I'm a King, and you are trekking through my lands and utilizing my resources. I will not allow you or any other Fallen free passage into my realm unescorted. You want the Mourning Star and that bitch, you come to me. Is that understood?*

The fury she felt in that empty bed chamber was of complete absolution. If she were there, she'd slice his throat and then watch him choke on his own vile blood. Since she still needed his services, she swallowed her anger like a bitter little pill and let the insults roll off her back like rain. As calmly as she could muster, she said, "I understand Mastema. No tricks. We do this together as we agreed."

Smart.

After sending her the address to his motel, he severed the connection.

Who can the damned pray to, Tzit wondered as he watched his King struggling to breathe on a mattress that's clearly seen better days, even in a seedy, rundown roach haven motel like this one. Things like crackheads blasting their filthy cum all over it or drunks pissing in their sleep – all of those things were better for it than what was happening to it now beneath Mastema.

All the blankets and bed coverings lay on the floor next to globs of the waitress's hair. The mattress itself was covered from top to bottom in a thick, black tar-like substance that oozed out of Mastema's pours.

And if that wasn't already bad enough, his meat suit lost most of its teeth, which the sick bastard Zozo collected and stacked on a nearby nightstand – 15 in total.

Yeah, things weren't looking good.

The girl and her baby worked in healing Mastema, but only temporarily. Within hours of feasting on their souls, he was back on the bed melting like ice cream dropped on hot summer pavement. Tzit wasn't sure how long the King had, but if he had to make an educated guess, it wasn't long.

But why?

This wasn't the first time Mastema switched bodies after losing one of his meat suits. Usually, he just got in, sieged control, and got back on with life. Easy-peasy. This time, however, it appeared his suit wasn't the only thing damaged during Lilith's attack – so was he. Whatever that evil bitch used; it was powerful enough to hurt a spirit like nothing he's ever seen before.

And that terrified him.

"Penny for your thoughts?" Zozo asked.

"You don't want these thoughts, even at such blowout prices," Tzit said as he watched his master sleep. "We need to have a serious conversation. Step outside with me for a moment."

Together they walked into the suffocating heat of another nightmarish Arizona afternoon. But at least the air out here was fresh, unlike back inside the room which smelled like greasy beer farts.

"We need to summon Shedim."

"Are you serious?" Zozo asked, not believing what he just heard.

"What other choice do we have at this point? Even if we hunt for another soul for Mastema, it won't help him. I'm not sure what Lilith used on him, but it fucked him up royally. Face it, Zozo, we need Shedim's magic."

"You think she'll help him?" Zozo asked. "She wants him dead as much, if not more, than Lilith. She'll come calling for sure, but not to aid our master, but to finish him off. You know there's a reason these two aren't in the same state. You remember what happened in Tangshan, China, in 1976 – a damn argument about what to have for dinner resulted in the death of 600,000 Chinese people! We bring these two together here, now, who knows what the fuck they'd do. I understand your concern, I do, but getting Shedim involved in any of this will only cause more problems, not solutions."

"Then what do we do?" Tzit asked, throwing up his hands in frustration. Leaning against the railing running along the motel's open patio, the Nonentity stared out across the parking lot at a pool packed with teenagers and a few overweight parents. Sighing, he said, "Maybe, I don't know, we can help them patch things up and reunite their fractured kingdom?"

"We'd have better luck convincing Lilith into a devil's threesome," Zozo said. "You know what we could do? A human soul might not work at this point, but a demonic soul would work wonders."

"A demon?"

"Not just any demon – Agrat."

"The Queen of Hell?"

"Bingo," Zozo said with a maniacal grin. "Think about it, man; she's a Fallen, one of the original castaways, which means she still has some of that yummy divinity flowing through her veins. Mastema gets his hands on some of that he'd be as right as rain."

"That's a bold plan."

"I'm a bold person," Zozo said with a laugh.

"You know…you're either a genius or just crazy; either way, this plan of yours just might work. Of course, we'll have to run this by Mastema first and see what he says. If he refuses, I don't know what we'll do."

"We'll be planning a funeral," Zozo said.

When they went back inside, Mastema was awake. He was propped up on the back of the bed with his fingers digging deep into his eye sockets. Fresh blood, bright and red, poured down his cheeks as he gouged out his own eyes.

Tzit and Zozo watched, stupefied, as Mastema removed them from his skull with a wet plop. Clutching them between his fingers like soft-boiled eggs, he popped them into his mouth and ate them. While he chewed, his true eyes flared to life in the empty sockets, burning brightly like a California forest fire.

"Mastema, are you alright?" Tzit asked.

"Better now," he said with a cough. "My eyes stopped working; I couldn't see a damn thing. Speaking of not being able to see, where the hell did you two idiots disappear off to?"

"We needed to chat, my Lord," Zozo replied.

"Chat? About what?"

"I think you know," Tzit said. "Those souls should have worked, but they didn't. In fact, since we've been here, all you've done is get progressively worse."

"You think I'm dying?"

"I know it, my Lord."

Mastema tried to speak, but instead of words coming out, only a hot spew burst from his throat. The once mighty King of the Nonentities threw himself over the side of the bed and puked violently all over the floor as his servants watched.

"Fuck the both of you," Mastema grumbled, sitting up, his chin doused in yellow stomach bile. "Do I have to remind the two of you I'm immortal! I cannot die."

"That was before encountering Lilith, my Lord. She's changed everything. But don't worry, we got a plan."

"You two?"

They nodded.

"In that case, I'm screwed. But I guess, considering the circumstances, I might as well hear you out. Amuse me with this so-called grandiose plan of yours."

Zozo told Mastema the plan while Tzit retreated to the bathroom, followed by a raucous round of heavy coughing by Mastema. They sounded like gunshots.

He closed the door behind him and flipped on the light, which bathed the small restroom in a piss yellow. He closed the curtains of the bathtub, which worked as the dead girl's makeshift crypt. Her body was covered in flies and scurrying cockroaches, and the smell, with the door closed, was gag-inducing. But Tzit wanted privacy.

Closing his eyes, he reached out to Shedim.

When they connected, the temperature in the room dropped instantly, filling it with a deep freeze. He watched as the moisture on the edges of the mirror frosted over.

Who summons me?

"It is I, Mistress, Tzit."

Ah, one of my husband's peons I see. What do you want?

"Your help, Mistress. Mastema is dying."

Impossible.

"A few nights ago, he encountered Lilith…"

More twisted lies from poison lips once sweet. We all know the bitch is dead. She's dust.

"She's returned, Mistress."

Then feed Mastema some human souls until he chokes beneath their weight and leave me alone.

"We did that, but it didn't work. He needs your magic."

If he needs me so much, why am I talking to you?

"He doesn't know I called."

He'd kill you if he knew.

"It's a risk I'm willing to take."

There was a long, uncomfortable silence as Shedim contemplated what to do next. Whatever her decision was, Tzit hoped she'd make it soon because the last thing he wanted was to get caught. Somewhere in the other room, he heard Mastema laugh.

So, Lilith lives, well, not for very much longer. I'll help Mastema, but that's only because I want the pleasure of the slow kill myself. Where are you?

It wasn't what Tzit wanted to hear, but it was better than nothing. Maybe once they see each other again, under different circumstances (especially one as tragic as this), they might be able to rekindle a bit of the love they lost and join forces. Maybe the thrill of hunting down Lilith and Lucifer would be the fire to reunite their passion.

He gave her the address.

Finished, he disconnected from Shedim and turned on the faucet – cranking the thing to its hottest setting. Within seconds, the bathroom was filled with steam. Once the icy chill in the room was gone, Tzit rejoined Mastema and Zozo.

"Where the hell have you been?" Zozo asked him.

"I had to take a dump."

Tzit looked over at Mastema, who was sitting up in the bed looking quite jovial for someone dangerously close to death's door. Walking over to Zozo, he asked, "Well, what do you think of the plan?"

"It's my kind of fucked up. Who would have thought Zozo had something like that in him? I'm impressed."

"Thank you, my Lord," Zozo said with a bow.

"And you, Tzit, had no plan?" Mastema asked. "This shocks me, for I always took you to be the creative one. Nothing?"

"Mine lacked the creative flair of Zozo's, my Lord."

"What was it?"

"It was stupid," Tzit said.

"Yeah, retarded, my Lord," Zozo added with a laugh.

"I could use a laugh. Tell me."

"We really should focus on getting Agrat here. Your strength…"

"Stop stalling and tell me," Mastema roared. "Or are you hiding something? Keep in mind I can crack open that pathetic meat suit of yours and rip it out of your black heart."

"I thought about contacting Shedim."

"Shedim?" Mastema asked, eyebrows cocked skyward. "You're right; your plan was dumb. Now, to make this work, I will need another soul – something that will give me enough strength to make a connection to Hell. Something young, something tender."

Agrat dressed and then bolted to the throne room to find Beelzebub. When she arrived, she saw him speaking to Toth, one of the wisest of the Fallen.

Lucious called him Hell's Dr. Frankenstein, rarely seen outside of his underground stronghold near the Spine. He was short and plump, with long dirty white hair growing past his ankles. The worst thing about him, if that could be narrowed down to a single offense, was his eye. He only had one and it swelled and oozed in its socket like an overripe peach. The other socket was as empty as Jesus's tomb after his resurrection.

"My Queen," he said, "you grace us with your presence."

"I know," she replied, walking past him and into Beelzebub's open arms. She squeezed him, then turned to face Toth, asking, "What brings you out of your hole?"

"News, my Queen, news of the most splendid variety," he said, cleaning some pools of yellow foam from the corners of his mouth. As you know, Lucious supported my work immensely—especially crossbreeding. Well, after centuries of many failed attempts, I have finally done it."

"Done what?" Beelzebub asked.

"Created life. My own beautiful moppets."

"I've never heard about any of this," Beelzebub said, frustrated. "Lucious never addressed any programs concerning Toth, let alone crossbreeding, with the Council."

"Lucious was trying to build a new army," Agrat said.

"An army of mutants?"

Toth nodded.

"What did you crossbreed?"

"A little of this and a bit of that," Toth said as he cleaned his pulsating eye with a handkerchief. "Living next to the Spine, as you can imagine, garnishes me access to certain…resources."

"Monstrosities!"

"Bingo Bongo," Toth said with a sick laugh.

Beelzebub may have been in the dark concerning Toth's mad pursuits, but Lucious had informed Agrat of them in vivid detail. The stronghold the demon used for his butchering and rape was called Rojus De, and it had a fearsome reputation throughout Hell as a house of horrors. Those unfortunates who got dragged off there spent a perpetuity of endless turmoil and misery under Toth's mad cruelty. But Hell's Mengele had never produced anything of genuine merit. Though she doubted Toth knew it, Lucious had no love or interest in anything he did at Rojus De so long as it kept him busy and out of his personal affairs.

"What can I do with a bunch of mutants?" Beelzebub asked.

"If I may be so bold, my new King, but I seriously doubt you'd be sitting there with his wife had my children been present."

"Mind your words," Beelzebub warned.

Toth bowed about as low as his pudgy body would allow and then said, "Truth, no matter how ugly Lord Beelzebub, is still truth. My children were not ready for Lucious and that proved ill for him. Don't let the same happen to you."

"How many do you have now?" Agrat asked.

"A handful, my Queen," Toth said as he ran his black, forked tongue across his lips.

"I will see these corrupted, but not at your butcher shop. You'll bring them here. And if they are as viable as you claim, I will ensure you get whatever you need. We all know Lucious's last attempt to invade Heaven crippled our armies and made Hell a shimmer of its former potency — I want that ratified, even if it's with an army of freaks."

Toth laughed. "Here, there…no difference, no difference. Give me three days," he said as he flashed the three remaining fingers on his left hand. With his knees popping, he rose off the floor. "I'll come at dawn with a small cavalcade of children for your viewing. I believe once you see what I can do, you'll grant me the opportunity to go into mass production so I can replenish Hell's tattered ranks."

"How many can you produce?" Beelzebub asked.

"As many as you desire, my new King," Toth said as he plucked lice from his hair. He popped them into his mouth like popcorn.

He truly was vile, maybe the most despicable of all of Hell's demons, but Agrat remembered a time when his beauty rivaled his intelligence. The Fall is what corrupted him; it warped his mind, body, and soul in many horrible ways.

"Three days," Toth repeated, "I will return with a sampling of Heaven's Armageddon in three days."

"That I have no doubt," Beelzebub said. "Now leave us."

Toth gave one last pathetic bow before hurrying out of the chamber. Once the large doors closed, Agrat turned to speak to Beelzebub, but before she could, he was kissing her. As much as she loved it, she pushed him away.

"What is it?" he asked.

"I have news."

"Why do I have the glorious feeling it's something exquisite?"

"Because it is. Mastema has found them."

"Where?"

"You know that prick, he refused to tell me until I returned top side," Agrat said as she took his hand and squeezed. "He wants me there so we can renew the hunt together."

"Any word on his health?"

"Still at question mark status."

"Mastema is quite the enigma."

"He's an asshole."

Beelzebub laughed.

"As much as I love you being here, you better return to Mastema while he still has their scent."

She kissed his cheek and then got up, strolling towards the big doors of the hall, ready to kick some serious ass. Beelzebub called after her as the doors swung open, their hinges screeching like someone being flayed alive.

"I will have Belial meet you at the portal in one hour."

Hearing his name being added to the mission was like having her tits sliced off. It was a slap in the face, a blatant sign of absolute disrespect. She didn't want his help, nor did she need it. Swallowing her white-knuckle rage like a bitter pill, she gave her love a quick bow and stormed out of the chamber.

CHAPTER 2

Belial was MIA.

Agrat wasn't surprised the douchebag was late, seeing as punctuality was never his virtue, but this was goddamn ridiculous at this point – thirty-five damn minutes! Though he had a history of arriving late to banquets and meetings, she kind of figured he'd move his ass a bit quicker seeing as they were under a heavy time crunch. But nope, the asshole was taking his time.

As usual.

Agrat selected a shift dress and buckle leather boots with small, silver skulls. Everything else she needed for the trip was in her purse: makeup, brush, pocket mirror, cash, and the keys to her awaiting transport. She had everything she needed for this trip except her unwanted acquaintance. Finally, she glimpsed him coming around the corner of the Keep wearing a gray hoody and jeans.

The idiot had it pulled over his head, hiding his face deep inside its interior. Though she didn't want to, she waved.

"Sorry I'm late," he said as he fidgeted with his gold-plated nose. "I haven't been to Earth in some time, so I needed to research modern garb."

"We're going to Arizona."

"So?"

"It's hotter than here, numb nuts," she said, "and you want to wear a hoody? Forget it. We're already running late; you burn, you burn."

She charged across the courtyard towards the transference chambers, with Belial racing after her, struggling to keep up. When they reached the chamber, they saw three Lords standing in front, with a young man bound in chains lying at their feet. She saw Xaphan, Moloch, and, of course, Abaddon.

"There you are," Abaddon said as he walked towards them. We were beginning to think you had changed your mind."

"Blame our lateness on the fashion diva over here," she said, pointing at Belial. The Lords laughed as Belial tried to shrink deeper inside his hood like a spooked turtle.

Agrat looked at the man lying on the ground with his hands and ankles shackled firmly to his chest. He was young, probably in his early twenties, with thick black hair and a muscle-ripped body.

"Does he work, my Queen?" Moloch asked.

"He looks yummy."

Xaphan said, "We're ready to proceed when you are, my Queen."

"Let's do it. Belial, bring the meat."

She followed them into the chamber, which already buzzed with dark energy. Careful not to flub the chalk markings covering the floor, Agrat and Belial entered the pentagram. Outside the circle, the Lords began chanting in the divine tongue. A few minutes later, a murky void opened between them, a perfect shaft of moonless midnight in the shape of a door.

Agrat was about to slip into its cold embrace when Xaphan suddenly shouted, "Be careful, my Queen! Mastema can't be trusted; he's a rotten scoundrel. If you need anything, reach out to us, and you shall receive it. Come back to us safe!"

"What about me?" Belial asked. "Am I invisible?"

Agrat shoved him and their sacrifice through the gate as the Lords laughed. She stepped through it a moment later.

One second, she swam through the vast coldness of the In-between, and the next, she stood inside the sweltering interior of the shack. Stepping out onto the dusty earthen floor, she expected to find the remains of their sacrifice, but there was none. She could hear them though, the monsters enjoying their tasty meal.

Heading outside, she found Belial sitting on the car's hood with his arms crossed and his pink eyes glowing.

"They were hungry. One of them tried to take my hand off."

"I hope it wasn't your masturbating hand. Aren't you hot?"

"I like heat."

"We'll see how much you like it once the sun is up," she said, storming over to the driver's side door and throwing it open. A strong gust of stale hot air blasted her in the face, causing her to break out in an instant sweat. Goddamn Arizona, she thought, climbing inside.

She started the car and flipped on the AC as Belial climbed in. Turning the car around, she pointed it back towards civilization. Agrat wasn't sure how Belial felt about this little mission of theirs, but she was more than a little anxious. She didn't like that Lucious was left undetected on Earth for a few days, which gave him plenty of time to plot his next move. That was incredibly dangerous—like giving a bunch of Islamic Jihadists access to nuclear bombs.

"You look serious, my Queen."

"What do you care?"

"I don't. I just hate silences. I find them deplorable," he said. Belial scratched alongside his fake nose. The skin around it was already red and badly irritated from his relentless scraping.

"I'm thinking about Lucious."

"Lucious?" he said, surprised. It's kind of soon to be longing for his touch, isn't it?"

She punched him hard in the arm. "It's not his touch I desire, idiot; it's his head on a stick. And if you don't mind your manners, I'll also take yours."

"Forgive me, it was an ill-timed joke."

"Lucious is a master schemer," she said as she steered the car in the path of an armadillo. She felt the little armored body squash beneath the weight of the front wheel. "Lucious isn't just sitting around doing nothing; he's plotting. And that's dangerous."

"Let him plot," Belial said nonchalantly. "What's he going to do, storm into Hell and take on everybody with his non-existent army?"

"He's done it before. Uprisings are kind of his thing."

The words seemed to sober Belial. He straightened in his seat, his fingers digging into the flesh around his nose deep enough to draw thin streaks of blood.

"Do you have to do that? It's gross."

He stopped scratching.

"Mastema isn't talking either," she said. "That troubles me too."

"As it should, he's a loose cannon who follows orders about as well as a rabid dog. Leaving him alone was a mistake, my Queen."

Belial was right. And that pissed her off.

He continued by saying, "Being earthbound leads him to believe he's above the laws of Hell, and so can do whatever he wants, answering to no one but himself."

"Yeah, but still, he was chosen," Agrat grumbled.

Twenty minutes later they reached the highway.

One minute later the fuel light came on. Annoyed, Agrat pulled off at the first gas station they encountered for a quick refueling and, of course, to get some much-needed directions.

Just as Agrat climbed back inside her death machine, she felt an alien presence in the back of her mind. It didn't take the superior intellect of Stephen Hawkins to summarize who it was trying to reach out to her.

"Where the hell have you been?" she asked sternly.

"You talking to me?" Belial asked, confused.

Agrat shushed him and pointed at her temple. She then focused all her attention on Mastema, whose words came spewing out of him like hot, sticky vomit.

What took you so long? It's been hours.

"Calm down. Going from one plain of existence to another takes time and preparation. We couldn't just up and go."

We? Who is with you?

"Belial."

Better to come with a dog, Mastema snarled.

"We'll be there soon," she fired back, ending the connection. Flustered, she said, "Christ, he's an annoying child."

"I guess that means he's still breathing," Belial said. "Lucky us."

"He doesn't deserve it, you know."

"What?" Belial asked.

"Lucious's soul. I may hate the prick, but even he doesn't deserve such an abysmal fate. It's too much."

"Contracts have been signed."

She started the car and sped off onto the highway, their own personal highway to hell. Dangerous thoughts danced inside her head as she hit the gas, throwing her middle fingers to the speed limit as she merged with traffic.

She was still furious with Beelzebub and absolutely loathed Mastema. And now she was trapped in a car with the biggest moron in all of Hell, Belial. This wasn't right and it was high time, she thought, to take control of the situation rather than remain a pawn in a greater game. Suddenly, a thought rose to the surface and it was diabolical brilliance. But to do it, she'd need Belial's assistance.

"Maybe we should burn it."

"Those are some serious words, my Queen."

"Well, I'm in a serious mood, Belial. Let me ask you something, something that's been on my mind for a while. Why did you join the insurrection? I know you and Lucious were damn near besties, but still you stabbed. I have to admit, your turn was the most surprising."

"You going to ask all the Lords about their loyalty?"

"No. Just you."

Belial shifted uneasily in his seat, which told Agrat she had him off balance. If she pressed too hard, he'd shift into defensive mode, and all would be lost. She had to change her tactic or lose the offensive. Gently, almost motherly, she told him to answer the question.

"Why did you do it?"

"Easy, I didn't love him anymore. You?"

"I did it for the glory of Hell."

"Yeah, right, Belial."

He rubbed the edges of his nose.

"I know you're hiding something, and I bet whatever it is...is delicious. Most secrets are. Tell me."

"What do you want me to say?" he asked. "That I did it for Beelzebub?"

"Those three words you've always wanted to say but didn't out of fear of Lucious's wrath. Well, he's gone, and we're alone, so what are you waiting for? You don't think I know? I've always known Belial."

"I don't know what you're talking about."

Why are men such pussies, Agrat thought, taking a Rest Stop exit. Finding a parking spot away from other cars and trucks, Agrat turned off the car and looked at Belial.

"You seriously going to play this game with me right now? This night of all nights?"

"My Queen…"

She reached over and flipped back his hood. There was nothing about his face that made her swoon, nothing about his persona that made her quiver; he was average in every way, shape, and form. Compared to the awe of Beelzebub, Belial was nothing more than a pimple on the ass of life and didn't deserve a solitary ounce of her affection. But for power, she leaned over and grabbed him by the scruff of his neck, pulling him toward her. She closed her eyes when she kissed him; she had to because it was the only way to fight through the revulsion. When his dry tongue slipped into her mouth it took every ounce of her will not to bite it off. Finished, she pulled away and stared at his flushed face, knowing she had achieved absolute victory over the mind and soul of the pathetic Lord.

"Going to confess now, Belial?"

He did. For the next few intolerable minutes, Belial professed his love for her. He went on and on in his declaration to the point she got bored and damn near drifted asleep.

Eventually, she said, "I knew you did. You might be able to hide it well from the others, but you can't keep your impure thoughts from me. It's kind of my specialty."

"I should have known."

"If what you say is true, then I want a demonstration of that love."

She watched as the idiot removed his engorged cock from his pants. Compared to Beelzebub, it looked like a broken pink pencil. With a sigh, she said, "What the hell? Not like that man and definitely not here. You think I want to get banged in the back of this stupid car at some damn rest stop?"

"Sorry," he said as he put it away.

"It's okay," she said as she kissed him again, this time on the cheek.

When he tried to kiss her on the mouth, she slipped away. Had he been thinking clearly with his head rather than his inflated cock, he might have noticed her eyes were void of warmth. They were cold, lifeless pools…those of a hunting shark.

"Declare your love to me," she demanded.

And he did.

"Show me how much you love me and proclaim your loyalty to me, the Queen of Hell, and no one else!"

He didn't hesitate. In a voice riddled with passion, he shouted to the heavens, "To Agrat, Queen of Hell, do I pledge my allegiance. Now and until death."

"Affirm your love to me by bequeathing your armies to me."

"Fully and without restraint," Belial answered.

"And I happily accept them."

They kissed again. And as Belial explored her body with his hands, she retreated inward to happier thoughts and better places.

CHAPTER 3

"You sure this is the place?" Belial asked as he massaged his nose for the thousandth time since arriving on Earth. "Looks like a dive. A place people go to commit suicide."

Agrat didn't know and she didn't care. She didn't come to the motel for a room but for information. Her goal was to get in and out before the bed bugs infested her clothes.

"Do people actually come here willingly?" Belial asked.

"Does it matter? Just keep your eyes open for room 42," she said. She drove past the office at a crawl.

The lights in the rooms and the many cars parked in the lot told her they did, though she didn't understand its rationale. If the condition of the buildings weren't worrisome enough, the small graveyard across the street should have sent any road-weary travelers seeking alternative accommodation. Though she couldn't see them from the car, she felt the presence of the restless dead watching them from among the stones.

"There it is," Belial said. He pointed at a room. "Second floor, far end…near the Pepsi machine."

"I see it," she said as she pulled into an empty spot. She turned off the car and dropped the keys in her purse just as Belial opened the door. Before he got out, she grabbed his arm.

"Wait. Before we go in there, you need to know something."

"I'm listening," he said. He looked at her.

"I'm going to kill that bastard and swallow his soul."

Belial's eyebrows shot up like a pair of nuclear blasts. "I'm sorry, what did you say? I thought you said you were going to kill Mastema."

"Damn straight."

"You do realize assassinating the Mad King will lead to open war with the Nonentities."

"Good. It's better than sitting around sucking their cocks."

"What about Shedim?"

"What about her?" she asked.

"As evil and revile as Mastema is, his wife is a hundred times worse. We take him out, and we'll have her on our ass like our own personal phantom. As much as I'd love to see that dickhead dead, I think killing him is a major mistake. How about we just see what happens first, okay? See what he has to say."

"I don't care what he has to say. He could tell me he knows the location of the Ark of the Covenant and I'd still kill him. If you don't want any part of it, fine, just stay out of my way."

Before Belial could protest further, she stormed out of the car with her decision made. She rushed up the steps and reached his room by the time Belial reached the first step.

She knocked.

The door swung open to reveal a middle-aged cowboy dressed in jeans, flannel, and a white Cattleman speckled with blood. Just behind him, seated on a chair, was a girl decked out in goth-style clothing. Judging by the girl's features, Agrat figured she was in her teens. Besides the odd appearance of the people in the room, what struck her the hardest was the smell.

The room reeked of death.

"Yes?" the cowboy asked in a thick southern drawl. "What can I do for you, ma'am?"

"I'm looking for someone. Mastema."

"Let her in!"

The cowboy took off his hat and bowed as he stepped aside. When he spoke again, his accent miraculously vanished. "I am Tzit my Queen, and that," he said as he pointed at the girl, "is Zozo."

The girl waved.

Agrat entered the room to find Mastema lying on the bed, still wearing the waitress from the diner. The last time she saw him, the girl was youthful and pretty. All of that was gone. The Mad King was lying on the bed, rotting in a pool of its own filth and decay. Most of the girl's hair had fallen out, leaving only a scabby, red scalp. Most of her teeth were gone, and her eyes were all Mastema. Everything leaked, leaving her exposed arms and legs slick with bodily discharge.

"Holy crap," Agrat gasped, covering her mouth with one hand.

"Hello, hell-bitch. Nice of you to join us," Mastema said, his voice firm. "Where is my old, sweet friend Belial? I've heard horrible rumors about a certain prosthetic."

Belial stepped into the room almost on cue. The only thing that would have made his entrance more dramatic would have been an ironic drum roll.

"There it is," Mastema gloated with laughter. "When I first heard the news, I thought it was a joke. But there it is, proof – you got a gold nose, and it looks freaking ridiculous!"

Belial quickly flipped up his hood as Tzit closed the door behind him.

"Don't hide it, boy, be proud of your artificial beak."

Belial reached up to itch it, but Agrat slapped his hand down. All the Nonentities in the room roared with laughter as Belial sulked in his hood like a scolded teenager.

"What's wrong with your body?" Agrat asked.

"Damn females," Mastema growled. "I should have never claimed a woman as my vessel – too goddamn weak. Too soft. After a long, dreamless slumber, I woke to find the body putrefying. It's dying Agrat and it looks like it's trying to take me along with it. Zozo, fetch me a cup of water."

The Nonentity filled a plastic cup in the bathroom sink and handed it to Mastema. Agrat watched in stunned silence as the Mad King raised the cup to his lips with shaky hands. He took a few greedy drinks and then returned the glass, its once clear liquid a shade of red.

"You told me you found them. Where are they?"

"Don't think you can come to my world and throw your weight around. Here you're not a Queen, just another bitch, a whore in service. So, do what you're supposed to do and serve. After that, I'll talk."

"What do you want?"

"To tell you the truth, Agrat, I wanted you. But seeing as you brought this worthless piece of shit along, I'll take him instead. This vessel is beyond repair, my soul damaged. I need a new puppet to inhabit and a demonic soul to heal me. You give me what I want, and I'll give you what you want. Lucifer's head is on a silver platter. What do you think? We got a deal?" he asked, smiling toothlessly.

"You want Belial?"

"Golden nose and all."

"I have a better idea," she said.

In a flash of black fury, Misandry appeared in hand. Tzit gasped as he staggered back, hands shielding his face. Agrat brought the sword down in a death march, cleaving his head in half.

Belial took care of Zozo with a fury of hell-forged projectiles from his mammoth revolver. The poor girl the Nonentity occupied was ripped to shreds by the bullets, sending blood and skull fragments all over the room as the head burst from the shoulders.

Agrat looked at Mastema.

"Is this the part where I'm supposed to beg for my life?"

"You can do whatever you want," Agrat said, "but I'm going to find out where they are, so you better start talking, or I'm going to start cutting."

"Eat a dick, hell-bitch."

Misandry vanished. She saw no point in holding it, Mastema would not be intimidated, and besides, the damn thing was heavy. Leaning against the wall, she asked, "Why prolong this? Does death scare you that much?"

"If death had a face, I'd slap it."

On the far side of the room, emerging from the shadows, was a tall man dressed in a black suit and topped with a wiry afro. Agrat and Belial couldn't see the Psychopomp, but Mastema could. It drifted across the room, over the smoldering remains of Zozo, and over to the bed, where it stopped.

"I'd like to see you slap me," it said.

Ignoring it, Mastema said, "Come on, Agrat, let's make a deal. One that makes all of us happy. Do you really care that much for this faggot? I'm offering you Lucifer. I'll even let you have his soul if you spare mine."

"Do we really have to listen to this drivel?" Belial asked, aiming his revolver at the Mad King. "Let me finish him. Put this prick out of all of our misery."

"Yes," the Psychopomp said with a jackal's grin. "Do it."

Before he could pull the trigger, Agrat grabbed his arm and pushed it back down to his side.

"Not yet."

"Why?"

"I got to get ready."

"Ready for what?" Mastema asked.

"To swallow your soul."

"Noooo," the Psychopomp shrieked in frustration. "Why does this keep happening? I was so looking forward to this."

The Psychopomp floated over to the Agrat, even though she couldn't see him. "Please, please sweet, dark angel – let me have this one. Just. This. One."

"Keep your gun on him Belial, though I seriously doubt he can do much of anything besides leak on you."

"Of course, my Queen."

"And if you kill him before I return, I'll rip your goddamn heart out. You got me?"

He nodded.

As she walked towards the bathroom, Mastema shouted after her, his voice full of hot venom.

"You ain't swallowing anything!"

She slammed the bathroom door shut and regretted it instantly. The stench in the small room was ungodly rancid and hit her like a kung fu kick to the face. She flipped on the light and found the source of the stink lying in the bathtub. Two bodies stacked up on each other. The one on the bottom was a young woman, and the other was a young boy. They were covered in bugs, their bodies bruised and dirty.

"What a sick dick," she said as she shut the curtains.

She returned to the mirror and turned on the faucet until the water steamed. Splashing it on her face, she cleaned away the funk and dirt of the road.

Feeling better, and more awake, she turned it off and headed out to finish what she came to do – murdering Mastema. Stepping out of the bathroom, she half expected to see Belial dead and Mastema ready and waiting for her with the fools' own gun. Instead, the status quo remained the same with Mastema still trapped in the bed with Belial holding him at bay with his big ass gun.

"You're a bitch," Mastema snarled. "A whore without equal."

"Both titles I wear proudly," Agrat replied, coming around the bed, strolling like a master predator stalking their prey. Why rush things, she thought, Mastema was practically dead anyway.

"Stay away from me hell-bitch. I'll give you what you want and tell you everything."

"You had your chance to cooperate, but instead, you decided to spit in my face. And nobody does that, not even failed kings," she said as she shoved a small nightstand away from the bed, causing a cluster of cockroaches to scatter for the hills.

"Any last words?"

"I hope you choke," he spat.

Her sword reappeared in her hand and she slammed that son of a bitch right into his chest so hard it went right through the mattress and box spring with zero resistance. The King screamed as the blade erupted into flame, burning the bastard's innards. Above the bed, nails digging into the ceiling, was the Psychopomp – hoping to snag Mastema's escaping soul before Agrat could eat it.

He failed.

As the Mad King, Lord of the Nonentities, soul drifted out of his body, Agrat inhaled it like a cocaine addict did a sweet line of white rock. It had no flavor, but the kick was instantaneous as an electric charge rippled through her body, making her incredibly horny.

Staggering back, her body humming, she bumped into the wall with her hands fumbling with her pants. She didn't give a damn Belial watched her with his pink eyes, she needed to garner access to her sweeter meats.

"Agrat? Are you…"

She unbuttoned them and slipped her hand into her panties, seeking the wetness between her thighs. Caressing her slick mound, her heart pounding in her ears like a death metal song's chaotic beat, she slipped her fingers deep inside and closed her eyes – letting the moment take her completely.

Though frustrated, the Psychopomp decided to stick around a little longer because there was no way he'd miss this show – not for any soul on Earth. Meanwhile, Agrat's legs quivered beneath an onslaught of heavy orgasms, with each one being more powerful than the last. Breathless, her brow slick with sweat, she collapsed to the floor, utterly spent. Panting, she withdrew her slippery fingers and cleaned off her saccharine juices with her tongue. And though she couldn't hear or see him, the Psychopomp gave her a quick round of applause before vanishing.

Rushing over, Belial knelt before her and asked, "Are you okay?"

"I may be bad, but I feel good."

"I bet," he said. He pulled her to her feet.

The room slowly filled with smoke as her sword continued to feast on Mastema's corpse with hellfire.

"We better get out of here," he said, ushering her towards the door as the smoke alarms shrilled.

But Agrat wasn't done; she was still hungry and caught in the mad frenzy of bloodlust. With a flick of her wrist, Misandry dislodged itself from Mastema's burning body and flew across the room. She snatched it out of the air and brought it down in a wild arch, cleaving Belial's head in half. Almost instantly, his confused soul began drifting upwards. Like a well-trained dog seizing a tennis ball out of the air, Agrat jumped up and ate it.

When she landed, most of the room was engulfed in wild flames. Outside, she heard a half-dozen concerned voices and, somewhere, not far away, the familiar catcall of approaching police cruisers.

She headed to the window and peeked out the curtains. The landing outside was clear, but the parking lot was full of curious onlookers armed with cameras and their annoying curiosity. Agrat took a breath as the initial buzz began to wane. Instead of the erotic heavy static, her mind began to clear, and body relax.

She threw open the door and bolted down the nearest staircase as the room's window exploded behind her.

She raced through the parking lot, knocking over onlookers like bowling pins as she made her way to the car just as the police arrived. One man tried to restrain her by grabbing her arm, and she rewarded him by breaking four of his five fingers. When she spun around to continue her escape, she came face to face with a pair of officers with their guns drawn and pointed.

Fuck.

PART SIX:

After Forever

CHAPTER 1

Lucious jolted upright on his cot with his ears buzzing. With his room still smothered by predawn darkness, he got up and flicked on the light. It took a moment for his eyes to adjust to the sudden bombardment of oversaturated neon, and while they did, he felt the dull ache of invasion digging its hooks into his gooey membranes.

It was Agrat.

He almost connected out of habit, but before he could his senses sharpened, and his temporary dip into lunacy faded. Fighting against the steady throb behind his eyes, he stormed over to the small washbasin and cleaned his face.

In the folds of his firing synapsis, he heard her say, *I'm not going anywhere until you speak with me asshole. I got all day.*

Lucious replied by smoking some of Adam's leaf. It wasn't the Tangerine Dream but one of his other mutated variants, something called Testament. It didn't push her out, but at least it diminished some of her unwanted presence.

He ate breakfast and chatted with Sage and Moragon about this and a bit of that, but by late morning, Agrat had returned in the form of a massive migraine. Fearing his head might burst, Lucious retreated to his dwelling to confront the heart-breaking cunt.

"Alright, Agrat, what do you want?"

Hello lover, she taunted. *Miss me?*

He actually did. He missed her a lot, but he'd rather castrate himself before ever admitting that to Agrat. Instead, he slammed his door shut and collapsed onto his cot, the springs groaning beneath the sudden assault of his weight.

"I have nothing to say to you, so you might as well piss off."

You may be able to deceive the masses, but you can't deceive me. I know you too well, my sweet Lucious. You're hurting. I can feel the heartache and it's making me wet.

"Shows how much you know – what you feel is heartburn. I had a burrito for lunch."

You're holding back. I wonder how long it'll be before you break and crumble beneath an emotional tsunami.

"Don't know what you're talking about you crazy skank," he said as he grabbed a Ziplock bag full of joints from off the floor. He opened it and fished one out with a trembling hand.

Do you know what I did last night?

"Don't care."

You do. I know you do.

Lucious scanned the room for the lighter but couldn't find it.

Last night, I had the best fuck of my life.

The joint slipped from between his fingertips to the floor, forgotten. Her words felt like nails to the back of the cranium rather than simple abstract constructs of linguistical communique.

I was pounded Lucious, with such aggressive fervor in all my holes that I actually felt virgin pain. It was amazing.

Inside his head, demonic visions penetrated. He saw Agrat on their bed riding atop a faceless phantom, screaming out in glorious rapture. And just when he felt he'd lose himself to his growing rage, Lucious saw the lighter on the rim of the sink. He grabbed the joint and rushed to it in a mad, desperate dash. He lit it and took a much-needed puff as his vision distorted beneath a blanket of tears.

I've never been fucked or loved so completely as I am now, Lucious. You were a pitiful husband, an abysmal father, and a wretched King.

She went on a bit more, but whatever she said didn't register, thanks to the devil's smoke, which thankfully worked enough to lower the volume. Agrat must have sensed the sudden shift because her voice lacked its previous tenacity.

Dumping you was…

"It's the best thing ever, right? Yeah, I get it—like being married to you was a picnic. Is that why you turned Brutus?"

She didn't say anything.

"You ever hear of a divorce? If you wanted to get cut loose to find another dick to sit on, you should have said something – you didn't need to lead some pathetic coup."

I hate you.

"Feelings mutual. Now that that's been established, can we end this already? I have better things to do than sit around here talking to your annoying ass."

Plotting?

"Damn straight I am," he said with a grin. "Mark my words…this revolution is nothing more than a temporary inconvenience. I'm coming back, and when I do, I'm slaughtering everyone involved in my expulsion. Family included."

Got to get back first, love. And to do that, you've got to get through me.

"Seriously, give me a proper challenge. I'll carve my way through you and all the Lords of Hell for a shot at the puppet master, this damn imposter you help put on my throne."

You'll never get back, Lucious. You may act all confident, but I know it's nothing more than false virility and wishful thinking. You're doomed. You're a dead man walking, and soon, you'll be dead. You're not the only one plotting, you know.

He loved it when she talked dirty.

You have no allies left. Those who did not bend the knee to the new King were dispatched without mercy, no matter their echelon or rank. As for the inhabitants of Hell, well, they couldn't have cared less. We expected civil unrest after the announcement, but nothing happened — not a single protest or riot.

"A lot of Hell's inhabitants are there because of their political dogmata. I suspect most are trying to keep their noses clean and out of the troubles."

Or they knew what the rest of us did.

"Knew what?"

You're worthless. How could you fail so appallingly in your war against Heaven? The last attempt alone wiped out more than half of our remaining forces, leaving us vulnerable to enemies beyond the Spine and those of the Angelic order. Your worst offense, though, Lucious, is how you retreated from the battlefield, leaving your own fucking child to be captured. That is unforgivable!

She was speaking of Eisheth, his eldest daughter. Hearing her name burned him like a branding iron. It stung deep and he cringed.

You are a failure and don't even deserve a respectable death. That's why you were dragged to Earth. We didn't want you to taint Hell's soil with your venomous fluids.

He laid back on his cot and rested his head on his pillow. Outside, he could hear the wind roaring like some irate beast. The rains had stopped, but leaden clouds fat with precipitation still lingered low in the sky, threatening Tucson with another barrage of storms.

Let's stop this pathetic game, Lucious. Tell me where you are so we can end this.

"Finished already? I expected more — at least another hour or two of your worthless blathering. I'm disappointed."

Good.

His smile widened.

He wished Agrat could see him and just how little fuck he gave about the drivel oozing from her vile lips like venom. Lucious knew her words were designed to cut, but they were nothing more than kitty scratches on his rhino skin.

"As for giving you my location — nah. I like being your incurable cancer. I like it so much that I think I'll drag this out a bit longer. How's that sound?"

I knew you didn't have the balls.

"Oh, I have the balls. You should know I used to put them in your mouth," he taunted with a dry laugh. This brought on a massive tirade of insults from Agrat, who went totally nuclear. He loved it and gobbled it all up greedily.

Hard to believe I actually loved you once.

"There's the victim mode I was waiting for, I knew it'd come eventually."

Fuck you.

"Who's the puppet master Agrat? Which Lord is it enjoying my sloppy seconds?"

How's the saying go, Lucious…loose lips sink ships?

"That's what they say about your vagina, Agrat."

There was a long pause after that cheap shot, one long enough to make Lucious wonder if she had closed the communication portal. But she eventually came back like a mouthful of cold sores.

I'm going to enjoy killing you, Lucious. And I'm not going to do it quick, oh no. I will draw it out until the trumpets of Armageddon fill the sky.

"Not me. I'm going to kill you quick and be done with it."

The connection ended, thank Christ.

For the next few minutes, he smoked, letting the leaf wash away the horrible aftertaste of their engagement. And of course, the images of his wife banging another cock, something he did not want to see.

Just when Lucious thought he'd get a bit of a reprieve, the door to his room slowly creaked open.

"Go away, I'm not interested."

"Give me a second, and I might just change your mind, dude."

It was Adam.

Lucious waved him over instead of giving him the finger, which is what he really wanted to do.

"Is this wise? This guy was just talking to himself like a complete loon," Dead Meat said as he stalked in behind him.

Lucious looked at the witch's cat and said, "I'm not insane. I was talking to someone."

"Says the loony," Dead Meat played.

"Aren't you supposed to be dead?"

"My, my, my…aren't we feeling testy," the familiar said as he hopped onto the bed. "What crawled up your butt and laid seed?"

"You ever been married?" Lucious asked.

"We felines aren't that suicidal."

Dead Meat, thankfully, was washed since their previous encounter. Though the stench of death lingered, the scent of sour apples helped suppress it somewhat.

"Who were you talking to?" Adam asked.

"The ex."

"Telepathically?"

"Cheaper than calling long-distance," Lucious laughed. "Where have you been, haven't seen you since yesterday?"

"I found him in the basement crying over a crate," Dead Meat said.

"A crate?"

"It's nothing," Adam interjected.

Lucious could tell it wasn't nothing, but he decided it best not to press—at least, not now. He could wait. Besides, there were much bigger things on his plate to contend with than Adam's mystery box, like trying to figure out how to give the Eld a possible life-saving jolt.

"Did you figure anything out?"

"Yeah dude, I got like a plan and stuff."

Everyone assembled in the former hospital's waiting room, which also served as their central meeting hub. Lilith sat away from everyone in the back row while Lucious and Moragon sat at the table. Sage took a spot near the wall, where he stood arms crossed and looked extremely disinterested. Adam, who was headlining this shindig, sat at the nurse's station with Dead Meat passed out next to him.

Look at these people, Lucious thought, taking everything in. We're supposed to be God's chosen Dirty Dozen, but we look more like

God's chosen chodes. He didn't understand how this motley crew of rejects was supposed to save the Eld. Hell, he didn't even think they could save themselves.

Supposedly, Adam had the answer. He figured if anyone could figure this out, it had to be someone possessing Eld-like knowledge because he sure as hell couldn't.

Dead Meat farted.

"Now that we're like all assembled and stuff," Adam said as he waved his hand limply in front of his nose, "I'd like to kick off this meeting with a question. Does anyone here like Tiffany Swan?"

"The singer?" Sage asked.

Adam nodded.

"Not my style bro, but I'd still bang her."

"She's underage," Adam said.

"Even better," Sage replied with a sick laugh.

"Well, I used to be a big fan of hers until I discovered her dark secret," Adam said. "She's a demon."

"Archdemon," Lucious corrected.

"Whatever. The point is the Eld needs us to make a quick and effective kill, and she's the perfect target. She'll be in town tomorrow for an album release party for her newest LP, Halo. She's scheduled to do it downtown tomorrow night at the Zen Club. And dig this, she won't be alone. Traveling with her is Harvey Nero, President of Global Music Group."

"Is he a demon, too?" Sage asked.

"He's one of the Lords of Hell, Hornblas."

Adam handed out vanilla folders containing their information and the latest pictures. Lucious recognized Hornblas right away even beneath the girth of a few extra hundred pounds. He had grown fat in this world, fat and bloated like a water-logged corpse. All his hair was gone, and he had multiple chins speckled with graying fuzz. In the picture, Harvey had his pudgy arms around the waist of a slim model in a sheik, golden mini dress.

"Is the girl Tiffany?" Lilith asked.

"Nah dude – that's just some actress. The one you really need to be focused on is like standing to his right."

In the photo was a tall, slender black girl with straight, blond hair down to her shoulders. She was pretty and had the curves of an

African fertility goddess. Lucious scanned her face and checked her eyes for a hint of the demon beneath the flesh.

"Wow, she's really changed a lot."

"How so?" Moragon inquired.

"In her true form, she has six tits – not two."

"Six tits, bro? Damn, that's kind of hot," Sage said. "Is it common for female demons to come so well-equipped?"

"For some."

"Fuck bro, you making Hell sound pretty awesome. But let me get this straight because I think being dead has seriously screwed me up in more ways than one," Sage said. "Are we actually going to be killing the biggest Diva on the planet?"

"Once this ball gets rolling, more stars are going to fall—and not just stars but heads of mega-corporations, politicians, and religious leaders," Lucious replied.

"Like Hornblas," Adam added.

"I don't care about Hardblast or whatever his name is, so check that noise, hippie. My concern is Tiffany Swan. I mean, like you say, she's underage. I think she's sixteen or something."

"That's how she looks in her current state," Lucious said, "but she's an ancient, pushing closer to 800 than 17. Don't let her innocent exterior blind you Sage, because she's a man-eater. She'd bite your head off and use your blood for her breakfast cereal if you got too close."

"Look, I'm no saint. I know I've lived a pretty messed-up life, but I had one rule—one code I refused to break no matter how much money was thrown in my face," the hitman said. And that was no women, no kids. Now, this is my first job with you guys, and you ask me to break both of said commandments on the same target. Demon or not, my mind is having a hard time grasping this insanity."

"I'll do it," Lilith said. "Never liked Tiffany Swan anyway. Her music sucks."

"Jesus! You be one cold-hearted bitch," Sage replied.

Lilith gave him a salute.

"You think you can handle Hornblas?"

Sage shrugged. "Don't know. Never killed a demon before."

"There's a time and a place for everything," Lucious said. "Besides, if the Eld has such confidence in your death-dealing capabilities, you shouldn't be so worried. And remember, she's not a kid. In fact, the bitch is older than Moragon."

Sage nodded.

"I'll kill her if Sage is having issues with it," Lilith said. "I mean, that is if you think you have the balls to take care of Hornblas?"

"I got no qualms sending this Hornblower back to Hell in a body bag, but tell me…how in the fuck do you kill a demon bro?"

"Same as killing a human," Lucious said, "just need more bullets."

"We have special weapons," Adam added.

"Doesn't this seem risky? I mean, we're planning to go into a party, guns blazing like some Islamic homophobic. We need another safer option before we accidentally execute a bunch of innocents during our first mission."

"You think that party is going to be attended by saints? I guarantee every single one of them will be tainted with sin. And that makes them fair game for eradication, at least, according to the rules established by the Eld."

"Can you really guarantee that Lucifer?" Lilith asked.

"Yeah bro," Sage added, "that is one big hypothetical."

"I know sin."

"Excuse me," Adam said, "if I may interject. I never said we'd go to the club, so I'm not sure why we're arguing about it. I hacked their daily planners so we could do a pre-party strike. They're scheduled to check in at three o'clock. She's in room 1408, and Hornblas is in the master suite, room 8435. They won't leave for the party until well after midnight."

"I like it," Lilith said. "We can put ourselves in their rooms and take them out without risking potential innocents."

"Sounds like a buzzkill to me," Lucious said glumly.

"I dig it. It's smart, bro," Sage said.

"Well, I guess I've been outvoted. So how exactly are we going to get into their rooms undetected?" Lucious asked Adam.

"The key, dude."

"And what will I do?" Moragon asked.

"Go and resurrect some more dead pussy," Sage taunted coldly.

The old hag spun around so fast that Lucious thought her neck might snap. She raised one of her bony fingers and pointed it like a knife right in Sage's face, saying, "I can put a hex on you—a hex that rots the flesh and fills your bowels with parasites."

Lucious figured he better step in before things escalated from threat to action. Calmly, he said, "Be civil you two – remember, we're on the same team. To answer your question, Moragon, I'm not sure what you can contribute to this particular mission. Just hang in there. We'll find something for you."

"Why don't you just hex our targets and save us the trouble of going in," Lilith said.

The old hag grinned toothlessly at them. Lucious could tell the witch was having some dark, dreary thoughts drifting through her head like toxic sludge.

"I'd love to infect them, but a hex works slower than a bullet between the eyes," Moragon said.

"I guess that means you can't do anything," Lilith replied. How about you prepare me and Sage a hero's feast? Do you think you can manage that, you old cow?"

Moragon snarled at Lilith and then stormed out of the room.

"Did you have to do that?" Lucious asked.

"What? It's not my fault she can't contribute. Remember, she's not even supposed to be here. Hey stoner," Lilith shouted at Adam, "did you remember to pack your weapons?"

"Duh, dude. I'll go and get them," he said as he slid off the countertop. Dead Meat raised his head, looked at Adam, and then went back to sleep uninterested.

"Lilith," Lucious said, "I just want to tell you…"

"Oh. My. God. Like I'm going to listen to you."

"I'm your leader, remember?"

"Keep dreaming, asshole, because you aren't leading jackshit, man. Especially not me."

"That's not what the Eld says."

Lilith shrugged.

"All I wanted to say is mind your words around Moragon. She didn't end up in Hell for doing simple parlor tricks. She's a Night Mother, and if you get on her bad side, not even I can protect you from her magic. Dead Meat alone should tell you about the powers she processes. If I were you, I'd go apologize before she curses you."

"Is that right?"

Lucious nodded.

Lilith gave him the finger and left the room.

"Wow, bro, there's never a dull moment around this place. So, what do we do now?" Sage asked, rising from his seat.

"Prepare for war."

CHAPTER 2

Adam's mind swam with an endless stream of advanced mathematics, and enough scientific breakthroughs he could have changed the course of mankind forever ten times over. Round and round his mind went, like a dog chasing its tail. Instead of taking rigorous notes, he scratched his balls. And in that satisfying instant, the solution to bending space time for interstellar travel came and went in a heartbeat.

Adam led Sage down the narrow steps to the hospital's basement while solving 3 of the remaining 6 Millennium Prize Problems. He would have solved another one if he didn't get struck by a small pebble.

"Whoa, who threw that?" Sage asked. He crouched down on the narrow basement steps to peer into the building's shadowy underbelly. "Someone down here, bro?"

"Just a ghost man," Adam replied.

"A ghost?"

"You afraid?"

"Shit, bro, I ain't afraid of no ghost," Sage protested.

"Good to know because this place is full of them."

Sage seemed to be taken aback by the 'full of them' statement and stared wide-eyed at Adam, almost unbelieving. "I ain't seen nothing. They all down here or something?"

"Not really," Adam said as he descended the last few steps. "I've seen them scattered throughout the hospital, mostly on the second floor. They don't venture down here much because he doesn't want them here."

"Who doesn't want them here?" Sage asked, looking around.

"The Top Hat Man."

"What the hell is a Top Hat Man bro?"

Somewhere in the basement's deeper depths, a steady banging, metal on metal, could be heard. Sage froze on the last step of the staircase, clutching the railing with his hand until his knuckles turned white.

"He doesn't like you."

"Sounds like the Top Hat Man is racist, bro."

Adam turned on the lights, revealing an impressive workspace. There were multiple computers and workstations comprised of such advanced gadgetry that it left Sage speechless. There were tables littered with weapons and various chunks of armor…all dissected. In the middle of the room were a pair of rusty embalming tables pulled together with futuristic guns spread out on them. And alone, sitting off to the side, was a military-grade footlocker.

"This is a pretty impressive setup you got here," Sage said as he soaked it all in. I feel like James Bond stepping inside Q's workshop."

The banging stopped as Adam took a seat at one of the computers. Sage didn't seem to care either; his attention was on the guns.

"Did you do all this on your own?"

"Yup."

Sage picked up one of the modified rifles and checked its weight. It was the same one used when liberating Lucious at the diner.

"This thing hums," Sage said as he held it up to his ear, listening.

"It's the cartridges."

"What do these things fire?"

Adam spun around on his chair so he could face Sage. "Killing a demon man, especially something as powerful as an actual like Lord and stuff, takes more than simple bullets. You need like extra oomph of the divine variety to do real damage."

Sage held the gun out at arm's length and studied it intently. It had the base body of a Barrett M468 carbine but with a different-style mag and modified barrel, both silver. He set it down next to a Zbroyar Z-15 and an M&P 15 Competition. He saw shotguns, handguns, and, of course, more rifles.

"This all of it bro?"

"Most of it. I have more in the locker over there," he said, pointing at the body fridge. I took these out to clean and prep for the upcoming mission."

"No military grades?"

Adam shook his head.

"Let me ask you something, bro. When did you get involved in all this?"

"The first time they contacted me was five years ago, man. I was living off the grid in the mountains when Metatron appeared with an offer."

"Metatron? Sounds like a Transformer."

"He's not," Adam said with a laugh. "He's the Prince of the Presence, an angel – works as the voice of the Eld."

"You guys keep referring to him as the Eld – is that God or what?"

"He has infinite names throughout the cosmos, but here He is known as God, Jehovah, Yahweh, Elohim, etc. The list is long and as complex as the Hodge Conjecture and then some dude. But in the end, it's just the name for the same magnificent being, the Eld."

"And this mother appeared before you?"

"Can we watch the language dude?"

"Just answer the question, bro."

"He did. He told me to start crafting weapons for what the Eld called the Great Event."

"Great Event? You mean Armageddon, don't ya?"

"I didn't know it at the time, but yeah, it looks like it. The idea was like to create weapons to arm the Army of the Eld against the forces of darkness. To do that, man, I was given access to divine light. It took me years to learn how to manipulate it with the Art just to channel it into these primitive mechanisms of modern weaponry."

"That's why you were tapped," Sage said. "You're like the world's biggest nerd. He knew if anyone could figure this out it'd be you!"

"We all serve a purpose, Sage."

"Do we?" Sage said as he scratched his ass. "What about Lucifer?"

"Even he serves."

"Wouldn't killing his ass save the Eld?"

"Probably, but that's not what He wants. Knowing what happens when you go against God's word, I'm not about to make that same mistake again by working against His orders."

"Why is he here?" Sage asked, crossing his arms.

"He was flushed out of Hell…like excommunicated and dethroned, all that good stuff."

Somewhere in the basement, something heavy went crashing to the floor. The sudden blast of sound caused Sage to jump. Adam, seemingly used to the strange spectral occurrences of the basement, continued speaking unabated.

"He has no power now man. Killing Lucious does nothing except make our job that much harder. We need him to see the patchwork of the Shroud so we can dismantle it."

"Not very comforting, is it," Sage said as he shook his head, "to know the Eld was so desperate that even He had to make a deal with the Devil."

"Sometimes a deal with the Devil is better than nothing."

"I need a drink, bro. I'm dying for one. Please tell me you got something stashed away down here. It can be our little secret."

"Sorry," he said.

"But you smoke dope, bro! Can you say double standard?"

"I can," he said fishing out his joints. "I could use a nice cold beer right about now, but that's not what He wants from us. We are here to plan and execute, not drink. Here," Adam said. He offered an exceptionally fat joint to Sage and asked, "Want some?"

"I don't smoke that trash. Pot makes you dumb."

"That's why I smoke it," Adam said with a wink.

"You don't drink?"

"Not for a long time."

"How long?"

Adam mulled it over for a second and then said, "About 500 years ago, give or take, dude."

"What made you stop?"

"The hangovers."

A rock zipped past Adam and struck his computer screen.

"That ghost is a real prick."

"He killed himself here. Over there," Adam said as he gestured down a rotten hallway littered with trash and broken furniture.

"He tell you that?"

Adam nodded.

"He tell you why he did it?"

"He was being investigated for some missing children."

Sage looked around the basement, rubbing the back of his neck. Though the dark murk of the cellar made him nervous, he tried not to let Adam notice his general uneasiness. With his hands in his pockets, he continued strolling around the workshop while Adam checked his cracked computer screen. He walked over to the faded green military footlocker with the words Army Intel itched into it, followed by the number 9906753.

Sage opened it.

He expected to find Adam's drug stash but instead found the mummified remains of a woman. She lay on her side in the fetal position with her skeletal legs pulled up against her bony chest. She wasn't wrapped like a traditional mummy but instead wore black lingerie and reeked of vanilla perfume. The hair was nicely combed, the skin freshly lacquered, and the face was covered in a fresh layer of makeup.

"What the hell?"

When Adam saw what he was looking at, he sprang from his seat and dashed over to him. He slammed the lid down and grabbed a padlock from off the table. With his hands fumbling, he struggled to lock the lid.

"Adam…bro…"

"Could you give us some privacy?"

After some difficulty, Adam eventually managed to lock the lid. With a sigh, he collapsed on top of the locker while Sage stood there, unsure what to do next. This was beyond creepy, and it got worse when Adam started stroking the top of it.

"Uh, you want to introduce me to your friend, bro?"

"Don't tell anyone about this dude. Especially not Lilith."

"It's cool, bro. While most people keep their skeletons in their closets, you like to keep them in a funky locker."

Adam collapsed against the table, knocking over a few tools and an AR-15 resting on a bipod. His face had drained of color as sweat trickled down his face.

"I bet you want that drink now, huh?"

Adam shook his head.

"Care to explain why you got some creepy ass corpse in a chest?"

Adam glanced over his shoulder and appeared to listen to something that only he could hear. Spooked, Sage inched closer to the embalming slab with the guns on it.

"Be nice, dude. You're going to hurt her feelings."

"Hurt her feelings? No offense, but she's dead."

Adam whispered something to the footlocker as he continued patting the top. He appeared to be consoling it…not the box, but the corpse locked inside.

"Who is she?"

"My wife," Adam answered.

"You mean that thing in there is Eve? Man, that is so fucked up."

They both heard a laugh. It seemed to be coming from deep in the bowels of the basement, where the shadows refused to die.

"Is that him? The Top Hat Man?"

"Probably. He's like a pretty pesky poltergeist."

"So, what's the deal bro – you take her like everywhere you go?"

Adam nodded as he ran his fingers through his greasy hair. "When she passed dude, I just couldn't let her go. She's the love of my life."

"Whatever happened to 'until death do us part,'" Sage asked. "You know she in Heaven watching over your ass, right? You want her to see you carry her around like that?"

"I never made that vow. When I got married, there was no Book of Common Prayer—it was just Eve and me in the Garden of Eden; our guests were the angels and the Eld, our vow master. It was a beautiful ceremony," Adam said as he cleaned away a few tears. "Have you ever been married, Sage?"

"Yeah. Like six times."

They both laughed. The Top Hat Man didn't join them.

"Can we get back to work? We got a war to start tomorrow."

"One more question."

"What?"

"Relax bro, it's not about Eve…it's about our arrangement."

"What about it?"

"You figure out your sin? I've been pondering it for days trying to figure out the one sin God found most troubling from a life full of debauchery. Any ideas or suggestions on how I can solve this riddle?"

"You ask anyone else?"

"Lilith."

"What did she say?"

"Pray on it," Sage said with a snicker.

"She's right, man. You need to do some serious soul-searching. I figured out my offense to the Eld and have fought, every day, to refrain from sinking back into the quagmire of wickedness ever since. And it hasn't been easy. It takes real strength."

"You mind me asking what it was bro?"

"On like one condition."

"I'm listening."

"It like stays down here, dude."

"You got it."

Adam gestured for him to come closer. Sage leaned in as the First Man whispered a dark secret into his ear. And after he did, Sage kind of wished he didn't. The word sent a shiver of repulsion down the dead hitman's spine like a flash of hot lightning. The word whispered was Necrophilia.

Lilith paused outside Moragon's room and listened to the witch's guttural ravings mid-invocation. The door to her room stood ajar, allowing a foul smell to disgorge itself from its gloomy interior into the hall.

"Oh. My. God. Is she actually hexing me?" Lilith murmured to herself in disbelief.

Enraged, Lilith got ready to kick some hag ass but froze when she spotted Dead Meat poke his head out from behind the door. The undead cat stared up at her with his big, yellow eyes. She wondered how many people outside the hospital would even notice that the feline was resurrected, a walking, talking miracle. She doubted they would, seeing as we live in the age of the sick when the wonder of the miracle was long dead.

"Lilith?"

She knelt down to Dead Meat's level and spoke in gossip-like whispers. "Tell me, what is your mistress doing in there?"

"What else would a witch be doing in a dark room speaking in tongues – eating pizza?"

"Do you recognize the spell? Is it a hex?"

"I just fetched the supplies, Lilith. I'm no Artist. Why don't you go in there and ask her? She's nearly finished."

The chanting stopped dead.

"See, all done," Dead Meat said with a smirk. "If you have any questions concerning casting or spell weaving, I'd speak to the Night Mother. Not a cat."

"Dead Meat?" Moragon called.

"Out here!"

"What are you doing out there, you dimwitted bag of fleas? Get in here, I need you."

"Well, it was nice chatting with you, Lilith," Dead Meat said with a bow, "but as you can see, duty calls."

He then disappeared back into the room.

With a sigh, she got up and opened the door. Inside, she saw Moragon sitting Indian style in a large circle surrounded by candles and dead animals. She saw four in total, each lying in the four cardinal positions of North, East, South, and West. There were the shredded remains of a garden snake, a headless mouse, and a couple of dead birds—which were no doubt Dead Meat's contributions to the incantation.

"Come in child," Moragon said. "What brings the First Woman to my humble lodging? Hungry for some pussy?"

"You're disgusting."

Moragon chuckled.

"What are you doing in here?"

"Isn't it obvious?" the witch asked, gesturing at her circle. "I'm casting spells."

"A hex?"

The witched laughed.

"What's so funny?"

"That my words caused such paranoia. There just words, dear one, not stones...they won't hurt ya none. To think, I thought you were made of sterner stuff."

"Then what are you doing?"

"I'm doing a blessing."

"A blessing," Lilith repeated, looking at the Satanic circle and animal corpses. "If this is how you bless, I'd hate to see how you curse."

"We're on the same team, which means we need to find a way to coexist, or we're all dead. And seeing as I just came back, I'm in no mood to die," she said with a smile. "Seeing as I want to save my soul, I thought it wise not to dabble in the blacker Arts—at least, not now. Do you remember where you found me?"

"I do," Lilith said with a nod.

"Good, I thought you might have blocked it from memory like a disappointing one-night stand."

Since the jaunt, Lilith usually woke in the morning drenched in sweat from nightmares full of hellish vistas and nightmarish creatures. She wanted to forget about the terrors of the abyss, but the abyss clearly wasn't done with her.

"What do you know about the glade you discovered me in?"

"Not much," she admitted.

"It belonged to the Blood Witch, Abyzou. She is a cruel mistress, a thing to be avoided like the Pope does religious piety."

"Why are you telling me this?"

"To garnish your trust, Lilith. You need to understand why I'm bound to do anything I have to do to avoid going back to that glade and the always-hungry Blood Witch."

"Fine, I'll listen," she said – though she didn't really want to.

"Abyzou's favorite food is unborn children, straight out of the womb. To get them, she sends out slaves – men she dubs Hunters – into the woods seeking potential females. These poor women are dragged back and bound in chains. Then come the rapes. One after the other until your clam is macerated and doused in blood and semen."

"Oh. My. God. That's sick," Lilith murmured, feeling phantom quivers in her most private places.

"He no help you…he doesn't care about the damned. Nor does His daddy-o in the sky-o! As the Hunters pound, bite, and claw – the bitch hovers over you to lick away the tears. You see the Hunters line up, girl, especially for the new flesh. They'll rape you until the seed takes, and then eight months later, she devours the babe right through your plump belly."

Without thinking about it, Lilith's hands went to her belly.

"I kept a tally."

Lilith didn't want to hear it, but the witch told her anyway, and the number was haunting.

"875 babes, Lilith, eaten right out of my womb. Too many. No more," she said. "I would not risk this chance at redemption on a proud bitch like you for anything. Sorry to burst your inflated ego, but I won't do it."

"You're being a bit harsh mistress," Dead Meat said.

"It's fine," Lilith replied, "it's not the first time I've been called bitch, and I seriously doubt it'll be the last time either."

"No, it won't," Moragon said with a laugh. "And I don't need the power of divination to make that prediction either."

The temperature in the hall suddenly dropped a few degrees, sending a frosty chill up Lilith's spine. Confused, Lilith hugged herself to stifle off some of the cold.

"Feelin' something?" Moragon asked.

"Temperature drop."

"It's the restless dead. There is one standing next to you."

Lilith remembered the little girl she encountered one dark, stormy afternoon – Valerie. She checked the hall, hoping to see her again, but all she saw was an empty hall.

"Not the child," Moragon explained. "The Top Hat Man keeps the younger spirits close to him most of the time so he can feed on them like a parasite."

"Like Abyzou."

Moragon smiled toothlessly at her. "You speak truer than you realize."

In the doorway, next to Lilith (though she couldn't see her), was a ghostly nurse dressed in an outdated fashion. Her head lay unnaturally against her shoulder, her skin the pigment of death. There were deep grooves in her neck, the remnants of the rope used to strangle the life out of her all those decades ago.

"Who is this Top Hat Man?" Lilith asked.

"If you're smart, you'll leave him be," Moragon snapped. "He's been nice so far by just throwing stones, but you piss him off, and there's no telling what he might do. You see that girl of yours, your sweet Valerie, smile and give her some of your time and no more. Remember, she's dead; we're not."

Lilith nodded.

"Besides, you got a war to prepare for. Enjoy this day before the world as we know it changes forever. Pleasure yourself, and if you get bored, come back and pleasure me," the witch said with another burst of vile laughter.

"Oh. My. God. That's disgusting. I'm outta here," Lilith said. She flashed the peace sign and headed back to her room, followed by their repulsive laughter.

CHAPTER 3

"It's going to rain," Lucious said.

He stood at the window in the waiting room, peering out at the decaying remnants of the hospital's parking lot. Most of it was overgrown with weeds and discarded trash, but a few concrete slabs of the former lot remained like vestiges of some ancient, lost civilization.

"The Earth is preparing for a cleansing," Moragon said as she joined Lucious.

"You think it deserves it?" he asked.

"Does it matter what I think?"

"I've learned the hard way that only one opinion matters in this twisted universe, and it belongs to the Eld. As for this place," he said as he waved dismissively, "needs to be destroyed, not saved. It was the rift that divided Heaven."

"If that's how you feel, then you're standing on the wrong side of history, my Lord. We're acting as its protectors, not its destructors," Moragon said.

"Don't I know it," Lucious said glumly. "Standing here is an insult. I should be battling to preserve the Shroud, not ripping it down. Especially not now, as we are so close to absolute victory. He's moments away from drifting into the long, cold dark of eternal sleep."

"What made you agree to the terms in the first place?" Dead Meat inquired. He sat on one of the chairs at an odd angle, which made his black, hairless testicles visible. "If you don't mind me asking. I'm a cat and being curious is my modus operandi."

"Vengeance brought me here," Lucious said. "A famous person once claimed revenge is an act of passion, vengeance of justice. I will have mine on those who pulled out their knives to stab me in the back. I will slaughter my Brutus. Mark my words."

"Do you know who it was?" Moragon asked.

"I only know one conspirator at this point, my ex-wife – Agrat."

"I wish I could," Moragon said.

"I won't risk your soul, Night Mother."

The door at the far end of the room opened with a loud bang as Sage, Adam, and Lilith entered with their arms full of gear. The time of death-dealing was upon them, and they all seemed well prepared, Lucious thought.

Lilith wore a wireless transmitter in her ear and had one of Adam's rifles strapped over her shoulder. On her hip was that wonderful, strange disc weapon she used to cut Mastema's hands off. Sage carried a modified AR-15 and extra mag pouches on a shoulder holster. Though hidden, Lucious saw a pistol of some sort wedged in the front of his pants. Behind these living fists of God came Adam, armed with a joint and the key.

It was the key that caught Lucious's eye. He stared at it, zeroing in on it as his head danced with unhealthy, violent thoughts. If he could sneak back into Hell and murder that bitch and her lover while they slept in their beds, he wouldn't have to follow through with the reaping of his precious Shroud.

He licked his lips.

"Hey man," Adam said with a wave, "they're ready to rock and roll."

"How we looking on time?" Lucious asked.

"You got me, dude," Adam said as he checked his bare wrists.

"Oh. My. God," Lilith said with a groan. She shoved her wrist in Adam's face, shaking her watch under his nose. He read it through a plume of smoke. "Can you read it, or do you need me to fetch you some glasses?"

"Harsh man," Adam said with a squint. "It's five past two, which means we got a cool fifty-plus minutes to sneak in and prepare for our potential targets."

Lucious walked over to them as thunder crashed somewhere close, causing the hospital lights to flicker. It was an omen — a taste of things to come. And when he reached them, the sky opened up and pissed upon the world.

"How you guys feeling?" Lucious asked. "Any questions or concerns before you go off and kick ass for the Lord?"

"I'm good bro," Sage said.

"Me too," Lilith added. "You going to give us a prep talk?"

"I was thinking about it."

"Well, don't waste your time. I'm not interested in anything you have to say unless it relates to dealing with my target."

"Shoot to kill," Lucious said. "Don't hesitate, because the last thing you want to do is allow them a chance to react. Aim for the head and remember to double-tap before returning – just to be sure. Keep in mind by taking out these two assholes, we are essentially setting off a chain reaction – a kind of unraveling."

"How so?" Lilith asked.

"I have a feeling we're about to see a drastic spike in overdoses, suicides, and mysterious disappearances all across the music industry as an internal power struggle ignites. Nothing is more appetizing to demons than power. Does that answer your question, Lilith?"

She shrugged, already disinterested.

"Does this bother you, bro? Killing your friends?" Sage asked.

"A little. I'll miss Durji's music and Hornblas's jokes—the guy had wicked humor."

"There demons," Lilith said. "And I, for one, can't wait to introduce them to the sweet sound of death. Are we done? Can we get this started already?"

"You are heartless," Moragon said.

"Sorry, witch, my heart doesn't bleed for the wicked."

"It's fine," Lucious said. "I don't expect any of you to show compassion for them. You don't know them the way I do, and perhaps for your own safety, that's a good thing. Is there anything else before we begin?"

Sage and Lilith shook their heads.

"Okay then – who wants to go first?" Lucious asked.

"I'm your huckleberry," Lilith said as her hand shot into the air like some know-it-all teacher's pet.

Adam walked over to the hospital's main door, stabbed it with the magic key, and opened it. Instead of leading into the hospital's rain-soaked courtyard, it opened into a posh interior of a resort hotel on the far side of town.

"Good luck, bro," Sage said, "don't get yourself killed."

"You do the same."

She saluted everyone in the room except for Lucious – for him, she gave the finger.

CHAPTER 4

Agrat sat crossed legged on the cold floor, eyes closed and her thoughts elsewhere. She tried to melt into the blackness of the cosmos, to fade into the oblivion of the in-between, but just before she could submerge herself completely, the holding cell door opened and shattered her concentration like a brick through a windshield.

She opened her eyes.

Being escorted inside was a large black woman topped with an enormous afro. She had tattoos on both her arms and one snaking around her neck, some name written in cursive. Her face was heavily pot-marked and covered with an expansive network of deep grooves and wrinkles. When she spoke to one of the guards, Agrat noticed her teeth were gold capped.

"Don't look at me," the woman snarled at Agrat as she entered the cell, acting as if she owned the place.

"Be nice in there, Ashanti," the guard behind her ordered. "Let's try and make this visit a quiet one."

"How about you choke on a bag of donkey dicks, piggy? I ain't got to listen to you. You ain't the boss of me. Fuck you, I'll say and do what I want."

The guard shrugged as she locked the door and left.

The holding cell's body count stood at five. Besides Agrat, there was a toothless drunk passed out on one of the bunks, a middle-aged woman with dirty black hair and a Latino with a pair of black teardrops tattooed beneath her left eye. They all looked like regurgitated dog food and were all ultimately hell bound.

Her kind of scum.

"Keep looking at me," Ashanti said as she marched past her, "and I'll gouge your eyes out. I'm already domed. I'm looking at ten years, easy. You think I give a damn what gets tacked on if I maul a pretty cracker like you? Hell no."

Agrat closed her eyes and attempted to drift once more. It didn't come easy, especially after the night she had. She was weak and off-kilter, thanks to a lack of sleep and the piss-poor food at the police station. But that wasn't the only thing preventing her from slipping into the in-between; there was something else. Something intangible she couldn't quite put her finger on.

What was it?

"Agrat…what the hell!"

Opening her eyes, Agrat saw Belial standing just outside the cell. He was a phantom, his body completely transparent. He had no eyes or nose, just empty black holes.

"Seriously," he said as he drifted between the bars, "why did you do it? I thought we were lovers!"

His last line was so pathetic she couldn't help but laugh.

"I can't believe you killed me. Not cool, Agrat, not cool."

How are you here? she asked. *Shouldn't you be dead?*

"You seriously don't know? Think about it; you'll figure it out. I'll wait. I've got nowhere else to be."

It didn't take long for reality to set in and punch her in the face. With a heavy sense of dread, she muttered, "Your soul."

"Yeah, genius, you ate it. Remember?"

Behind her, Ashanti stirred like some great bear rousing from uneasy dreams. "What'd you say, cracker? You best keep your trap shut before I ram my fist down your cock sucking throat."

"I see you making friends," Belial said.

Shut up. Is Mastema with you?

"He's in here somewhere. Sulking."

Though she hated being bothered by Belial, it was far better than the alternative, which was a pissed-off Mastema. Flustered with her inability to connect to Hell, she retreated to one of the open beds and sat down.

Belial focused his skeletal gaze on her as he shook his head in dismay. "I can't believe you did it. I thought we had something, something special."

Jesus, what is it with men and pussy? It's like their Goddamn kryptonite, I swear. Look, I did what needed to be done, babe. It's not my fault I was the only one using my brain.

"Why did you do it?"

Power. I'm done being bossed around like I'm some weak, little puppy. I'm taking control of my destiny and killing anyone who gets in my way.

"I wasn't in your way?"

No, but you're still an annoying male. You'd still be alive if Beelzebub hadn't forced you on this mission. I didn't want you here and I didn't need you here. Kind of like now. Can you piss off?

"Hate to burst your bubble, but I'm not going anywhere."

She groaned.

The longer this conversation continued, the harder it was for her to keep her words restricted to her mind space. She wanted to scream; she was desperate for it.

In her lap, she clenched her hands into tiny balls of concentrated hatred. Belial drifted right up on Agrat. He was so close that the temperature around her dropped several degrees, turning her sweat into small beads of ice.

"Cold?"

A bit, yeah.

"Do you know what it feels like to be dead?"

Shitty?

Belial laughed.

His tormentable guffaw reverberated off the walls of the cell, penetrating both her mind and soul alike. It washed over her like a toxic spill. She asked him to stop, but the snicker grew in both potency and volume. She realized if she didn't give Belial what he wanted he'd drive her well beyond the mountains of madness.

"What do you want from me you sick fuck? An apology?"

She was surprised by the fury in her own voice as it bounced around the cell. All the women, except the passed-out drunk, stared at her with their mouths agape.

"Who are you talking to, you crazy ass cracker?" Ashanti asked angrily.

Lilith ignored Ashanti's outburst. She didn't care about what some ignorant human cunt had to say, but the phantom floated in front of her with a face only a mother could love.

"Go on then," Belial said, "I'm all ears."

Whose dick do I have to suck to make you evaporate?

"I wish I knew because I'd happily watch that show."

Jesus…you really are a pig.

"Oink, Oink my Queen. Now say it."

I'm sorry. Okay?

"Say it out loud."

"Sorry."

"With more compassion, you cold bitch."

"Sorry, you dickless fuck!"

"Enjoy rotting in this cage with the rest of this riffraff. I'll be seeing you. The next time I appear, you better say it right, or I'll shatter that mind of yours and leave you in a cationic state."

Belial faded from view.

Agrat got up and began pacing the cage, her heart pounding in her ears. The desire for slaughter was so intense that she nearly unleashed Misandry. Instead, she focused all her thoughts and energy on the one light in her pitiful, wretched life…Beelzebub. It helped a little. Agrat sat down beside the prisoner with dirty hair and did her best to calm her rattled nerves.

From beneath oily bangs, the woman stared at her with big, dark, muddy eyes. In a soft voice, she asked, "Bad night?"

"What do you think?"

"I hear voices too."

Jesus.

"Satan talks to me," she whispered. "He tells me to do things."

I wish he'd tell you to wash your dirty hair.

On the other side of the cell, Ashanti rose from her seat and approached them with sinister purpose. "You two bitches done gibber jabbing or what?"

The woman nodded frantically at the opposing alpha female, but Agrat simply stared at her – completely unimpressed.

"What about you, cracker? You done?"

"Is that supposed to be an insult – calling me a thin, flaky wafer?"

Ashanti didn't answer verbally but with the language of the street. She took a swing at Agrat. If she had wanted to, she could have dodged it or snatched the aggressor's hand mid-swing, but in the end, she decided to do neither. She was curious about Ashanti and the power this explosively unstable ape contained. The punch landed just below her right eye with decent force. Agrat wasn't impressed, nor was she harmed.

"You hit about as well as you shit-talk," Agrat said flatly. "Perhaps if you imagined me as your Uncle Willis or that drunk cousin who raped you, maybe you'd put a bit more oomph behind that punch of yours."

"How do you know…"

"I know more than that, Ashanti. I know you've had three beautiful babies slaughtered in that venomous womb of yours because you couldn't get your boyfriends to wear a rubber. You also killed your best friend, Tamika Jordon, by introducing her to meth."

Ashanti backed away from Agrat with her eyes wide in absolute horror. Enjoying herself, Agrat slipped off the bunk and advanced on the retreating woman, grinning as she approached.

"You're a corrupter, a cancerous vessel spreading death and ruin to everyone around you. But I've got good news, Ashanti – all that is about to end."

"You going to kill me?"

"I got better things to do than get my hands dirty with your blood. But when it happens, I'm going to sit back and watch."

"You're a devil."

"No, but I used to fuck him."

Out in the hall, two female officers came to collect Agrat. As the storm swelled outside and the thunder boomed, she was led to room 47B.

The room was nothing special.

It had four walls covered in crisscrossing black and white soundproof Styrofoam. On the wall opposite Agrat was a two-way mirror to film the confession that wasn't coming. She waved at her disheveled reflection and did her best to fix the rat nest that was her hair. She was sitting at a small table with a couple of chairs. The one assigned to her was an uncomfortable leather seat with a wobbly leg while the other, reserved for the law, was a simple office chair.

Agrat sat there with the flickering lights for a good thirty minutes before the door eventually opened, and a lanky man wearing a dark blue suit entered. He was bald with pasty white skin and extremely bushy eyebrows. In his hands were two cups of coffee. He gave her one and then closed the door.

"Sorry to keep you waiting, but this weather is…"

He didn't finish the sentence; he let it wither and die on its own. With his free hand, he reached into his pocket and pulled out his badge, flashing it at her like it meant something. "My name is Special Agent Dan Milton. I'm with the FBI."

"Congratulations."

"Thanks," Dan Milton said as taking a seat in an empty chair. He took a drink and then set his cup down in front of him. "Not thirsty?"

"Don't like coffee. It gives me cramps."

"You want something else? Water? Tea?"

"I'm good," she said.

"I understand you refused your right to legal counsel."

"I'm allergic to lawyers."

"Who isn't?" Dan laughed. He sipped his coffee and said, "My brother-in-law is a Criminal Defense attorney in D.C. I can't stand him; the guy is a massive prick."

"It might cheer you up to know that the shafts of Hell are clogged with them; they are like plaque in an old man's arteries."

The door opened and in came an officer with a cup of water. He handed it to her without a word and then left. She drank while Dan Milton watched her with his cold, calculated stare.

"Isn't this the part where you start prodding for answers, love? I didn't wave my rights for nothing."

"Why did you?"

"I wanted to speed up this laborious process."

"Did you now?"

She sipped her water as he pulled out a small blue notepad from his breast pocket. He flipped it open and read, "Your name is Mary Migdal, correct?"

"Yup."

"How long have you been in town?"

"Since yesterday," she said nonchalantly.

"Ever been here before?"

"Sure. Arizona is my favorite place to visit next to Disney Land."

Dan chuckled, then asked, "When were you here last?"

"I don't know the exact date," she said with a shrug. "A few days ago, I think."

"Here?"

"No."

"Where?"

"Elephant Head."

His eyebrows shot up like a pair of mushroom clouds. Agrat wondered if the agent was connecting the dots between one bloody murder scene to another because she wasn't about to give that to him for nothing. She wanted him to dig like a dog with a bone.

He wrote something down.

"What happened at the hotel?"

She laughed.

"You consider that hell hole a hotel? That's bad comedy."

"I've been in worse," Dan Milton replied. He chewed on the badly gnawed portion of his pen a moment while looking at his notes. After a short pause, he said, "Something terrible happened inside that room. We pulled four bodies from the fire, one of them being a sixteen-year-old girl. Did you set the fire?"

"I don't play with matches Mr. Milton."

Dan started to speak, but a shotgun blast of thunder gave him pause, and the entire building shook beneath its force.

"This is one mean storm, isn't it?"

The door opened, and in came a woman dressed in a gray suit and topped with blood-red curly hair. She was cute, even for a stiff. In her hand was a folder.

"This is my partner, Special Agent Tabitha Flamingo."

"Charming name," Agrat said. "You guys banging?"

"No," Dan said.

They were. She knew it. All kinds of nasty stuff right behind their spouse's backs like last night in their hotel. Dan liked Tabitha because she was nasty, did things his prissy, Christian wife would never dream of doing, like anal. Tabitha liked Dan's fat cock, which ripped into her like a power drill.

The woman handed the folder to Dan, her eyes never leaving Agrat's. It was a pathetic display of power, one Agrat batted away like an annoying fly at a Presidential debate.

"Your driver's license claims a Chicago residence. Do you really live at 2800 N Pine Grove Ave?" Dan asked.

"I think you already know the answer to that one, don't you love?"

"We do. You don't."

"You caught me! Congratulations," Agrat said. She took a drink of water. It was tap and tasted like rust.

"The people in the hotel room…"

"Where just a bunch of assholes," Agrat said. "If you knew who they were, you wouldn't arrest me; you'd give me the Nobel Peace Prize."

"You said you wanted to talk, but you keep playing these games of misdirection," Dan said.

It was clear to Agrat that he was already getting flustered. He probably thought he was walking into a confessional with some guilt-stricken little woman, not someone with the cool confidence of the Riddler.

"Am I not talking?"

"You are, but you're not saying much."

"I want you to beg for it. Get down on your knees and grovel like the federal pig you are, Mr. Milton and I'll tell you such deliciously sweet secrets you'd bust a nut in your pants faster than you do your partner's mouth. If you don't want to do it, have her do it. I'm all about equality of the sexes."

There was a knock at the door.

Tabitha opened it to find an officer standing in the hall. Agrat didn't know her name, but it was one of the officers who escorted her to the cell the previous night. She didn't look so well, and she smelled even worse. She reeked of fear.

"What is it, Officer Manis? We're in the middle of an interrogation," Dan Milton protested angrily.

"I know, but this is urgent."

The lights flickered again.

"Tabitha…go with her, see what the hell she wants."

Tabitha and Officer Manis left the room. Even though they were isolated at the center of the station and behind soundproof walls, Agrat still heard the thunder. It sounded like a car bomb.

"Sounds bad out there," Dan said.

Agrat laughed.

"What's so funny?"

"I have a feeling it's about to get worse."

"How so?"

"Wait and see – I don't want to spoil it for you."

He stared at her while he chewed on his pen. He was trying to keep his emotions in check as he struggled to figure out how she knew about his relationship with Tabitha.

"You're confused, Mr. Milton."

"Why do you say that?"

"It's written all over your face in big, bold letters. You want to know how I know about you and Tabitha."

"I told you…"

"A lie," she said. "We're both adults, Mr. Milton; how do you expect me to confess my sins if you don't confess your own. I don't blame you fucking your partner – she's a looker."

"I'm not."

"I can smell her on you."

"Is that right?"

"She's on your fingers. On your cock."

"Okay, that's enough," he said. He slammed the folder on the desk, spilling its contents.

"When you going to tell the wife, Mr. Milton?"

She drank her water while a nearby lightning strike shook the building's foundation again. Though she couldn't see what was happening outside from the windowless interrogation room, but it must have been nightmarish.

"Let me handle the questioning."

"Well, ask better questions because I'm getting bored."

The door to the interrogation room flew open as Tabitha rushed in looking grim.

"What's wrong?" Dan asked.

"The station is surrounded by an army of lunatics."

Slaughterama

CHAPTER 1

Lilith passed through the portal with her head spinning. One second, she was in the hospital lobby, and the next, she stood inside a luxury suite on the far side of Arizona under the same bleak sky.

The room she found herself in was the suite's living area, which was filled with expensive furniture and one of the biggest TVs she had ever seen. To her right was a mini-bar and a door leading to a private patio. On the opposite side of the TV was a hallway, which probably led to the bathroom and bedroom.

Before she could even take a step, a violent burst of static filled her ear as Adam called her.

"Oh. My. God. What the hell do you want, Adam? I mean, I just left. You miss me that much?"

"Just making sure we, like, have a connection and stuff."

"Well, it works. Happy? Anything else?"

"How's the room?"

"Seriously? It's a room, Adam. If you want to experience this lifestyle so badly, book your own room. Now can you piss off so I can get this job done?"

"Oh right. Sorry dude. Good luck."

Click.

"What an idiot," she said as she watched the portal close, officially abandoning her behind enemy lines.

She stood there a moment, waiting for the last bit of vertigo to fade as thunder shook the windows. Seeing as she had time to spare, she thought she'd raid the mini bar. She walked around the counter and found six Louis Vuitton bags behind it; half submerged in shadow.

"Oh crap."

Listening carefully, Lilith heard the steady pounding of rain outside, but the room itself was eerily silent. Something was off. Nervous, she radioed Adam.

"Adam? Adam, do you hear me?"

"That was fast," Adam said with a chuckle. "Miss me already?"

"No, dumb ass, she's here."

"Who?"

"Who the hell do you think, asshole, the demon."

"Impossible, dude. I totally checked their itinerary. They're not supposed to be there until about 3."

"You might want to tell her that because I'm staring at her luggage."

From down the hall, she heard the creaking of door hinges. Remembering what Lucifer said about giving no quarter, she crouched behind the counter and unslung her rifle.

"Hang on, someone's coming."

Footfalls, unrushed and approaching. Peering down the length of the barrel, her finger tightening on the trigger, she heard the electric hum of divine energy humming in her ears. The first chance she got, she told herself, she was going to blow her head off regardless of flight arrival times.

"God," she whispered, "make my aim true."

Coming around the corner was a short woman dressed in a business suit, but it wasn't Tiffany Swan. Unlike the beautiful singer, this woman was plump with poorly dyed hair. In her hand was a gold cosmetic bag. When she spotted Lilith and her gun, she froze.

"Don't move," Lilith said. "Run, and my bullets give chase. Understood? Now put your hands up but do it slowly."

As the woman's hands shot up, Lilith came around the bar. Studying the woman's face, she searched for indicators about the woman's origins, struggling to determine if she was human or just another godless demon.

She couldn't tell.

"What's your name?"

The woman answered with sobs.

"I asked you a question. For your sake, I'd advise you to answer it before I lose my patience, and you lose your life. Now tell me, what's your name?"

"Kenzie," she blathered. "Kenzie Walters."

Lilith stopped a few feet away from the woman, keeping her gun out of reach just in case she wanted to play hero.

"Where's Swan?"

"Please," she begged, "I have kids. Two little girls."

"Shut up."

Kenzie fidgeted with her hands as her lips quivered, and tears streamed down her chubby, flushed cheeks.

"I asked…where's Swan?"

"Are you going to kill us?"

"Swan, most diffidently. I don't know about you yet. You her assistant or something?"

"Yes."

"I thought you assholes weren't supposed to be here until three?"

"We left early…to beat the storm."

"I see. Where's your boss?"

Before Kenzie could answer, Lilith heard Tiffany Swan's muffled cry from deeper inside the suite, sounding almost phantom-like. She recognized her voice instantly, having listened to countless songs of Swan's over the years, like *Partition, Burn it Down, Fire Dancer,* and *Take it Off.* She hated all the songs because the radio played them on an endless loop, and she found the lyrics beyond insulting. Killing her was going to be an absolute pleasure.

"Kenzie," Swan called, "did you find it or not?"

The assistant stared wide-eyed at Lilith, clearly waiting for instruction.

"Tell her you're still looking. Say anything else, and I'll rearrange your face so badly your two children won't even be able to identify your body."

Kenzie nodded and then shouted back, "I'm still looking, ma'am."

"Hurry up!"

"Is that what she wants?" Lilith asked, looking at the cosmetic bag.

"Yes."

"What, no ma'am?"

Kenzie swallowed hard and then said, "Yes, ma'am."

"That's better. Open it."

She shook her head.

"Are these secrets really worth dying for, Kenzie? Now open the bag, or I'll do it after I rip it out of your cold, dead hands."

She opened it. Lilith glimpsed inside to find a couple of syringes filled with a dark, red liquid.

"What's that – heroin?"

"Blood."

"Blood? Whose blood?" Lilith asked.

"I prefer not to say…ma'am."

"And I'd prefer not to redecorate the room with your brains. Now answer the question – whose blood is it?"

"Nobody special. Just some girl."

"She dead?"

Kenzie nodded.

"You sick bitch."

"I didn't do it, I swear."

"Bet you paid someone to do your dirty work, huh?"

"Yes."

"How old was she?"

"I didn't ask. All I can tell you is that Miss Swan likes them young."

"I bet she does. Where's the body?"

Kenzie didn't answer; her lips were sealed as tight as a dead girl's tomb. Before Lilith could press further, Tiffany Swan started calling again for her assistant, her voice sick with want.

"Did you find it or what?"

"Tell her you're coming," Lilith said as she lowered the rifle.

Kenzie relayed the message.

"Good girl. You just might survive this."

She smiled.

"Just not unscathed."

Lilith ran up to the girl and struck her in the head with the stock of her rifle. Kenzie staggered back with blood oozing from a deep gash on her forehead. After two drunken steps, her legs buckled, and she collapsed to the floor in a heap.

With her down and out, she called Adam.

"Hey, Adam – you there?"

"Reading you loud and clear."

"Good, now shut up. Where's Sage?"

"About to pass through his portal."

"Were they scheduled for the same flight?"

"Who?"

"Who do you think Adam – Santa Claus?"

"I'm sorry, but Santa Claus does not…"

"If you were standing in front of me right now, Adam, I'd drop-kick you in the damn nuts. Nero, you idiot, Nero! Was he on the same flight with Tiffany or what?"

"Yeah. They were scheduled to take his private plane."

"Well, then, you better warn Sage. I don't want him to accidentally walk into an ambush."

"Oh right. I'm on it."

Click.

And people think dope should be legal, what morons. Taking a deep breath, she raised her rifle and headed down the hall towards the source of Swan's voice. It was coming from behind a closed door. She offered up a quick prayer and then opened it.

Turns out the room was the suite's bathroom. Inside, the room was full of steam and the overpowering stench of flowers. In front of her was a large vanity mirror completely misted over. Scattered around the sink were bottles of pills, a mirror dusted with powder, and a couple of empty bottles of wine. On the floor, haphazardly scattered about, were discarded clothing: a skirt here, panties there, and a dainty black bra dangling from a towel rack.

It appeared as if someone was having a bit of a pre-party party.

Lilith stepped inside, gun at the ready.

To her left was an enormous shower, and inside it was Tiffany Swan. The superstar demon was pressed against the glass, fingers buried inside her pink innocence between her curvy, black thighs.

Not a bad way to go, Lilith thought raising the gun. Just as she started to pull the trigger, Kenzie burst through the door. The crazy assistant jumped on Lilith's back, digging her nails into her skin, puncturing flesh and drawing blood. Screaming, Lilith tried to flip the unwanted monkey off her back, but the woman refused to be bucked.

In an act of desperation, Lilith threw herself hard against the wall. With Kenzie pinned there, she swung her head back straight into the bitch's face, pulverizing bone and cartilage.

Kenzie cried out in agony as blood sputtered out of her broken nose. Lilith stepped forward with one of her arms hooked and flipped her off. As she flew, one of the assistant's legs bounced off the sink on her way down to the cold, unforgiving floor. She went for her gun, but the assistant knocked it away.

Lilith went for her disc, fumbling with it on her belt as Tiffany stepped out of the shower. The demon was still naked, her flesh slick and damp. Without all the Photoshop work or the assistance of makeup, the teen idol was nothing special to behold. She was average at best, a product sculpted by the media and a massive corporate machine.

"Hello," Tiffany Swan said as an unseen force sent Lilith somersaulting backward through the air in a mad spiral. It slammed her into the wall and pinned her there like a toad on a dissection tray. She tried to move but every joint in her body was locked up tightly.

"Hand me the gun," Tiffany ordered.

"She broke my nose," Kenzie groaned, clutching her damaged face as bright blood oozed between her fingers. She knelt, grabbed the gun, and handed it to Tiffany, saying, "I'll call the police, ma'am."

"Not yet."

"Not yet? This woman tried to kill you."

"And she failed, did she not? If you want to make yourself useful, go clean your face and then bring me what I asked for."

Kenzie bowed low and then sulked out of the room.

Tiffany examined the rifle briefly before setting it down on the sink, uninterested. "You're an oddity, aren't you? A hitman armed with weapons fueled by the divine. If I ask you questions, I wonder if you'll humor me with actual answers or play the silent game. Should I even bother?"

Lilith tried to respond, but like the rest of her body, the invisible force prevented her from speaking. Her mouth felt like it was superglued shut.

Tiffany drew closer. "You look…familiar."

The demon waved her hand, and instantly, Lilith felt the force waver slightly. Instead of having everything frozen stiff, she had limited mobility. She could wiggle her toes, fingers, and mouth. She suspected the demon relaxed the power enough to interrogate her.

"Have we met?"

"Nope."

Tiffany cocked her head to the side, her eyes narrowing in silent contemplation. After a short moment, she said, "It can't be. Lilith? Is it really you decorating my wall?"

Lilith answered her with an iron-clad stare.

"I heard you were killed at the Battle of Châlons."

"Guess I'm a ghost."

Tiffany smiled as she said, "Not yet, but you soon will be."

Kenzie returned with her face clean of both blood and damage. Her broken nose was straight, her skin healthy and pink. It was then Lilith realized her grievous error; Tiffany Swan wasn't traveling around with a mortal assistant but one of the demonic persuasions.

"Should I call Mr. Nero?" Kenzie asked handing Tiffany the cosmetic bag with the syringes full of blood.

Tiffany took out one of the nozzles and tapped it with her finger; her eyes remained firmly locked on Lilith's. "Do you not realize we have a celebrity in our midst, Kenzie? This woman is no mere fanatic; she's an Elder blunder – a first man, an immortal apparently."

Kenzie looked at her.

"No bells ringing inside that head of yours?"

"No ma'am."

"That's Lilith, the first wife of Adam."

Kenzie leaned in closer, gawking at her in disbelief. Eventually, she said, "I thought she was dead. Killed during the Blitz."

"Clearly not, for there she hangs."

The demons laughed.

Tiffany plunged the needle into the inner curve of her thigh as Lilith watched. Before learning she was demonic, Lilith hated her. She hated her music, her overly produced dance numbers, and, of course, the shallow lyrics of her songs. But now, having learned the truth of the creature standing before her, her hate transformed into pure abhorrence.

"So, what's going on here – you working for the Eld?"

Lilith didn't say anything.

"That's an interesting turn of events, don't you think Kenzie? She once spit in the face of God and now she kills for Him. Imagine that."

"How do you know?" Kenzie asked.

"Her bullets are full of divine energy. That stuff only comes from one place, and it's not on trees."

Kenzie looked at the rifle and then back at Lilith, her face twisted in shock and awe.

"Want to hear something else interesting about this slut? She once kicked Lucious in the balls."

"What? No way," Kenzie gasped.

"Yes, way. Right in the old bean bag."

"You guys want an autograph or what?" Lilith asked. While the demons mocked her with their taunting laugh, she stretched her free hand, the one not holding onto the disc, towards her radio, knowing that if she failed to reach Adam, she was dead.

"Finally, you speak," Tiffany said with a childish clap. "I was beginning to think I'd have to twist your nipples off to loosen those lips of yours."

"I just don't like socializing with morons."

Tiffany pulled out the syringe and handed it to Kenzie, who licked the needle clean.

"What made you crawl back into service of the Eld?"

"Your new album."

"Cute," Tiffany said. "Nice to see the millennia haven't changed you much, still a cunt. Soon to be a dead cunt."

Lilith's fingers brushed across the talk button, skimming it. She knew if she didn't get a message to Adam, she would soon be worm food. Straining against the magical field that pinned her body to the wall, turning her muscles to rust. She tried again. Just a bit more, she prayed, just a…little…more.

"What is she holding, ma'am? It looks like the weapon used by the Predator in the horrible sequel."

"I don't know what you're talking about, Kenzie; just tear it loose."

Kenzie walked over and sniffed around her wrist and weapon like a curious puppy dog. And then she bit. Lilith felt her fangs dig into her wrist with a flash of hot fire. She tried to hang on to the disc, but it was just too much. Her fingers straightened, causing the death frisbee to fall to the floor with a loud clang. Kenzie quickly kicked it behind the toilet.

"That's for the nose," she said as she stepped back, her face splattered with blood.

"How does she taste?" Tiffany asked.

"I've never tasted anything so sweet ma'am."

Tiffany paraded over to Lilith and lifted her shirt to reveal the smoothness of her flat belly. She placed her hand against it and said, "How interesting, it's empty. You've never been with child?"

"Go fuck yourself."

"I already did," Tiffany said. With a sick grin, she shoved her still-moist fingers down Lilith's throat.

Gagging on the demon's sour juices, Lilith thankfully managed to press the talk button on the radio. There was a sudden flash of static in her ears as the connection was made.

"How does the mistress taste?" Kenzie asked.

"Like a McDonald's Filet-of-fish."

"What do we do with her, ma'am?"

"That's a great question Kenzie. I'd like to kill her, but I know that wouldn't please the master. He'd want to question her. But that doesn't mean we can't sample the meat."

Kenzie started clapping.

"Just try not to eat all the good parts. Leave some for Hornblas."

"Of course, ma'am."

Lilith watched as Tiffany's tongue's pink tissue turned a cancerous black and then split right down the middle. The two appendages were heavily pockmarked with razor-sharp barbs, reminding Lilith of a whip. The demonic superstar threw them at her exposed midsection, tearing flesh and leaving deep hideous gashes. For the first time in centuries, Lilith screamed.

Sage entered his target's suite.

It was a nice place, a significant upgrade to the one he died in just a few days ago, en route to his retirement Mecca in Jacksonville, Florida. It was in the sweltering heat of the long Florida days he planned to spend the rest of his days, drowning in booze and cheap pussy until death got the balls to come and claim him. He figured he had a solid ten, maybe twenty years left to enjoy himself and his immoral habits. But then his former boss's thug, Two Tall Tony had to come along and spoil his fun. The prick killed him mid-thrust on some underage beauty seconds before he climaxed all inside her sweet, tight slit.

He pushed aside the thought as he explored the suite, absorbing his surroundings. While checking out the bedroom he heard Adam's obnoxious voice in his ears.

"Come in, Sage – how's everything looking?"

"Fine and dandy so far," he said as thunder crashed outside.

He peeked inside the bedroom's private bathroom and saw an insane shower. The thing had a typical showerhead in the center, but it also had six smaller ones running parallel on three of the four walls inside. Sage decided if he survived this hit, he might have to pop in for a quick washing.

"You alone?"

"What do you think bro?"

"I just spoke to Lilith, and she told me Tiffany is in the room."

"Well, I don't know what to tell you," he said as he left the bedroom. He walked down the hall as the rain outside came down in a mad torrent. Continuing, he said, "Place is empty. They may have come together, but he isn't here."

Back in the living area, with its expensive furniture and mind-boggling flat screen, something caught Sage's attention. He stood there; his eyes transfixed on the object sitting in a bucket of ice on the mini bar.

And smiled.

"You there, Sage?"

"Keep your panties on, bro; I can hear you."

"If I were you, I'd find a good hiding spot and get ready. He could show up there any moment."

"Thanks for the advice," he said as he walked to the bar. Wedged among a mound of melting ice cubes was a bottle of champagne. The bottle was a slick back and expertly crafted. And on the decanter was a Swarovski crystal shaped like the Superman logo. Below it, nestled in the pewter, he saw the words Goût de Diamants.

"My, my, my – what do we have here?"

Somewhere in the back of his mind he heard the voice of his ex-wife, Meredith Shaw Jenkins, pleading for him not to do it. Even in death, his old ball and chain was a controlling, no fun having bitch.

He ran his tongue across his lips, which had suddenly gone dry. He had never been as parched as he was then and there, his hand clutching the neck of the bottle, with the cold condensation oozing between his fingers.

"Walk away, Sage – walk away."

The annoying voice was pissing him off. He never liked it before, and he hated it now. Hearing the voice of his long-dead wife violating his head space made him want to drink even more. With trembling hands, he started to open the bottle.

Outside, thunder boomed.

"Imagine that," he thought admiring the artistry of the bottle. "A bit of heaven found in the darkest of places, on the very precipice of Hell no less."

He uncorked it and drank deeply. He didn't know much about champagne outside of it being expensive and usually the drink of rich, snobby assholes like his old boss. His drink of choice was beer and whiskey, which was a thousand times better than this floral, creamy bullshit. But booze was booze and until he found something more his speed, it would do.

He guzzled it.

With the bottle half empty, Sage figured he'd check out the mini fridge. He squatted down in front of it and flung it open, causing a few bottles inside to topple over. Inside, there was another bottle of champagne, but he didn't care about that because something else caught his eye—smaller bottles. It was like a treasure trove of liquor in there as his eyes danced from bottles of whiskey to rum to tequila in a happy musical waltz.

"Hello old friends," he said with a grin. "Oh, how I've missed you."

He ditched the champagne and seized a tequila. Using his teeth, he twisted off the cap and drained it in two Kraken-sized gulps. He tossed the rejected bottle aside, not caring where it landed and grabbed two whiskeys: a Blue and Black label Johnnie Walker.

Sage drained the Blue first and quickly opened the Black. Outside the thunder roared like a ravenous prehistoric beast.

Inside his head, Adam's voice buzzed in his ears like an annoying fly. Angrily, he turned off the radio and finished the last of the Johnnie Walker. Grumbling to himself, he said, "I didn't need a wingman before, I sure as don't need one now."

He stood up.

Almost instantly, the world around him spun like a broken carousel. He closed his eyes and leaned against the counter, waiting for it to pass. He wasn't sure if it was the lack of booze or his alien body, but alcohol never affected him like this. Back in his old body, this was nothing but a child's warm-up to the real drinking.

"Fuck me," he belched.

Suddenly, the electronic lock disengaged in the door.

He opened his eyes and looked down at the counter. Instead of seeing one gun, there were six, and all of them were spinning.

The door opened.

Sage's hands fumbled across the countertop. For half a heartbeat, he thought he'd miss it or, worse yet, knock it to the floor. But somehow, probably thanks to the blessed Jesus, he found it. With the gun in hand, he dropped behind the counter.

"Be careful with those bags," someone snarled in a deep, gruff voice. "Those are Mark Cross bags. They cost more than your entire college education, boy."

"Wow, Mr. N, this room is amazing," a girl said. "I love it."

"Do me a favor, Brittany, run me a hot bath."

"Sure thing, Mr. N."

There was a smooch followed by rushed footsteps. Sage figured her to be Mr. Nero's current cock rest. Men like him, demon or not, always had a plethora of willing, able bodies of young flesh to molest.

"Anything else I can do for you, Mr. Nero?"

"Yeah. Disappear."

There was a shuffling of papers as Nero figured out the kid's gratuity. Sage couldn't help but wonder how much demons tipped. Was it the usual 15%?

He heard the door slam shut.

Sage listened as the footfalls of the dreaded Mr. Nero approached the bar. He didn't panic. He took a deep breath as he raised his gun, ready for the kill the shot. He figured once the prick stopped by the empty ice bucket on the counter, he'd pop up like an evil Jack-in-the-book straight out of hell and blow his stupid head clean off his shoulders.

"Come on bro," he whispered, "just a little closer."

Sage popped up from the bar ready to do God's work, but nobody was there. The sitting area was deserted outside a stack of black leather bags near the door.

"What the hell?"

Somewhere deeper inside the suite, back by the bedroom, he heard the girl laughing. With a burst of new fury, he stormed around the bar determined to redeem himself. Creeping down the hall as best he could, which was no easy task, thanks to the bulk of his new body, he approached the rear bedroom.

When he reached the door, he kicked the bastard open and stormed inside. Harvey Nero stood near the bathroom with his dick lodged halfway down the girl's skinny throat. He was tall, well over six feet, and fat as hell. With one hand pressed on the back of the girl's head, he gently guided her in the art of the suck. They were still dressed, Nero in a business suit and the girl in jeans and a white tube top. He recognized the girl instantly as the upcoming popstar Brittany Pelosi.

She was 17.

"What the hell," Harvey blathered fishing his cock out of the girl's mouth. With shaky hands, he awkwardly stuffed it back into his pants as the girl cleaned slaver off her chin.

"Hell is exactly what I bring, bro," Sage replied, raising his rifle.

Harvey yanked Brittany off the floor and attempted to hide his bulk behind her. In the past, this did little to stop the Nigerian because he'd simply kill them both. But things changed, of course, when he agreed to work for God, who expected him not to slaughter innocent lives. Staring at the girl, who just a few seconds ago had the cock of a demon in her mouth, and wondered if she was really innocent.

"Is this a joke?" the girl asked with a playful smirk. "I mean, come on, Mr. N – that gun is clearly fake. I think I saw one similar in one of my dad's crappy sci-fi movies."

"This is no joke," Nero grumbled. "I don't know who this man is or what he wants."

"Listen to the man, Brittany," Sage said, "for I am the Grim Reaper, and I've come to collect his soul."

"Look," Nero pleaded from behind his underage shield, "can't we make a deal or something? I've got money…a ton of money, and it's yours if you just let me go."

"Shut up bro. Does it look like I'm here to play Let's Make a Deal? I'm the personification of God's wrath motherfucker and it's about to be unleashed on your wicked ass. So how about you let the girl go, because I'm not here for her. Just you."

"Mr. N?"

"Shut up you stupid cunt," Harvey snarled, tightening his grip on her arms. "Whoever you are, you clearly don't know who you're messing with. I'm Harvey Nero, the closest thing to a god you'll ever come into contact with. Now get out of this room!"

"I know more than you think, Hornblas! Now let the girl go and die with some dignity."

Harvey shook his fat head as the girl tried to tear herself free, but he pulled her in tighter. She pleaded with him to let her go as tears streamed down her face.

Sage knew he wouldn't. Demon or not, the man was a coward and didn't want to get shot. No matter, he thought as he took careful aim. Even though he stood behind Brittany, Harvey was so fat, so grotesquely obese, he offered a lot of surface area to attack. With confidence, Sage fired twice.

CHAPTER 2

Dan Milton stood in the visitor area of the small police station wishing he was someplace else. Someplace far away because what he stared at scared him shitless. Cloaked figures stood perfectly still in the midst of a raging maelstrom. All of them wore long black hooded robes with dark red symbols itched along the hoods. And they were armed. He saw rifles and handguns, pitchforks, and machetes. One guy even carried a chainsaw. These odd enigmas stood in a semi-circle with about five to ten yards between them.

In the parking lot were a half dozen smashed vehicles, and one squad car was completely engulfed in flames. The ground was littered with broken glass and chunks of discarded metal. Pressing his head against the door, Dan saw the way in was blocked by a couple of vans.

And then there was the woman.

She stood alone from the others, dressed all in crimson. She was tall and extremely beautiful. Arguably, the most attractive woman Dan Milton had ever seen, with her long, flowing blond hair, penetrating blue eyes, and body to kill for. She was lust personified. And oddly enough, though she stood in the pouring rain, she remained dry.

A pair of officers rushed past him and positioned themselves along the sides of the door with shotguns.

The station chief, Terrance Bell, strolled over to Dan with his hand on his Glock. He stood a foot taller than him, had a thick goatee, and wore a black cowboy hat. To Dan, he looked like some ancient gunslinger teleported to the modern age.

"This don't look good, does it?" Terrance said in a gruff voice.

"No."

"She's pretty for a crazy bitch."

"How bad is it?" Dan asked.

"Bad. We're surrounded. I positioned men at all entry points and moved civilians to an empty cell. I don't know what's about to go down, but I want them out of sight and out of mind as much as possible."

"Did you hit the panic button?"

"And the fire alarm," Terrance said as he shook his head. Nothing works. Not even the phones—landline or mobile. And the internet is down to boot. It looks like we're on our own."

"How is this even possible?" Dan asked, checking his phone. Sure enough, no connection. He tried switching the thing over to cellular to use data, but the damn thing remained dead.

"You got me," Terrance said. This is straight horror movie stuff right here. I don't suppose you've ever encountered anything like this before."

"I don't think anyone has," Dan said putting away his phone. "Anyone try to establish contact with them – see what the hell they want?"

"You can," an officer by the door said, his voice rising a few panicked octaves. "You want to talk to them so damn bad, be our guest because I ain't going out there."

"That's fine, I'll do it," Dan said.

He ordered the doors unlocked and then stepped out into the cold torrent; gun drawn. He came in peace, but if anyone wanted to get physical, he had no qualms about putting a little hot lead in their diets.

As he drew closer to the woman in red, his eyes danced from one cloaked figure to another, watching for any aggressive movements. Nobody moved – they all stood their ground like cemetery statues.

"Special Agent Dan Milton," the woman in red said, her voice calm and collected. "You have come to negotiate?"

"How do you know my name?"

"Magic, of course," she said with a smile.

"Magic?"

"The darkest of varieties, I assure you, Officer Milton."

"Who are you?"

"That's inconsequential to what's about to transpire here if you don't give us what we want," she said, her eyes sparkling with sinister intent.

"And what's that?" he asked, his heart pounding in his ears.

"A blood bath."

"What do you want?"

Before she could answer, a rogue lightning bolt struck a utility pole across the street from the precinct in a blinding flash of lavender. Staggering back, he watched as the lines snapped and hit the ground, shaking beneath the rage of their own internal power. The woman and her odd followers didn't react to the ear-shattering boom, which sounded like a pissed-off Japanese Kaiju.

"We want a prisoner. One in your custody Officer Milton."

"Mary?"

"Is that what she goes by these days? Her name, like her tits, is fake. Her real name is Agrat bat Mahlat. You will deliver her to us within the next ten minutes or we'll start killing. And we won't stop until every pig in there is slaughtered or until we get what we came for. Either way, she is coming with us."

In one insane swoop, all the hooded figures laughed in unison. It was a mocking laughter, the type a bully makes after stealing their lunch money.

"Make your decision Officer Milton, but be quick," the woman said, "for the countdown to your extinction has begun."

As the hooded figures chanted in a low growl, he backpedaled towards the station. The same word repeatedly, and that word was death.

Rushing inside, the officers quickly locked the doors. Out of breath, he walked over to Terrance, who was talking to a group of officers on the far side of the lobby.

"Get anything we can use?" Terrance asked.

"They want us to hand over a prisoner," Dan replied brushing his bangs from his face. "Mary Migdal. They say they'll attack the station if we don't hand her over in the next couple of minutes."

"Is that right?"

Dan nodded.

Terrance walked back to the door and peered out into the storm. The hooded figures remained, but the woman was gone. In her place stood a large, shirtless man holding a pair of massive swords. The dude's body was a steroid's wet dream, completely ripped. He still wore a hood, which shrouded the man's face from view.

"Why don't we give her up?" one of the officers asked. He was young, probably fresh out of the academy. "I've got a newborn at home, man, who needs his daddy. I don't want to die protecting some convict."

"She's in our custody, so you know what that means," Terrance said. "We have the duty to keep her safe, even under such fucked up circumstances as the one we're facing. That's our job. Our duty."

There was another ear-shattering thunderstrike. A second later, the lights in the station went out.

"This place is about to become the goddamn Alamo. If any of you are religious, I'd start praying before the bullets start flying. You might not get another chance once shit hits the fan," Terrance said.

"Holy crap," one of the guards by the door shouted. "There's more of them!"

Dan ran to the door and peered out to see more armed, hooded figures arriving in droves. The newcomers came from the outlining streets. He didn't know how many there were in total, but there were a lot of these freaks.

"You still so sure about not handing her over?" Dan asked.

"Barricade the doors," Terrance shouted.

Dan ran his fingers through his soggy hair, watching the impossible become possible. Who would have imagined, he thought soberly, a siege on a police station happening today? Jesus, give me strength.

Somewhere inside the station, a gunshot echoed.

Tabitha escorted Agrat back towards her cell as waves of visitors were escorted in the opposite direction by armed police officers. The look on the visitors was grim and pathetic. They looked like sheep being led to slaughter.

"Place is a madhouse," Belial said. He materialized next to her.

What are you doing here?

"Came for the show."

You must be loving this.

"I'm gobbling it up," he said with a sour smirk.

Do you know who's out there?

"I do actually."

Who?

"I wouldn't worry so much about that now, Agrat, because they're about to introduce themselves directly here soon."

They rounded a corner and passed through a series of doors to the holding cells, uninhibited since the power was out.

Once they returned to the holding cell, Agrat saw a pair of female officers positioned outside, keeping everyone in check. Both were more butch than half the men she saw in the halls. One was tall, while the other was short, and donut shaped. Neither of them had a single ounce of femininity in their entire body outside of their biological requirements to be classified legally as female.

"What's going on out there?" the tall one asked.

"Your guess is as good as mine," Tabitha said as she handed Agrat over to the donut. "It appears a group of armed assailants have surrounded the station, and with this storm in full effect, communications appear to be down."

"Please tell me you're kidding," the donut said.

"I wish I were. Look, I don't have a lot of information at this time. Stay here, look after the prisoners, and I'll go and see what I can find out. Don't panic. We got this."

And without another word, she stormed off.

Agrat was escorted back into her holding cell as the rest of the prisoners stared at her in childlike wonder – all except the drunk, who still dozed on a bunk without a single care in the world. Out of all the people in the cell, the drunk was quickly becoming her favorite person.

"Did you see anything out there?" the dirty-haired girl asked nervously. She sat in the corner still playing with her filthy locks.

"Yeah."

"What?"

"Death."

The girl gasped.

"You're full of it," Ashanti said. "How about you just sit down and stop trying to scare my girls."

"You'll find out soon enough," Agrat said as she found a spot along the wall. Sitting down, she tried to figure out how things got so terribly fucked. Getting incarcerated was planned, seeing as the last thing she wanted to do was return to Hell, a bigger loser than when she left.

Armed with fresh souls, she needed time for the essence of her ingested souls to merge with her blood before she could unleash it. Once she could, the hunt would continue.

What really bothered her was how she failed in trolling Lucious into revealing his location and the crazy shit transpiring at the police station. She expected a possible backlash from the Nonentities after assassinating their King, but nothing like this.

"Bet you never thought you'd go out like this," Belial taunted as he passed through the cell doors. "It's almost poetic justice, isn't it? You brought Lucious here to die, but in the end, you will ultimately perish on this rock."

Could be worse.

"How?"

I could have let you fuck me.

"You're such a childish bitch."

And you still love me, don't you, Belial? Even in death, you can't cut yourself off from me. You're pathetic.

Belial didn't protest or dispute her claims; he just shrugged his shoulders as a wickedly loud crash of thunder rocked the building. So many near strikes in such a short amount of time could mean the storm was supernatural. And if it was, it meant Shedim was here.

"I see you finally figured it out," Belial said as rubbed the edge of his nonexistent nose again. "I was beginning to wonder if you ever would."

How did she find me?

"This is their dominion; they have emissaries everywhere. What did you expect would happen, Agrat? You killed her husband? Your actions just started a war."

Do I look like I care?

Agrat noticed the drunk woman push herself off the cot with her skeletal arms, which were riddled with drug marks and faded tattoos. Her spidery hair was a cluster of tangles and knots, and the entire left side of her face was slick with drool. She looked like a lifetime of bad days and piss-poor decisions all rolled into one.

"It looks like time hasn't been kind to Sleeping Beauty over there," Belial mocked. "The best part of being dead is not having to smell that crow. She's riper than a three-week-old bloated corpse."

Belial might not have been able to smell her, but Agrat could. And the inebriated cow did not smell fragrant. She was so pungent she cleared out her portion of the cell. The only one who didn't budge was Ashanti, who sat the closest to the drunk.

The drunk swung her gaunt legs over the cot's edge and then sat there, staring off into space. She ripped another fart, a foul wet one that could peal the paint off of walls.

"Jesus, I think I can smell that one," Belial said.

The drunk turned to stare at Agrat with mismatched eyes, one brown, the other a milk white. "Agrat bat Mahlat," the drunk grumbled as huge globs of spit and phlegm flew from her mouth. "I see you, I see you well."

"Hey, you crazy ass cracker," Ashanti snapped, "Why don't you…"

Ashanti never completed her sentence, because the drunk lashed out at her throat like a coiled serpent. With one quick slash of her gnarled hand, the bitch's neck was slashed. The women around her screamed out in terror as her big ass head rolled off its shoulders. From her neck, a fountain of bright red blood sprayed out like a Yellow Stone geyser.

The drunk stood as the cell door flung open. The guards rushed in with their guns drawn.

"Looks like things just got interesting," Belial said. "Curious to see how you get out of this one."

Me too.

"Agrat bat Mahlat," the drunk roared as viscous liquid oozed from between her yellow teeth.

The walking, talking donut ordered her to stop.

She didn't.

The donut warned her again, but Agrat knew the woman wouldn't stop. She couldn't. The drunk was no longer in control of her body because she was possessed by a Nonentity. The only way she'd stop now is if the donut shot her.

"I'm going to kill you," the drunk shrieked in a voice forged in the darkest abyss in Hell. "I'll feast on your eyes and then piss in your empty eye sockets."

The drunk charged.

She only got a few steps before the drunk's head burst, splattering the wall and floor with skull fragments and brain matter. In the corner of the cell, Belial applauded.

"Now that's what I call entertainment."

Donut ordered everyone out of the cell. Nobody had to be told twice as they bolted towards the exit, doing their best not to step in large pools of blood on the floor. Coming at them from the opposite direction were the FBI agents Tweedledee and Tweedleslut. Behind them, in hot pursuit, was a black guy wearing a ridiculous cowboy hat.

"What's going on back here?" the black guy asked. "Who fired their gun?"

"I did," the donut said as she stepped forward. "I had no choice. One of the prisoners was, I don't know how to describe it, acting crazy. She beheaded one of the prisoners with a karate chop to the throat and then went after another one."

The tall officer nodded behind her like a broken bobblehead.

Dan and the other officers checked out the carnage inside the cell while Tabitha vomited in the corner. The donut explained, in length, what happened while everyone gathered there, convict and law dog, stared at Agrat.

"Did you know her?" Dan asked Agrat.

"Don't need to know someone for them to want to kill you."

"It hurts more if you do," Belial said as he appeared beside Dan. "But it kills you when you love the person stabbing you in the damn back."

Oh, cry a river you little bitch.

The temporary hush of the station ended in a nightmarish instant when an insane amount of gunfire erupted. The Latina screamed and dropped to the floor, crossing herself and muttering a prayer in Spanish. The tall guard tried to yank her up, but the woman was deadweight, a toddler with liquid bones.

"Take these prisoners to the interrogation room from earlier and bar the door," Dan said to Tabitha. He had to shout just to be heard over the rampaging chaos.

"What about you? Don't go playing hero and get yourself killed."

"Need to help hold the fort."

Tabitha kissed Dan on the cheek and then grabbed Agrat by the arm. Just as they started running through the dark halls, something exploded on the far side of the building – filling the place with the suffocating stench of Nitroglycerin. As they raced down another hall, Agrat heard a window shatter.

"How long will you pretend to be this damsel in distress?" Belial asked as he drifted alongside her, keeping perfect pace with them. "Reach out to Beelzebub for aid or, at least, draw your sword!"

Why do you care so much? I thought you wanted to see me die.

"I did. I do."

Then shut up and get ready for the main event.

They rounded a corner to find a police officer lying on the floor, dead as disco. The poor bastard's throat was slit. His tongue dangled, half bitten off, between blue lips – his skin the color of toilet paper. He was slumped against the wall, right next to the interrogation room.

Tabitha threw open the door and shoved Agrat and the dirty-haired girl inside. After checking the hall one last time, she ran inside, slamming the door shut behind her as a low, angry grumble of a chainsaw filled the air.

Tabitha quickly locked the door and, with the help of dirty hair, dragged a large table in front of it. To add a little extra weight, they tossed a couple of chairs on top for good measure. It was a feeble barricade at best, but something was better than nothing.

"Get down," Tabitha ordered, "and stay quiet."

The FBI agent pointed at the floor below the two-way mirror. It made sense, Agrat thought because if someone peered in, they would just see a terrified woman hiding behind a lopsided barricade. Under normal circumstances, an assailant might have seen her and just kept on walking, but this siege was anything but normal. These weren't insane occultists or Jihadis; these were pissed-off spirits, and they wouldn't be so easily fooled. Meanwhile, outside, the muffled snarl of the chainsaw grew closer.

"Who are these people?" Tabitha asked stepping away from the door, gun raised. "What makes you so damn special that they'd risk their lives to save you?"

"Who said they're here to save me? These bastards want me dead. And they'll kill all of you just to get to me. I kind of figured you FBI types would have already figured this out – I mean, you guys are supposed to be of a higher intelligence."

"Then what are we waiting for," dirty hair screamed. "Hand her over. We don't need to die for her."

A second later, the chainsaw's guide bar ripped through the door, spewing wood chips and smoke into the room. The cutting saw made short work of the cheap wood as their attacker brought the metallic teeth down in a violent arch, splitting the wood into a V-shape.

Dirty hair fainted.

With the door sliced down the middle like a butchered hog, the attacker withdrew the blade and peered inside at them through his manic incision like a knock-off Jack Nicholson from The Shining.

Tabitha shot him in the face.

The sound of the gunshot was deafening. Even Agrat, who once heard the Doomsday Trumpets blast their cryptic sounds during Lucious's exile, needed to cover her ears. Belial didn't; he just stood disinterested in the corner, watching events unfold.

"Well, that sucked," Belial said. "I thought I was about to see a live, reenactment of the Texas Chainsaw Massacre."

Disappointed love?

"A bit."

Get used to it because I'm not going anywhere.

"There's a score of Nonentities out there that say otherwise."

Bet on them if you want to, it doesn't hurt me none. All I'm saying is don't get your hopes up.

"I think your ears don't work."

What the hell are you blathering about now, Belial? I'm kind of busy.

"That woman is screaming at you," he said as he pointed at Tabitha.

Agrat turned to see the FBI agent yelling something at her, but she couldn't hear anything. All she saw was a pair of lips flapping with mad urgency.

Does she not realize I can't hear her?

"She wants you to get down, you moron," Belial explained flatly. "But you and I both know that won't do much. These things are hunting you with a different set of senses."

Tell me something I don't know.

"You got a big ass."

The ringing in her ears abated, only to be replaced by the screeching of a disgruntled FBI agent. Agrat respected Tabitha, but she had no intention of listening to her erratic commands no matter how loud she shouted. She was the Queen of Hell and the Queen of Hell died on her feet, not on her knees.

You wondered earlier how much longer you'd have to wait before I shed this sheep's skin? Well, hold onto your butts.

She flicked her wrist.

There was a flash of dull, red light at the center of a cloud of black smoke as Misandry appeared.

"Holy crap – how did you…"

Tabitha never got the chance to finish her sentence because Agrat cut her head off in one swift, clean stroke. She died painless, but her soul's agony was just beginning as it found itself in the slums of Hell.

"That was a bit uncalled for don't you think?" Belial said. "Did you really have to kill her?"

"Probably not, but when has that ever stopped me?"

He shrugged.

Agrat looked at the dirty-haired girl lying on the floor, lying in a pool of piss. And raised her sword.

"That one too?"

"Death has robbed you of your balls, Belial."

Agrat knelt down and brushed the girl's dirty locks out of her face, surprised at what lay hidden beneath the filth. The girl had the face of a lost angel, youthful and sweet. Instead of cleaving off her head, Agrat stood up and started towards the makeshift barricade.

"Looks like I'm not the only one who's lost my balls."

She flipped him off, tossed the furniture out of the way, and then kicked open the door like the Terminator. Before stepping out into the hall, she grabbed Tabitha's gun.

Out in the hall, she did her best to navigate around the chainsaw freak's corpse, trying not to slip in his juices. All around her, she heard the sound of war as absolute hell broke loose in the middle of butt fuck nowhere, America.

"What's your plan?"

"To not die, for starters. Outside of that, I'm just going with the flow," Agrat said.

A terrified police officer came running at her from down the hall, his uniform drenched in blood.

The poor bastard was also missing his right arm. He didn't stop when he saw her; he just kept running on his way to die elsewhere. She kind of felt bad for the guy, too; he was handsome.

A moment later a pair of hooded goons came scrambling around the corner. One had a gun; the other was armed with a blood-splattered machete. Agrat hurled Misandry at the one with the machete with such rage that it took the dude right off his feet.

She shot the other one.

"That was fun," Agrat said.

She snapped her fingers, causing Misandry to reappear in her hand, the blade hissing angrily with burning blood. She started walking as Belial glided along her side.

"I wouldn't get cocky, Agrat – there's a lot of bodies between you and freedom."

"Let them come."

Up ahead came a series of rapid gunshots. Pressing herself against the wall, she raised the gun and got ready. And though she didn't see them, the hall was full of Dead Wranglers. They were working overtime as they collected the souls of dead police officers, and they did so with heavy hearts.

Dan Milton staggered into view; his clothes blood splattered. The left side of his face was completely drenched in crimson from a nasty gash running from temple to chin. Though he was a cheating asshole, Agrat kind of felt bad for him, especially knowing the fate of his recently departed beloved. She knew once he found out what happened to her, he'd take that gun of his and shove it in his mouth.

When he spotted her, he raised his gun and pointed it at her – legs apart in the Weaver Stance. Shouting, he said, "Drop your weapons!"

"I can't do that. As if you didn't notice, hon, we're in a war. So instead of pointing that thing at me, maybe you should keep an eye out for the real threat, those assholes wearing hoods."

Speaking of hoods – three more appeared on the scene. Dan blasted one, but when he turned his attention to the others, his gun jammed. Agrat's didn't; she executed them until her gun went dry. Finished, she dropped it while Dan watched, stunned.

"This is where you thank me," she said.

"Who are you? Really?"

"Nobody of any special magnificence."

She threw the sword at Dan, striking him hard in the head with its hilt. Knocked stupid, the FBI agent collapsed to the floor with stars dancing around his head. He wasn't dead, but he'd wake with one mother of a headache.

"Sparing another one," Belial said, shaking his head in disgust. "You are on a downward spiral, my Queen. Soon, you'll want to find Lucious, not to kill, but to beg for forgiveness."

"If you weren't already dead Belial, I'd kill you for that."

"Agrat!"

Turning around, she saw a woman in robes the color of a heavy period. She was at the end of the hall with a couple of fresh heads dangling from her belt. Behind this feminine reaper of death were more hooded figures, six in total.

"I've been looking for you," the woman said.

Oh no. Is that really Shedim?

"Yup. You're fucked."

Thanks, Belial.

"I've been looking for you," Shedim said.

"Well, you found me, congratulations."

Just then, a disruption, almost electrical, slammed into Agrat with diabolical authority. It knocked her to the floor, causing her head to bounce off the floor. Something was wrong, something was dreadfully wrong, but Agrat didn't know what it was. But she knew who was responsible – Lucious. He was out there somewhere screwing up the status quo.

She tried to get up as Shedim's goons rushed her but slipped in the blood and went back down. This time she didn't get back up, as one of the goons struck her in the face with the stock of his rifle.

Lucious watched Sage disappear through the portal as Dead Meat circled his ankles, purring lightly while the storm raged on and on outside like a bad dream.

"You think they'll come back?" Moragon asked.

Lucious shrugged, disinterested.

"Maybe I should ask – do you want them to come back unscathed?" she corrected with a sinister smile.

"I want them to succeed. If they get maimed, they get maimed."

Not in the mood to converse with the hag, Lucious kicked Dead Meat out of the way and marched over to Adam with sinister intent. He wanted the portal key. With it, he could slip back to Hell and reclaim his throne without jumping through the Eld's hoops.

"What's up, dude? Need a smoke?" Adam asked. He was sitting at the nurse's station with a pack of Oreos on his lap.

"Sure."

Adam stuck the key in his pocket as he hopped to his feet. He quickly cleaned the cookie dust off his pants and popped his neck as thunder boomed outside from an iron-black sky. Lucious knew if he was going to get his hands on the key, he'd have to play it smart since he was competing with the most intelligent man in the universe next to the Eld. At least when he wasn't as high as fuck.

"Cool, give me a quick tick," Adam said as he walked away. "I need to like check the radio."

He disappeared into the back as Moragon came over with a disgruntled pussy glaring at him. She stood a couple of feet away with Dead Meat perched on her scrawny, liver-spotted shoulder, looking almost stuffed.

"Lucious, what are you doing?"

"Nothing that concerns you."

"Everything concerns me," she replied sternly, "especially when my soul hangs in the balance. I've been to Hell, and I'm not going back if I can help with it. Now you can tell me what you're doing or I'll invade your mind and discover it for myself. Your choice."

"What makes you think I'm up to something?"

"Your Lucifer. It's what you do."

"You don't want her squirming around inside your head," Dead Meat said. "It sucks. I don't recommend it."

"Neither do I because this is one place you don't want to tread," Lucious said, pointing at his head. I've seen things, dark things, that will shatter your soul like glass. If you want to know what I'm up to, just wait and see because it's going to be spicy."

Adam returned from behind the nurse's station armed with a lit joint. Though he wasn't really in the mood to smoke, Lucious took it anyway and took a drag.

"How they doing so far?" Lucious asked.

"Both in like Flynn dude – though there might be a little snag in, like, our original plotting and stuff. Seems the targets arrived early, probably to beat the storm."

"You call that a little snag?" Moragon asked. "Are they okay? Do we need to adjust our strategy?"

"They're on their own," Lucious said as he passed the joint back to Adam – who took his own lengthy toke as the world continued to explode outside.

"The storm is getting worse," Adam said.

"It's not natural," Moragon said as she stroked Dead Meat. "Something very powerful is at work out there – manipulating the weather for their dark purpose."

"An elemental," Lucious said. "And they're clearly pissed off about something."

Outside the sky exploded. Hail, the size of golf balls, pelted the hospital as if reacting to their conversation.

"Adam," Lucious said gently, "where's the portal key?"

"In my pocket dude," he replied, staring at him through a veil of pot smoke. "Why?"

"I just wanted to make sure it's safe."

"Oh. Well, it's perfectly safe, dude."

"May I see it?" Moragon asked. "I'm curious about enchanted objects, especially those with divine influence. I'd like to read it."

She held out her hand.

Lucious was so annoyed he wanted to snap it off at the wrist and then shove it up the familiar's ass. He looked at Adam and then over at Moragon, who smiled toothlessly at him.

"Hold that thought a moment," Adam said as he adjusted his headset. I'm going to do a quick check-in with Sage and see how he's doing and stuff."

Adam flashed them both a warm smile and then walked away so he could speak undisturbed. As soon as he was out of sight, Lucious focused all his attention on the Night Mother.

"What game are you playing?" Lucious asked.

"I don't know what you're talking about?"

"Asking for the key."

"I wanted to look at it."

"Why now?"

"I'm curious about it," she said innocently, even batting her stupid eyes at him. "I'm curious about it, Lucious. And I'm insanely bored sitting here with nothing to do."

"Bull. Remember Night Witch? I read lies like a blind man does Braille. You are up to something."

"So are you."

Adam returned shaking his head glumly. He looked defeated. Broken. It was a new look for the First Man, one Lucious wasn't used to seeing. Adam usually was just so damn jovial – a walking, talking sunbeam.

"What's wrong?" Lucious asked.

"It's officially begun," Adam said. Lilith has engaged the enemy while Sage—I don't know—turned off his radio."

"Why would he do that?" Moragon asked.

"You got me, dude."

"He's an arrogant asshole," Lucious said, not really caring what happened to the pigheaded jerk. If he really thought taking out Hornblas was the same as assassinating a fat Italian mobster, he deserved whatever he got. Besides, he thought, there were bigger fish to fry than just Hornblas – there was the usurper. If he got the key, he'd slip back to Hell and strangle the bastard.

This thought made him smile.

From behind him, he heard Moragon whispering something. Turning around, he saw the Night Mother speaking into Dead Meat's ear. The pesky, undead feline nodded before leaping off her shoulder. He tried to see where the pecker was off to but lost sight of him beneath the chairs.

"What did you tell him?" Lucious asked.

"Nothing of interest."

More lies.

Adam stuck his hand in his pocket and pulled out the key, which glowed slightly. He held it out towards Moragon, but before she could take it, Lucious went for it, dreaming of a violent retribution dancing around inside his head.

And then Dead Meat took it.

The maggoty bastard flew out of nowhere, snatching the key from Adam's fingertips like a dangling sardine. Lucious tried to catch him mid-flight, but he slipped through his hands like water.

At some point during their little exchange, Moragon had distanced herself from their childish huddle. She stood on the far side of the room near one of the boarded-up windows, her arms outstretched towards her returning familiar, grinning like death. Jumping in her arms, Dead Meat dropped the key in her hand.

"I want that key," Lucious demanded.

"No."

"Are you seriously telling me, the goddamn Mourning Star, no?"

"I think that's what I said."

"It is," Dead Meat said in agreement.

That's when she swallowed it.

Lucious couldn't believe what he saw the witch do and stood there completely stupefied. As for her, she had a calm, almost euphoric look on her face. He wanted to smash it.

"Dude," Adam gasped, "why would you do that?"

"For purpose. What good is a Night Mother who can't cast spells, Adam? Nothing. But," Moragon said as she patted her stomach, "a witch who can open doors, aye, that is a witch with a purpose."

"Purpose, my ass – all you did was swallow our key and screw us," Lucious fired back hotly. "You screwed us."

"You can have it back in a couple of hours I'm sure," she said with a sickly cackle. "But it will do you no good, for it will be nothing more than useless brass."

"What are you talking about?" Adam asked.

"Whatever power it had now flows through me. I can feel it."

"You can have it back in a couple of hours," she cackled. "But it will do you no good for it will be nothing more than useless brass. Whatever power it had now flows through me. I can feel it."

"Feel it? We can, like, see it," Adam said in surprise.

So did Lucious.

Time, it seemed, began regressing for the Night Mother as wrinkles faded and her once saggy flesh tightened. Her spidery, white hair thickened and turned blood red, while her milky white eyes transformed into healthy emeralds. Moragon had transformed from an ancient hag into a stunning beauty in ten short seconds.

It was a miracle, a complete rejuvenation.

"Holy crap," Dead Meat gasped. "You look amazing."

"I feel alive. Reborn," Moragon said.

Adam rushed over to her; his face completely flushed. In a panicked voice, he said, "We need a doorman…like right now."

"What's wrong?" Lucious asked.

Almost on cue, there was an ear-shattering crash of thunder outside. The storm was raging before, but it was fuming now as the winds intensified and the rain came down in a wicked gush. Lucious glanced outside to see the hospital's grounds mostly submerged beneath pools of muddy water. And above it all—the rain, the wind, and the never-ending grumblings of a pissed-off sky—Lilith came in loud and clear over Adam's headset.

She was screaming.

Lucious glared at Moragon and said, "A witch who eats my key and then fails to open the proper door gets crucified. Do you understand me? Now open the goddamn portal!"

Moragon scrambled to the center of the room and plopped down with her eyes closed and her legs crossed. She took a deep breath, held it, and then let it out agonizingly slow. Watching her prep for whatever she was doing was torturous for Lucious, who was aching for things to get chugging along. The witch leaned forward and knocked three times on the floor, and it opened.

Well, it opened somewhere.

"Is that Tiffany Swan's room?" Lucious asked, peering down into a dark room. He saw no indications of it belonging to the superstar demon, so he wasn't keen on just jumping in.

"It should be."

"How do you know?"

"I just let the magic work through me," she said.

Though she was attempting to sound confident, Lucious could see right through her false façade. She didn't know shit. And she was terrified.

"It better be…for your sake."

Lucious got ready to pass through the portal when Adam grabbed him by the arm.

"Where you going, man?"

"To save Lilith."

"I should go, dude. I mean, like, you're too important."

"I love the heart Adam, but you've never fought a demon before. I have. You stay here and hold the fort. Keep the home fires burning, the doobies lit, and I'll save Lilith."

"Good luck, dude."

"To all of us," Lucious said and then crossed over.

Lucious found himself standing in a hotel room.

Somewhere.

Maneuvering through the dark room, he approached a table stand and turned on the light. He saw a stack of leather travel bags over by the mini-bar, which he hoped belonged to Durji. He was about to look at them when he noticed a vase on the table packed with a dozen white flowers.

Hellebore – the Demon Rose.

He doubted that American hotels had a habit of decorating rooms with this particular fauna, as it was heavily associated with occult and demonology. Not to mention, it was Durji's favorite. When he visited her home when she was still a musician in his court, it was full of the stinky shit.

Maybe I am in the right place after all, he thought. But if I am, where the hell is everybody?

Lucious decided to check the bedroom.

He started down the hall but didn't get very far before his senses were overwhelmed with the scent of blood. There was a door to his left, slightly ajar. Making his best ninja impression, he quietly crept over and peeked inside.

It was a bathroom.

He saw discarded clothing on the floor and a bra lying on the edge of a sink. Next to it, he saw one of Adam's specially designed rifles.

Bingo.

Lucious kicked the door, sending it flying off its hinges. Charging in, he saw Durji and some short bitch crowded around Lilith, their faces slick with blood.

Behind them was Lilith, planted against the wall like a butterfly to a paper strip. Her stomach was completely shredded, and in between strips of ripped flesh, Lucious glimpsed intestine, glistening in the neon light.

"Lucious?" Durji called in surprise. She cleaned some of the excess gore from her mouth, asking, "What brings you here?"

"You're eating it."

"Lilith?" the demon asked confused.

Lucious grabbed Adam's gun from the sink and shot the short one. He made her dance with a bombardment of divine death before swinging the weapon around on Durji.

"My Lord…"

"Not anymore," he said. He shot her in the face.

When her body hit the floor, so did Lilith's.

Slinging the rifle over his shoulder, he grabbed a few towels off a nearby rack and ran to Lilith. He placed them gently against her mangled midsection as she grimaced in pain.

"Why…did…it have to be you?"

"James Bond was busy."

"Fuck."

"Looks like we're even Steven," Lucious said with a smile.

"Eat…a bag…"

"Of dicks, yeah, I got it," he said. He scooped her off the floor.

Grabbing the murder disc from behind the toilet, he carried Lilith back to the portal as she drifted unconscious. Though he found her annoying, he was happy to see her alive and kicking. And he planned on keeping it that way.

CHAPTER 4

Death nor drink affected Sage's marksmanship, for his shots were executed with deadly meticulousness.

The problem was his target wasn't human.

Just before the bullets hit their target, Hornblas shielded himself by lifting his human shield directly into the line of fire.

Brittney ate both bullets.

Sage cringed in mortified horror as the young girl's face and neck were pulverized by Adam's modified weapon, spraying blood and chunks of the girl all over Harvey's face. The demon, whose name he still didn't remember, tossed Brittney's body aside before charging bull-like at the Nigerian Cannibal.

Before he could squeeze off another round, the demon rocketed past him like a superhero straight out of a Marvel movie. One second, Nero stood in front of him, and the next, he was behind him, clutching a fist full of Sage's entrails.

Sage followed the path of the stringy pink tubing back to his own disemboweled midsection. His shirt was in tatters, and where his belly should have been was now a massive hole outlined by mangled flesh.

"Motherfucker," Sage said as he raised his gun. Before he managed to squeeze off another round, the demon cut him in half.

Sage's torso wobbled a moment on his hips, before sliding off. He hit the floor with a sickening squish. Propping himself up on his elbows, he stared in disbelief at his intestines floating in a pool of bile and blood. As for his legs, they still stood in the middle of the room, swaying back and forth.

"I thought something was off when I first entered the room," Nero said calmly, "but I couldn't quite put my finger on it. It was an intangible. I thought I was imagining it."

Nero stepped into view, his eyes glowing a dull beige. He stood there momentarily, studying Sage and his wicked carnage with mild interest.

"How are you still alive? You should be dead."

"What can I say – we niggers die hard."

Nero chuckled as he knelt over Sage, his hands dancing over his severed torso as they sparked and fizzled with spats of unnatural light. Sage watched, hypnotized, as the bastard's hands engulfed in green flame. The strange thing was, even though the hands were just a few inches above him, Sage felt no heat radiating off them. His mother, who grew up in the thick of New Orleans would have considered this craziness Voodoo. But this was way worse.

"This body does not belong to you," Nero said. "You invaded it like a virus, but you're no Nonentity. This is most strange."

"What the hell is a Nonentity?"

"Never mind," Nero said as he waved his hand dismissively. "I can read your soul – and I don't think I've ever encountered something as vicious as yours, and I knew Hitler. It's black, blacker than pitch, and drenched in the blood of countless victims. And there's something else too, hidden deep."

"Go to hell."

"Been there, done that," he said with a sinister smile. You have the taint of the Eld on you—faint but still present. How is this possible?"

"Wouldn't you like to know, bro?"

The demon struck him hard across the face; hard enough to break teeth. Rolling onto his side, Sage spit them on the floor.

"Keep up those witticisms, and I'll tear that contemptible tongue of yours out of your mouth. All I want to hear from you are answers—answers to my questions and nothing more," he said as he yanked the rifle out of his hands.

He sniffed it.

"Bullets drenched in the lifeblood of the universe," the demon said, his face twisted in disgust. "You truly are a beautifully perplexing oddity, assassin. How did you come across a weapon like this?"

"Found it in my Christmas stocking."

"Why don't you feel pain?"

"I have a high threshold, bro."

Nero tossed the gun aside and then jammed his hand deep inside Sage's midsection and began fishing out handfuls of innards. Soon the whole room stank of his rotten, dead organs.

"You are a living miracle, but I doubt the Eld had much involvement in your resurrection. I feel other hands involved. Tell me, assassin, who made you?"

"The Lord created me from the dust of the earth."

"Let us end this mystery," Nero said placing his sticky hands against Sage's moist brow. "Your name…is Sage Williams, but to many, you are known as the Nigerian Cannibal. You used to be a hitman for the mafia up until your death. Oh my," the demon said with a child-like giggle. "You were killed by your own protégé while banging a disease-infested prostitute. How sad. How pathetic."

"You can…read my mind?"

"It is nothing but a closed door needing opening," Nero taunted. "The answers I seek will come, assassin; it's only a matter of time. Do you wish to tell me willingly or do I need to crack this skull open like a coconut and find them for myself?"

"Fuck you!"

Nero latched on to the side of his head and let his dark magic seep into it with invisible tendrils.

"This is delicious."

"Get your goddamn hands off me!"

"The prostitute was underage," Nero said as his powers wormed deeper into his mind mush. "Like them young, do we Sage? Very young it would appear, seeing as this former child of God was barely fourteen when you plowed her."

"Get out of my head?"

"Why? I like it here," Nero replied with a snicker. "You have no shine, none at all – your soul is darker than the center of a black hole. Would you like to know the moment when you lost it?"

Sage tried to figure out what he was going to do. His primary weapon was lying somewhere in the room, discarded, and forgotten. Even if he knew where it was, it wouldn't help – he had no legs to fetch it. His only chance was his pistol.

"You lost the shine," the demon continued, "all the way back in junior high when you raped Casey Southgate in the girl's locker room. Do you remember her?"

He did.

She was a sweet white girl with long blond hair and big tits. The first time he saw her walking in the halls, she caught his eye, flaunting her curves in a tight-fitting cheerleading outfit. He asked her out a few times, but she refused his advances. She even told him once she didn't date black dudes.

Ultimately, it didn't matter; he got what he wanted by taking her down in the locker room. Unlike most women he raped, he didn't kill her, but instead he left her with a threat. Talk and die.

She never talked.

Lying on the floor, Sage could feel Nero slithering through his memories as he bore into his mind deeper than the Kola Borehole.

"Assassin, you have a graveyard worth of sin in here. You were a mass murderer long before you started killing for money. Women. What made you hate women so much, Sage, Mr. Cannibal?"

"Keep searching, bro. Maybe you'll stumble upon it," he said slowly as he carefully inched his arm across his abdomen towards the pistol. He hoped Nero was so enthralled with him as an enigma that he'd fail to notice. So far, he had been lucky, and he hadn't.

"You abducted your first victim back in 97. A fifteen-year-old girl walking home from school. When you finished with her, you dumped her body a few hours later in a junkyard, forever entombing the poor child in the truck of a 1982 Renault Fuego. A goddamn Fuego of all things you sick bastard."

"Get out of my head you mother…"

"Tell me what I want to know, and I'll spare you from all these ghosts. Don't, and I'll unleash them."

Sage wanted to confess everything to the demon like a priest at the Confessional, but he fought – with everything he had – to repress the temptation. But the struggle was quickly becoming too much as his strength declined. He felt like he was battling against an undertow threatening to drag him out to sea.

"Still refusing? Fine, let's take this to the next level."

And then, just like that, Sage was teleported from the hotel suite to the cramped backseat of his old Honda. He was pinning a girl down by her wrist as he buried his cock inside her battered and torn pussy. The girl's makeup was streaked, her bottom lip swollen from an earlier stiff backhand.

Her Catholic school uniform was tattered, and her small, underdeveloped breasts peeked out from her ripped shirt. Sage didn't know her name, and he didn't care either – all he cared about was her sweetmeats. Later, she'd find herself in the Keegan Landfill with a snapped neck.

In the vision, he felt her heat – the frantic pounding of her heart against his chest. He could taste her blood in his mouth and the wetness of her womanhood. The fight in her was all about fucked out of her, so she just lay there motionless – waiting for the assault to end.

And then she spoke.

"Why did you do this to me?"

He stopped thrusting and stared down at her confused. Having lived out this memory a thousand times over in his mind, she never spoke. In fact, he didn't even know what her voice sounded like.

"Why did you kill me?" she said as she turned to face him, with rage in her eyes. "You stole everything from me – my family, my friends, my damn life! I hate you!"

Suddenly, the once lifeless girl sprang back to life – kicking and clawing as she fought against him. She scratched his face and kicked him hard in the balls as he struggled to get out of her reach. His back hit the passenger door, throwing it open.

He slipped out into the pouring rain and kicked the door shut as soon as his ass hit the mud. Scrambling to his feet, he pressed his full weight against the door and trapped the girl inside. Cleaning the blood out of his damaged face, Sage turned around to see a half dozen women standing in various states of decomposition. Some had their heads bashed in, necks snapped, and one was completely decapitated. Sage cried out; his voice ripe with madness as his former victims came lumbering forward.

"Shall I unleash them upon you?"

Then something clicked inside the firestorm that was his mind, instantly giving him hope against his potential slaughter. If only he could focus his attention on getting his hand on his gun. His hand was nearly there, just a few more inches.

"There's so much darkness here," Nero laughed. If you hadn't tried to kill me, I'd have given you a job. I could always use more people like you in my ranks."

"Fuck your ranks," he said as he drew his revolver. He slammed it against Nero's head and pulled the trigger. The whole left side of the demon's head exploded, showering the room with skull fragments. The once talkative demon was silent as it collapsed to the floor dead.

With a sigh of relief, Sage collapsed to the floor with his eyes closed. He thought some of the lingering dead would be there to greet him, to finish what they started. But they were gone and his haunted mind was again at peace.

"Kudos on a job well done Mr. Williams," someone said.

His eyes flung open to see a handsome young man with blond hair and piercing blue eyes standing over him. He was dressed in blue jeans and a Dokken t-shirt.

"Who are you?"

"My name's Gabriel. And let me just say that was a stellar performance, Mr. Williams. Absolutely stellar. Of course, I wish the outcome had resulted in you taking less damage, but we'll take this win any way we can."

"Gabriel – as in the angel?"

"Rightly so."

"You don't look very angelic. Where are your wings?" Sage asked, pointing his gun at the so-called angel's chest. He wasn't going to take any chances with this prick. For all he knew, he could be a demon, too.

"Don't shoot," Gabriel said as he stepped back. "I assure you I'm of the angelic order. I didn't think this meeting required such a grandiose appearance, so I decided to downgrade to a more humanistic manifestation. Besides, my robes are being dry cleaned."

"Doesn't explain the wings."

"Their retracted."

"Show me, or I'm going to call your bluff."

"Very well," Gabriel said taking off his shirt.

His chest was hairless and sickishly pale white. But what caught Sage's attention was a glowing ball of light just beneath the rib cage. And it was organic, too, because he could see it beating. A second later, unfolding in all their splendid majesty, were an actual pair of white wings. They were beautiful.

Sage said as he lowered his weapon. "I can't believe it. You're a real angel."

"I am," he said with a slight bow. "May I put back on my shirt?"

"Sure."

"Thank you," he said as picked it up off the bed. After his wings retracted, he slipped back into it and fixed his hair.

"So, what's next? Do I get a new body or what?"

"I'm afraid not Mr. Williams. Lucifer told you how you could absolve your soul of sin and return to the Father, but you had to avoid falling back into your old vices. And I'm afraid you did that."

"Was it the girl? I didn't mean to shoot her."

"It wasn't her. As much as I wish her death could have been avoided, her soul was sold a long time ago for a shot at fame and all the pleasures that came with it. She paid her debt."

"Then what?"

"Alcohol."

"Alcohol? You serious, bro?"

"To reduce your inhibitions and psych yourself up before a murder, what did you do? Drink. How did you deal with the guilt – not in the arms of your lord in confession, but at the bar smothering it in booze. This demon destroyed your marriage; it prevented you from finding your way back to the light, and today, of all days, it nearly cost you this hit."

Before Sage could even wrap his mind around what was about to happen to his soul, poof – he was gone. Within seconds, he was back in the Grey Wastes and ready to enjoy Hell's splendid torments.

CHAPTER 5

Just as Lucious passed through the portal with Lilith, a thread to the Shroud got axed. Almost instantly, he suffered a violent reaction, one that surprised the Mourning Star. Stumbling into the hospital, he hit the floor with his head and guts on fire.

Outside, the storm stopped.

Adam and Moragon rushed over and grabbed him by the arms. It took all their strength to pull him out of the portal's mouth, which buzzed all around him. As soon as his feet cleared it, it closed with a thunderous crack.

"Lucious?" Adam called.

"Forget about me," he spat. "I'm alright. Just save Lilith."

Adam dragged her off to the side and then flipped her over, exposing her torn midsection. Frantically, he took off his shirt and pressed it against the bloody wound. To Moragon, he screamed, "Get towels. And be quick!"

"Lilith? Lilith, can you like her me?"

No answer.

"Well, if you do – hang in there."

With the discomfort fading, Lucious got up. Though he was a little dizzy and his stomach feeling like an absolute ass, he was already starting to feel better. Seeing all the blood, he removed his jacket and offered it to Adam, who snatched it away.

"She's losing a lot of blood."

"I can see that," Lucious said.

Moragon came back over, running like the devil. She handed the towels to Adam, looked at Lucious, and asked, "What can we do? I can feel her life fading."

"Pray," Lucious said.

"I don't know how."

"That makes the two of us."

The shirt and jacket were utterly saturated in blood, and when Adam tossed them aside, they hit the floor with a sickening squish. Lucious noticed black lines snaking up and down her arms, meaning she was poisoned.

With tears streaming down her cheeks, she asked, "Can you do anything to help her?"

"Sure," Lucious said, "I'll give the last rites."

"Mr. Williams didn't make it."

Spinning around, Lucious saw Gabriel standing in the center of the room dressed like a time-traveling punk in his jeans and rock t-shirt. Though he looked stupid, Lucious was thrilled to see the jackass ditch his usual angelic garb.

"Too bad, so sad," Lucious said. "His loss is no skin off my back and probably not off yours either, so long as he got the job done. And considering how I felt a couple of seconds ago, I'm guessing he did."

"He did. And you could feel it?"

"Yeah, and it sucked. So, tell me, Gabe – are we all forgiven now that the Eld's worthless existence has been prolonged?"

"Sadly no. Things are just getting started."

Moragon ran over to Gabriel with Dead Meat hot to trot on her heels. When she reached him, she collapsed at his feet and began kissing them.

"Arise," Gabriel said softly. "There's no need for that. Who are you? I don't remember you being on the list."

"She's a tag-along from Hell," Lucious said. Her name is Moragon Cuttleback. She's a Night Mother."

"Oh."

"Lilith, she's dying. Help us. Please, I beg you," Moragon pleaded.

"Even though victorious," the angel said. He looked at Lucious. "It appears your first mission was nothing short of disastrous."

"Casualties are a part of war, you know that. And it wasn't like I didn't warn you and that asshole Michael about them not being ready. You wouldn't listen. You see all this," he said as he pointed at Lilith and the blood-covered floor, "it's on your hands, not mine. I wash my hands of it."

"Lucifer…"

"Call me Lucious, or I'm turning off my ears."

"Look, I will call you what I want," Gabriel fired back. "You are not my keeper, nor do I follow thee. As for this mess, you can make all the excuses you want for your lack of leadership today, but in the end, the outcome remains the same: one dead and one dying."

"Speaking of someone dying," Moragon called, "can we get a little help here? We can argue about who calls who what later."

Gabriel knelt down beside Lilith, stared at her half-devoured midsection, and sighed. He took a deep breath as his hands began to sparkle like diamonds, charging with divine energy. Glancing at Moragon, he said, "I make no promises, but let's see what I can do."

Moragon watched threads of gammy flesh as it mended, twisting and churning back into place, while patches of missing skin reappeared pink, healthy, and alive. While Gabriel worked his magic, Lilith groaned as she battled against the eternal void of death. The Archangel ran his hands over the wound three times. When he finished, she was healed but not completely.

There was a scar.

A small price to pay for such a violent close encounter with a couple of demons, Lucious thought.

"She going to be okay?" Adam asked.

"Perhaps, but she's not out of the danger zone yet. She'll need rest. And a lot of it before she's ready to charge back into the fray," Gabriel said. "In the meantime, how about you and Moragon take her to her room. Lucious and I need to talk."

Adam nodded as he ran into one of the adjacent halls. Returning a few seconds later, he came back with a gurney. It was an old, rusty thing, but it still rolled. He brought it over to where Lilith lay, and with Gabriel's help, they got her on it.

Once they left, Gabriel turned to Lucious and asked, "What's next? Do you have any ideas for potential targets?"

"I got a couple in mind."

"Like what?"

"You'll see. But I'm going to need an army to accomplish these next ones. They're big—big enough to blow a hole right through the Shroud."

"Just recruit wisely. And remember, whoever joins your ranks is bound by the same rules and restrictions as everybody else. So, teach them and teach them wisely! Understood?"

Lucious nodded.

"Good. Now, before I go, I have something to tell you—this comes directly from the Eld," he said as his face morphed into one of complete mischievousness.

Lucious didn't like it.

"The Eld decided to offer you some additional support."

"Support," Lucious repeated, crossing his arms. "What kind?"

"An assistant."

"We don't want one, and we don't need one, Gabe, especially one selected by the Eld. Look what happened to his last pick. Got his overrated ass killed on his first mission. Go back to the Eld and tell him thanks, but no thanks. We're fine."

"I'm afraid this is non-negotiable."

"I'm running this show, remember? We got a contract."

"You still are," Gabriel said. The assistant is not coming here to challenge your authority but only to support it."

"Who?"

"Hi, Lucy. Long time no see. How have you been?"

Lucious spun around to see the Archangel Michael standing on the far side of the room wearing skinny jeans and a Goddamn Jesus Saves t-shirt. Like Gabriel, Michael hadn't changed a bit since the Fall. He was still good-looking and ripped like a WWE superstar.

"What are you doing here?"

"I'm the assistant."

"This is who He has in mind? Hell no! Screw that, fuck this, and definitely fuck that ass hat," he said. He pointed at Michael, who laughed in the face as his frustration mounted. "I don't like you Gabriel, but I'd rather have you here than him."

"It looks like God is trolling you," Dead Meat said as he emerged from between a pair of chairs.

"You got that right," Lucious said.

Gabriel walked over and tried to put his hand on Lucious's shoulder, but he batted it away like an annoying fly. Angry, he said, "Touch me, and you lose teeth."

"Look, Lucious," Gabriel said. "I'm no military strategist, but he is. You want to know who stopped your invasions? Who outwitted you on the battlefield—it was him?"

Lucious stared at Michael as he fought the urge to punch him in the face.

"Don't look at me like that, Lucy; I don't like this any more than you do. You think I want to work with you? Give me a break. The only reason I'm here is to make sure we're victorious in this war. And to do that, I'll work with just about anyone. Including you."

"The only thing I want to do is put your face through a wall."

"Is that right?"

"Oh yeah," Lucious said, balling his hands into fists. "You have no idea how often I've sat in Hell dreaming of spoiling your good looks. The word hate doesn't even begin to describe how much I despise you."

"I'm right here Lucy," Michael said, "let's see you do it."

Lucious started towards Michael with his chest puffed out and his hands ready to pound some ass. Since the Fall, there wasn't a day that passed in Hell with him not imagining him unleashing unholy amounts of violence on this guy.

"Brothers," Gabriel said as he jumped between them. "I will not allow this violence."

"Brothers?" Michael snarled. "Don't kid yourself; we aren't brothers and haven't been for a long time, Gabriel. Remember what he's done to us with his foolish pride. It has doomed the world and practically killed our Father."

"Calm down," Gabriel said gently. "Don't let the wrathfulness inside consume you."

"Yeah Michael," Lucious taunted, "listen to your master like a good dog. Seeing as you're my assistant, like the little bitch you are, I'll have you cleaning toilets and washing my feet by nightfall."

Michael tried to lunge forward, but Gabriel wrapped himself around him, using his weight as an anchor to secure the enraged Archangel in place.

It was working.

But barely.

"I beg you, brother," Gabriel pleaded, "stop this madness! Remember the Eld and the oaths you took."

"And the dicks you sucked."

Just before breaking free of Gabriel's grasp, the angel began speaking to Michael in the language of the angels. Having not heard it in such a long time, most of the conversation was lost to Lucious. However, the parts he did understand chilled him to the bone.

According to Gabriel, he was here — not just because of the Eld, but because 'she' wanted him here. The rest of the conversation consisted of a lot of blah-blah-blah, followed by a bit of this and a lot of that, and then something Lucious could finally sink his teeth into. This part he listened to intently.

"You promised her you'd keep him safe. Keep on the path of salvation," Gabriel said in that ancient, flawless tongue. "How would she react learning you killed him?"

Michael seemed to relax.

"Who sent you?" Lucious asked.

"The Eld," Gabriel replied.

"That's not what you said. You talked of a woman wanting this piece of shit here. Who is it…the Mother?"

"No," Michael answered, his voice better composed. "If you want to know the truth, I volunteered my services."

"For a woman," Lucious said.

"Yes, for a woman."

That's when Lucious noticed the ring on Michael's finger. It was a unique golden halo, binding two for an eternity. Weddings between angels happened, but they were rare.

"Looks like, at some point after my Fall, you tricked some poor slut into marrying you. Was it even the Eld's idea for me to have an assistant or was it something you personally pushed for? Just to score some pussy points for the bitch you tricked into marrying your dumb ass. Tell me."

"The Eld wanted Cassiel," Gabriel said.

"I'd take a Cassiel. Hell, I'd take a Moroni over this chub. But what I really want to know about is this mysterious woman. I can't think of anyone in Heaven who would give a damn about little ol' me, let alone dumb enough to marry this fool."

"Watch what you say about my companion," Michael snarled as his anger rose once more. "I'm here for her, not you. Remember that."

"Does she have a name, or should I call her whore?"

"Eisheth," Michael said. "Her name is Eisheth."

"My daughter?"

Michael nodded.

Lucious didn't know what to say, which is nothing short of a miracle in and of itself. He stared at the Archangels, his jaw slack and his mind caving in on itself beneath the weight of heavy revelation. It took him a moment to find his voice, but when he eventually did, he said, "That's why the Eld refused to release my daughter. It's because she married you."

"It's true," Michael answered. "She wants me here to assist you, so you can be reunited in Heaven. In short, she gave me the greatest task possibly since the dawn of creation – saving your black soul. Honestly, seeing you here now in the flesh, I don't know if I have the strength to do it."

"You can't because I have no soul left to save."

"I told her that, but she claims otherwise."

"Can I see her?"

Gabriel and Michael exchanged glances.

"Please."

"I don't see the harm," Michael said after a short pause. "We are trying to cleanse the air between us and create a path towards peace. Let it be remembered that I offered the first olive branch."

Lucious thought he could call it whatever he wanted; he didn't care. All he wanted was to see his child.

CHAPTER 6

Lucious retired to his makeshift dormitory with extra pip in his step because he was about to see his daughter for the first time in two years. The last time he saw her was on the battlefield outside of New Jerusalem. Among the fires of a burning city, he saw his daughter charge headlong into a throng of angels with her sword and shield, screaming for blood. He tried to follow her, but a swell of opposition swallowed him up like the whale did Jonah, and he lost track of her. The battle went south from there, and Lucious and the remains of his tattered army retreated to Hell in defeat.

His wife never forgave him.

Hell, he never forgave himself.

While he waited, he quickly tidied up the room and then sat down on the edge of his lumpy cot and counted crosses on the wall. He got to 42 when the door opened, and his sweet, sweet princess entered dressed in a spiked leather jacket, jeans, and a pair of combat boots. Her hair hung past her shoulders and was dyed a mossy green. She wore black lipstick and, of course, ash-colored eyeshadow – her personal favorite. Though she now called Heaven home and was married to that prick, it was nice to see none of that changed her.

Almost instantly, his vision blurred with tears.

Embarrassed, he got off the cot, walked to a corner of the room, and tried to collect himself and his out-of-whack emotions. The last thing he wanted to do was cry like a soy boy in front of his daughter.

"You okay?" she asked.

"I'm cool," he said with a sniffle.

"You crying, Dad?"

"It's all the dust."

She ran over and hugged him from behind. "I've missed you," she said. She squeezed him like a hungry boa constrictor. She smelled of frankincense and rosemary. "The worst part of Heaven is being separated from you."

That's when the tears started flowing, steaming as they raced down his cheeks. Drying them off with the back of his hand, he said, "Look what you done did, girl, make me cry like a sissy."

"I'd be more upset if you didn't cry," she said. "And what's this Michael tells me about you not having a soul?"

"He told you that?"

"He tells me everything. He has to, or I'll kick his ass."

Lucious laughed.

"I don't like hearing you think so lowly of yourself. You have more light inside you than you realize," she said. "It's just grown a little dim. The Eld would have never gone through all the trouble of saving you if He didn't see it lurking just beneath the surface."

"Is that right?"

She nodded.

Glancing down at her hand, he noticed her wearing a similar ring to Michael's on her ring finger. But unlike the Archangel, the flesh from the tip of her appendage all the way down to the base of the ring was completely black. The purity of the halo killed the appendage like lung cancer does a smoker.

"Your finger."

"Yeah," she said. She held it up so he could see it better. "It looks way worse than it feels."

"It's dead."

"I like it – it's very goth."

Lucious pulled her in close and gave her a big, fatherly hug two years in the marking. It felt terrific having her in his arms again with her face pressed against the nape of his neck.

This was his Heaven.

"I never thought I'd ever hold you again after New Jerusalem," Lucious said. "I should have never abandoned you. It was one of the greatest regrets of my worthless existence."

"Don't do that, Dad," she said, "you did what you had to do. If you tried to save me, you'd be dead now, and this little happy reunion we're sharing would have never happened. And if you try to apologize for it, I'll kick you in the nuts."

When she smiled at him, it melted his heart like ice on a hot plate. This time, instead of fighting against the oncoming waterworks, he let them come. This time, it was his daughter who wiped them away. With their hands intertwined, they sat on the cot.

"So, Michael, huh?"

"Yeah."

She bowed her head in shame, but Lucious wouldn't let her. Gently, he lifted her head so he could see into the dark pools of her eyes and, further still, down to her very soul. And yes, she had one, and it burned bright.

Had it always, he wondered.

He didn't remember.

"What made you decide to marry that schmuck?"

"Have you seen his cock?"

"Eisheth!"

She rolled her head back, laughing.

"That's the last thing I need circulating around inside my head," Lucious said playfully as he punched her in the arm.

"I'm Sorry; this conversation was getting too serious for my tastes," Eisheth said. Don't tell me you lost your wicked sense of humor while being trapped here."

"Just tell me the story."

"Well, as far as Michael and I are concerned, I don't know what to say; it just sort of happened."

"A spell of diarrhea after Taco Bell sort of happens, not a union between a demoness and one of the highest ranking of the Eld's angelic order."

"Fine, Dad, but just the Cliff Notes version – okay? Basically, I was left to die on the street when Michael found me. I thought he was going to kill me, but instead, he rushed me off to a healer to save my life. Of course, he only did it, at the time, because he wanted to interrogate me."

"Did he?"

"What do you think?"

"Bastard," he said as he shook his head.

"It started business as usual for him, Dad, asking about our defenses and the size of our legions. But I didn't tell him anything," she said. "He tried to press, and I told him, point blank, to go fuck himself."

"I wish I could've seen that."

"The more we talked, the more our conversations evolved from just the strategic to just…talking. Michael was incredibly interested in learning of our struggles with the monstrosities, our laws, and how we governed our cities. From there, things just started to…develop."

"Like cancer."

"Cancer," Eisheth repeated, laughing. "No, silly, we started to fall in love. I discovered beneath his militaristic nature he could actually be charming. Even funny. You might not believe this, but he's very romantic. Once we started courting…"

"Is that what they call it in Heaven? Courting?"

"Yeah, Heaven is a bit old fashion."

"You mean outdated."

"Do you want to hear this story or not, Dad?"

"Fine, go on."

"Like I said, once we started courting, Michael made a confession. He told me he fell in love with me the moment our eyes connected. He said he tried to fight it, because he knew it violated Heaven's laws. Eventually, he couldn't take it any longer and went before the Eld. In front of Him and the Order of the Angels, he confessed his love for me. And do you know what the Eld told him?"

"Keep it in your pants?"

"He told Michael to listen to his heart."

"Bullshit."

"It's true," she said. "Believe it or not, after your revolt, things in Heaven changed for the better. The Eld realized if He had just listened to your grievances the war, all the misery and death, could have been avoided outright. As a result, He amended the laws, rolled back angelic restrictions, and learned to listen. I can't say how these changes altered Heaven because I wasn't there during your time, but it's not that bad. A bit conservative for my tastes, but not bad."

"So, while your mother plotted my murder and I drowned in guilt, you dated and got married in Heaven. Nice."

"Sorry, Dad," she said. She kissed him softly on the cheek. "If it makes you feel any better, I tried to kill the Eld once. And like you told me before, that dude is one hard mother to kill. I'll tell you that story another time."

Lucious laughed.

"Face the music, Dad. You don't belong in Hell anymore. You belong in Heaven with me.

Lucious shook his head.

"Why?"

"I will never submit to Him again."

"You don't have to submit, Dad. Does it look like I took a knee?"

"You took a husband."

"Hell is lost to you. Why would you want to go back to a place that chewed you up and spit you out? Your friends have betrayed you and swore allegiance to the usurper to save their own pathetic skins. Those loyal to you are dead. There is nothing there for you."

"You just described Heaven."

"You need a fresh start, a freaking reboot. Don't you think you deserve as much?"

"Do I?"

The hard-bitter truth was, he didn't. He spit in the face of the Creator, tainted and all but destroyed his prize position, and slaughtered hundreds of thousands of his children down through the ages. And the sad thing was, his daughter didn't realize it, but he'd do it all over again.

"Remember Psalms 86:5 – 'You, Lord, are forgiving and good, abounding in love to all who call to you.'"

"Did you…did you just quote the Bible at me?"

"I did."

"Well, you have to understand that some of us are beyond forgiveness," he said. "My hands are stained with too much blood."

"Let Him wash it. The Eld wants you home, Dad. He's wanted you home for a long time, and it has nothing to do with the war. He misses you," Eisheth said.

"That's rich," Lucious chuckled.

"He does."

"I don't know what to say because the feelings are definitely not mutual."

"Judge not, and you will not be judged; condemn not, and you will be condemned; forgive, and you will be forgiven. Start learning to forgive yourself, Dad, for crying out loud, and then you can receive His forgiveness."

"It's not that easy Eisheth."

"Why not?"

"I have nothing to be forgiven for. This might be hard for you to understand, but I'm absolutely at peace."

"You can bluff your way with most," she said. She patted his hand, "It doesn't work with me. I can sense the lingering anguish in you. You want closure."

"That anguish you're picking up on has more to do with recent wounds than anything from my past, let alone my rebellion against that dictator."

"Mom?"

He nodded.

"I'm sorry," Eisheth said, "I know how much you adored her."

"I worshipped her. And like a junkie, I'm going through withdrawals. Painful ones. From your little perch on high, I don't suppose you know who the usurper is?"

"I haven't the foggiest."

"What about the Eld? You think you could ask Him and then send back word once you return to Heaven?"

"I could try," she said.

"Someone corrupted your mother, Eisheth, and I want to know who it was because I'm going to stick a knife in his belly."

"Repay no one evil for evil but give thought to do what is honorable in the sight of all. Beloved never avenge yourselves, but leave it to the wrath of God, for it is written, 'Vengeance is mine, I will repay, says the Lord.'"

"Sounds like something Michael would say."

"Actually, it was Matthew. Anyway," she said as she got off the cot, "I can't change your mind. Not yet at least. Just promise me you'll consider it, Dad. I can live with that for now."

"Fine, I'll consider it."

She leaned over and kissed his cheek as the cell door opened. Stepping inside, Michael asked, "Is everything okay?"

"It was great until you showed up."

"Lucy, I…"

"Will you two stop," Eisheth said as he stepped between them. "You have to learn to somehow bury the hatchet and work together. Newsflash, guys, you're on the same damn team! And Michael," she said as she glanced at her husband, "I expect you to take great care of my dad – and to listen to what he says. Will you do that?"

"I guess."

"And Dad, promise you won't try and kill my husband."

"Do I have to?"

"Dad?"

"Fine."

"Now shake hands."

The two stared at each other, neither moving an inch. But after a bit of encouragement from Eisheth, they swallowed their pride and shook. But they both shook extra hard.

"Was that really so bad?" she asked.

"Yes," they said in unison.

"Look at that," she said with a laugh, "you guys already agreed on something. I have a good feeling about this relationship. I do. Well, Dad, I'm going to head out."

"So soon? You just got here."

"You've got a war to wage, Dad. You need to focus. I'll come back soon—I promise. Maybe I'll even bring you an early Christmas present if I can figure out who the usurper is."

"The usurper?" Michael asked, confused.

"It's between me and my dad," she said. She kissed him on the lips. Before walking out, she looked back at Lucious and said, "Love you!"

"Love you too."

"Be careful and stay safe," she said. "I expect the both of you to return to me in one piece when all this ends."

Lucious watched as Michael escorted his beloved daughter out of the room and back towards an awaiting stairway to Heaven. She paused in the golden light of the Most High and waved; he waved back. And then she was gone, leaving him in the hospital with Dumb and Dumber. And a war to win.

So it goes.

CHAPTER 7

Lilith opened her eyes and found herself back in the modest dwelling of her temporary residence, a dilapidated hospital on Tucson's outskirts. The last thing she remembered clearly was being unceremoniously saved by the biggest asshole in the universe, Lucifer. What a joke.

Gently, she sat up on her elbows and tugged up the shredded remains of her t-shirt. She figured to find some gaping hole in her midsection from where the demonic bitches feasted, but instead, she found smooth, unaltered flesh. The only thing remaining from the vicious attack was just a hint of scar.

Relieved, she collapsed back onto her pillow and stared at the ceiling. It was covered with water stains and crisscrossing hatch marks snaking this way and that chaotically without purpose, reminding her of her long life on earth post-Eden. Since her self-imposed exile, she had wandered the globe from country to country, never really feeling at home anywhere she went. She was a true nomad, a pointless drifter without a goal or end game. That ended the day Gabriel appeared out of the ethos with an offer she couldn't refuse.

Motherhood.

Not long after leaving Eden behind, it took root. The desire to have a child was a constant itch she could never scratch no matter how many times she let men fill her with their seed. When, eventually, science caught up with her desperate longing, she visited doctors the world over to fix her barren womb. But no matter where she went, their answers always carved her insides apart like a basement abortionist's coat hanger. She was infertile, barren, and sterile. She tried treatments and half a dozen different surgeries to course-correct her eggless womb.

Nothing worked.

Nothing, at least, until Gabriel appeared. The offer presented by the Eld was a no-brainer. To kill demons, she was offered the chance at forgiveness and motherhood! She agreed and signed the contract that afternoon. Running her fingers across her belly, smiling, her thoughts drifted away from flesh-eating demons to the future – where she'd have a fresh babe pressed against her breast, suckling.

"You gave us quite the scare, my sweet."

It was Moragon.

Though she wasn't in the mood to interact with the witch, at least she wasn't Adam or Lucifer. With a sigh, she glanced toward the open door at the Night Mother peering in at her.

Instead of a shriveled, old hag, she saw a beautiful young woman. Throughout her unnaturally long life, she had never encountered one as fair or lovely as the girl standing there with her blue eyes blazing in the dirty sunlight.

"Moragon?"

"The one and only," she said as she entered. "How you feeling?"

"Not as good as you are, obviously. How did this happen, and where can I get some?"

"This blessing is a one-and-done, I'm afraid."

"Lucky duck."

"At least until I shit," she said. She put her hands on her stomach. "To get all this, I had to eat Adam's magic key."

Though she looked absolutely stunning on the outside, Moragon was still the same old, vile witch on the inside. Lilith figured there were just some things magic couldn't fix, like a horrible personality. Confused, she asked, "Why would you do that? Did you know it would do that?"

"The makeover was a pleasant side effect I wasn't expecting. But you see," Moragon said. She sat beside her. "As a Night Witch, my contributions to the team are going to be restricted due to the dark nature of my spellcasting. Eating the key gave me a purpose."

"How?"

"I open all the doors."

There was a flash of discomfort in her midsection, which made Lilith cry out. Grabbing onto the edges of the mattress, she waited for the pain to pass.

"You're feeling the demon's venom. Painful as all hell, but not usually lethal. Give it time, and it'll pass."

"I hope so because this sucks."

What happened next surprised Lilith. Moragon held her hand gingerly like a mother comforting her child experiencing her first menstrual cramps.

"How long was I out?"

"A couple of hours at most."

"You here the whole time?"

"Not very long," Moragon said. "Adam just left."

"Adam?"

"He's been at your side since you returned. He looked exhausted, so I told him to piss off downstairs to get something to eat. If I hadn't done that, I don't think he would have moved. He was really worried about you."

She was surprised he cared so much about her, especially after all the stuff she did to him in the Garden before she walked out. Once she felt better, she might mosey down to his workshop and hug the dude.

Maybe.

She would have to see.

"Did I miss much?" Lilith asked, squinting.

"Breathe, child – breathe through the pain, or it'll smother you. As far as the going-on in this place, you better believe things have been rocking and rolling while you slumbered. Gabriel was here. He was the one who actually healed you," she said. She pointed at her midsection. "Do you remember any of that?"

Lilith shook her head.

"The Eld didn't like how Lucious handled this mission, so He slapped him with an assistant."

Lilith took a few deep breaths as the pain intensified. At first, she thought they wouldn't help calm the fire ripping through her guts, but after four or five of them, the pain surprisingly subsided slightly. In between gasps, she asked, "Who is the assistant?"

"Michael."

"Oh. My. God. Lucifer must love that."

"Love what?"

Lilith's eyes flung open. Lucifer stood in the doorway, leaning against the jab with Dead Meat cradled in his arms. He was dressed casually, with his shirt saturated in blood.

Her blood.

"I just came to see how my favorite trash-talking ass-kicker was doing," he said as he entered the room.

"Like you care."

"If I didn't care, why would I risk life and limb saving your ass from a couple of demons? I could have left you there to bleed out like a gutted pig. But I didn't, did I?"

"No, you didn't," she admitted. "I suppose I can give you that."

"Thanks."

"I heard about Michael."

"It is what it is," he said with a shrug. "Not much we can do about it now, seeing as he's setting up his room as we speak. As much as I detest the dude, he's a master strategist. And in the upcoming war, we'll need him. Since you've been sleeping, the music industry has already begun to spin out of control. Hell, three of his biggest starlings have already died under mysterious circumstances."

"That fast?"

"Power gaps have to be filled, Lilith."

Dead Meat jumped into Moragon's arms as the witch rose from her seat. She wished Lilith a speedy recovery, bowed at Lucious, and then exited the room – leaving them alone with the weight of the world hanging between them.

"You come fishing for a thank you?"

"To pay my respects mostly, but if you think saving your life warrants one," he said as he sat down. "I'll take it. But knowing you and your serious lack of creativity, you'll probably just say we're even or something equally uninspired. Regardless, I'm glad you're here. This would get real boring without you keeping me amused."

"You going to get all emotional on me, Lucious?"

"Hey," he said as he perked up. "You called me…"

"I know, don't make me regret it."

Smiling, he said, "As for crying…hell no, I'm too exhausted to cry. I think we can both agree it's been a long damn day. I'll have Adam send you up some food, but as for me, I'm going to crash. I'm going to need all my strength to get through tomorrow."

"Why?"

"I'm going to be doing some heavy recruitment," he said as he rose. We need an army of deplorables if we're going to remove this Shroud successfully, so I decided to reach out to my followers."

"You mean Satanist?"

"Hey, they've been praying to me for a long time – might as well make an appearance at one of their little orgies, see if I can't recruit some of them."

"You think they will?"

"You never can tell can you," he said with a smile. "I'm going to try a small gathering in the predawn hours in Michigan, where a ritual is being planned by a local Satanic chapter – and from there, start hitting up some of the bigger organizations."

"This is crazy."

"And it will only get crazier, so we must strike while the iron is hot. In about two weeks, demons will be celebrating one of the most unholy days on the Satanic calendar."

"Two weeks? But Halloween isn't…"

"Who said anything about Halloween?" Lucious asked, cutting her off. "That day is for posers and future diabetics, not serious occultists. I'm talking about the Day of the Unveiling Lilith, July 25th."

"Never heard of it."

"Exactly," Lucious said. "It's one of the darkest days of the year for Satanists, a celebration of absolute wickedness. And sadly, it comes at the hands of children."

"Those sick assholes," Lilith said.

"You got that right. You see, there's an island where some of the most powerful people in the world go to partake in the blackest of rituals. Rituals that involve cannibalism, torture, and rape. You'd be surprised who attends this place, a real who's who of A-listers, all dining on flesh and blood. It's a vicious affair that brings out the elitist and some powerful demons, like Leviathan. If our strike hasn't already spooked them, we'll have an awesome target to take out. One big enough to blow a major hole in the Shroud."

"I'm glad you're taking so much pride in this mission, where innocent children are being victimized."

"I'm excited because we're going to stop it," Lucious said. "I've never asked for any of this to be done in my name. It makes me sick, especially when things are done to children. That's why we need an army, and I'm not just speaking about humans either – we need some of the supernatural variety, seeing as what we're going up against. And that's where you come in," he said. He pointed at Lilith.

"What are you talking about – supernatural variety?"

"Vampires," Lucious said. "We need to fight fire with fire, and vampires are the perfect counterpunch against demonic forces. They're fast, have superhuman strength, and are hard to kill."

"And you what…want me to talk to them? I hate to break it to you, Lucious. I know nothing about vampires other than what I've seen in movies. And as far as those go, I haven't seen very many. I think the last one I saw was Lost Boys."

"You only have to talk to one," Lucious said, "their Queen."

"That Nova chick you told me about?"

"Not Nova, Neva. Neva Rios. And from what I've been told, she's hiding out in Ransov, Romania – in some kind of self-exile. You and Adam will go there and see if you can't convince her to join our little cause. I think she might be interested."

"Why?"

"She's been sucking on necks for the last eight-hundred years. You don't think she might want a damn hamburger? I already told Adam about it, and he's down."

"I'm sure he is," she said as she sat up on the cot. "But what makes you think they won't attack us once we arrive? I mean we are their food of choice."

"I'll explain all that later. Just get some rest, okay?"

She nodded as the pain began to slowly intensify again, bringing her dangerously close to crying. Not wanting to break down in front of Lucious, she chewed on the inside of her cheek – wishing Lucious would get out of the room.

Just when she thought she'd have to yell at him, he walked out, closing the door behind him. As soon as Lucious was gone, Lilith grabbed her pillow and smashed it against her face.

And then she screamed.

EPILOGUE

"This can't be happening."

Father Abbott sat in the backseat of his 1957 Volga as it roared down the rain-slicked cobblestone streets of Riga, Latvia. His sweaty fingers fumbled with his Rosary as his heart pounded. His mind wasn't on the mysteries of the Rosary, or the many prayers associated with the symbol of his faith but on what awaited him at the Domus Inanis Exstinctique on the far side of the city.

Built 500 years ago on Zakusala Island, a small islet in the middle of the icy Daugava River, was a church built to be forgotten. It didn't offer mass and its bells remained silent on Sundays. It was a tomb for one of the Catholic Church's dirty little secrets, and no, it didn't involve altar boys.

But something else.

Something linked to Armageddon.

They were still far from their destination and kept farther still with the traffic-congested streets of morning rush hour.

"No worry," his driver, Timur, said. "I get you there. Main road not only road in Riga, Father Abbott."

He made a hard turn, sending them down a narrow alleyway, cutting between coffee shops. Timur hit the gas, pushing the old clunker as hard as its timeworn engine would allow as it kicked up gutter water.

"Good thinking, Timur," Father Abbott said. "You get us there in under fifteen minutes; I'll give you an extra hundred American."

"You got it, Father."

They merged on a one-way street, with the car's wheels squealing angrily as they struggled for purpose on the slick, wet stones of the ancient city. With angry horns blaring behind them, Timur probably cut ten minutes or more off their route with his reckless driving.

Off to their right, Father Abbott saw Our Lady of Sorrows Cathedral. It was a beautiful building with an impressive blue spire at its apex, pointing towards the grandeur of Heaven. Today, the majestic building looked almost skull-like with its white walls and black lancet eyes. Had it always looked like that, he wondered, or was it the result of the strange phone call?

It came in the predawn hours, around the witching hour of 3 a.m. While most of the residents of Riga slept, his private phone rang, stirring him from a night of uneasy dreams—dreams packed with terrifying visions of burning cities.

He answered it, his mind still locked in a heavy fog.

Phone calls from the Domus Inanis Exstinctique were standard enough considering who it housed in its archaic walls. There were the modern prophets, the demon-possessed, and those suffering strange, religious inflictions. It was a house that never slept and where suicide was as common as the cold.

As a ward, he oversaw the house's day-to-day functions and approved researchers' and religious scholars' access to its occupants. Built sometime in the fourteenth century, the Domus—also known as the House of the Sightless—became a sort of asylum. It was a three-story building with a vast network of catacombs, where they kept the demonically possessed. The reason for its name wasn't the clairvoyants or prophets but the blind monks.

His mind drifted to them as the car sped through the bustling streets of an awaking city. All of the monks were born with a rare genetic defect called Anophthalmia, which causes a child to be born without eyes. Most of the monks were abandoned by the church after their parents gave up dealing with their infliction or were simply bought off by human traffickers. As dark as it would appear to outsiders that the Roman Catholic church would partake in human smuggling, there was a purpose behind it.

A prophecy.

At the late hour, while his mind pulled itself free from nightmarish fantasies, Father Abbott listened to the caller – trying to push back his exhaustion and the caller's thick accent.

"Calm down, I can't understand you. What did you say?" Father Abbott asked the caller.

"I say – they see."

"See?"

"Yes! Yes! You must come. You must. Now."

And then it hit him, and he snapped instantly awake. He sat up in bed, nearly dropping the phone in his panicked haste. Could it be, he wondered with mounting dread? Could it really be happening? Now?

Logic told him there had to be some rational explanation for the late call because considering otherwise meant the beginning of the End Times, the time of the Great Dying.

"Did you hear me?"

"I did," he said. "When did it happen?"

"Not long. Five minutes."

In the background, Father Abbott heard some people screaming. It was terrifying. It was how he imagined people sounded in Hell as their flesh melted off their bones.

"What is going on?"

"Madness. Absolute madness, Father. You come. Now."

Before he could ask any other questions, the caller hung up. Father Abbott quickly dressed and then called his driver, Timur. They were on the road in ten minutes.

"You look flustered, Father."

Timur's words snapped him back to reality, back to their old car, which reeked of communism. Confused, he asked, "What did you say, Timur?"

"I said you look flustered, Father. Everything okay?"

"I don't know," he said.

If the caller's statement was true, it meant the blind monks were no longer blind. And if that was the case, it meant the second coming of Christ was upon them.

In Paul's secret prophecy, a section of the Bible never published, he wrote: When sight returns to the sightless, look for Him, and you will see Him in all His glory.

The pages were locked in the vast vaults of the Vatican, along with many other forbidden sections of God's gospel, like the Books of Judas, Mary Magdalene, and Jesus Christ. There was even a very interesting section written by Jesus's father, Joseph, which explored Jesus's young life and the trials and tribulations of a mortal father raising the son of the one true God.

As they came around a sharp turn, Father Abbott prayed that this would be nothing more than another false alarm and that the blind monks would remain blind.

He swallowed hard as the car weaved and danced through the traffic, gracefully yet determined. Timur was an excellent, cool-headed driver, and the way he worked his magic this morning was proof enough of that.

"Is it my driving, Father?"

"No."

"Perhaps something you ate?"

He shook his head.

Unlike him, Timur was not a man of the Church. He was a hired driver, a former KGB operative with ice-cold nerves, the type needed to ensure secrets remained that way.

"I know not my business, but you want talk?"

"No."

Timur nodded.

They sat quietly as they made their way through Riga along the Daugava River, which ran parallel to their right. Father Abbott stared at the water and watched a ferry drift along its surface, cutting through the water beneath a turbulent sky.

A storm was coming.

Under normal circumstances, he wouldn't have thought much of it. Rain was, after all, rain. But today, after the startling call, the dark storm clouds looked ill-omened. They passed Riga Castle and then, a little later, the Virgin of Anguish Church. Father Abbott didn't pay much attention to these familiar Latvia landmarks. His attention was locked on the looming thunderheads stacking up on the horizon. The wind was really picking up as they neared the A8, which led directly to their destination.

"I had dream," Timur said. His voice broke the silence like a lightning strike. "Last night, horrible dream. I saw Riga consumed by a wall of flame as winged demons swooped down, slaughtering all. It was terrible; I woke up in a cold sweat."

Listening to Timur describe his dream brought the Father back to the forefront of his mind. He didn't see Riga burning but the Vatican.

"I no like dream," Timur said. "Drank vodka to wash it away. Happy when you called me when did, or I'd still be drinking, Father."

"I can understand," Father Abbott replied. "Nightmares can make even the strongest man weak in the knees."

"You dream?"

"I don't remember," he lied.

"Many years I work for government. Interrogate many people. In some cases, I had to break'em to get them to speak. I know when man lie," Timur said coldly.

Glancing at the rearview mirror, Father Abbott could see Timur staring at him with his gun-metal eyes. Since arriving in Latvia three years ago, Timur worked as his driver. Not once, during the entire time together, had he ever looked at him like he was now.

"Man, of cloth should not lie, Father. I work for your sect long time," he said, focused on the road again. "Two Fathers come before you. Father Mitchell you know, but did you know Father Manolo?"

He shrugged, not really liking where this was going.

"Came from Spain, where…no remember. Big man, built like a shithouse. He like drink as much as bible. Deep voice. Loved talk about God. One night he returned from House, look lot like you. Sweating. Clearly worked up. No want to talk either. Stubborn you Catholics be," Timur said. He paused at a busy intersection before eventually turning onto the A8. The storm was nearly upon them as thunder roared overhead like an enraged lion.

"I ask him like I ask you now, what wrong? You want to talk. He brushed me off. So, we no speak. I respect his wish and drove car. That night, hung self."

"I didn't…"

"Know? Of course, no. Why they tell you. This years ago. Forgotten to everyone except us with scar to remember. I fail him that night. I no fail you. Need talk, talk. I no judge. Secrets," he said as he bobbed his head side to side, "I keep."

Everything turned pure white as lighting blasted across the sky, followed closely by a wicked crack of thunder. Its vibrations were so strong that they felt it inside the car.

"I thank you for your words and oath of secrecy Timur," Father Abbott said as he cleaned sweat from his brow with the back of his hand. He continued, saying, "But even I don't really know what is happening there, not fully at least. Whatever it is is strong enough to rattle Kir into calling."

With a hot flash of static, the sky ripped, and the rain fell. Timur had to slow the car or risk losing control of it in the maddening weather. They got off the A8 once they reached Zakusala Island and took a series of back roads and offshoots until they reached the House of the Sightless.

It was a feudal structure, crafted with dark gray stones which were covered with thick ivy. In the raging storm, it looked like something one might see in some late-night horror film with its gothic style straight out of the century it was spawned.

When Timur stopped the car, the rain was coming down in a mad torrent, killing visibility. The day light was gone, completely swallowed by the intensity of the storm. From the car they could see the front door of the House stood open. Standing there, peering out at them, was Ailie Lucas – a residential scholar researching the possessed.

He was pointing to something.

Father Abbott turned in the direction he indicated just as a streak of blazing silver cut across the sky. For a brief second, he saw the entire house and the land around it light up brilliantly. He saw the large elm in the yard bending from the rain's bombardment.

And a man.

Just as he began questioning the legitimacy of what he thought he saw, a naked man ran into view, wielding a knife and screaming.

Father Abbott and Timur watched, stunned, as the man threw himself at the car like a wild animal. He stabbed at the front window as white foam oozed out of his mouth.

"This no-good Father."

"That's Omar Hays, an American who just arrived a few days ago," Father Abbott said. The man was a deranged psycho, arrested for the murder and cannibalization of six underage girls in the name of Satan. He was sent to the House for observation after his arrest because he was demonstrating abnormal behavior like speaking in tongues, Stigmata, and levitation.

"Well, he no like us much, Father."

Merging from the darkness on the passenger side of the car was another man, this one armed with an axe. The man was Kane Armin, one of the House's long-term residents. Another of the demonically possessed. In the car's headlights, he saw Kane carved a bunch of Satanic symbols into his flesh.

"Now I know what phone call about," Timur said as he popped open the glovebox and pulled out a Glock. "No wonder you no want to talk. I wouldn't want to talk about this either."

Father Abbott watched as Kane came around to the rear passenger door. Before he could fling it open, he quickly reached over and locked it as the lunatic watched, grinning slightly. Stepping back, Kane brought the axe down on the window, shattering it.

Crawling across the seat, his hands being sliced by the glass, Father Abbott tried to put some distance – the little he could – between him and the madman.

"Dead is better Father," Kane shouted as he reached inside, unlocking the door. "Dead is peace. Dead means no more dreams, no more voices arguing inside your head."

"Then shut up and die," Timur said as he shot Kane in the face. As Kane stumbled back into the rain, the man with the knife continued stabbing the car unscathed by the sudden burst of violence.

He, too, was screaming about death being better as lightning streaked across the sky in intense tones of silver and gold. Timur took care of him next, hitting him with three clean shots to the chest – sending him rolling off the hood and into the stormy darkness.

With his ears buzzing, Father Abbott got out of the car and stepped into the maelstrom, instantly drenched. Doubled over, hands resting on his shaky knees, he threw up. The vomit was hot and sour, full of last night's modest dinner consisting of a few greasy sausages, rice, and beans. Every time he thought he was done, more would come coursing up his throat, hot and thick. He gagged on the rice, which clogged his throat and filled his nostrils.

Timur rushed over to him and placed one of his murderous hands on his back. He was saying something, but over the storm and the ringing in his ears, Father Abbott couldn't understand him.

Timur leaned in close and said, "They'd have killed us both, Father. I had to do what I had to do. They rabid."

Father Abbott nodded, knowing his driver was right. But that didn't mean he wanted to see Kane and the other patient shot dead. He could have shot them in the leg or something, just enough to slow them down or make them less of a threat – but to murder both? No, that didn't sit right with Father Abbott.

Ailie ran down from the house, holding an umbrella. Putting one arm around Father Abbott's shoulder, the scholar escorted him towards the house, speaking as he went with cold calculation. "Kane killed Rada after escaping his room. I tried to call the police Father, but the lines are down."

"Dear God," Father Abbott said, his thoughts turning to sweet Rada, the resident cook. She was beloved by all, a gentle creature, and a mother of three. It broke his heart to hear she was dead.

The three of them entered the main hall, which was where the receptionist area was located. The small station stood deserted – just like the rest of the room. All over the floor were discarded pieces of stationary, and all the furniture was overturned.

"What is going on here?"

"I wish I knew Father," Ailie said with a shrug.

From there, the manor was a hodgepodge of chaos. He heard talking and, somewhere else, the blood-cuddling scream of a woman. Like the storm outside, the House was in a state of absolute pandemonium. He didn't want to explore further, but he knew he had to overcome his fear and get to work. It was, after all, his duty as ward.

"Where are the monks?" he asked Ailie.

"Cafeteria."

"Take me."

"If you need a moment to collect…"

"I don't need a moment. Now take me," he fired back hotly. He felt bad for shouting at Ailie but couldn't take it back any better than he could a fart at mass.

The lights flickered as Timur helped him to his feet. They passed through an empty hall and into the central lobby just as thunder boomed nearby, strong enough to shake the old manor. The main hall had a pair of doors on both sides, one leading to a library, the other to a study. In the center of the room, snaking in a large arch, was a pair of dual staircases leading to the second landing. Between them, half submerged in deep shadow was the door leading to the cafeteria.

Father Abbott took a deep breath as he approached the closed doors, terrified about what might lurk behind the large, heavy oak. In his head, he heard Kir's frantic words, "Blind no more. They see."

He opened it.

Inside, he found the monks seated throughout in their dark, brown robes. Some still had their hoods up, shielding their faces, but most were drawn back or hung like dead roadkill around their necks. He recognized all of them. Some were young and youthful, others old, wrinkled and bearded.

Out of the fifteen monks calling the House of the Sightless home, only one was female, and it was her eyes that he met first.

Kir was right, the monks could see. And they saw with new eyes. Instead of empty sockets, he saw actual eyeballs – all sticky in wet in their new heads. The pupils of these miracles were an amazing shade of violet. All of them the same, exact color. The new eyes were glorious and perfect, just like God's love. Instead of revulsion and fear, he felt calm and the static buzz of the Holy Spirit.

"The prophecy is true," he muttered in complete disbelief. "When sight returns to the sightless, look for Him, and you will see Him in all His glory."

"Father?" Timur asked.

He wanted to tell him, all of them, that the end was near. That this miracle, this amazing showcase of God's infinite power, came with the heaviest of prices. That of the world.

But he didn't.

"There is more," Ailie said.

"More?" Father Abbott asked, confused.

"Yes. After Kir called you about this," he said as he gestured at the monks. "There was an explosion in the cellar. He went to investigate and what he found…"

"What?"

"An ancient sepulcher."

"Here?" Father Abbott asked, surprised. The House of the Sightless was old and had many passages below, but none of them were tombs. When the Templars built it, they used the passages below for storage.

"I'll take you."

Father Abbott nodded and then followed Ailie through the swarm of monks, happy to be away from them and the terrible news they brought. Silently, the trio made their way through the House and eventually to the vaults below.

Down here, the raging storm sounded distant, and so did the screams. The stench of dust and mold was overpowering and made Father Abbott's overly sensitive nose instantly run. He cleaned away the clear mucus as he followed Ailie into the catacombs, which had dimly lit corridors. Outside of a few of the House's most dangerous occupants, most of the area was left unused.

Passing by rooms housing the most dangerous of the house's occupants, Father Abbott, and Timur followed Ailie down shadowy halls as the voices of the possessed shouted in a dozen different languages. They shouted threats among their insane laughter and fits of hysterics, their voices shifting and changing from male to female almost on a whim. Father Abbott was used to it and even found their taunts somewhat comforting considering the day's momentous circumstances.

Coming around the corner, they found a collapsed wall. Chunks of brick, dust, and mortar littered the floor in a heap. Father Abbott crept forward and peered inside. It was dark beyond, but the light from the hall provided just enough to illuminate the remains of a vault.

"Look there," Ailie said as she pulled out his phone. He turned on the light and shone it on the wall just beyond the opening. There was a carving. A hammer. Below it were the words he didn't recognize, some ancient text long lost to time.

"Do you have any idea what it says Ailie?"

"Afraid not, Father."

"Timur?"

"I have gut feeling tell me – something bad. We should go."

Father Abbott stared at the etchings, running his finger along the grooves in a sort of trance with the storm and the dark miracle of the monks forgotten. The world seemed to melt around him as the hammer and words scribed in the rock called out to him, demanding to be solved. Timur put his hand on his shoulder and snapped him out of his thoughts. He looked at the KGB agent, confused.

"Someone inside," Timur said. "I saw a shadow."

"Kir?" Father Abbott called; his voice low.

"Maybe 'nother mad man. I go first."

Father Abbott and Ailie didn't protest as the former KGB officer entered the room with his gun drawn. Ailie went next, Father Abbott last. With his heart pounding in his ears, Father saw what spooked Timur because it stood in the center of the room – their hand completely engulfed in fire.

At his friend lay Kir, who had his head cracked open – his brains decorating the floor like spilled jelly. Timur stepped between him and Father Abbott and Ailie, gun pointed at the murderer's chest.

"Get down on your knees," Timur shouted, "hands on the back of your head, or I'll shoot."

"Shoot then."

Timur lit him up, unleashing the remainder of the mag into the strange man. He danced against each impact, but he didn't fall nor did he die. Instead, he walked over to Timur and struck him hard in the face – sending him flying across the room.

"Who…are you?" Father Abbott asked, retreating back.

"I am Methuselah."

"Impossible," Father Abbott protested, his eyes transfixed on the hulking figure with the burning hand. Methuselah was the father of Lamech, father of Noah – and died, according to the good book, at the tender age of 969.

"Impossible, you say? Like the blind being able to see," the man said. "Today is a day of the impossible becoming possible—a day of God's miracles."

"You killed Kir," Ailie said.

"I killed no one," Methuselah said.

"I see a dead man at your feet."

"And I see one standing before me. Dead to the world with a soul black as pitch. You dare cast judgment on me with your hands drenched in blood? The man before me is dead, but not at my hands. It was his," Methuselah said. He gestured towards the darker shadows of the crypt.

It was then that Father Abbott noticed Methuselah was holding a chain in his opposite hand. He tugged on it, which caused a dwarf-like creature to stagger forward out of the darkness. Though human-like, there was truly nothing human about the monster standing before them with its oblong torso and stubby arms and legs. It looked like a penis with its pink-tinted skin and dark purple veins. There were globs of black hair speckled on its shoulders, knees, and chest. Black as pubes. And on its mushroom-topped head were a pair of goat-like horns.

It was a demon.

"I have come to help in the upcoming war," Methuselah said. "The war against Lucifer and his demonic forces."

"Why you?" Father Abbott asked.

"Because I am a demon slayer."

Thank you for reading *The Wretched!*

If you enjoyed it, I would appreciate your recommendations and reviews – they mean so much to us indie authors, because we tend to be members of the unseen and unheard. Show the corporate machine that you love and support your indie authors!

To learn more about book signings, future releases, and read blogs from your favorite Battered Brains authors, please check out our website batterbrains.com.